Sarra Manning is an author and journalist. She started her career on the music paper *Melody Maker*, then spent five years working on the legendary UK teen mag *J17*, as Entertainment Editor. Sarra was also editor of *Ellegirl* and *What To Wear*.

Sarra now writes for *ELLE*, *Grazia*, *Red*, *InStyle*, the *Guardian*, the *Mail on Sunday*'s *You* magazine, *Harper's Bazaar*, *Stylist* and the *Sunday Telegraph*'s *Stella*. Her teen novels, which include *Guitar Girl*, *Let's Get Lost*, *The Diary Of A Crush* trilogy and *The Fashionistas* series, have been translated into numerous languages, and in 2008 and 2010 she was shortlisted for the Book People's Queen of Teen award. Sarra's first grown-up novel, *Unsticky*, was published in 2009, and her latest teen novel, *Nobody's Girl*, was published in 2010.

Sarra lives in north London.

Also by Sarra Manning

Unsticky

You Don't Have To Say You Love Me

Sarra Manning

CORGI BOOKS

TRANSWORLD PUBLISHERS
61–63 Uxbridge Road, London W5 5SA
A Random House Group Company
www.rbooks.co.uk

**YOU DON'T HAVE TO SAY YOU LOVE ME
A CORGI BOOK: 9780552163293**

Simultaneously published in Australia and New Zealand
in 2011 by Bantam Press
an imprint of Transworld Publishers

Copyright © Sarra Manning 2011

Addresses for Random House Group Ltd companies outside the UK
can be found at: www.randomhouse.co.uk
The Random House Group Ltd Reg. No. 954009

The Random House Group Limited supports the Forest Stewardship
Council (FSC), the leading international forest-certification organization.
All our titles that are printed on Greenpeace-approved FSC-certified paper
carry the FSC logo. Our paper procurement policy can be found at
www.rbooks.co.uk/environment

Typeset in Meridien by Falcon Oast Graphic Art Ltd.
Printed and bound in Great Britain by
CPI Cox & Wyman, Reading, RG1 8EX

2 4 6 8 10 9 7 5 3 1

To the girl I used to be who had the good sense and the determination to go on a diet and stick with it.

Thanks

As always, thanks to Gordon and Joanne Shaw, Kate Hodges, Sarah Bailey and Lesley Lawson for loyal, long-suffering support. Fittingly I should also thank the staff of the Manor Health and Leisure Club in Fortis Green where I've whittled down my body, like Neve, and mended most of my plotholes while swimming lengths and going hell for leather on the cross-trainer.

Finally I'd like to thank my agent, Karolina Sutton at Curtis Brown, for her wise counsel and supreme un-flappability, and Catherine Cobain at Transworld for being my biggest cheerleader and silk-pursing my prose style.

http://twitter.com/sarramanning

It is far harder to kill a phantom than a reality.

Virginia Woolf

PART ONE

Wishin' And Hopin'

Chapter One

Neve could feel her knickers and tights make a bid for freedom as soon as she sat down.

She shuffled to the edge of her seat so she could plant her feet firmly on the floor, straighten her back and yank in her abdominal muscles. It didn't work. Her doubly re-inforced waistband suddenly gave way and she could feel her tummy gleefully push against the seams of the vintage dress that she'd told her younger sister, Celia, she couldn't get into without the aid of Spanx and bodyshaper tights.

As usual, Celia had refused to take no for an answer, in the same way that she'd refused to listen to Neve's pleas to be allowed to stay at home with a pot of tea and a good book. That was why Neve was perched uncomfortably on a neon-pink chaise longue in a hot stuffy club in Soho surrounded on all sides by hordes of fashionably dressed people who were all shrieking at each other to make them-selves heard over the reverberating bass-heavy music.

'I hate you,' she hissed as her sister plopped down next to her.

'No, you don't, you love me,' Celia replied implacably. 'Here's your drink. There was no way I was asking for a spritzer, so you'll have to drink your white wine neat.'

Neve took an unenthusiastic sip as she tried to suck in her gut. 'When can I go home, Seels?'

'I'm going to pretend that you didn't even say that,' Celia said, eyes narrowed as she scanned the room. 'Now, anyone here take your fancy?' She nudged Neve. 'I love that we're going out on the pull together now. It's so much fun.'

Going out on the pull was not at all fun. And anyway . . . 'I am not out on the pull,' Neve said primly. 'I said I wanted to try talking to single, straight men and maybe work up to a little light flirtation. I'm not at the pulling stage yet. Not for ages.'

'We'll see,' Celia said. 'What do you think of Martyn from the subs desk?'

Neve looked at the man Celia was gesturing towards. He didn't look as aggressively trendy as the other men present, but he was still out of Neve's league. But then, even the *Big Issue* seller they'd passed outside Leicester Square tube station seemed out of Neve's league when she had as much experience of men as an eighteen-year-old, convent-educated Victorian girl attending her first regimental ball.

Celia insisted that putting down her books and actually going to places where single men were likely to congregate was all it took. 'You just smile a little, make eye-contact, think of something to say about the music or how crap the bar staff are and you're golden,' she'd proclaimed blithely. 'But mostly you need to get out of the house.'

So, here she was, out of the house at Celia's office Christmas party. In Neve's experience, office parties usually involved a few tired paper streamers, stale crisps in plastic bowls and one of the secretaries weeping in the Ladies. Except Celia worked on a fashion magazine called *Skirt* so there were tempura rolls, light installations and a bevy of beautiful girls wearing the kind of cutting-edge fashion Neve had seen in magazines but didn't think anyone wore in real life. Also, it was the end of January but apparently the *Skirt* staff were too busy attending other people's Christmas soirées in December to have one of their own.

'Oh, Celia, please don't,' Neve begged as she realised that her sister was frantically waving at the infamous Martyn from the subs desk, who detached himself from the throng with an eager look and hurried over.

His eagerness turned to rapture when Celia threw her arm round him. 'Martyn, this is my older sister, Neve. She's super-smart and knows tons of long words, you two have *so* much in common.'

Martyn from the subs desk looked at Neve, then back to Celia, with disbelief. They didn't even remotely resemble sisters. Neve was good Yorkshire peasant stock from their father's side of the family, while Celia had soaked up every single one of their mother's Celtic genes and was all angles and gawky limbs – and even though her face had a pinched, sharp look, that didn't matter when she always wore an easy grin that was echoed in the sparkle of her green eyes. Her legs wouldn't have looked out of place on a Vegas show-girl, and her long curly hair was so fiery and red, no one ever had the nerve to call her a ginge.

Neve, on the other hand, was sturdy, that was a given. But she was soft too. Sometimes Neve felt as if everything about her was vague and indistinct, from the way she looked to the way she could always be talked out of what she thought were deeply held opinions. Celia and her mother insisted that Neve's navy-blue eyes and straight, thick, dark-brown hair were her best features, and she had a good complexion but everything below the neck still needed a lot of work. Young men were never going to catch their breath as Neve walked past; she could deal with that, but she wished Martyn from the subs desk didn't look quite so dismayed at the prospect of being stuck with her as Celia muttered something about going to the bar and disappeared.

'It's nice to meet you,' Neve said, holding out her hand. She knew she should stand up instead of receiving him like an elderly monarch but she didn't want her tights sliding down to her knees. Of course, Martyn could always sit down but he stayed towering over her. 'So, um, do you like being a sub-editor?'

Martyn shrugged. 'It pays the mortgage,' he said. 'I get free grooming products. That's about as good as it gets.'

'Terrible queue at the bar,' Neve continued doggedly. She hoped that Martyn wouldn't think she was angling for a drink, but he just nodded and continued to look everywhere but at her.

Neve knew that her flirting skills were so non-existent that they were invisible to the naked eye, but she was beginning to get rather irritated with Martyn from the subs desk. OK, she wasn't Celia, but if he ever wanted to get inside Celia's electric-blue jumpsuit, it might be an idea to get her elder sister on side first.

Still, he'd do to practise on, Neve decided. 'What's your favourite word, then? I think mine's carbuncle. Or maybe bus-station. I can't decide. Also, is bus-station all one word or should it be hyphenated?'

Now she had Martyn from the subs desk's full attention. 'Seriously?'

'I just wondered,' Neve said, and knew it would be bugging her for the rest of the evening until she could go home and check the *Oxford English Dictionary*. 'Are you enjoying the party?'

'Look, Eve . . .' Martyn was looking at her now with a rueful smile, his hands spread wide. Neve might not know much about flirting but she knew when her number was up.

'It's Neve,' she corrected him gently. 'And it's OK. You only came over because when Celia waved, you thought she wanted to talk to you and instead you got stuck with me.'

'No, no. It's not like that,' Martyn protested. 'I'm sure you're really nice. You *are* really nice but I left my friend getting a round and he probably needs a hand. Nothing personal.'

Neve nodded understandingly. 'You should get back to him.'

'It was really nice talking to you, Eve,' Martyn said, already backing away. 'Maybe I'll see you later.'

'Sure.' But Neve was already talking to Martyn's back. Now that she knew she was boring and physically repulsive, even to a man who did spellchecking for a living, there was no harm in standing up and giving her tights and knickers a really good yank. Then she gingerly lowered herself back on to the sofa and stared at the toes of her black patent Mary-Janes until Celia and Yuri, her sister's flatmate, sat down on either side of her.

'How did it go with Martyn?' Celia asked eagerly, replacing Neve's glass, which she didn't remember draining, with a full one.

'It didn't. Can I please go home now?'

'I told Celia that it would never work with you and that sub-editor,' Yuri said conspiratorially. Douglas, Neve and Celia's elder brother, insisted that Yuri was the most terrifying woman in the world, which was ironic considering who he'd married. If Neve hadn't seen Yuri in her pyjamas practically every morning as she came up the stairs to borrow teabags, milk and occasionally a clean teaspoon, she would have been terrified of her too. Neve had never met a Japanese person with an afro before, or one who sounded like Carmela Soprano, courtesy of the language school in New Jersey where Yuri had learned English. If Celia hadn't come back from New York a year ago with Yuri in tow and Neve wasn't Celia's older sister, which according to Yuri automatically gave her 'eleventy billion cool points', Neve wasn't sure that Yuri would ever have acknowledged her existence. Or happily list all the reasons why Martyn from the subs desk wasn't the right man for Neve.

'He drinks shandy and he sweats a lot,' she finished scathingly. 'Hey, Celia, Neve can do *so* much better.'

'I just wanted to ease her in gently.' Celia made her thinking face. 'What about a male model? They're not as out of reach as people think. Like, they're dead insecure about their looks so the bar isn't that high.'

'Thank you very much,' Neve said, wriggling her

shoulders in annoyance. 'Look, it was sweet of you to ask me along but I don't fit in here. Everyone's beautiful and cool and I feel like a dowdy maiden aunt.'

'No, you don't,' Celia gasped. 'You're rocking the little black vintage dress.'

'Not so much of the little,' Neve reminded her. 'I don't feel comfortable here and that man standing by the bar has been staring and smirking at us for the past five minutes.'

As Yuri and Celia looked over, he raised his glass in acknowledgement and didn't seem perturbed that the three of them were talking about him.

'He's not smirking at us, he's eye-fucking us,' Yuri informed Neve.

'What does that even mean?'

'Max eye-fucks everyone,' Celia said nonchalantly. 'He's our Editor-at-Large, he's a complete slut and he is not, repeat *not*, the kind of man to practise your light flirtation skills on, Neevy. He'll eat you up for breakfast and still have room for a full English afterwards.'

Although she'd been trying to ignore him, Neve squinted through the dry ice and the strobe lights to get a better look at this fashion magazine Lothario, but he was now eye-fucking two pretty blonde girls instead.

'I think he was probably just eye-f— looking at you two, not me, and even if he was, I can take care of myself,' Neve insisted, patting her sister's hand because all of a sudden Celia was looking very hot and flustered. Though that could have been because her vintage jumpsuit was made of Crimplene.

'You can't take care of yourself,' Celia insisted shrilly. 'You have zero experience of men like that. You've led such a sheltered life.'

'You do give off a virgin vibe,' Yuri mused. 'You've had sex, right?'

Neve choked on a mouthful of wine. 'Of course I have! Well, I think I have. I started to, but it hurt a lot and it was just horrible . . . God, I am not having this conversation.' She folded her arms and fixed Celia with a stern look. Celia was the only person who ever got her stern look. 'I'm older than you by three years, so stop trying to pull rank on me.'

'Just warning you off the big bad wolf.'

'Well, there's no need,' Neve started to say as she glanced over to the bar again to get a third look at *Skirt*'s infamous Editor-at-Large, who now had an arm looped round each of the blonde girls' shoulders. 'I've never seen a genuine cad in the flesh before. He should have a pencil moustache really, shouldn't he?'

Celia looked at her sister with fond exasperation. 'He's not a cad like they have in those mouldy old books of yours, Neevy,' she said witheringly. 'He's a twenty-first-century manwhore, bless him.'

'Yeah, he's a tart with a heart of gold,' Yuri added.

Celia dug Neve in the ribs. 'Anyway, enough about Max. You're not going to meet any men stuck here in the corner.'

'But wouldn't you say that just leaving the house and being in the corner of a club is progress? Baby steps . . . Please, Celia, stop manhandling me!'

Celia had one hand wedged into Neve's armpit and with Yuri's help she hauled her sister to her feet. 'We're going to mingle. It will be fun,' she said with grim determination.

It wasn't fun. It wasn't even a little bit fun. Neve switched to spritzers and stayed glued to Celia's side, apart from the times when she held her bag while Celia was throwing energetic shapes on the dancefloor or wheeling over a steady stream of men who all looked the same with their skinny jeans and skinny tees and hedge-trimmer haircuts. Like Martyn from the subs desk, they were all monumentally uninterested in Neve but were vague and polite because she might put in a good word with Celia.

One more spritzer, then I'm definitely going home, Neve vowed to herself as Celia dragged her over to the bar. 'Now, standing at the bar is a great way to meet a man,' Celia told her. 'Especially if there's a queue,' she added, using her elbows to negotiate her way through the crowd waiting to be served. 'You look around and make sure you catch a fit bloke's eye so you can share a smile about how long you've had to wait. Then you'll get served first, because hello, you're a girl, then you offer to get his drinks and because he thinks he has a chance, he'll pay for yours and you're in there.'

'I'll be sure to remember that,' Neve muttered, but Celia was already commiserating with the man standing next to her about how long he'd been waiting to be served.

'Oh, poor Neevy, you look so miserable,' she cooed, when they were finally clutching a free drink each, courtesy of Celia's superior flirting skills. 'Tell you what, we'll sit down for five minutes, before we start Operation Manhunt again.'

'I'm not calling it that. I'm calling it Operation Light Flirtation,' Neve insisted, as she followed Celia over to a shadowy alcove where there were a couple of sofas and a pair of easy chairs arranged around a low table.

'Whatever. We'll just scooch in here.' Celia was already clambering over people's legs to get to a patch of unoccupied sofa. She sat down and patted the three inches of seat next to her. 'Come on. Plonk your arse down.'

Neve didn't clamber over people's legs so much as trip over them and apologise profusely, which was nothing compared to how profusely she apologised to the girl who scowled and got up rather than be squashed against Neve and the arm of the sofa.

Celia checked her phone for messages as Neve tried to surreptitiously yank at her tights and knickers, which were at half-mast again.

'Are you sure neither of you are models?'

Neve and Celia grinned at each other, Celia's nagging and Neve's moaning instantly forgiven as they shared an eye-roll, then looked over at the corner where the infamous Max was living up to his reputation.

Neve had imagined Lotharios to look a lot more suave. Max was handsome enough, with wide-spaced dark eyes framed by outrageously long boy-lashes, pronounced cheekbones and a pillowy, pouty bottom lip, but his face was saved from being too pretty by his nose, which was slightly hooked and bent as if it had been broken by someone's boyfriend, and the hair that he kept pushing off his face looked like it could do with a good wash. He was wearing a crumpled black shirt, a pair of herringbone tweed trousers with frayed hems and a bashed-up pair of Converses.

It took Neve less than five seconds to give Max the once-over and decide that he wasn't her type. And she certainly wasn't his, judging by the two blonde girls he'd been talking to earlier who were now perched on his lap and giggling wildly as he tried out another line on them. 'Well, at least tell me that you're twins, then? I've had triplets before but never twins.'

Celia snorted with mirth. 'Hysterical, isn't he?'

Neve could think of a few other words to describe him but she'd only got as far as 'popinjay' when she felt something cold, hard and wet hit her squarely on the chest. She squealed in shock as the ice cube slid down her cleavage and into her dress. 'What . . . you . . . how dare . . .'

'Hey, dickwad, did you just chuck something at my sister?' Celia snapped at Max. Neve tried to fish the cube out of her tight bodice but it melted fast against her hot fingers and all she got for her trouble was an icy trickle of water that only stopped trickling when it reached the insurmountable barrier of her firm-control tights. 'What is wrong with you?'

Max glanced at Neve, then his gaze skittered away as if she wasn't even worth looking at for more than a second. 'Yeah, sorry about that,' he said breezily, turning to Celia and flashing her a smile that seemed to come with its own lighting rig. 'Was meant for you, Brat. Don't suppose you speak Russian or Polish or something like that. Not sure these girls speak the mother tongue.'

'No, I don't.' Celia made a big show of trying to wipe Neve down, even as Neve wriggled to get away from her because, really, this was humiliating enough without Celia treating her like a messy toddler who'd just had an accident with a ketchup bottle. 'This is my sister, Neve, whom you just assaulted with an airborne missile.'

'Shut up,' Neve hissed out of the side of her mouth, her every molecule throbbing with mortification. Not that Max noticed; he was giving Celia his rapt attention, even as he nuzzled the neck of one of the giggling, not-English girls on his lap. 'You're making everything worse.'

'I said I was sorry. Look, is there an app for the iPhone that one of them can giggle into that will tell me what language they speak?' Max asked earnestly. 'And then I need an app that will translate what I'm saying into that language, because I'm wasting my best lines here.'

He was absolutely poisonous, Neve thought as Celia joined in with the giggling. Obnoxious. Shallow. A nasty piece of work who wouldn't even acknowledge the presence of a woman who didn't measure up to his clichéd standards of female pulchritude.

'Celia, I'm going home now,' Neve said in her iciest voice, but Celia was now happily consorting with the enemy and wittering on about how she wished there was an iPhone app that would tell her if she was about to purchase an item of clothing that one of her friends already owned. 'Celia!'

'OK, OK, keep your hair on,' Celia grumbled, getting to her feet. 'There's only half an hour before we get kicked out, might as well stay to the end. See you later, Max.'

Max didn't even deign to reply because he was neck-nuzzling again, so he just waved one languid hand in their direction.

'What a horrible, horrible man,' Neve said when they were free from the sofas. 'It was like being back at Oxford

22

and having bread rolls lobbed at me by vile posh boys.'

'If it's any consolation, Max is much nicer when there aren't scantily clad blonde women about.'

'Well, it isn't.' Neve sighed, then stuck out her lower lip. 'I'm off. I don't want to miss the last tube.'

'OK, but will you hold my bag for a second – just want to have one more dance,' Celia said, not waiting for Neve to reply but shoving her clutch at her sister.

Chapter Two

It wasn't until they stepped out on to the street half an hour later and the cold January night threw a hundred icy daggers at her face and she gave a comedy stagger that Neve realised she wasn't exactly sober. Not drunk either. But somewhere in between. She stood outside the club shivering in her winter coat and fretting about catching the last Piccadilly line train while she and Celia waited for Yuri to get her skateboard out of the cloakroom. Yuri never went anywhere without it, though Neve had never actually seen her ride it.

'Come on, we're going to Soho House for an after-party,' Celia said, tucking her arm into Neve's. 'Grace is going to sign us in.'

Grace was more important than Celia in the *Skirt* fashion food chain; she was also the sulkiest-looking girl that Neve had ever seen, although she did manage a wan smile in their direction.

'I'm going home,' Neve said firmly, disentangling herself from Celia. 'I've had quite enough excitement for one night.'

'You've barely had any excitement,' Celia said, pouting. 'It will be fun.'

'I've exceeded my fun quota for the month,' Neve told her. 'Now before I go, can we make sure that you or Yuri have your keys, because I don't want you ringing my doorbell at three in the morning.'

'That only happened once . . .'

'I think you mean once this month. Show me your keys.'

The keys were finally produced after a frantic search of Celia's two bags, her coat pockets and her third bag, which Yuri gave her when she finally emerged from the club with her skateboard tucked under her arm.

As Neve was insisting that she wasn't drunk and actually she had gone home on the tube after dark by herself on many occasions, she could hear a commotion behind her. She turned to see Max surrounded by a gaggle of *Skirt* girls, as he mournfully proclaimed, 'Well, I wasn't sure if they were legal, and neither of them spoke English so I had to make my excuses. Pity, they looked very bendy.'

There was a chorus of 'Poor Max' from the cheap seats as Neve turned back to Celia and Yuri. He really was absolutely odious. 'Don't stay out too late,' she reminded Celia. 'You said you had an early shoot tomorrow.'

Celia pulled a face. 'Yes, Mum.'

'Anyway, which one of you lovely ladies is coming home with me?' Max demanded behind them. 'Gracie, don't you think you owe it to yourself to slip between my sheets just once? I'll even make you breakfast and walk you to the bus stop in the morning.'

'Hmmm, tempting offer, Max, but I've given up shagging manwhores for Lent,' came the tart reply.

Neve rolled her eyes, as she checked the side pocket of her bag for Oyster card and rape alarm. 'Right – well, I'm off,' she said briskly.

'Celia? Skate Girl?' He was still trying to drum up business as Neve kissed Celia on the cheek, and she was just about to turn round and head off to the tube when she felt a hand land squarely on her bottom. 'Or what about you? You've got plenty of cushion for the pushing. I like that in a woman.'

Neve let out a furious gasp, her eyes blinking rapidly as

tears welled up. 'Right, I'm going,' she choked out, as Celia gazed at her in horror. 'See you.'

'I take it that's a no, then?' Max shouted after her, as Neve scurried to the safety of the other side of Dean Street and scrubbed one gloved hand furiously at her watering eyes. Max wasn't a cad. A cad would never treat a woman quite so badly. Max was, quite simply, the lowest of the low. Exactly the same as those well-bred, boorish boys at Oxford who'd only ever noticed Neve when they wanted to have a cheap laugh at her expense.

She paused for a second, to take a deep breath and gather herself. She still felt ungathered as she started to walk again, but at least Neve didn't feel as if she might burst into tears. Not all men were like Max, she knew that for a fact, and she shouldn't let that . . . that *manwhore* get to her, even if he had drawn everyone's attention to the size of her bum and physically assaulted her.

Though it was a bitterly cold night, Neve had to side-step throngs of people smoking outside pubs and bars. It was well after midnight and she wished she was snuggled in bed under her winter-weight duvet with her feet resting on a hot-water bottle. Just the thought of it made Neve quicken her pace, especially when she realised that someone had fallen into step beside her. She was just working up the courage to say, 'No, I don't want to get into your unlicensed minicab, thank you very much,' when she saw that it was Max.

'God, you walk fast,' he said cheerfully. 'I've been trying to catch up with you since Wardour Street.'

'You needn't have bothered,' Neve ground out, as she came to a halt so she could stand there with her hands on her hips and glare at him.

In the glow of the streetlamps and the glare of neon signs, Neve could see that his hair wasn't dirty but a glossy dark brown, and his skin had an olive tinge that suggested he'd tan at the first sight of the sun. Which wasn't important right then. It didn't matter how pretty he was when he had such an ugly soul.

Max spread his hands wide. 'Look, I'm sorry I slapped your arse. It was inexcusable and it's been pointed out to me in no uncertain terms that most women don't have the same relaxed attitude to inappropriate touching as the girls in the office do.'

It was a really poor excuse for an apology. 'You implied . . . you said . . .'

'To be honest, I don't know how cushiony your bum is, it was just a line. I really didn't mean to upset you.' Max sounded sincere and he was looking at her with a furrowed brow.

'Fine,' Neve said, though it was a very huffy kind of 'fine'. 'Apology accepted, I suppose.'

She started walking again. So did Max. Walking alongside her, as if they were friends.

'So, where are you heading?'

'I'm going to the tube,' Neve said, because she didn't have the guts to pointedly ignore him.

'Where do you live?' he asked casually.

If by some bizarre twist of fate, Max had decided that she'd do for the night, then he was going to be sorely disappointed. 'Finsbury Park,' Neve said tersely.

'I'm going that way too. I live in Crouch End. Do you want to share a black cab?'

Black cabs were an extravagance that Neve couldn't afford, not this far away from payday, but that wasn't the reason why she declined. 'No, thank you. I'm perfectly all right with catching the tube.'

'OK, tube it is,' Max agreed, because he was quite obviously emotionally tone deaf and couldn't sense the huge 'kindly bugger off' vibes that Neve was sure she was emitting. 'You're still mad at me, aren't you?'

'You apologised, why would I still be mad at you?'

'One day we'll laugh about this. When little Tommy asks

how we met, I'll say, "Well, son, I threw an ice cube at your mother, then slapped her arse, and we've been inseparable ever since."'

Neve could feel her mouth doing something very strange. It felt as if she was smiling, and when Max smiled back at her she could understand why the *Skirt* girls forgave him for being such an obnoxious flirt. It was a suggestive smile that stopped just short of being a leer, and when it was aimed in Neve's direction, it made her feel as if she was sexy and desirable and worthy of it. In fact, it was such a good smile that Neve was powerless to resist its potent charm. 'Come on, then,' she said. 'I don't want to miss the last tube.'

Threading their way through the bustle of Old Compton Street meant that they didn't have to talk, and soon they entered the welcome warmth of the station. Neve always walked down the escalators (and up them too) so she didn't even think to see if Max was following but lurched down the stairs, the strumming of a busker playing 'Hey Jude' getting louder and louder, until she stepped off with a shaky dismount. Max was right behind her, not quite touching her, but close enough to steer her in the right direction when she got confused between the northbound and south-bound Piccadilly line platforms.

'It's so crowded,' Neve complained as they stepped on to the packed platform. 'It's as bad as rush hour.'

Max cupped her elbow. 'Let's walk down to the end – more chance of getting a seat.'

As they reached the end of the platform, the train screeched into the station. Max had been right; there were plenty of empty seats. Neve plopped down and pulled off her woolly hat. 'You should never get in the first or last carriage,' she said. 'If we had a collision with another train, we'd bear the full force of the impact.'

'Well, I'm willing to risk it if it means I can get a seat,' Max said, sitting down next to her and stretching out his long legs. He gave Neve a sideways look from eyes framed with those outrageously long lashes. 'So, here we are.'

'You didn't want to go to Soho House with the others?'

'Fancied an early night for a change,' Max said with a smile that definitely verged on lecherous this time. 'Normally I'm the last to leave but I have a breakfast meeting at the Wolseley with my agent. The man's a sadist, always forcing me out of bed at some ungodly hour.'

'I know what you mean,' Neve said feelingly. Not about breakfast meetings with agents at very fancy London restaurants, but five days a week her alarm chirped insistently at six. She looked at her watch in dismay. 'I've got to be up in five and a half hours.'

'Not really much point in going to bed, is there?' Max shifted in his seat so his arm and leg were pressed against Neve's. 'I'm sure we could find something else to do to pass the time.'

He said it lightly and with that cheeky little smirk so Neve decided not to take offence. She smiled instead, secure in the knowledge that there was every point in going to bed, alone, to sleep for a solid five hours. 'So, why do you have an agent?' she asked, mostly to change the subject. 'Do all Editors-at-Large have one?'

'Only those who write best-selling novels,' Max revealed with just the slightest edge, like he couldn't believe that Neve needed any clarification. 'Well, technically I ghost-write them, but between you and me, Mandy isn't going to give Iris Murdoch any sleepless nights.'

'Well, Iris Murdoch has been dead for quite a few years,' Neve murmured. However, Max was still looking at her expectantly, as if his bestselling novels merited more of a reaction. 'I'm sorry. Who's Mandy?'

Max stopped lolling in his seat and sat up straight. '*Mandy*,' he repeated impatiently.

'I can't quite place the name,' Neve said. 'Is she one of those very famous people who don't need to have a surname?'

He made a tiny scoffing noise. 'Yeah, right. Mandy McIntyre. She's only the most famous WAG in Britain.'

'Hmmm – what does WAG stand for again?' Neve asked. 'I always forget but I know it's something that doesn't make sense.'

'You don't know what a WAG is? For real?' Max asked incredulously. 'Wives and girlfriends. *Footballers'* wives and girlfriends.'

'Oh! See, that's the bit that I don't understand. If they're footballers' wives and girlfriends, then really they should be called FWAGs. Though it doesn't really roll off the tongue that easily.' Neve mouthed the unwieldy acronym to herself a couple more times as Max stared at her. 'No, it really doesn't work. Anyway, I've never heard of her but I don't watch much TV. So she writes novels, does she? Or you write them for her?'

Neve was trying not to sound too disapproving that some girlfriend of a footballer could get a book deal, when she knew of at least three would-be novelists with good degrees from good universities who were working for minimum wage and couldn't even get a short story published. She guessed that she'd managed to keep her outrage to herself because a faint smile was tugging at the corners of Max's mouth.

'Well, Mandy and I go way back,' he said. 'I interviewed her for *Skirt* and we really hit it off so she asked me to ghost her memoirs.'

'Oh, she must be quite old if she's already had a memoir published.'

'She's twenty-two,' Max said. 'Then, after Mand's auto-biography, we wrote a *Style Guide* and now I'm working on her fourth novel.'

'But I thought you said that you wrote them together?' It was all very confusing, especially when you'd had too many white-wine spritzers.

'The publisher came up with an idea about a young girl

who's working in a supermarket when she starts dating a footballer, then Mandy and I brainstormed some scenarios, I fleshed it out and three novels later, we've sold over a million books. The series has been translated into twenty-three different languages and it's in development with a film production company,' Max said proudly. 'You *must* have read one of them. Every woman I know has secretly read at least one of them.'

'Look, I don't read that kind of novel,' Neve said – and immediately realised how snotty she sounded, if the curl of Max's top lip was a good indicator. She frantically tried to backtrack. 'Well, that doesn't sound very fair; I mean, you do all the work and she gets all the credit and the royalties.'

'Not *all* the royalties,' Max demurred. He shook his head. 'Why don't you know who she is? Have you just come out from under a large rock?'

'The truth is, I'm not really that interested in celebrities,' Neve explained carefully. 'It just all seems rather superficial, and anyway, I have to do a lot of serious reading for my job, so—'

'What is your job?' Max demanded rather belligerently. 'I suppose it's something completely worthy and *un*superficial, like finding a cure for cancer or solving world hunger.'

She hadn't said that *he* was superficial so there was no need for Max to be quite so snippy. 'I work at a literary archive,' Neve informed him coldly. 'I'm the senior archivist.'

'What? Like a library or something?'

'It's not the least bit like a library,' Neve snapped. 'And safeguarding literary papers for future generations is actually a very worthwhile and rewarding job.'

'If you say so,' Max said dismissively. 'Sounds kinda boring to me.'

Neve was saved from having to tell Max she didn't appreciate his philistine views on her choice of career by the train pulling into Finsbury Park station.

As soon as the train came to a halt she was out of her seat and through the doors before they'd even finished opening. She then lurched up the stairs in shoes which had now officially become Instruments of Torture, and would have tried to run down the long tunnel that led to the street if she wasn't stuck behind a man wheeling a large suitcase behind him.

It wasn't long before Max caught up with her, though Neve couldn't imagine why. If their positions were reversed, she'd have skulked on the platform for several minutes until she was sure he'd gone.

'Is this going to be the pattern for our relationship?' he asked, body-blocking the Oyster card reader so Neve had to yank him away before somebody intent on swiping their ticket hit him. 'I say something mildly controversial, you storm off in a huff and then I'm forced to chase after you so I can say I'm sorry?'

'We're not in a relationship,' Neve reminded him. She was resolved that this time, she wouldn't smile or let herself by swayed by Max's effortless but considerable charm, but God help her, she found herself smiling.

'Fine. You've apologised. *Again*. Isn't that your bus?'

They both watched the W7 sail around the corner. 'Of course, instead of apologising, we could kiss and make up instead?' Max suggested lightly.

They were standing in front of the London Underground map, hands shoved into respective pockets. Neve looked up at Max to see if he was joking, because, quite frankly, he *had* to be joking. Men who looked like Max and had glamorous jobs and were on first-name terms with WAGs didn't kiss girls like her. 'You want to kiss me?' she asked tremulously.

'Well, it will be a nice ending when I tell little Tommy the story of how we first met,' Max said, and Neve wasn't just smiling, she was giggling, even though, as a rule, she didn't giggle. 'The question is, do I kiss you here or at your front door after I've walked you home and just before you invite me in for a coffee?'

Neve frowned. This whole situation was running away from her. She was just starting to get the hang of light flirtation and now Max had raced ahead to kissing and . . . 'For a coffee?'

'Are we really doing this?' Max sounded exasperated. 'Not for a coffee. For this.'

His hands were out of his pockets and around her waist before Neve had time to blink or pull in her tummy. All she could do was watch Max's face get nearer and nearer. The kiss was inevitable but she still thought she was imagining it when Max's lips brushed against hers.

Neve didn't pull away, but she didn't move closer; she just stayed absolutely statue-still to see where this was going to lead.

'I love your red lipstick,' Max murmured, as if they were already alone in her flat and not standing outside a tube station with the wind whistling around them and discarded take-away containers and fag ends at their feet. 'It's so sexy.'

Neve knew it was just a line to get into her knickers, though if Max could see the firm-control reality of them, then he'd have wished he hadn't bothered, she thought sadly. She opened her mouth to say something, to tell Max the red lipstick was just false advertising, supplied by Celia, but her words got lost when Max lifted his thumb to her mouth and slowly and deliberately wiped it away.

'What did you do that for?' Neve touched her fingers to her lips, which were tingling as if he'd been kissing her for hours.

'Because I want to kiss you again and I don't think red's my colour. I usually go for the pinker shades,' Max said, and Neve wondered how many girls he'd practised on before the right words came tumbling out of his mouth without him even having to think about it. He'd undoubtedly kissed a lot of women, really knew what he was doing, so why not treat this whole confusing encounter as an educational experience?

'Well, go on then,' she said in what she hoped was a challenging tone. 'Kiss me if you want to.'

This time Neve was ready, tilting her head back as Max cupped her cheek and slowly kissed her. Just his lips on her lips, nothing more than friction, but it sent a thousand sparks shooting down her arms and legs so Neve was flexing her fingers and trying to curl her toes in her too-tight shoes. It was only her third ever kiss. There'd been an horrific collision with her second cousin's tongue at a wedding where she'd also got drunk for the first time, and there'd been the dreadlocked Philosophy student who may or may not have taken her virginity, and that was after she'd consumed a huge number of fudge brownies, which she'd later discovered had been heavily laced with marijuana. They barely counted. Whereas this was stellar kissing, the kind of kissing that she'd only read about in the lurid bodice-rippers she'd sneaked from her grandmother's bookshelves.

Neve did what any self-respecting Regency heroine would do and wound her arms around Max's neck with a rapturous little sigh so the kisses could get deeper, more heated, and they only stopped when someone across the street bellowed, 'Get a fucking room!'

Her hat had fallen off in all the excitement. Max crouched down to pick it up, as Neve tried to get her breathing under control. She really had to try to be more blasé about this.

'So, what do you think?' Max asked as he placed the hat back on Neve's head, pulling it over her eyes and grinning when she scowled and adjusted it. 'Back to yours or am I catching the last bus home?'

Neve was never very good at making split-second decisions. Even choosing a DVD from Blockbuster could be a fraught experience and she needed at least a week to debate this question, but Max was tapping his foot impatiently.

'Well, I . . . I don't . . . I think you've already missed the last bus,' she choked out, staring at the top button on Max's black wool coat because she'd lose her nerve if she had to look at his face. She'd give him coffee and have another half-hour of those dark velvet kisses, then she'd kick him out. 'I suppose that would be all right.'

Max nodded. 'Cool.' He paused. 'By the way, I don't think I ever caught your name.'

Chapter Three

Finsbury Park was an area of London that was meant to be up-and-coming but still hadn't quite up and come. If you turned right when you came out of the tube station and walked under the bridge, it was a soulless morass of minicab offices, fast-food joints and gangs of hoodies.

But Neve always turned left and walked past the little supermarkets, their stalls displaying exotic fruit and vegetables, the Afro-Caribbean beauty store that had row after row of be-wigged mannequin heads in the window, the fishmonger's and up to the Old Dairy, which was now a gastro pub. When Neve's parents had first got married and moved into a maisonette a couple of streets away from her grandmother's pub on the Stroud Green Road, the area was a grimy collection of betting shops, off-licences and crumbling terraces converted into poky flats; the sort of place where one didn't linger too late after dark. In the last ten years though, the streets of solidly built Victorian terraced houses, the huge park and the ten-minute trip on the Victoria line to Oxford Circus had reeled in the middle classes.

Neve could never imagine living anywhere else. She'd spent three years at Oxford, but the dreaming spires, medieval churches and punts bobbing on the river had completely lacked the poetry of the roar of the crowds spilling out of the station when Arsenal played a home game or the sun falling in dappled shadows on the Parkland Walk.

Besides, who'd want to live anywhere where you couldn't get a can of Coke and a bag of chips after midnight within two minutes of opening your front door?

It was, however, the first time Neve had walked these familiar streets with a man who wasn't a member of her immediate family or gay. Neve wasn't sure what a suitable topic of conversation would be for an almost stranger that you were taking back to your house solely for kissing and possibly some of the other things that went hand-in-hand with the kissing. But then Max started talking about the tramp who could usually be seen under the railway bridge swigging from a bottle of cider and, 'Have you ever been in that charity shop? It smells like the bowels of hell.'

All too soon they came to her gate. Max paused for a moment as if he was giving her time to back out, but Neve simply unlatched the gate and hurried up the path to the house that had once been her grandmother's. When she'd died, her son, Neve's father, had converted the property into three flats and divvied them up between his three children. Celia was still seething that she'd been in New York when the conversion was completed and so she'd got stuck with the ground-floor flat.

Celia was currently pickling her liver somewhere in Soho and the house was dark and silent, but Neve didn't turn on the hall light, and as soon as Max stepped through the door he crashed into her bike, which was propped against the wall.

Neve's heart shuddered. She looked fearfully upwards, expecting the landing light to snap on and a shrill voice to start screaming. When nothing happened, except Max swearing under his breath, she sagged in relief.

'Um, can you take your shoes off?' she whispered.

'Why?' Max asked in his normal voice, which sounded loud enough to wake the dead.

'You have to keep your voice down,' Neve hissed. 'My brother and my sister-in-law own the first-floor flat and she's . . . *an evil psycho bitch* . . . very noise sensitive. Please, Max.'

It was too dark to see anything, but Neve was sure she could *hear* Max rolling his eyes with great force. 'OK,' he said in a stage whisper, toeing off his Converses.

They crept up the stairs, Neve holding her breath until they'd cleared the first-floor landing and she could exhale very quietly. When they reached her door, she carefully inched her key into the lock.

'This reminds me of being sneaked into girls' homes when I was a teenager and their parents were asleep upstairs,' Max grumbled as Neve frantically shushed him and pushed him through her front door.

'Sorry about that,' she muttered, snapping on the hall light. She went to unbutton her coat and froze because now in her hall with Max looming over her, reality was beginning to sink in. She had a man in her flat who'd come home with her for the sole purpose of getting his hands on her body, and suddenly taking off her coat felt like getting naked. And though there was no way in hell she was having sex with Max, there'd still be touching, and the way she'd kissed him outside the station meant that Max would expect . . . God, she didn't know what he'd expect, and in some ways that was the most frightening thing of all.

Neve didn't even know what to do with her hands but just let them flutter helplessly as Max unwound his scarf and took off his coat. 'Shall I hang them up here?' he asked, gesturing at the wall hooks.

'Yeah.' Neve did a slow turn as if she'd never been inside her flat before and was trying to get her bearings. 'The living room is through here.'

She imagined that she could feel Max's breath on the back of her neck as she bustled into the lounge and turned on a couple of lamps; the only way she'd get through this with any measure of dignity still intact was with very subdued lighting.

Max sat on the sofa that Neve pointed at jerkily and looked around with interest. The lounge had originally been two bedrooms; now it was one huge room lined on two walls with floor-to-ceiling bookshelves. Neither Celia nor Douglas had wanted their grandmother's old furniture so Neve had claimed the battered leather Chesterfield and the two threadbare red velvet armchairs. In the furthest corner of the room was her desk, pushed in front of the window so she could look out over the railway lines and the woods. And then there were the books, not just on the shelves but stacked on her desk and in piles on the scarred wooden floorboards, which her father had begged her to sand down and varnish, and even books fighting for space with the collection of Clarice Cliff pieces on the mantelpiece. The computer, television and iPod dock looked as if they'd been imported from another universe.

Max simply nodded and smiled. It was a secret sort of smile as if he wasn't just pleased with the room but with something else that he didn't feel like sharing. 'I don't know why your sister-in-law gets so bent out of shape by the completely reasonable noise levels of someone going up the stairs when you live right by a railway track,' Max remarked.

Neve had often wondered the very same thing. 'Apparently I'm very heavy-footed,' she confessed, but Max snorted as if the notion that Neve could stomp up and down the stairs 'like a herd of fucking elephants' was ridiculous. Though at that moment, still wearing her coat and with her knickers and tights on the downward slide yet *again*, Neve felt more lumpen than she had done in months.

'Have you got something to drink?' Max asked, settling back on the couch. 'And are you going to take your coat off?'

Neve was still standing in the middle of the room on her plush art deco replica rug from IKEA. 'Yes, sorry, yes. Wine. I think I've only got white. Except there's some red but it's pretty nasty. It's cooking wine . . .'

'White will be great,' Max assured her. 'There's no need to look so scared, by the way. I don't bite.'

At least he hadn't added *unless you want me to*, Neve thought as she took off her coat and stared at her reflection in the hall mirror. She had a severe case of hat-head, her hair a mass of static, and her flushed cheeks were a perfect match for her smeared lipstick, but her face would do; it was the rest of her that she was worried about.

Neve flipped up her skirt and hoisted her tights so high that they almost touched her bra band, then smoothed her dress back down and peered at herself critically. In profile her waist looked tiny, but that was only because of the wide flare of her hips, and even with the finest shapewear that Marks & Sparks had to offer, her belly still pooched out. The sweetheart neckline of her fitted, black vintage dress didn't show much cleavage, which was just as well, and the tight sleeves were keeping her upper arms in check. Neve looked down at her stockinged feet; the hem of her dress swished pleasingly and covered her legs to mid-calf. Yes, fully clothed she passed muster so she'd just have to stay fully clothed but the tights would have to go, Neve decided, as they slowly began to unpeel for the gazillionth time that evening.

With the kitchen door shut firmly behind her, Neve pulled off her tights and stuffed them in the empty bread-bin to be dealt with at a later stage. There was an unopened bottle of Pinot Grigio in the fridge and Neve poured herself a glass, drained it, then, wedging the bottle under her arm, went back into the living room, where Max was lounging back on the sofa as if he ended up in some strange girl's living room every night. Point of fact, he probably did.

'I hope you don't want cheese and crackers,' Neve said doubtfully, placing wine and glasses on the coffee table in front of him. ''Cause I don't have any. I do have some oatcakes.'

'Just the wine will do,' Max said easily, watching intently

as Neve sat at the other end of the sofa, curling her legs beneath her as she grabbed a polka-dot cushion to shield her tummy. 'Shall I pour?'

'Yes, please.'

Once her fingers were curled around the stem of the glass, her other hand clutching the cushion to her like a motherless child she'd sworn to protect, Neve willed herself to relax. She was feeling all fuzzy round the edges and everything in the room, except Max, was in soft focus as if someone had smeared her corneas with Vaseline.

Max sipped his wine and Neve waited for him to make a move. She'd imagined that they'd move straight to more kissing, not this awkward silence while she racked her brains for something to say. Not that Max seemed ill at ease; he was leisurely sipping from his glass and gazing at her stuffed bookshelves with a slightly bemused expression on his face. Then he glanced at Neve, just in time to see the anxious look she was giving him from under her lashes.

'So you and Celia are sisters?' Max asked suddenly. 'You don't look at all alike.'

It was the single most predictable thing that anyone ever said when comparing the Slater sisters. And even after all this time, it still hurt. 'Yes, well . . .'

'Because she's always banging on about her Celtic roots and you don't look at all Irish,' Max continued, not seeming the least bit put out that Neve was sitting there with a stony face. 'You're more of an English rose.'

'I take after the Yorkshire side of the family,' Neve explained, forcing herself to relax muscles that were rigid with tension. It was going to be all right. Max appeared to be chatting her up and surely, after chatting her up, kissing would be the next item on the agenda. 'Celia is the spitting image of our Irish grandmother. She had a really mean right hook.'

'How do you know she had a mean right hook?' Max wanted to know. 'She didn't use it on you, did she?'

'Of course not,' Neve said, though her Granny Annie had never been able to resist pinching her cheeks hard enough to leave bruises. 'She owned the roughest pub on the Stroud Green Road and she was always wading into the middle of fights to throw people out and tell them they were barred for life.'

'And you weren't tempted to go into the family business?'

Neve shook her head. 'No. I punch like a girl and the smell of beer makes me dry heave.'

'You and Celia: you're really not at all alike,' Max murmured again. Maybe Celia was more his type. Maybe Celia and Max had already . . . No! Celia would definitely have said something. She always over-shared to a horrifying degree about her sexual escapades, even though Neve clamped her hands over her ears each time. But if Celia was more Max's type . . .

'We have tons in common,' Neve insisted. 'In fact, I taught Celia everything she knows.' Which was the only reason that Celia had managed to pass her GCSE in English. 'Apart from the fashion-related stuff.'

'Is that so?' Max enquired with a sultry purr to his voice that hadn't been there before. 'Why don't you snuggle in a bit closer?'

'Are you going to kiss me again?' It probably wasn't the sexiest thing to ask but Neve wanted to know that Max was on the same page as her. The page where there were passionate kisses and her heaving bosoms were crushed against a manly chest and . . .

'I was definitely thinking about it,' Max agreed. He patted his knee invitingly. 'Well, come here then.'

Sitting on Max's lap really wasn't viable but Neve scrambled to her knees so she could shuffle along the couch and drape herself carefully over him. It wasn't very comfortable, but with some wriggling and an elbow in Max's ribs, which made him grunt in surprise, Neve could mash her lips against his.

The first moments of kissing were all teeth and tongue as Neve attacked Max's mouth with a lot of enthusiasm and absolutely no finesse. But then Max retreated, regrouped and showed her how to do it slowly so each kiss was like biting into the richest darkest chocolate and pausing to savour the taste. Neve could feel herself getting more and more light-headed, not from the alcohol, but from being drunk on kisses and the feel of Max's fingers threading through her hair, then sliding down to stroke her neck. When his hand cupped her breast, Neve moaned approvingly and flattened her hand against Max's chest so she could feel the thud of his heart.

It would have been perfect if it weren't for the crick in her neck.

Neve rose up on her knees, one hand resting on the back of the couch while she caught her breath, and she didn't care that her belly might be sticking out or that Max was still caressing her breasts as if they were his absolutely favourite thing in the world. She just wanted to stay on the sofa, kissing him, for ever.

'So does this flat of yours have a bedroom?' Max drawled, and Neve had never made anyone drawl before.

She'd planned to keep this kissing experiment within the controlled environment of her lounge, but snogging furiously on the sofa seemed so adolescent. Max already thought that Neve was cut from the same glittery cloth as Celia, and maybe she was because in the space of one evening she had mastered light flirtation and aced kissing. Now it was time to maybe kiss in a room with a bed in it. She might even let Max slide his hands into her bodice, Neve decided recklessly. She'd play it by ear, after she'd downed what was left in her wineglass.

'This way,' she said, attempting to get off the sofa gracefully and hearing her dress rip in the process. Inwardly she winced but outwardly she held out her hand and tugged Max up. He squeezed her fingers tightly in a gesture that was strangely comforting as Neve led him out of the lounge, up one half-flight of stairs, pulled him back from the bathroom, and up another half-flight into her attic bedroom.

Chapter Four

Neve let go of Max's hand so she could turn on the old-fashioned standard lamp in the corner, then felt his arms envelop her as he kissed the back of her neck, hands smoothing down the slippery faux satin of her dress. She half-heartedly sucked in her tummy though Max didn't seem to mind that her belly went out rather than in.

'Never thought you'd have such a messy bedroom,' he whispered in her ear.

'I wasn't expecting visitors.' Neve closed her eyes as she leaned back against Max's chest so she wouldn't have to look at the havoc Celia and Yuri had wreaked when they were helping her select a party outfit. They'd pulled out practically every single item of clothing in Neve's closet and drawers and dumped them on her bed, on her vintage 1950s' sideboard and her matching pair of Lloyd Loom wicker chairs. It didn't help that 95 per cent of her clothes had an extremely muted colour palette so there were mounds of black material marring the pretty pink and whiteness of her room as if the guests at a funeral had performed an impromptu mass striptease.

With Max still wrapped around her, Neve staggered over to her bed – about the only thing she'd bought new because she'd wanted a proper girly bed with an ivory curlicued frame that she could heap with floral-sprigged linen. 'I'll just chuck them on the floor,' she said, scooping up a pile of skirts and flinging them on to her white floorboards. 'Normally, though, I'd put them away properly.'

'Of course you would,' Max said, as if he didn't believe her.

'I *so* would!'

'OK, you get this stuff off the bed and I'll get this dress off of you,' Max said playfully, lifting up her hair so he could fiddle with the hook-and-eye closure.

'No, don't do that,' Neve yelped, turning quickly so she could wind her arms round Max's neck. 'You haven't kissed me for at least five minutes.'

'I'm sorry about that.' His lips were on hers before he'd even finished the sentence, as he backed her on to the bed and came down on top of her.

It was so much better than kissing on the sofa – not only was Neve's head supported by her memory foam pillow, but the weight of Max on top of her and grinding slightly into her was more arousing than Neve had expected. It also meant that all he could see was her flushed face, so even when the skirt of her dress got tangled between them and he started stroking a path up her legs, there was nothing to freak out about. Touching wasn't the same as looking and anyway, she'd shaved her legs earlier in the evening, even though Celia had insisted that the one way you were guaranteed never to pull a guy was if you shaved your legs before you went out. Which just showed how little she knew.

'You're so pretty,' Max murmured against her skin, as he kissed a path along the neckline of her dress. 'Shall we get a little bit more naked?'

He pulled back so he could start unbuttoning his shirt and looked at her expectantly. Neve propped herself up on her elbows because lying flat on the bed wasn't very becoming. The room *was* dimly lit but not dimly lit enough because Max would be able to see all of her just as clearly as Neve could see every inch of Max's chest slowly emerging from its black cotton confines. His chest wasn't just good to lean against; it was good to look at too. Not especially hairy, but just broad enough and toned enough that she couldn't resist poking one of his pecs with a tremulous finger. There wasn't much give. Neve fanned out her fingers and rubbed her thumb over one of his nipples; it was smaller and flatter and browner than hers and then she was running both hands over his chest because she could. Because Max wanted her to and he wouldn't be smiling and shrugging his arms out of his shirt if he wanted her to stop.

She dipped her fingers in and out of his clavicles and slid them down his chest, over his abdomen, then stopped when she reached his worn leather belt. When she lowered her eyes she could see the outline of his hard-on because she'd made him hard. It was a concept that Neve couldn't even begin to process.

'OK, I've shown you mine, now you show me yours.' Max grinned as he tugged free his belt buckle.

There was a part of Neve that was slowly liquefying on her Cath Kidston duvet cover even though she felt as if she should be running around the room, arms and legs flailing wildly as she emitted high-pitched shrieks of terror.

Neve knew it was her right to say no at any time during any type of sexual activity. She knew that, but when you were lying on your bed while the sexy, glamorous, experienced man you'd invited back to your flat for the flimsy promise of coffee, even though he was light years out of your league, was slowly unbuttoning his fly, 'no' felt like the wrong thing to say.

If she said no, she'd appear gauche and prudish and a repressed freak who wasn't even sure whether she was a virgin or not. Besides, virginity wasn't such a big deal. Celia and Chloe at work had both shucked off the shackles of their maidenhood by the time they were sixteen, and she was twenty-five and she should have got round to doing this years ago, and though having a no-strings sexual

47

encounter hadn't made it on to her dating to-do list, at least she could stop worrying about it and—

'Look, I don't have such a great body,' Neve blurted out. 'I'm not thin or, like, toned and stuff.'

Max snorted. 'I know at least ten women who would kill for curves like yours.' He patted her knee and let his hand rest there so he could trace patterns on Neve's skin with the tip of his finger as he began to inch up the hem of her dress with his other hand.

Neve gritted her teeth but forced herself to remain calm. This wasn't going to be easy, but she'd made her mind up to do this and she never had to see Max again, especially if she made a solemn vow that she'd never attend another *Skirt* party.

'C'mon, Neve,' Max said softly. 'If you weren't sexy, then why would I be this hard? Here, feel . . .'

Her hand had been resting limply by her side but Max picked it up and placed it on his covered cock. She could feel it twitching, and when she tentatively curled her fingers around its length, it gave a little leap.

'I did that,' she said incredulously.

'You did that,' Max said, his other hand sliding up her leg and pushing up her dress – and that was when Neve saw the hem of her slip.

She was wearing a slip under her dress! She was saved, because she could easily do damage control on her bingo wings, and having sex with your slip on was textbook sexy in a *femme fatale*, film noir-ish sort of way.

Neve reached for her zip and slowly inched it down as Max stood up and started unzipping his trousers so there was a stereophonic symphony of rasping metal. They were both staring at each other, eyes widening when Max suddenly stopped, and bent down.

'Seeing me in nothing but my socks would kill the mood,' he remarked casually as Neve took advantage of the moment to quickly skin out of her dress and press her arms tight to the side of her body so there'd be no unsightly flab on display. Even her breasts looked perky framed by her nicest balconette bra and the black lace edging of her slip.

And Neve didn't think she'd ever felt quite so validated as when Max raised his head and gave a long, low whistle when he caught sight of her. 'God, you look just like Liz Taylor in *Butterfield 8*,' he said fervently. 'You have truly amazing tits.'

'They're OK,' she agreed shyly, because they did look pretty spectacular at that moment thanks to underwiring and padded cups – and that was all that Max was going to see of them.

Max didn't share her shyness. He slid his belt off so his trousers hung low on his hips, then quickly and efficiently pulled them off like he couldn't wait to get naked and move on to the next part. Neve knew that she was staring but she couldn't help it. She'd never seen an erect penis before, not in the flesh anyway, and what had happened with the Philosophy student had happened under the covers and in darkness. All she could do was sit there and stare half in horror, half in fascination at Max's straining cock. It looked painful and it looked much bigger than she'd imagined, and it looked as if it was never going to fit inside her and it looked so *other* that all Neve wanted to do was keep looking at it until it became more familiar. The way she did with a particularly troublesome crossword clue.

But that wasn't really an option when Max was walking towards her with a foil square in his hand and his dick leading the way, like a divining rod made flesh. Neve did the only thing she could do in the circumstances and dived under her duvet.

'Is there room for me in there too?' Max asked.

Neve folded back two centimetres of quilt. 'Of course,' she squeaked. And just to show she was totally on board, she took one of her full-length body pillows and threw it on the floor. 'See, there's tons of space.'

Then suddenly her bed was invaded by acres of warm, male flesh as Max took her in his arms. It really was a watershed moment; there was a naked man in her bed, moulding himself to the curves of her body, and even though Neve felt as if this was all moving too fast and it was jumping-from-a-burning-building scary, she couldn't remember the last time she'd been held by someone who wasn't Celia.

Max traced her eyebrows with the tip of a finger. 'I know I keep saying it, but you're so pretty.'

Neve knew she wasn't. It was just something that guys said when they wanted to have sex with you, and now that they were in bed and it was a foregone conclusion, Max really didn't need to say it, but still the words meant something to her. It was the first time a man had ever said it to her, apart from her dad, and that didn't count; besides, she really didn't want to think about her dad at a time like this.

'You're pretty too,' she said, touching the bump in his crooked nose. 'You remind me of Caravaggio's painting of David holding up the head of Goliath.'

Max screwed up his face in mock indignation. 'As long as you don't mean Michelangelo's *David*,' he said and he arched his hips, so she'd be sure of his meaning, not that Neve was in any doubt.

'You wish,' she said dryly, the way she'd talk when she was teasing Celia or chatting with Chloe and Rose at work. In fact, the way she normally was when she wasn't half drunk and half giddy with horror and her own daring.

Neve had never thought that she'd be cracking jokes when she was in bed with a man. Or that he'd pin her to her mattress and tickle her ribs until she choked out, 'Sorry,' in between giggles. She lay there, hair fanning out across the pillow, with Max looking down at her, and all it took was one arm hooking around his neck to persuade him to kiss her again and again.

It wasn't often that Neve felt she could escape the confines of her body, but in those hot, sweet moments, she imagined herself transformed into a creature of nothing but pure sensation. She didn't care about anything but Max's mouth and hands on her, and even the feel of his cock, hot and hard, against her inner thigh was something new and exciting.

'Can I touch it?' she asked, when Max let go of her mouth so he could kiss a spot on her neck that made her grind against him. But her hand was already skittering down his body so she could wrap her fingers around his dick, gauging the length and heft of him, smoothing her thumb over the rounded tip and snatching her hand away when Max groaned as if she'd hurt him. 'Sorry,' she whispered.

He bit her neck gently but deliberately. 'Don't stop,' he said hoarsely. 'Just carry on doing what you were doing.'

Her hand was back on him in a second, marvelling at how a penis could be both hard and soft at the same time, and she kind of wanted to have another look at it, even if it meant shucking off the covers, but her thought processes got derailed as Max's hand slipped up her legs.

'Let's get your knickers off,' he said lightly, tugging down the reinforced cotton and elastane with a speed and dexterity that Neve couldn't quite grasp. 'That's better. Now why don't I show you how good I am with my hands too? I'm also pretty spectacular with my tongue.'

The creature of pure sensation exited stage left and Neve was back in her own unwieldy flesh and arching her hips away from Max's fingers. She could handle the sex because she was going to insist on nothing fancier than the missionary position so Max would be on top with nothing much to look at but the framed Modigliani print above her bed. But there was no way she was going to spread herself out like a sexual smorgasbord. Sex was definitely the safer option.

'You don't have to do that,' she said, pressing her legs tight together and shuffling away from him. 'I'm ready to go.'

'You're sure? 'Cause I don't mind if you want to go twice.'

Celia had painted Max as a love 'em and leave 'em, cut-price Casanova, and instead he was being sweet and considerate and doing more for Neve's bruised ego than the week-long Goddess Retreat that her mum had bought her for her birthday, when she'd specifically asked for a Wii Fit, but she had the winning hand so to speak.

'No, honestly, I'm good,' Neve said firmly as she applied the same pressure to Max's cock as she had when she'd milked a cow on a school visit to the City Farm in Kentish Town. The farmer said she'd been a natural and it turned out he was right because Max closed his eyes and flung his head back.

'You keep doing that, and it's going to be game over before we've even started,' he muttered. 'Condom.'

'What did you do with it?' Neve said, loosening her grip on him.

'Nightstand.'

'Why are you only talking in one-word sentences?' Neve asked, as she groped for the foil packet.

'You know why,' Max gritted. 'As you're so attached to my dick, maybe you could do the honours.'

Neve tried to cast her mind back to her sex education classes and the unripe banana she'd sheathed in slimy rubber. Except Charlotte had said she needn't bother because no one would ever want to have sex with her. The entire class, apart from her friend Paula, had roared their approval and Neve had been so upset that she'd eaten her unsheathed banana while everyone else was watching a film about STIs.

Just the memory of it made Neve shudder. She thrust the condom at Max. 'I always put my nail through it,' she lied with an ease that surprised her. 'You do it.'

Neve wouldn't have thought it possible to put on a condom so quickly without even looking, but Max was pressed up against her in a matter of moments so he could kiss the corner of her mouth, which was drooping downwards. Those bad memories had killed Neve's mood but that didn't mean she was going to back out now. No. She wasn't a quitter. When she decided to do something, she saw it through to the bitter end.

They were lying on their sides, face to face, knees knocking together, but Neve pulled gently away from Max to lie flat on her back and tried to think of something sexy to say to hurry things along.

'Come on then,' she said in what she hoped was an alluring manner.

Max propped himself up on his elbow. 'You sure about this?' he asked. 'Ready to be ravished?'

'Quite sure,' Neve said shortly, tugging at his arm. 'Please, can you just . . .'

'God, you're impatient,' Max said, like he didn't really mind, but at least now he was looming over her, pausing to kiss her while Neve obligingly parted her legs.

Neve lay there completely still, until she remembered that she needed to tug her slip down where it had ridden up over her belly because the quilt wasn't covering everything she wanted it to.

Max was fumbling at her girl parts now and Neve was sure her clitoris was actually recoiling as it tried to evade his touch. She stared at the ceiling and tried to divorce her mind from her body, just like she did when she was having a smear test. What was taking him so long?

'Neve? I know you said you were ready, but you don't *feel* ready . . .'

She lifted her head. 'Believe me, I'm completely ready.'

Max frowned, a lock of hair flopping over his forehead. 'Could you tilt your hips a bit? No, tilt them towards me.'

Now it felt like she was in her Pilates class and trying to find 'neutral spine'. Though actually breathing in through her nose and exhaling through her mouth seemed like a good idea as Max began to enter her slowly and laboriously, lower lip caught between his teeth. It seemed to take for ever, as if they weren't two people having sex but two satellites docking.

At least this time, Neve knew for absolute certain that she was being penetrated. It didn't hurt but it was extremely uncomfortable and not something she was planning to do again any time soon. But it would be different when she was having sex . . . no, *making love* with someone she was in love with. Only love could make this more bearable.

Max was pulling out and Neve wished he wouldn't, because he'd only have to push in again and he was hissing slightly, teeth bared, features tight, his hands on her hips. Neve shut her eyes so she wouldn't have to look at him, and how could she have been so stupid? She'd been too impatient and decided that sex was something she could rush through, then cross it off her to-do list. But it wasn't an item that could be scored through; it was special and it was really, really intimate. If someone had never really got inside your head and your heart, then they shouldn't be inside your body. Neve got that now, but her epiphany was too late. She'd reached the point of no return about ten minutes ago.

She steeled herself for re-entry, eyes screwed tight shut, fists clenched until she realised that nothing was happening. Max had stopped.

'Is something wrong?' he asked tersely, taking his hands off her hips so he could move back.

'No, I'm fine. You can carry on if you like.'

'Well, I would, but it's not easy staying hard when the girl underneath you obviously wishes she was somewhere else,' he bit out.

The searing flush of utter mortification was like being plunged into boiling hot water. He thought she was crap in bed. She *was* crap in bed. *And* she was so utterly repellent that he'd lost his erection. Neve willed her eyes to open but they decided to stay shut so she wouldn't have to see the obviously repulsed look on Max's face. It was bad enough that he swore under his breath and slid out from under the covers so he could sit on the edge of the bed and put as much space between them as he could.

Neve said the only thing she could in the circumstances. 'I'd like you to leave, please.'

'I asked you if you wanted to do this. Not just once but several times.'

'Please, will you leave?' Neve rolled over so she was cocooned in her quilt and wouldn't have to look at Max when she finally opened her eyes.

'You should have said something, because I would never have . . . I don't force myself on women. Did I hurt you?' He was angry, not without good reason, but Neve could hear other things in his voice: shame, guilt, uncertainty. All the things she was feeling too.

'You didn't hurt me,' she said woodenly. 'You didn't force yourself on me. Not at all. But I really need you to go now.' She couldn't stand to stay in the same room with him so she inched her legs out of bed and when she felt the floor underneath her feet, threw back the covers and snatched up her dressing-gown from the chair in one fluid movement. 'I'll give you some privacy,' she mumbled as she sped for the door.

Neve scurried for the safety of the lounge so she could curl up in an armchair and huddle miserably in her ratty old dressing-gown, arms round her knees and listen to the sounds of Max getting dressed. Her heart thudded painfully in time with his tread on the stairs and she waited for his footsteps to keep going and for the front door to open, but they stopped – and when she looked up, he was standing in the living-room doorway.

She cringed back from his steady gaze, though it wasn't angry or accusatory as much as thoughtful.

'Bad break-up?' he asked.

Neve blinked at him. 'I'm sorry?'

'You've just broken up with someone and you thought you could go out and grudge fuck some random guy but your conscience got the better of you.' Max smiled thinly. 'Usually it happens about ten minutes after, not during.'

'You think I've dated? That I have had a boyfriend?' Neve shook her head in disbelief. She'd turned on all the lamps because the darkness had just made everything seem, well, darker, so Max could really see her in all her tarnished glory. The smudged make-up, the voluminous dressing-gown, and her calves were pressed up against her body so there was no disguising how stocky they were. He could see all that and still think that she had at least one other notch on her bed-post. 'It's nothing like that.'

Max folded his arms. 'So, what is it then?'

'It's not anything I want to talk about,' Neve said stiffly. 'I really need you to leave. Now. Please.'

'I'll see myself out then, shall I?' Max snarled and Neve couldn't blame him for being mad at her. She totally deserved it.

The sound of her front door opening was the sweetest symphony, although Max slammed it shut behind him. Neve heard Charlotte start shrieking and the familiar sound of a broom handle banging against the floor but she ignored it and listened to Max thumping down the stairs, then another slam of the street door – and only when she was sure that he was gone, she stretched out on the sofa because she wasn't sleeping in her bed until she'd run the sheets through on a boil wash.

Chapter Five

Neve woke up a few scant hours after the tumultuous night before and wondered why she was asleep on the sofa. There were a few seconds of blissful ignorance, then the events that had cast her out of her own bed came flooding back. She stared at a spot on the rug where she hoped a handy vortex would open and swallow her up. Alas, those handy vortices never appeared when you really needed them so Neve settled for Plan B.

An hour running on the treadmill at the gym helped immensely, and by the time she arrived at work Neve was calmer and the exercise seemed to have staved off her hangover too.

Neve had worked at the London Literary Archive for the last three and a half years. It would have been impossible to continue in higher education without a part-time job, unless she'd had a huge trust fund, so Neve had supplemented her tiny British Academy grant by toiling away part-time at the LLA, which was situated in the grimy hinterland between King's Cross and Holborn. Once she'd finished her MA and realised that she didn't have the appetite or the funds to spend another four or five years turning it into a PhD, she'd gratefully accepted the full-time position of Senior Archivist, even though her mother insisted on telling everyone that Neve was a librarian. Which she wasn't. The LLA's dusty files and even dustier books could only be seen by prior appointment and after sending in references from two accredited educational establishments.

Not that many academics wanted to search their archives because the bulk of the LLA's collection had already been turned down by every other archive in the western hemisphere. Their roster largely consisted of obscure writers who'd yet to be rediscovered, and they rarely turned down a donation from a literary estate, which usually consisted of collections of mildewed books with their spines battered and their pages heavily foxed. Every six months or so, rumours spread among the staff that the archive was closing due to lack of funds, but another pot of money always turned up from the unlikeliest sources: a bequest from a recently expired philanthropist; one of 'their' dead authors' books suddenly getting adapted for an arthouse Hollywood movie; or that Holy of Holies, National Lottery funding.

Even their building was entirely lacking in architectural merit. The LLA occupied the ground floor and basement of a small, squat building that they shared with a firm of accountants and a solicitor who specialised in Legal Aid cases and ambulance-chasing. The Reading Room, reception and the office of the Head Archivist, Mr Freemont, were on the ground floor. Neve worked in the basement where the only natural light came from a tiny window in the tiny kitchen at the back of the building, and where everything – walls, floor, ceiling, even the Health and Safety notice pinned to the corkboard – was nicotine yellow.

Neve wended her way through the huge open-plan basement office which was an obstacle course of cardboard boxes stacked in precarious piles, dilapidated metal filing cabinets lined up against each wall and anywhere else there was room for them, and stopped to say hello to pretty blonde Chloe, who was meant to be in charge of new acquisitions but spent most of her time filling in job applications to become a literary agent. She then greeted Rose, the Office Manager, who'd been at the LLA for donkey's years and was a good person to have on side because she was in charge of the petty cash and could quell Mr Freemont with a raised eyebrow and one terse word, and Neve's work 'husband', Philip, who put in time at the archive when he wasn't writing his PhD thesis. The other members of the staff were a motley collection of socially inept academics who'd been unable to find employment with even the most lowly universities. 'The ones that used to be polytechnics,' Mr Freemont was fond of sneering when he was hauling someone over the coals for inaccurate cross-referencing.

Once she'd established that Mr Freemont was out for the morning, Neve hurried to the little ante-room that she'd commandeered as her office, to switch on all three bars of the portable heater. She turned on her computer, which was still running on Windows 98, and wriggled around on her hard-backed chair in a futile attempt to get comfortable. Then she slotted a cassette into a battered Walkman, which had to be tapped gently in just the right place to coax it into playing.

A large part of Neve's workday was spent listening to crackling cassettes because an awful lot of minor literary figures had dictated their memoirs on to tape before they died, and Mr Freemont insisted that they were all trans-cribed. He honestly believed that one day they'd stumble upon an undiscovered Shakespeare play or even a lurid sex scandal featuring members of the Bloomsbury Set that would put the LLA firmly on the academic map.

Not today. J. L. Simmons (1908–97) had a peevish, querulous voice and was so verbose that Neve had to keep pausing the tape to consult from three different dictionaries on obscure words that had the spellcheck on Microsoft Word completely flummoxed. It was boring and her mind kept wandering back to the night before. It didn't take any effort at all to conjure up the awkwardness and embarrassment that had been the overriding themes of the hours she spent with Max. That was when she wasn't diving into his mouth tongue-first.

But the moment Neve kept coming back to again and again was the excruciating part where Max had stopped and slid out of her because he'd lost his erection. In fact, she didn't even know how he'd managed to get hard in the first place, because she wasn't the sort of girl to make a man feel that he might just die if he couldn't be inside her. After last night's débâcle, Neve felt as if she was destined to be alone and unloved, which would mean that the last three years had been for nothing.

She had six months to get her act together. Six months to be the best Neve she could be. Six months until William came back from California and saw the new improved, streamlined her.

Neve paused the tape again so she could rummage in her bag for the letter she'd received a fortnight ago. The pale-blue airmail sheets were creased and crumpled because she reread the letter at least once every hour, even though she'd already memorised the contents. She loved that they wrote letters, proper letters that they posted to each other, though Celia had been appalled.

'Why can't you just send each other messages on Facebook like everyone else?' she'd asked.

Because friending William on Facebook so he had full access to her daily status updates and photo albums would give the game away. It wasn't as if either of them were technophobes, they talked on the phone once a month, sent each other emails with links to articles from literary journals, but mostly they exchanged letters because, 'We studied English literature and there's a rich tradition of epistolary . . .'

'Oh God, you know I don't like the long words,' Celia had whimpered.

'Writing letters is more romantic,' Neve had clarified, and

Celia had rolled her eyes and said she needed to get out and meet real, live boys so she wouldn't still be crushing on her student adviser from Oxford.

Neve stared at her computer screen but all she could see was the encouraging look on William's face when he'd ask her to go to the pub with the rest of her seminar group. How he'd always want to know her opinion on the book they were reading or what she thought of the article by their Dean that had just run in the *Times Literary Supplement*. How he'd always smile and nod and really listen to what she was saying, in a way that no one else ever did. There'd been a hundred of those soft looks, a multitude of those tiny kindnesses until he'd accepted a three-year teaching post with the English Faculty at UCLA, and it felt like he'd taken a piece of her heart with him in his carry-on luggage when he'd flown to California. But now he was coming back to her. She read the letter out loud, under her breath:

You're the absolute first name on my list of people to see when I get back to London. It's odd that three years and an ocean between us have made us so much closer. There are so many things I have to tell you, but not in a letter – I need to see your face. You never hide anything or hold yourself back; everything you think and feel is reflected in your eyes and the curve of your mouth when you smile at me or bite your lip because I'm talking utter nonsense and you don't want to tell me because it might hurt my feelings.

This is why I can tell you anything and everything with no fear of censure or judgement. I know that you've changed since we've been apart; grown stronger, more sure of yourself, and I'm intrigued to meet this new incarnation of the girl you used to be.

Neve sighed. She was so fed up with unrequited love and platonic love and all the other kinds of love that weren't passionate, romantic, can't-live-without-you, I-have-to-have-you-right-now, the-beat-of-your-heart-matches-the-beat-of-mine love. She loved William like that, and the three years that he'd been away had just honed and refined it, made it burn that much brighter. She could tell from his letters that he felt something new for her that was more than just intellectual respect. So when he came back from LA, she couldn't afford to screw it up; everything had to be perfect, nothing could be left to chance because Neve was determined that when she and William began their relationship, it was for ever and ever. And for ever and ever was going to mean a lot of forward planning for Neve. For starters, she needed some real-life experience of a successful relationship. She also needed to be a lot more worldly and fit into a size ten little black dress. Currently, Neve still couldn't get into a little *anything*.

Suddenly, everything clicked into place. Of course she'd been awkward and embarrassed last night. She was still a long way from a size ten. When she *was* a size ten, everything would be different. *She'd* be different.

It was such a relief to know that it wasn't really her fault, that Neve went to lunch with a spring in her step and a new resolve that had her walking briskly around Holborn for an hour and only having soup and salad for lunch. The bad decisions of last night weren't forgotten, but she was going to try really hard not to think about them.

In fact, she didn't think about them until five minutes before her lunch-break ended and Celia rang her mobile at exactly 1.55 like she did every day. It always meant that Neve was late back to the Archive basement where there was no phone reception unless she climbed on top of the draining board in the kitchen and tried to get as close to the window as humanly possible.

'Hey, Seels,' she said, when she answered. 'What's up?'

'What's up with *you*?' Celia rapped back.

'Not much. In Transcribing Hell, went to the gym before work, same old, same old.'

'I know about last night,' Celia said flatly. 'I can't believe you're trying to be all evasive about it.'

Neve tried to ignore the icy dread that washed over her. 'What am I being evasive about?' she asked carefully.

'You always do that when you're being shifty! You answer a question with another question – it's so annoying,' Celia snapped. Neve hadn't heard Celia or Yuri come home last night, which meant that her sister was both sleep-deprived *and* hungover – a deadly combination. 'I know about you and Max! Didn't I warn you about him?'

Neve had to clutch on to the nearest lamp-post for support. 'Well, yes, but—'

'Beth from Features saw you going into the tube together,' Celia said.

As usual with Celia, it was something and nothing. Neve let go of the lamp-post she'd been gripping because she could deal with this unaided. 'We got the tube to Finsbury Park together because he lives in Crouch End,' she explained. 'It was perfectly innocent. Don't jump to conclusions.'

'Well, if I'm jumping to conclusions it's because I've seen Max this morning and your stories don't match,' Celia said grimly. 'He said he came home with you.'

'He saw me to the door . . .'

'And then came right up the stairs because he said you had more books than Waterstone's.'

Neve felt chilled in a way that had nothing to do with the icy gusts of wind that were lifting strands of her hair and whipping at her cheeks. She tried hard not to groan down the phone. 'What else did he say?'

'Not much,' Celia admitted. 'He just said that you had serious issues but then he asked if I'd spoken to you today and if you were all right. He tried something, didn't he? Did he hurt you?'

'No. No! Look, he came in for a drink and . . .' Neve racked her brains for something to tell Celia. Not the truth, obviously. Although Celia didn't know the meaning of TMI, Neve tried to keep her own counsel. Usually it wasn't difficult as nothing remotely exciting ever happened to her. But she couldn't tell Celia about last night because something *had* happened and it had been awful – but it hadn't been Max's fault at all. She'd lured him into her attic room under false pretences. Not that Celia would ever believe that. 'It was just a drink. Did he seem angry?' she added.

'Hmmm, not so much angry as well – troubled, I suppose,' Celia mused. 'But that might be because he's having a nightmare with the June cover. But seriously, Neevy, I swear if he tried to date-rape you, I'll cut off his dick with the Fashion Department scissors!'

'Seels, do you really think that someone who looks like Max and who's probably slept with models and—'

'No "probably" about it. He's definitely slept with models and that girl who did that stupid song about—'

'Then why would he try it on with me?' Neve asked her. 'And if he had, which he didn't, I can take care of myself. I box with Gustav.'

'Well, I s'pose when you put it like that . . .' Celia said slowly, and Neve could tell that she wasn't planning to exact revenge on Max's manhood any more. 'Don't get me wrong, you're gorgeous and pretty but it's the kind of pretty that's like a Marc Jacobs collection. Most people don't get it on first viewing, you know what I mean?'

'No, I haven't got a clue, but thanks for the compliment. It was a compliment, wasn't it?'

'Of course it was!' Celia giggled. 'Look, don't worry, we'll find some totally lush guys for you to snack on before William comes back. Sensitive guys who go to art galleries and hold doors open for you and shit.'

Max hadn't held any doors open for her last night, but he had walked on the road side of the pavement and enquired after her well-being during every perilous step of their climb towards sex. 'I think I'm going to hire a male escort and practise on him instead,' Neve said. She was thinking no such thing but wanted to hear Celia's gasp of shocked delight.

'I'm so telling Mum,' she said gleefully before she rang off and Neve was left to sneak back into work ten minutes late.

Neve really couldn't settle to transcribing and cross-referencing after speaking to Celia. That morning she'd been so involved in her own pity party that she hadn't even considered how Max might be feeling.

Recalling the sequences of events was painful and felt a lot like picking at a scab that should have been left to heal, but Neve forced herself to do it, to see herself lying there with her eyes tightly shut and a pained expression on her face that her family called her 'eating kippers look'.

'When the girl underneath you obviously wishes she was somewhere else.'

Max had sensed that something was wrong and he'd stopped and he hadn't got mad until she'd acted like a crazy woman. God, she couldn't even pick the right guy for a one-night stand. Celia had said Max was a ruthless seducer of women and he'd certainly lived up to his reputation, but hadn't Neve given every impression that she was ripe for being seduced?

Instead of wringing her hands and behaving like the innocent victim in last night's debauchery, Neve was forced to confront the unwelcome truth – that it was actually Max who was the injured party.

Oh, *bloody* hell!

After a hazardous journey home where she'd almost been knocked off her bike by a cabbie suddenly swerving into the bus lane without warning, Neve opened the front door and steeled herself for the unpleasant task that awaited her.

Right on cue, as she propped her bike against the wall and took her satchel out of the pannier, she heard Charlotte and Douglas's door open. Inevitably, the shouting started before Neve even saw Charlotte's head pop over the banisters.

'I didn't get a fucking minute of sleep last night,' she shrieked, because Charlotte always went from nought to ear-perforating in a second. 'What the hell were you doing?'

Neve knew that to the rest of the world she, Neve Slater, was a fully functioning grown-up. She voted, ate her greens, let old people get on the bus first, had a job and paid her bills on time, but with Charlotte she instantly regressed to the shy, bumbling, inarticulate fifteen year old that she'd used to be.

'I'm really sorry, Charlotte,' she whimpered. 'It won't happen again.'

'Well, you bringing home a man isn't something that's likely to happen more than once in a decade anyway,' Charlotte sneered, and even with her face contorted with the rage that Neve always roused in her, Neve was still struck by how pretty she was.

You had to strip away the fake tan and the fake eyelashes and the highlights that transformed her mousy-brown hair to blonde, but Charlotte was still an easy, effortless pretty. She was toned and tall, so whether she was wearing one of her beloved Juicy Couture tracksuits or a tiny black dress and teetering heels, she always looked groomed and pristine. Even tonight's ponytail and jeans combo looked as if it had been pulled together by a top stylist.

Neve's mother, who didn't know the half of it, always said that Neve should make more of an effort to be friends with Charlotte. But as far as Neve was concerned, you didn't attempt to cosy up to the girl who'd made your teen years a living hell, even if she was now your sister-in-law. It had been just about bearable when they'd first moved into the house because Neve and Charlotte had given each other a wide berth, but then there'd been that fateful weekend when Douglas had gone to Sheffield and Charlotte had had her horrible friends to stay. The same horrible friends who'd tormented Neve at school all the way through Years Seven to Eleven.

They'd all been trooping down the stairs in stripper heels and a cloud of cloying scent as Neve had been coming up them, and she'd heard that awful name that had followed her all the way through school. Worse, someone had shouldered her into the wall. And even worse, when they'd come home drunk at three in the morning, they'd proceeded to get even drunker and crank up *SingStar* to an unimaginable volume so that even Celia (not Neve, but Celia) had banged on their door and told them to shut the fuck up. That was when they'd started singing 'Nellie the Elephant' followed by 'Hey Fatty Bum Bum' and even 'Fat Bottomed Girls' until the Barcardi Breezers ran out.

Neve had spent all of the next day crying on Celia's shoulder. Celia had told their mother, who'd passed it on to Mr Slater, who must have had a word with Dougie and *he'd* definitely said something to Charlotte because after that, the gloves had come off. It was open warfare. Celia and Charlotte had had a screaming match in the middle of Stroud Green Road. Mrs Slater could hardly bring herself to be civil to Charlotte, and Charlotte took it out on Neve. *Plus ça* bloody *change*.

'I'm sorry,' Neve repeated, because it never did any good trying to explain or, God forbid, argue with Charlotte. She just gave back a hundred times worse and she always made it personal, so Neve had decided long ago that repetition was better than reason. 'I'm really sorry.'

'What do you think you're doing?' Charlotte snapped as Neve took a step forward. 'How many times do I have to tell you? Shoes off!'

With all the grace of a baby elephant, Neve wobbled on one foot as she tried to yank off her boot and succeeded in crashing into her bike.

'The bike shouldn't even be in the hall,' Charlotte exploded all over again, not at all concerned that Neve was gingerly feeling her hip to see if it was broken. 'You're so fucking selfish. I tore a new pair of tights on it, which you should totally pay for.'

It was a double-fronted house with a hall so large that even if there were bikes stacked three deep, there'd still be room to pass unhindered. But Neve wasn't going to get into that. 'I suppose I could try and mount it on a wall rack but I'm not sure the plaster's strong enough to take it.'

'I don't fucking care! Leave it outside! It's not like cycling anywhere is having much impact on your figure, is it?' Charlotte demanded nastily, and when she smiled like that, her face lit up with malice, she didn't look so pretty.

It was just Charlotte throwing out the same tired old insults that weren't even true any more, but Neve still looked down at her body just to make sure it hadn't swelled in size since Charlotte had started shouting at her.

'Sorry,' Neve offered again and she stood there, hands hanging limply by her sides, head bowed until with one last muttered curse, Charlotte went back into her flat and slammed the door shut behind her.

Neve crept up the stairs, tensing as she reached the first-floor landing in case Charlotte decided that she was ready for an encore performance because she did that sometimes. Just to keep Neve on her toes.

Once she was inside her own flat, Neve made herself an omelette very quietly, making sure to carefully place plates and utensils down on the rubber mats she'd bought. She'd even fixed rubber stops to her cupboard doors so it was impossible to slam them shut, though she hadn't had much luck with her cutlery drawer. She ate her dinner at the kitchen table and then it was seven thirty and Charlotte would be settling down to *EastEnders* and not liable to start banging on the ceiling because the sound of Neve's fingers on her computer keyboard or turning the pages of a book could be classed as noise pollution if you were the most heinous, evil, black-hearted witch that had ever walked the earth.

As she washed up, Neve thought about Max. But then she'd been thinking about Max all afternoon. She longed to be the kind of girl who could metaphorically shrug her shoulders, find some perspective on the situation and then turn it into a funny anecdote to tell her friends. As it was, Neve knew she'd take the sordid secret to her grave and never tell a soul, and she could only hope that Max felt the same way. Maybe he was already holding court over cocktails in some private members' club in Soho and making his glamorous, jaded friends roar with laughter as he gave them a blow-by-blow account of how he'd spent the previous night.

Neve clutched her head in her hands and felt a wave of shame and revulsion shudder through her. She was still sitting on her kitchen chair and rocking gently when the phone rang ten minutes later.

'Hello?' she said warily into the receiver, because her mother always called about this time and she wasn't sure that she could handle Mrs Slater loudly lamenting about how cold it was in Yorkshire and how many inches of snowfall they'd had in the last twenty-four hours.

'Neve? It's William. How are you?' Just like that, just with six words from William, Neve went from despair to delight.

'I'm fine,' she gasped, face pinking up from pleasure. 'What a lovely surprise. How are you?'

'All the better for hearing your voice. How do you do that?'

'I don't know,' Neve said, resisting the urge to giggle girlishly and preen at William's compliment. 'I thought we were going to speak on Sunday. Is something wrong?'

'Not exactly.' But William sounded so forlorn that Neve felt her heart ache in sympathy. 'Neevy, I've got myself in a terrible bind with the footnotes on that paper I'm writing about Rossetti. Honestly, I'm thinking of giving up academia and getting a job in a bookshop.'

'Oh dear,' Neve cooed, her tone getting so saccharine that

she actually wanted to gag. 'I don't think you'd be a model bookshop employee; you'd be too busy reading under the counter to do inventory and you'd refuse outright to sell books to customers if you thought they were badly written or without any literary merit.'

'And you wouldn't?' William enquired, and he didn't say it snidely but with such rich amusement that Neve couldn't take offence.

'Oh, I totally would,' she assured him. 'So is there any way I can help? I mean, the Romantic Poets aren't my strongest area, but would you like me to read your latest draft?'

'Would you?' William's relief was palpable. 'Also, are you going to the British Library in the next week, because I need to check a couple of references but the inter-library loans take for ever and I'm not even sure that they'll have—'

'It's no trouble. I'm due a visit,' Neve said eagerly. Every few weeks or so, she'd invent a reason to slope off to the British Library, and after she'd spent ten minutes diligently checking a source note, she'd while away a couple of hours on non-Archive business. She always felt guilty about it and lived in fear that Mr Freemont would suddenly appear to check up on her, discover the awful truth and sack her, but she still did it nevertheless. 'Why don't you email me the references and I promise I'll have them checked before the end of next week.'

'Thank you so much,' William breathed, and Neve clutched the phone tighter because even though there was a tiny transatlantic delay each time he spoke, she imagined she could feel his breath stirring her skin. 'I don't know what I'd do without you.'

'Really, it's nothing,' Neve said, turning her head away from the receiver so she could momentarily grin like a loon. 'Always happy to help,' she added, when she could trust herself to speak.

'Well, now we've got that business out of the way, maybe you can explain why you lied to me,' William said briskly.

'What? I haven't lied. What have I lied about?' Neve demanded, even as she racked her brains for anything she might have written to William that veered away from the truth. Maybe he meant lying by omission because she hadn't told him about . . .

'I can tell that you're not fine, even though you said that you were. I knew as soon as you picked up the phone and said hello that something was troubling you.' William's voice softened. 'I'd like to think that you trust me enough to confide in me.'

'I do trust you,' Neve said quickly, and though she'd give anything to be able to tell someone about last night and beg for some sound advice, William was the last person she'd tell. She'd tell her mother before she told William. 'And really, I'm fine. It's nothing.'

'You are *not* fine and it's obviously something rather than nothing. I'm going to have to resort to cliché and tell you that a problem shared is a problem halved.'

'Well, I'm not sure that's true,' Neve groused and William tsked, and more to keep him on the phone than anything else, she said, 'I, well . . . um, I made an error of judgement and it led to all kinds of er . . . wrongness and there was someone else involved and I think I may have upset them.' She frowned, and if she hadn't been holding the phone, her head would have been back in her hands. 'Or they might have told other people what I did. Oh God, I'm in such a pickle.'

'But what did you do?' William asked. 'I'm sure it couldn't have been something *that* bad.'

'But it *was* bad. Very, very bad.'

'Neevy, you haven't got a bad bone in your body and if you did upset this other person, I'm sure you didn't mean to,' William said soothingly, and it was at times like this, when he was so *simpatico*, that Neve wondered if he took a

71

pill every morning that gave him the ability to always know exactly the right thing to say.

'I just don't know what to do to make the situation right,' Neve admitted. 'Or to make myself feel better.'

'You could apologise to them,' William suggested. 'Explain the circumstances that led to this um . . . error of judgement and I'm sure they'd realise that you'd never normally behave like that. You haven't been plagiarising, have you, Neve?'

'God, no! Of course I haven't,' Neve spluttered, shocked that William could even think such a thing. 'I would *never* do something like that.'

'Well, then it really can't be so bad. You do have a tendency to fret. Just explain, apologise, move on,' William said firmly, and it was just the advice Neve had been hoping for, except . . .

'When you say apologise, do you mean in person? Or on the phone so that I'd actually have to speak to them – because I'm not entirely sure I could do that.'

William sighed. 'Oh Neevy, what am I going to do with you? Write them a letter . . . you do write beautiful, eloquent letters.' He sighed again. 'It's always lovely to see a blue airmail envelope waiting for me in my mailbox.'

Neve couldn't help sighing too, though her sigh was the sigh of pure longing. 'That's such a nice thing to say,' she said in a voice that was verging on a simper. 'And such good advice. I'll write this person a letter and then I might even be able to sleep tonight without worrying about it.'

They shared a few more pleasantries about the weather and how Neve would absolutely go to the British Library at the earliest opportunity, then William was ringing off and Neve was left to clutch her head in her hands for entirely different reasons.

She'd let Max touch her in ways and places that only belonged to William. William would never have tried taking those kinds of liberties with a woman he'd only just met.

Neve suddenly remembered how Max had kissed her and asked to come home with her when he didn't even know her name. He was a cad and he was probably moving in on another victim as Neve sat in her kitchen and brooded.

Neve tiptoed to the lounge, sat down at her desk, opened her top drawer and selected a sheet of Basildon Bond. Then she pulled out her best fountain pen, because if she was going to write a letter, then she was going to do it properly. Besides, it was bad manners to type personal correspondence. She prevaricated a while about putting her address in the top right-hand corner, but Max already knew where she lived and she couldn't write a letter without putting her address in the top right-hand corner – that wasn't the way she rolled. That done, she could get down to the real business in hand:

Dear Max

I just wanted to apologise for my behaviour the night that we met. It was completely out of character and something that I sincerely regret. Not least, because Celia has told me that you were rather upset about what transpired.

I'm not making excuses, but in my defence I had had rather a lot to drink and I'm not used to alcohol. It lowered my inhibitions and coloured my judgement, and I found myself acting in a way that has left me feeling deeply ashamed.

This is very hard for me to write but I feel that I owe you an honest explanation for my actions. When you asked me if I was recovering from a love affair gone awry, you couldn't have been more wrong. I've never been in a relationship or even been on a date, which I know is very unusual for a woman my age, but you see I am deeply in love with a man who's been out of the country for the last three years.

During this time, I've made several huge lifestyle changes, one of which is losing a considerable amount of weight. Not because of William (that's his name), but I must admit that his absence has been a motivation in wanting to transform myself for his return.

I had this foolish idea that as part of my journey of self-discovery, I needed to embark on some interaction with the opposite sex. Nothing too onerous to start with: some light flirtation, a few dates and then, hopefully a short-lived affair that would ease my passage into this new world. A pancake relationship, if you will, so that when William comes back from overseas, I'll have gained some experience and insight into what makes a relationship work and won't make any mistakes. I would hate it if our life together were ruined before it ever really began because of my nerves and my ignorance in matters of the heart.

But last night, as I've said, I had too much to drink and I was so flattered (and also confused) by your attentions, that everything became derailed. It suddenly seemed terribly important that I get the sex part of my plan out of the way, but my inexperience and my issues with my body overcame the alcohol and well, you know the rest.

I can't stress enough that none of this was your fault. I gave every indication that I wanted to have sex with you, and you were very conscientious in soliciting my consent throughout each stage of our unfortunate encounter. I am very grateful that you stopped when you did, as I fear that today I would feel an entirely different kind of regret if we'd seen it through to the bitter end.

Please don't think I was using you in any way. I got the impression that you had a very relaxed attitude to these sorts of intimacies and I think I gave you the impression that I shared the same casual disregard for sexual relations.

I know that I don't have the right to ask anything of you, but I would be eternally grateful if you kept the contents of this letter to yourself. I love my sister to pieces but she can be very protective of me and has a tendency to over-dramatise.

Once again, I apologise if I've caused you any distress or inconvenience.

With kind regards

Neve Slater (Celia's sister)

Neve read the letter back with mounting horror. She had often been complimented on her prose style; she'd even won a national short story competition at the age of eleven and she'd had several pieces published in *Isis*, when she was at Oxford. But this letter . . . God, it was so stilted and prim, as if it were written by a spinster of the parish who had too many cats and a big interest in the chapel.

But she was still reaching in her desk drawer for an envelope and a book of stamps, because posting the letter meant that this whole tawdry episode was done. Dusted. Never happened.

Chapter Six

Neve never heard back from Max, which was a huge relief. It meant that she could put the whole unfortunate incident behind her and move on. At least she'd learned from the experience – and what she'd learned was that she wasn't ready to interact with the opposite sex. Not emotionally. Not mentally. And certainly not physically.

At least she could do something about the last one. After all, she had a proven track record when it came to losing weight, and as it was the second Saturday in February, and time for her monthly fitness review with her trainer, Gustav, Neve was hoping for some good news. It was the only time that Neve was allowed to step on a scale. Gustav was emphatically anti-scales but very pro-tape measures.

'You've lost another inch off your . . .' He gestured at his chest. Neve didn't know if it was because Gustav was Austrian or gay but he didn't like to ever say the b words – boobs, bust or breasts – but preferred to use hand gestures instead.

'They've gone down? *Again*?' Neve looked down at her chest in dismay.

'Half an inch from your upper waist, nothing from your lower waist, no change on your hips. Maybe a quarter of an inch off your left thigh, nothing off the right.'

There had been a brief, blissful window of time when Neve thought she might end up with a classic hour-glass figure, but those halcyon moments hadn't lasted and now she was a definite pear-shape.

'But when is the fat going to shift from below the waist?' she asked desperately, clutching a thigh so Gustav could see it jiggle. 'How many squats and lunges is it going to take?'

Gustav wheeled his chair back even as he gave her his sternest look. They were in his tiny office on the top floor of the gym Neve went to in Highgate. She'd started off in a far less swanky gym in Finsbury Park, but when Gustav had moved to the one in Highgate, he'd wangled her a heavily discounted membership and made this stiff but heartfelt speech about how they were on a journey together and, 'We don't stop, not even when we reach the finishing line. It's a journey for life, Neve.'

Neve wasn't entirely sure, because it was hard to know with Gustav, but she thought it had been his way of saying that their professional relationship had become a friendship. A very co-dependent friendship.

'Neve, I tell you this again and again, you don't decide where and when the fat comes off. It comes off when it wants to. You have to be realistic. What else do I always say?'

' "I didn't put the weight on overnight and I'm not going to lose it overnight," ' Neve parroted back dutifully. 'But being realistic I still need to lose a good forty pounds, sorry, eighteen kilograms. And *realistically* can I do it in six months?'

'If you're very good and very patient and do exactly as I tell you,' Gustav said implacably. Normally it was good that he reacted with a stony face when Neve was having a crisis of faith, but sometimes it was just really, really irritating.

'But I've plateau-ed. I know it, you know it. I put on five pounds when it's my special lady time and then I lose five pounds after it's finished. It's been like that for three months now!' Neve finished on an aggrieved wail. 'I already work out six days a week and I cycle everywhere and always take the stairs and I—'

'You've been weighing yourself in secret, haven't you?'

Gustav asked huffily, folding his arms so his biceps bulged even more than they did in repose.

When they'd first met on that fateful day when Neve had entered a gym for the first time in her life and had been dripping gallons of sweat on an exercise bike and trying hard not to have a heart attack, she'd been terrified of Gustav. He looked like something out of Leni Riefenstahl's *Olympia* with his tanned, muscled frame, icy blue eyes and icy blond flat-top, and the Austrian accent had been the cherry on top of the Aryan cake. Over the last two and a half years, he'd been impossibly kind to Neve in an uncompromising, 'tough love' way, and she was incredibly fond of him. Even now, when his eyes were flashing and his thin lips had thinned so much that they'd ceased to exist.

'I said right at the beginning of this that there was to be no unsupervised weighing,' he said. 'You promised.'

'I know I did and I'm sorry, but sometimes I need numbers.'

'Only measurements count,' Gustav reminded her, his voice gentle now that Neve was suitably repentant. 'You know that when you break a promise to me, you break a promise to yourself. I told you the last fifty pounds would be the hardest to lose.'

'I didn't think it would be this hard.'

'Your metabolism is so unpredictable,' Gustav sniffed. 'We'll change things up a little.' He eyed her thoughtfully. 'Maybe you should take an exercise break for a week so you can reboot your system.'

'I can't do that!' Neve looked at him in horror. 'I'll balloon up overnight and anyway, I'm used to expending a certain amount of energy every day and I won't be able to sleep.' She could feel her brow pulling together as she gave Gustav a beseeching look. 'Anything but a gym break.'

Gustav caved in immediately, the way he always did when Neve showed a commitment to her fitness and training regime above and beyond what he expected of her. 'You've come such a long way,' he murmured, his clipped vowels softening, which was a sure sign that he was touched. 'I'm so proud of you. It's why I got you this.'

He reached into his desk drawer, and Neve's spirits, which had sunk at the prospect of cutting back on the gym, lifted. Maybe Gustav had relented and was going to let her have a pedometer, after all. But pedometers didn't come in big red envelopes.

'Happy Valentine's Day,' Gustav said with a straight face because he never joked during a personal consultation.

Neve took the envelope gingerly. Even though there'd been the usual card from her mother that morning and a text from Celia, she'd been trying to forget it was Valentine's Day. At least it had the decency to fall on a Saturday this year because she hated the smug girls on the tube in the evening with their smug bouquets of smug red roses.

'Do you usually get your clients Valentine's Day cards?' Neve asked, as she opened the envelope and was confronted by two red hearts nestling against each other.

'Of course I don't.' Gustav shuddered. 'Harry and I are still very happy with each other, but you're not just my client, Neve, you're my friend.' He paused. 'One of my best friends.'

'And you've changed my life,' Neva said, all humour wiped from her voice. 'And I would hug you but we've just been doing body conditioning and we're both very sweaty.'

Gustav nodded. 'Harry's making me dinner tonight but I've got twenty minutes if you want to do some light sparring?'

As Neve pulled on the boxing gloves she looked around the deserted gym (just one man pounding away on the treadmill, but he had appalling body odour so it was no wonder that he didn't have plans for tonight), and had a sudden epiphany that this would be the last Valentine's Day she'd spend alone. This time next year, William would be back and she'd be in a size ten and everything would be perfect.

Neve felt exhausted yet invigorated from punching away her demons then cycling home in the pouring rain. Her revelation that these would be the last few months that she'd spend single had put a smile on her face that wouldn't budge. As she freewheeled up Abelard Road and saw all the lights off at number 27, life seemed pretty good. Neve usually went out on a Saturday night, even if it was only to the cinema, but her coupled-up friends were having romantic dates and all her single friends had, quite rightly, decided that going out on Valentine's Day and having to fight their way through smooching couples was a recipe for rage black-outs and suicidal thoughts.

Neve was content to stay in because it looked as if Charlotte had harangued Douglas into taking her out so they could celebrate the absolute farce that was their marriage, which meant that Neve could run up the stairs with her shoes on and stomp about as much as she liked. Even listen to Radio Four and bang utensils about as she made dinner. She slid off her bike to unlatch the gate and saw a shadowy figure sitting on her doorstep.

Celia and Yuri were at a 'Fuck St Valentine and the Horse He Rode In On' night in Dalston, so Neve reached for her keys, which she could wield as a weapon. Then the figure stood up and the lamp-post across the road revealed who her supposed attacker was.

'What are you doing here?' she yelped at Max.

'I got your letter and I had a hunch you'd be home alone on a Saturday night,' Max explained as Neve remained half in and half out of the gate. 'I want to talk to you.'

'There's nothing to talk about,' Neve insisted, fingers clenched tight around her keychain as she ignored the dig about her supposed Saturday-night spinsterdom. 'I said everything I had to say. I *apologised*!'

'Well, yeah you did – in between casting me as some sort of man slut. Look, I'm not here to have an argument. I just want to . . . chat,' Max finished as if it wasn't the right word but was the only one he could think of.

'I don't think we have anything to talk about.' The rain was still coming down thick and fast and dripping down the collar of Neve's cagoule. 'Look, it's not convenient. I've been to the gym and cycled home and I'm soaking wet . . .'

'I could come in while you have a shower and get changed,' Max said easily.

Neve eyed him suspiciously. There was absolutely no way he was coming into her flat and sitting in her lounge while she was naked in her bathroom. Not unless he thought that, despite everything she'd said in her letter, she wanted another bash at it. 'No, you can't,' she hissed in a scandalised whisper. 'Wasn't last time bad enough?'

'Believe me, I'm still having nightmares about it,' Max snapped back. 'I only want to talk. Look, what about the pub on the corner?'

'What about it?'

'Meet you there, say, in half an hour?' Max stepped out of the porch and Neve had no choice but to wheel her bike back so he could remove himself from the premises.

'You have got an umbrella, haven't you?' Neve heard herself ask. 'I could lend you— oh.'

Max was opening a huge golfing umbrella that appeared to have started life at the Four Seasons in Beverly Hills. 'So does that mean I'll see you in thirty?' He was level with her now, only her bicycle between them to act as a chaperone.

'Well, I s'pose,' Neve said ungraciously. 'Though I can't imagine what we have to talk about.'

'Great,' Max said. 'I'll have a white wine waiting for you.'

'I'm not drinking,' Neve called after his departing figure. 'Not ever again!'

Neve wanted to meet Max at the Hat and Fan about as

much as she wanted a week's gym break. But she'd seen the resolute look in his eyes as they'd passed and she could just imagine him marching back to the house and leaning on the doorbell until she let him in.

As she had a quick, perfunctory shower, Neve couldn't think of any logical reason why Max would want to talk to her about the letter. Besides, it was one thing to be honest and real in a letter, but doing it in person was something else entirely. She quickly towel-dried her hair, because it was only going to get wet again and stood in bra, knickers and woolly socks, inspecting her outfit options. She wasn't getting gussied up again, it would only give Max the wrong idea – not that he seemed to have any fond memories of the time they'd spent together. Still, she had her pride and wasn't going to turn up in a tracksuit and a bad attitude.

Neve pulled on her Long & Lean Gap jeans, which did nothing to stop her from being Short & Stumpy, then after some brief dithering she slipped on a slate-grey, empire-line wool tunic that ended mid-thigh and covered a multitude of sins – or at least it covered her hips.

A quick glance at the clock and Neve realised she had ten minutes to present herself at the pub. She gathered her hair in a loose ponytail, swiped at her mouth with her trusty Black Honey Clinique Almost Lipstick and pulled on her Primark faux Uggs, even though Celia had tried to make her promise that she'd never leave the house in them.

The rain had eased, so, tugging on hat and gloves, Neve ran along the street and one minute before her half-hour was up, she pulled open the door of the Hat and Fan.

Normally Neve hated going into pubs on her own, but the Hat and Fan was like a second home, even though she hadn't stepped foot in it for nearly three years. She was delighted to see that it was still the hostelry that gentrification had overlooked. There were still horse brasses mounted behind the bar, along with packets of pork scratchings, a truly terrible reproduction of the *Monarch of the Glen* hanging above the simulated blaze of the fake log fire, and on the other side of the bar, there was a snug. And everyone still called it the snug.

Ida and Jack were still sitting at their usual table in the little nook by the door, nursing a port and lemon and a pint of bitter respectively, and as Neve stepped further into the toasty warmth of the bar, over a paisley-patterned carpet that hadn't been taken up to expose the wooden boards beneath, every head turned to look at her. It was that kind of pub.

'Neevy, my darling!' cried Bridie, the landlady. 'Will you look at this girl? She's wasting away.'

'Not really,' Neve said, removing her hat and waving at the three O'Leary brothers who always sat at the bar.

'There's nothing left of you,' Bridie insisted. 'I'd have barely recognised you if I didn't know you better than my own flesh and blood.'

Bridie had recognised her just fine when Neve had bumped into her in Tesco the week before, so Neve just smiled vaguely and looked around for Max. 'He'll be in the snug then,' one of the O'Leary brothers said – Neve was never sure which one was which. 'The young fella who came in earlier.'

Neve grinned. Max wouldn't have been allowed to buy a bag of crisps without a fierce interrogation and the suggestion that he'd be much happier in the Old Dairy on the corner where 'they have all that poncy imported lager'.

She opened the frosted-glass door that led through to the stuffy little lounge that always smelled of mothballs, and there he was; sitting on one of the pockmarked imitation-leather sofas and looking like he wished he had an elsewhere to be.

Chapter Seven

'You were the one who wanted to meet here,' Neve said, as Max's lips twisted in greeting.

'You could have said it was your regular watering-hole.'

'Not really, but this was my gran's old pub so I kind of grew up here,' Neve said, looking around with a half-smile as she remembered Sunday lunches at the long table in the main bar and standing on her grandpa Fred's feet while he waltzed her around to her grandmother's old Frank Sinatra records. 'It feels like home.'

'As long as I'm landlady, this will always be your home,' Bridie said as she bustled in. 'Give me your coat, love, and tell me what you want to drink.'

'Can I get a cup of tea?' Neve asked as she handed Bridie her coat.

'I could make you a plate of sandwiches or how about a nice bowl of soup? I've got some homemade Oxtail upstairs.'

'Just tea's fine, thank you,' Neve said, sitting down on the sofa that was arranged at a right angle to Max's.

Bridie shot Max a look that seethed with suspicion. 'And will your young man be wanting anything else?'

Max looked fairly harmless in jeans and a stripy woollen jumper, and he really hadn't done anything to warrant such open hostility, but just having a penis and knowing Neve by name was crime enough.

'He's not my young man,' Neve said softly, with an

apologetic smile in Max's direction, which got her a raised eyebrow in return. 'This is Max. He works with Celia.'

As Bridie's face curdled as if someone had trodden in dog shit and tracked it across the carpets, Neve inwardly smacked her hand against her forehead. Celia was the black sheep of the Slater clan with her outlandish clothes and her poseur friends and the way she'd run off to New York after her A-levels and 'broken your poor mother's heart' as Bridie would have it. Neve didn't remember her mother's heart breaking. She'd been really annoyed when Celia had landed uninvited on Auntie Catherine's doorstep in New Jersey, but that was as far as it had gone.

'Well, I'll be getting you a cup of tea then,' Bridie said, one hand on the snug's door. 'Just yell if you need anything.' She left the door ajar, all the better to hear Neve's pained cries if Max was overcome by lust and forced himself on her.

'So one word from you and there'll be a procession of flaming torches as they throw me out?' Max asked, draining the contents of his pint glass.

'I think they'll just run you through with pitchforks,' Neve said calmly because she was on home turf, as it were, and felt slightly less at a disadvantage.

'You do have a sense of humour, then?' Max shrugged. 'I was beginning to wonder.'

And just like that, Neve felt awkward and unsettled again. 'Look, about that night. I really am sorry,' she began uncertainly. 'I tried to explain in the letter. I don't understand why you had to hunt me down to hash it out all over again.'

'No one's ever sent me a letter apologising after a one-night stand.'

'It wasn't a one-night stand,' Neve interrupted in a fierce whisper. 'Not really.' Surely there had to be actual prolonged penetration for it to qualify as a one-night stand?

'It kinda was,' Max whispered back, and Neve was grateful that he'd realised that every ear in the main bar was straining in their direction. 'Anyway, it freaked me out and then I was worried that you were even more freaked out and I wanted to make sure you were OK.'

It wasn't at all what Neve had been expecting and she let herself relax slightly. Or at least exhale and unclench.

'So, are you?' Max prompted, reaching over to gingerly nudge Neve's arm as if he was afraid she might break if he touched her, or more likely scream for help.

'Am I OK?' Neve considered the question, but the burn in her cheeks answered it for her. 'I think so, apart from wondering if it's possible to die of shame.'

'See? That's what I was afraid of.' Max scooched right to the very corner of his sofa, so he was as close to Neve as he could get while still keeping a respectable distance between them. 'Sex is nothing to be ashamed of. It's no big deal.'

'But it is a big deal,' Neve said, pausing as the sheer magnitude of the act hit her again. 'Or it should be. It's just about the most intimate thing you can do with someone and I had too much to drink and ploughed straight into the sex without any thought. I've spent longer debating whether I should buy a pair of shoes.'

Max's eyebrows had risen higher and higher as Neve delivered her speech, and just as he opened his mouth to plead the case for free and easy love, Bridie was back carrying a tray with a pint of lager on it, a steaming mug of tea and a plate of doorstep sandwiches.

'Now I know you said you weren't hungry but you look as if you haven't had a decent meal in weeks,' Bridie insisted forcefully, even though Neve knew that if she ever survived a plane crash she had enough fat reserves to last at least a month if she couldn't find any nuts and berries. 'Cheese and pickle. You used to love cheese and pickle.'

Neve felt her nostrils twitch as Bridie ceremoniously placed the sandwiches in front of her. Never mind the cheese and pickle, she could *smell* the butter. Thick, creamy, salty butter.

Max was talking to Bridie, who was dialling down the hostile vibe as he smiled at her and told her that she didn't look old enough to be running her own pub, but all Neve could hear was a rushing in her head as she looked at the plate of sandwiches. There had to be at least one thousand and five hundred calories there. That was two full hours at the gym doing high-impact cardio. But, God, that butter . . .

Neve blinked slowly and tore her gaze away from the plate as Bridie's voice became sharper. 'Sorry?' Neve said. 'Did you say something?'

'I was just asking if your mum's in Yorkshire or Spain at the moment?' Bridie's eyes gleamed inquisitively.

'They're in Yorkshire,' Neve admitted, knowing full well that her mum would be getting a phone call within the hour to let her know that her eldest daughter was out in public with a man, whose intentions were, as yet, undeclared.

'I really should give her a ring,' Bridie said predictably, as she practically ran to the door. '*Midsomer Murders*' about to start so best keep this shut. Don't want to disturb you.'

Neve had visions of Bridie putting her mum on speakerphone so Ida and Jack and even the taciturn O'Learys could come in on the chorus. 'My dad persuaded my mum to move back to Yorkshire after my gran died,' she told Max, who probably wasn't the least bit interested, but if she was using her mouth for talking, then she couldn't be eating sandwiches. Sandwiches that had been liberally spread with butter and were heaped with really sharp crumbly cheddar and Bridie's home-made pickle, which tended to take the top layer of skin off the roof of your mouth, in a really good way. 'But they bought a place in Spain too, on the Costa del Sol, so they spend half the year there. God, you have to eat these.'

Even putting the tips of her fingers on the plate so she could push it over to Max made Neve's resolve weaken. Visualising her size ten self waltzing down the street in a slinky black dress wasn't having its usual effect.

'I've already had something to eat,' Max protested. 'Just leave them.'

'I can't! You've spent ten minutes with Bridie, so you must know that she'll stand over me until I've eaten them – and I do not eat stuff like this.' Neve looked around wildly for a handy wastepaper basket or a window that would actually open, while Max stared at her like she was frothing at the mouth. It did feel as if her saliva glands were working overtime.

'Why don't you just have one?' Max suggested reasonably, as if he was talking to a reasonable person with a reasonable attitude to food.

'Just have one?' Neve echoed incredulously. 'Would you tell a drug addict to have just one rock of crack?'

'It's a cheese sandwich, not a Class A narcotic.' Max was still sitting on his sofa, though Neve had half-expected him to run to the door by now. She'd much rather re-enact every excruciating moment of their night together than have him witness one of her food freak-outs. 'Just wrap them in the napkins, put them in your bag and chuck them in the bin when you leave.'

Neve spotted Max's messenger bag, emblazoned with the Marc Jacobs logo, propped against the table leg. 'Can't you put them in your bag? Please.' She could feel the first warning throb in her tear ducts. 'I'm begging you, Max.'

Saying his name plaintively worked like a magic incantation because Max was carefully wrapping up the sandwiches in the red napkins provided by Bridie. He was doing it with a really put-upon air, but he was doing it and that was all that mattered. 'I hope these don't leak pickle juice on my phone charger,' he grumbled.

Only when the sandwiches had been concealed and Max had tucked his bag behind the sofa so Neve wouldn't have to look at it did she settle back down, reaching for the mug of tea with a trembling hand. 'I'm sorry,' she muttered. 'I'm OK if I know in advance that there's going to be food I can't eat, but when it takes me by surprise . . .' She tailed off because no one really understood that food wasn't just fuel or that there was no harm in a little bit of what you fancied; every meal, every morsel was a battle in a never-ending war.

'You said in your letter . . .' Max began, then stopped as his eyes trailed over her. 'You look fine to me and I saw enough of you that night . . .'

'You saw only what I wanted you to see,' Neve confessed, remembering the way that she'd kept her arms pinned to her sides, hadn't even taken her slip off.

'I think I saw a little bit more than that, when I was under the covers,' Max said in this slow, amused way that should have made her hackles and every hair on her body rise. Instead, Neve felt a tiny shiver run through her that had nothing to do with the aftershocks from the cheese sand-wiches and more to do with the way Max's voice dipped down so low as if the memory of being between her thunderous thighs was a pleasant one.

'It was dimly lit, you'd been drinking,' Neve insisted. She swallowed hard because this was never easy to say, even if she'd been able to write it in a letter. 'My body . . . if I'd been this weight all the time, my body would look different. But I weighed a lot more than this and it shows.'

'So you've lost a couple of stone.' Max shrugged again. 'You women. You're all so fixated on your weight, and really, unless you're morbidly obese there's nothing to worry about. You always think you weigh more than you do.'

On some level, as soon as she'd seen Max sitting on her doorstep, Neve had known that they'd have this conver-sation. At least that would be one thing she'd be spared with William because he'd known her back then. Anyway, after tonight, she was 100 per cent certain that she'd never see Max again so she might as well go for broke.

'I always know exactly how much I weigh,' she said,

hoping that Gustav hadn't fitted her with a bugging device. 'And I was morbidly obese.'

'Oh, please . . .' Max was all set to start scoffing, but Neve had expected that too, which was why she'd taken down the photo that was usually taped to the fridge door and stuck it in her bag so she could pull it out and slam it down on the table.

'Morbidly obese,' she repeated. 'I used to weigh three hundred and fifty-eight pounds. That's twenty-five and a half stone. I'd say I was a size thirty-two because that was the largest size that Evans did – but even that was tight.'

Max stared down at the photo with a horrified expression. 'Fucking hell! That's not you,' he breathed. 'It can't be.'

The picture had been taken at the family Christmas dinner four years ago. Neve had been caught unawares, because normally she ran, or waddled, away from the camera lens. But on this occasion, Celia had managed to snap her just as she was manoeuvring a cocktail sausage wrapped in bacon towards her mouth, jaw open wide to receive the offering so the camera had really captured the full glory of her several chins. The rest of her wasn't pretty either; a black-clad mountain of amorphous flesh with a round pale face perched unsteadily on top of it.

Neve didn't have to look at the picture on the table because she saw it at least five times a day when she was getting skimmed milk or leafy green things out of the fridge. Maybe it was the familiarity that had lessened the shock value, but these days it was like looking at a girl she used to know, rather than a girl she used to be.

'It is me,' she said simply, because she was used to people's disbelief when they saw the picture. Even Celia, who'd taken the bloody thing. 'You weren't *that* big,' she'd always stubbornly insist. 'It's just a bad angle.'

'Now that you've seen it, do you understand why I am like I am?' Neve asked quietly.

'Wow,' Max said. He looked at Neve sitting there, and even though the grey tunic was as voluminous as a size sixteen could get, there was no mistaking the whittling of her body. 'You're half the woman you used to be, quite literally.'

Neve never tired of the look that Max was giving her, the look she'd received from so many other people who hadn't seen her since her transformation. It was a look of dopey stupefaction, usually followed by a swift, 'Fuck me!'

'More than half,' she said a little smugly, but she'd earned the right to be smug. 'I've lost two whole Kylie Minogues.' Then her expression grew serious. 'So you see, that's why I've never had a boyfriend or been in a relationship.'

Max pushed the photo away as if he couldn't bear to look at it any longer. 'But lots of f— larger people have relation-ships.'

'You can say the f-word, it doesn't bother me,' Neve told him, curling her legs up beneath her because she could do that now. And cross them too, if she wanted. 'I know there are lots of fat people in happy, healthy relationships, but I wasn't one of them. I mean, I had friends but I was miser-able about the way I looked so I'd eat to cheer myself up and that just made me bigger, which made me more miserable. I wasn't exactly in the right frame of mind to put myself out there to try and find a boyfriend. I was sure that most men hated the way I looked too.'

'But this guy, this William, he didn't hate you?'

Neve shook her head. 'No, he didn't hate me. Not at all.'

Max rested his elbows on his knees and stared serenely at Neve. 'And he feels the same way about you?'

His unblinking gaze was like truth serum. 'Well, I think so.' She squared her shoulders and forced herself to look Max straight in the eye. 'The heart knows, isn't that what they say?'

'If he loves you, then he won't care what size you are or what experience you may or may not have,' Max said softly. 'Not if he really loves you.'

'It's not just that.' Neve closed her eyes momentarily. 'He'll ask me if I've been seeing anyone and I'd have to say no, and he knew that I wasn't involved with anyone when I was at Oxford and that night we had . . . if I was like that with William, it would ruin everything and I'd want to die.'

It sounded so silly and melodramatic when she said it out loud, but Max just nodded. 'Look, you should have said it was your maiden voyage,' he remarked cheerfully. 'We could have taken it slower, much slower. I guarantee you'd have had a good time.'

'Oh God,' Neve said faintly, because sex was not something you discussed in such a jovial manner or in a public place or with someone who wasn't Celia and even then it was under extreme duress.

'No, really,' Max insisted, mistaking Neve's mortification for disbelief. 'There's no point in being modest about it; I'm really good at sex. Fantastic at foreplay, never have to be asked to go down on a girl – in fact, I love it, especially when—'

'Please, for the love of God, will you stop,' Neve begged. 'Just stop talking about *it*.'

'You really are very repressed. You can't even say it, can you?' Max frowned. 'Look, that night, you said that you'd taught Celia everything she knows and believe me, she knows a lot, and you—'

Neve clutched a hand to her frantically beating heart. 'Oh, sweet Jesus, you've slept with my little sister!'

'Of course I haven't,' Max said indignantly, and Neve wanted to smack him – because even though she was hugely relieved he hadn't shared Celia's bed, there was no need for him to sound so affronted. Celia was quite the catch. 'I never sleep with the *Skirt* girls – well, apart from the interns and I've sworn off them too lately – but I've been away on location shoots with your sister and she's not a shy little flower and I thought you were cut from the same cloth. You practically dragged me to your bedroom.'

Even though it was hot enough in the snug to have Neve red-faced and slowly roasting in her grey wool tunic, she shivered. 'Look, I said I was sorry in the letter so why are you subjecting me to this postmortem?'

She must have sounded really forlorn, because Max shifted uncomfortably on his sofa. 'I really did want to make sure that you were all right,' he said. 'That you weren't still beating yourself up over what happened.'

'Well, I wasn't until you showed up on my doorstep and now I'm back to castigating myself,' Neve sighed.

Max leaned forward so he could take Neve's limp hands in his cool grasp. Neve longed to tug them away but Max tutted as he felt her fingers flutter. 'Look, Neve, you're a pretty, intelligent girl and you shouldn't be spending Valentine's Night sitting in a crappy pub – no offence.'

'None taken,' Neve said, because the only reason she loved the Hat and Fan was because of the memories, not the actual funky-smelling reality of it. 'But you're also spending Valentine's Night in a crappy pub too.'

'Yeah, but I have three other places to be after this,' Max informed her loftily. '*I'm* not going to spend the rest of the night home alone.'

Neve did try to tug her hands away then, but Max refused to let go. 'Stop being so huffy,' he said. 'I'm here to help you.'

'I don't need your help!'

'Here's what's going to happen,' Max said, as if she hadn't spoken. 'We're going to go back to yours so you can change into something that's a lot less, well, sackclothy, and then we're going into town and we're going to get you laid. What do you think about that?'

Neve thought quite a lot about that but she couldn't get any words out as she was coughing and spluttering. 'I don't want to get laid,' she said eventually. 'I never did. Not for ages. There are other steps.'

'If I were you I'd forget the other steps for now and just

get the shagging out of the way,' Max advised her, like he was some kind of shagging expert, which actually, fair point. 'Think of it as like ripping off a plaster really quickly so it doesn't hurt, and once you've got the sex out of the way, then you can get on with the other stuff.'

'I don't want to get sex out of the way,' Neve hissed. 'In fact, I think sex is completely off the agenda for now.'

'So, you're going to wait for this William bloke to do the honours?' Max clarified, absent-mindedly stroking Neve's wrist right where her pulse was pounding away. The movement was like a mantra, calming and comforting even as Neve wanted to pick up her mug of rapidly cooling tea and fling it in Max's face. 'You're saving yourself for him because he's your one true love? Christ, that's a lot of pressure for someone to live up to.'

Max was right, which was infuriating. But if their stalled sexual encounter had taught Neve anything, it was that she wasn't ready for sex. 'I need relationship experience, not sex experience,' she told him.

'Come on, I'll take you to Black's. It's always stuffed with literary types and I'll sort you out some bloke who can bang on about books and then, er . . . well, bang you.'

Neve did manage to snatch her hand away. 'Ugh, that's disgusting!' She pointed one quivering finger at Max, who grinned at her. Caddishly. '*You're* disgusting! It's not funny to be twenty-five and have no idea how any of this is meant to work. There's no earthly way that someone like you could possibly understand how terrifying and confusing sex and relationships and dating is when you've never done any of it.'

She was close to tears, close enough that she had to sniff loudly before continuing. 'I wasted so much time in this cycle of fat and self-loathing, and now there's *no* time and it feels like an impossible task to go out and try to meet someone and flirt with them and laugh at their jokes.' She shrugged. 'Then, what? You start to date and there's all this rigmarole and leaving two days before you call them and that could drag on for weeks and weeks. I want to skip straight to three months into the relationship.'

She wasn't sharing so much as ranting, but Max looked like he was hanging on her every word and Neve saw there was a crumpled piece of Basildon Bond in his hand that looked horribly familiar. 'What's a pancake relationship?' he asked, tracing that particular line with the tip of one finger.

'It's so dumb. Just this really tortured analogy . . .'

'I love tortured analogies. They're my favourite kind.'

It was hard to know when Max was laughing at her. 'Well, when you make pancakes, the first pancake tastes all right but you're basically testing out the consistency of the batter and it's never quite the right shape or thickness so it gets chucked away.'

Max looked confused. 'I've never heard of that.' He frowned. 'So when you make pancakes, you throw the first pancake away?'

'Well, I don't eat pancakes any more and when I used to make them, I always ate the first one,' Neve recalled dryly. 'And the second one and the third one and the one after that, until there was no more batter left. But generally people who aren't compulsive over-eaters throw the first one away. And I want a relationship like that.'

'So a relationship that's OK as relationships go, but it's not quite the right consistency so you can just dump the poor bloke when this other guy gets back from wherever he's been,' Max summed up, then smiled faintly as he picked up his pint glass.

'It sounds terrible and heartless when you put it like that,' Neve protested. 'It's just a fun little affair, nothing serious, and with no hard feelings when the time comes to go our separate ways.'

'And what's in it for the guy in this pancake relationship? Does he know he's going to get his marching orders or are you going to pretend that he might really be the one and—'

'Stop! Please, stop.' Neve picked up her mug but the tea was stone cold. She was tempted to bellow to Bridie to stick the kettle on, because then she'd bustle in and make Max stop talking, but from the sound of raised voices in the bar, *Midsomer Murders* had reached a particularly exciting bit and Neve didn't have the heart to disturb her. 'Obviously I haven't ironed out all the kinks in the plan, but Celia says that ninety-nine per cent of all men are commitment-phobic and a three-month, no-strings affair is about all they can handle.'

'I don't think a no-strings affair is anything that *you* could handle, though. Not at the moment anyway,' Max noted, and all of a sudden Neve felt as unclothed and vulnerable as she had done that other night. Underneath all that hackneyed charm and scruffy clothing, Max's perception was razor-sharp. 'So what would this faux relationship involve?'

Neve wasn't going to say another word on the topic. She really wasn't. Except her mind was already going to that happy place where there'd be 'long Sunday-afternoon walks, even if it was raining, because it's invigorating walking in the rain with someone else, rather than being on your own. And then when you got home and dried off, there'd be tea and toast and a black and white film on BBC2 with Bette Davis in it. Or maybe there wouldn't, but it wouldn't matter because then we could do the crossword together. But if the weather was dry then we could go for a drive in the country and visit National Trust houses. I really must get round to joining the National Trust,' she heard herself say dreamily.

Then Neve blinked her eyes and came back to earth where Max was looking at her as if she'd been speaking Mandarin.

'Really?' he said. 'Is that what happens in relationships?'

'Well, I'm sure you know more about relationships than I do,' Neve said shortly, stiffening her spine and attempting to look more in control.

Max pulled a face. 'You know how Mariah Carey doesn't do stairs?' Neve shook her head but Max didn't seem to notice. 'Well, I don't do relationships. Just can't see the point in being with one woman, and not being allowed to have sex with anyone else. I'm far too young and pretty for that kind of commitment.'

'You're absolutely unbelievable,' Neve told him, but it was impossible not to be amused and maybe a tiny bit envious. Life must be so easy when you looked like Max. 'Look, I don't expect you to understand, but I just want to get a feel for the kind of relationship and see what areas I need to improve on.' That sounded better – more businesslike.

'I see.' Max was straight-faced, but his eyes gleamed with amusement. 'And do you have any candidates lined up?'

'Well, no. It's more in the planning stage.' Neve fixed Max with a stern look. 'All that Sunday-afternoon stuff I'll do with William; it's the meat and potatoes stuff that I need to practise – like knowing what to say and do when I go out on dates and well, I've never even shared a bed with a man, and how do you negotiate who sleeps on which side and when to turn the light out and who's going to get stuck with the lumpy pillow?' Neve didn't know why she kept talking and talking. Because the more she talked, and the more she tried to justify her fuzzy ideas on relationships to Max, the more fuzzy they became and the more out of reach.

'So, can I put my name down on the list? Do you have a list?' Max asked, pushing away his empty glass and looking hopefully at the door as if he expected Bridie to materialise with another pint of Stella.

'What list? I don't have a list! You're not taking this seriously.' Neve realised that her grey tunic had become rucked up and was displaying her splayed thighs, so she made adjustments. 'You just said that you don't do relationships.'

'I don't, but you made them sound such fun and if you

don't want to have sex, then you're not going to mind if I get my jollies somewhere else.' He lowered his lashes. 'I have *needs*.'

Neve didn't know why she'd bothered trying to shine some light on the darkest, most secret places of her psyche. In fact, she didn't even know why she'd come to the pub to suffer this emotional abuse when she could have been tucked up on her sofa with a nice bowl of home-made vegetable soup and the new issue of the *London Review of Books*. She got to her feet and stuck out her hand in Max's general direction. 'It was nice to see you again but I really have to go now.'

'Oh, don't be like that.' Max took her hand but only so he could stroke her knuckles. 'You really have to stop taking everything so personally. It must be exhausting.'

'Goodbye,' Neve said sharply, removing her hand from Max's grasp and snatching up bag, coat, scarf, hat and gloves, and wishing that it wasn't winter because it was impossible to make a speedy getaway when you had so much cold-weather gear to put on first. 'Tell Bridie to put your drinks on the Slater tab,' she added, because God forbid that Max should think ill of her. Or *more* ill of her.

'So you don't fancy meeting up again?' Max persisted, though Neve didn't know why, because she thought she'd made her position perfectly clear. 'Swap war stories?'

'I don't have any war stories,' Neve said, and in that moment she felt that she never would. That every night would be spent creeping round her flat in her socks with the telly turned down so low that she could barely hear it, so in the end she'd have no other option but to escape into the pages of books where there were other girls falling in and out of love but not her. Never her. She stared down at the scuffed toes of her faux Ugg boots in sudden and tired defeat.

'If you don't have any war stories, then at least you don't have any war wounds,' Max said, so quietly that Neve had to strain her ears to catch his words. 'Take my number.'

It was impossible to tell someone to their face that you didn't want to see them again because everything they said rubbed you raw, as if they'd taken a gigantic Brillo pad to your soul. It was much easier to limply hand over her phone and watch Max tap in his number, though Neve vowed she'd delete it as soon as she got home.

Chapter Eight

On Monday morning, after her second sleepless night brooding over the conversation she'd had with Max in the Hat and Fan's snug, Neve trudged down her stairs with heavy feet and a heavy heart. She was still mentally berating herself for how much she'd over-shared, and planned to spend most of the day trying to sort out her confused thoughts about light-hearted affairs and no-strings relationships. Then she caught sight of the blue airmail envelope waiting for her on the doormat.

Neve snatched it up with an excited cry, all thoughts of Max instantly banished, and only the fact that she had forty minutes to cycle to Holborn to meet Philip for breakfast before work stopped Neve from plopping down on the bottom stair and tearing it open. Instead, she had to make do with stroking it against her cheek and imagining she could feel the phantom touch of William's hand as he wrote her name and address in his beautiful copperplate script until she caught sight of the moony smile on her face in the hall mirror.

Still, it was hard to concentrate on Philip's latest thesis-related angst when the envelope was burning a hole in her satchel. Philip was a mature student who'd been made redundant from his job in derivatives, got divorced and come out of the closet all in the space of six months. That had been four years ago and Neve wasn't sure that Philip had entirely got over the shock. He was an anxious-looking man in his forties who'd had to downgrade from a four-bedroom house in Chiswick to a studio flat in Ealing, and had embraced academia along with an anti-quarian bookseller called Clive, although neither one was bringing him much joy.

'. . . and now he says that we should be free to sleep with other people,' he told Neve morosely as she waited for her porridge to cool down.

'So, are you splitting up then?' As ever, Neve resisted the urge to tell Philip that he'd be much better off without Clive, who'd tried to stick his tongue down Gustav's throat within five minutes of being introduced to him at Neve's birthday drinks last year. It wasn't just that Philip had terrible taste in men, there was also the ex-wife who was currently living in the four-bedroom house in Chiswick with her twenty-three-year-old boyfriend and frittering away what was left of Philip's redundancy package. He was really, really, really bad at choosing his life partners.

'No, apparently we're having an open relationship,' Philip sniffed, his eyes suspiciously red-rimmed, as if he'd only stopped crying just before he stepped off the tube at Holborn. 'I can't believe that I'm forty-five and I'm still having to go through all this *Sturm und Drang*. You don't know how lucky you are to be single and unencumbered.'

Being single didn't feel unencumbered. It felt extremely cumbersome. 'Well, I really think I'm almost ready to start dating,' Neve ventured because Philip was a good candidate to test the idea on. Or maybe not, because he was looking at her with undisguised horror, eyebrows raised so they jutted out from above his half-moon spectacles.

'Do you?' Philip asked. 'Really?'

Neve took a hasty gulp of her skimmed-milk latte and scalded her tongue, but that was better than having to defend her decision to date in the face of Philip's zero encouragement. 'I have to start sooner or later. I don't want to end up like Our Lady of the Blessed Hankie.'

Philip shuddered. 'No one would want to end up like that. So how were you planning to dip a toe into the choppy waters of romance?'

There was the rub. Making eyes at total strangers hadn't worked out too well. 'I did read a thing about speed-dating in *Skirt*.'

'Neve! You can't! You'd be eaten alive,' Philip gasped. 'It would be like throwing a paraplegic Christian to the lions.'

'You could be a little more supportive,' Neve grumbled. 'I said I was *almost* ready to start dating and I do have some experience of the opposite sex, you know.' Which was true because she'd now *almost* had sex twice and she knew lots of straight men like her brother and her father and she was on first-name terms with Aziz from the all-night convenience store and Dave from the second-hand furniture shop who always called her when a new bookcase came in, and Mr Freemont at the LLA, though Neve wasn't sure that he counted as a straight man. She didn't like to think that he had genitals of any description.

'Of course you do,' Philip said soothingly. 'Well, what about Adrian, Clive's Assistant Manager?'

Adrian was a willowy youth whom Neve remembered from Oxford. Even when he wasn't languidly lounging in a punt, he looked as if he should be. 'Adrian's gay.'

'No, he's not.' Philip clicked his teeth. 'You may have some experience with the opposite sex but your gay radar is a little shaky.'

'It's called a gaydar, Philip,' Neve said gently. Philip was a terrible gay man. Since he'd plunged into further education, he tried to dress the part in corduroys and tweed jackets, but Neve always got the impression that he yearned to be back in his grey pinstripe suit. 'Anyway, I think you have to say to Clive that you don't want to be in anything other than a committed relationship,' she added, anxious to steer the conversation back to Philip's love-life rather than her own lack of one.

'But even an open relationship is better than being without him,' Philip said quietly, as if he was talking to himself rather than Neve. He gave her a brave but watery smile. 'Be sure that a relationship is something you really want. Here be dragons . . .'

But there wouldn't be dragons. There'd be only fun and frolics and her heart safely tucked away until William returned to claim it. Or maybe it was more important to work on reducing her girth rather than her relationship skills. Neve gave a non-committal, 'Hmmm,' and it was actually a relief when Philip decided they were done with the personal stuff and could get down to business. He pulled a ringbinder from his leather satchel and Neve spluttered into her coffee.

'My God, that's a lot of paper,' she said accusingly. 'Just how much have you written of your thesis since I last saw you?'

When he wasn't beavering away at the Archive, Philip was writing his PhD dissertation on the poet Stephen Spender. Neve, for her sins, had agreed to 'beta-read' it for him.

'I'm about thirty thousand words into the second draft,' Philip said proudly. 'But I've still got miles to go.'

'OK, hand it over,' Neve sighed, holding out her hand and mentally bracing herself for thirty thousand words on one of her least favourite poets.

Philip tutted and shook his head. 'You know the deal, Neevy. I show you mine, if you show me yours.'

Neve kicked her satchel further under her chair. 'But you've written another ten thousand words and I've written much, much less than that.'

'Where are you up to?' Philip asked, pushing his glasses up his nose so he could glare at her more effectively.

'Lucy's at Oxford and she's met Charles Holden, although she thinks he's an absolute pig at the moment,' Neve revealed. 'It's odd, really, when you and I both know that meeting him set her on a path that would change her life for ever but she doesn't even know that herself right now.'

'Please, just hand it over,' Philip said. 'I want to know what happened with her father before she left for Oxford. Stop withholding.'

Neve reluctantly reached under her chair for her satchel. When the twelve cardboard boxes containing failed novelist and very, very minor poet Lucy Keener's life and works had arrived at the Archive, Neve had left them gathering dust in her office for weeks. There were so many of them and Neve couldn't find any details of Lucy Keener or her writings in any dead author databases, so she didn't hold out much hope that she was going to discover one of the great unknown writers of the twentieth century. Then one after-noon when she'd run out of tapes to transcribe, she'd started flicking through Lucy's autobiographical novel *Dancing on the Edge of the World*, about her Second World War years working at the Ministry of Information. And that was it – Neve had fallen in love, in the same way as she had when she'd opened up *Pride and Prejudice* at the local library one Saturday morning when she was twelve, or the time she'd seen her first Katharine Hepburn film, or when William had knocked on her door at Somerville College and introduced himself as her student adviser.

She'd spent the rest of that week devouring every single yellowing page in the Archive boxes. She'd read Lucy's poems, letters and diaries and fallen in love with Lucy too; a working-class girl from Leeds who'd won a scholarship to Oxford, despite the opposition of her tyrannical father. At Oxford, she'd met the Right Honourable Charles Holden, whose family owned huge swathes of Gloucestershire and a Mayfair mansion. Lucy's love affair with Charles would survive the war, his marriage to the second daughter of a viscount, even Charles defecting to Russia in the . . .

'Neve! I'm waiting,' Philip reminded her. Neve dug out a folder which contained ten single-spaced pages: Chapter

Five of the biography she'd started writing about Lucy Keener. She didn't even know why she was bothering because Mr Freemont had refused to see any literary merit in Lucy's writings, when Neve had gone to him with her discovery.

He'd skimmed one page of *Dancing on the Edge of the World* with his hardboiled-egg eyes. 'Well, it's easy to see why she never found a publisher,' he'd announced. 'This is very pedestrian. Tiny ideas from a woman with a tiny view of the world; is it really necessary to spend an entire page pontificating about the hat she plans to buy? Send it back where it came from.'

But Neve hadn't. She'd argued her case, which had surprised Mr Freemont because usually Neve did what she was told without any backchat, but he refused to budge. When Neve had distributed a photocopy of *Dancing on the Edge of the World* around the other members of staff who'd all loved it, he'd threatened her with a written warning for gross insubordination so Neve and Chloe had packed everything up, borrowed Chloe's boyfriend's car and ferried the boxes to Neve's spare room. That was after they'd spent an entire week surreptitiously scanning every last piece of paper so there'd be back-up if Celia left a scented candle burning *again* and 27 Abelard Road went up in flames.

So Neve had started writing the biography because she was angry with Mr Freemont and silent rebellion was the only kind of rebellion she knew. She'd also wanted to exercise her writing muscles, which had got flabby since she'd finished her MA. Mostly though, she couldn't consign Lucy's sad and beautiful life to twelve cardboard boxes and simply leave it there unread and unknown.

Even with working full-time and a punishing gym schedule, Neve still had a frightening amount of downtime. She used this to sort and collate and write about Lucy's life, farming out each new chapter to Philip, who'd then pass it on to Chloe; next on the list was Rose, before it came back to Neve with lots of margin notes in red ink.

She looked anxiously across the table at Philip who was already skimreading the first page of her new chapter. 'Don't read it now,' she berated him. 'Not when I'm sitting here.'

'I'm sorry. That's so rude,' Philip mumbled, still reading even as he slid the sheet back into its plastic folder. With a sigh, he tucked it away in his briefcase and fixed Neve with what he considered to be a winning smile. 'So, can you get that draft back to me in a week?'

Neve stared at him without blinking, without even the faintest flicker of her facial muscles.

Philip squirmed. 'Two weeks?'

'Call it three,' Neve decided.

'All right, three,' Philip conceded unhappily. 'And please don't write on it. Your handwriting is completely illegible.'

Half an hour later, Neve was sitting behind the reception desk in the Archive's Reading Room. She was supposed to be writing out index cards in her completely illegible handwriting, but was reading William's letter instead. Then reading between the lines of William's letter. Then looking for hidden meanings in the way that William dotted his i's (there was one on the second line of the third paragraph that looked a little like a heart), crossed his t's and looped his y's. It was very time-consuming.

Neve forced herself to slow down and savour each word. William started off with a quick weather report and a request for a large box of Sainsbury's Red Label teabags and a box of Carr's Water Biscuits. She impatiently skimmed over that so she could get to the good stuff.

It was so lovely to talk to you last week. The sound of your voice always leaves me feeling nostalgic for those long Oxford afternoons where we sat by the river (as I recall, the sun always had that soft golden glow, but surely that can't be the case? Because I also remember a lot of rain and you gifting me a set of Tupperware

containers to catch the streams of water that poured through my
leaking roof) and talked about the books we loved the most. Do
you remember the ferocious argument we had about Jane Austen
versus the Brontës? I think it was the only time I ever saw you get
really cross. 'Mess with Miss Austen and you mess with me,' I
seem to recall you growling.

It's always sunny in California – that much is the same. But
there are no rivers and no Neve to sit with and talk about
literature, philosophy or anything else that takes my fancy.

Neve had to pause there to sigh rapturously. There were
moments of self-doubt, of course there were, when she
worried that she was getting ahead of herself and that
she was building herself up for a spectacular fall when
William got back. But he couldn't write things like that if he
didn't feel it too: that tugging sensation in her chest, as if
her heart was constantly straining in William's direction,
Atlantic Ocean be damned.

I'm reminded of all those long afternoons by the river because my
current crop of undergraduates would be hard-pressed to name
even one novel by either Miss Austen or the Miss Brontës, let alone
deconstruct them. One of the girls in my sophomore tutor group
actually played Lydia Bennet in a big Hollywood adaptation of
Pride and Prejudice *set in New York. (I can actually hear your*
sudden and swift intake of breath!) She's personable enough,
pretty even, if you like that kind of thing. But she's also as dumb
as a box of rocks and apparently her infrequent appearances on
campus are more to do with her agent marketing her as an
intellectual while the university is happy with the publicity they
receive. I also have two models in my freshman class; the Dean has
asked me to turn a blind eye when they need deadline extensions
on their coursework because they're modelling bikinis or jetting off
to New York for castings.

Yes, Oxford seems like another lifetime.

Neve thrust the letter away from her in horror. Hollywood actresses? Models? She'd been worried enough about golden-skinned, blonde-haired Californian girls, but an actress? *Models?* They'd eat William up with a spoon. He had perfect, patrician features, as if he'd just strolled off a cricket pitch, and a posh, abstracted air just like Hugh Grant. And William wasn't a monk. OK, he wasn't an utter Casanova like Max, but he'd had plenty of girlfriends at Oxford. Wispy, weedy little things who'd cultivated a bohemian chic by way of Topshop and read a lot of Rilke. There were probably girls like that at UCLA too but they'd be called Tiffany and Brittany and Courtney instead of Sophie, Camilla and Tamara.

William had been in California three years and even if he only dated casually, he'd have had sex with at least fifteen women. Five women a year actually seemed like a very conservative estimate. Whereas, in three years, the only man who'd really touched Neve was Gustav when he was helping her stretch out her muscles after working out. Plus one bout of almost-sex with Max. It wasn't good enough. *She* wasn't going to be good enough. William had a sexual past while there were sixteen-year-old girls who had more experience than Neve.

She glanced across the Reading Room to see the Archive's most regular visitor, Our Lady of the Blessed Hankie, sniff and pull out the massive wad of tissues she always kept up her cardigan sleeve. It was like looking at her future.

Neve folded up William's letter and stuffed it back into its envelope so its contents wouldn't torment her any longer. There was no time to prevaricate and procrastinate and keep faffing about with a vague plan to work her way up from light flirtation. She had to do something now. And the something she had to do was find a man, any man . . .

Chapter Nine

By the following Monday, Neve still hadn't found a man but she had five dates lined up for that week and had developed a stomach-churning terror that had completely killed her appetite, which was an unexpected bonus.

She'd decided to keep Celia in the dark about her decision to date because her sister would be encouraging her to hook up with male models and forcing her into clothes that she didn't want to wear. Instead, she'd thrown herself on the mercy of Chloe.

On the surface, they didn't have much in common. Chloe was cool and Neve wasn't. Chloe wasn't edgy fashion cool, like Celia, but the kind of insouciant cool that you could only be when you'd spent your formative years travelling round Europe in a VW Campervan with your hippy parents. She spoke five languages, had got a Double First from Cambridge even though she'd only started attending a regular school the year before her GCSEs, made beautiful purses from vintage silk headscarves and sold them on Etsy, but she also played bass in a band called The Fuck Puppets and could down a pint of lager in eleven seconds. Neve had timed her.

Maybe it was because of her crazy, transient childhood, but there was a side of Chloe that was deeply conventional. Neve often thought that that was the side of Chloe she connected with. At exactly four thirty every afternoon, they discussed what they were going to have for dinner that evening; they shared a love of Georgette Heyer novels and a common hatred for Mr Freemont.

Chloe didn't actually date because she'd been going out with the same boy (now a fully qualified Chartered Accountant) since she was fifteen, but she had lots of friends who dated and was always on the phone to them commiserating over bad dates and offering sound relationship advice, so Neve had waited until Mr Freemont went off to meet the Board of Trustees the previous Thursday and scurried out of her little back office. 'Can you come in here and look at something?' she'd begged.

Chloe had come, muttering because she thought Neve was going to make her look up obscure literary references in big, dusty dictionaries, but was confronted instead by Neve's *match.com* dating profile.

'I need you to read this and tell me if you'd date me,' Neve had said nervously. 'If you were a guy.'

She'd stood there waiting anxiously as Chloe sat down and started to read. Every now and again there'd been a stifled groan, or a, 'Christ, Neve, for real?'

'Is it that bad?' she'd asked, when Chloe had declared herself done.

'It's worse than bad. You are never going to get a date with this profile,' Chloe had said forcefully, because her angelic looks masked a steely inner core. She had blonde ringlets, Wedgwood-blue eyes and a deceptively demure face so even Mr Freemont never told her off, though she turned up for work most days wearing jeans and sneakers and insisted that taking only one hour for lunch was an affront to her civil liberties. 'You need to cut out all words of more than two syllables.'

'All of them? But "archivist" has three syllables.'

Chloe had looked at Neve as if she'd just admitted to being Britain's most successful serial killer. 'You can't say you're an archivist. You have to say you work in publishing and oh my God! "I like long walks and have always dreamed of visiting the New York Public Library but I don't understand the whole fascination with backpacking. Trekking through the Hindu Kush would be my own personal ninth circle." *Seriously?'*

'What? *What?'*

Chloe had patted her arm gently. 'They're not really going to get the Dante reference.'

'So I should change it to . . . ?'

' "I like travelling and long walks," ' Chloe had said firmly, fingers already poised over the keyboard. 'This list of favourite authors has to go too. Even I haven't heard of half of them. Change "I don't really listen to music" to "I like all different types of music", and "a few extra pounds" to "curvaceous".'

'But isn't this false advertising?' Neve had fretted as Chloe began to delete huge chunks of text.

'Oh, don't worry. Everyone lies on these things,' Chloe had assured her. 'It's just a little calling card; it's not until you meet them that you'll know if they have potential.'

'How am I going to meet anyone if they're lying and I'm lying and I don't know if we have anything in common?' Neve had tried to nudge Chloe so she'd relinquish control of the keyboard but she'd refused to budge.

'They send you a message, then you go and meet them,' she'd said, fingers flying over the keys as she'd described Neve's personality as 'bubbly and outgoing'. 'I know you, miss. You'll spend weeks exchanging wordy messages about French cinema and never meet anyone.'

'I wouldn't do that!' Neve had gasped without much indignation because that was precisely what she would do.

'Honestly, sweetie, my flatmate finds all her boyfriends on the internet and it's all about the numbers,' Chloe had said. 'Quantity, not quality. The only way to weed out the ninety-nine per cent who are total freaks of nature is to meet them in person.'

Neve hadn't liked those odds. She'd liked it even less when Chloe had called in Rose, the Office Manager, for moral support and they'd both ganged up on her and deleted the arty black-and-white profile shot she'd uploaded. They'd taken her shopping during the lunch-hour and bullied her into buying a push-up bra and a low-cut top that she couldn't really afford so they could take new pictures of her on Rose's cameraphone.

'Tits and teeth,' Chloe had kept chanting as Neve bared her lips in what she hoped was a warm and friendly smile.

Despite her grave misgivings, the dumbed-down profile and cleavage-tastic photo led to thirty responses the next morning. Rose and Chloe had whittled down the non-contenders and stood over Neve while she sent saccharine messages to the shortlist. Now it was Monday afternoon and she was getting ready to meet Tom, a software engineer who liked martial arts, Asian cinema and graphic novels.

Neve also had a long list of dos and don'ts from Chloe's flatmate.

1. Don't give out your last name, phone number or email address.
2. Do let Chloe know where you're meeting him and send a text message when you're on your way home so she knows you haven't been Roofied and date-raped.
3. Don't talk about diets, weight-loss or your crazy fitness regime.
4. Do ask lots of questions and try to look interested when he answers, even if he's duller than mud.
5. Do offer to split the bill, but don't be too forceful about it.
6. Don't put out. A kiss on the mouth is acceptable but only use tongues if the second date is already locked down.
7. Check all exits on your way in, so you can make a speedy getaway while he's having a wee.
8. Try to have some fun.

Neve didn't think she'd ever been so terrified as she slowly walked along High Holborn to meet Tom outside the tube station. She could feel beads of perspiration popping out on her forehead, though it was the coldest February in thirty years, and she was sure that when she opened her mouth, she wouldn't be able to speak. Even breathing was an ordeal.

'It's only a date,' she kept telling herself as she reached the traffic-lights opposite the station and scanned the crowd for Tom. He'd looked quite cute in his photo – a boyish face smiling shyly out at the world – and his punctuation had been absolutely perfect in the two messages he'd sent her. But Neve couldn't see anyone boyish and shy outside the station, just a stream of commuters dodging the hapless men brandishing free copies of the *Evening Standard*.

Somehow her feet carried her across the road so she could stand outside the station and peer anxiously at the sea of faces.

'Are you Neve?' said a voice behind her, and she turned to see an ageing goth who was neither boyish nor shy, to judge from the quick but comprehensive once-over he gave her.

Tom was nearer to forty than the thirty he'd claimed to be, and Neve suspected that the closest he'd ever got to martial arts and Asian cinema was watching Kung Fu movies.

Once they found a corner table in a pub that stank of stale chip fat, he crossly told Neve that she didn't look anything like her profile picture, and while she was still thinking, Kettle meet pot, you're black, Tom started talking about something called Linux for ages while staring at her breasts, until he got up to go to the bar and Neve slipped out of the side door without a second's hesitation.

As she walked back to Gray's Inn Road to collect her bike, Neve felt strangely exhilarated. She'd done it! She'd actually been on a date. Her first date. And yes, it had been horrible and scary, but nothing could be as bad as that first foray into the unknown. Now she knew what to expect – as little as possible – and maybe on the second or the third date, she might even get the opportunity to talk about herself for a few minutes. Right now, Neve couldn't wait to get home and confess everything to Celia because she was beginning to understand what Chloe's flatmate had meant when she'd said that the debrief was usually more entertaining than the actual date.

On Tuesday she had early-evening drinks with an ambient trance DJ, who made it pretty clear that Neve didn't have one iota of cool ('You've never heard of David Toop? You have to be fucking kidding me!').

Wednesday night was a date with an estate agent. Neve had had grave misgivings about it even though Chloe had insisted that there had to be some nice estate agents. It turned out that David wasn't one of them. His hands had brushed the underside of Neve's breasts when he'd gallantly helped her remove her coat, and she'd only had time to take one sip of her white-wine spritzer before he asked, 'Are we going to fuck later? If we're not, then this is really a waste of my time.'

By Thursday, Neve was seriously flagging and in no mood for her date with Adrian, but Philip had gone to great trouble to set it up, incurring the wrath of Clive who thought that his staff were his own personal property. With zero enthusiasm, she set off to meet Adrian outside Foyles on Charing Cross Road.

Her heart was somewhere around her knees, but when Neve saw Adrian waiting for her with a sulky expression on his pretty face, it plummeted all the way down to her ankles.

'I'm gay,' he snapped, as soon as she was within earshot.

'Oh! I kinda knew that,' Neve said, and when she tried a tentative smile, Adrian smiled back. He really was very pretty. He wasn't quite so pretty when he looked at her properly and his eyes bulged in their sockets.

'Neve from Oxford?' he queried. 'Fucking hell! Have you had one of those gastric bands fitted?'

'I did it the old-fashioned way,' she said, failing to dial down the smug tone. 'Diet, exercise, blood, sweat, tears. Still a way to go though.'

Adrian gave her an appraising look as if he was about to send her off to market. 'You look fabulous.' He paused and

Neve could see him come to a decision. 'Let's go for a drink. You don't mind if we go where there's eye candy, do you?'

It was the most fun Neve had had all week. They spent a very enjoyable hour bitching about the vile, perfidious Clive and how Adrian had to pretend to be straight at work as it was the only way to fend off his lecherous advances.

'Though he keeps telling me that once I have cock, I'll never go back,' he confessed to Neve, who squealed in horror.

Adrian even promised to think of single, straight friends to set her up with and the evening only came to an end when the barman that Adrian had been flirting with all evening finished his shift.

And on Friday there was Edward, who Neve had a really good feeling about. He'd sent her twelve messages in the last two days praising her intellect, prose style and beauty, and it was a huge relief to correspond with someone who knew who the Poet Laureate was.

Edward was shorter than she'd expected but, by this stage, Neve was adding five years to the age of all her dates and shortening them by five inches, and he was even more nervous than she was, which was a nice change. He was sweating profusely and once they were seated in a little pub by the Law Courts, he swayed from side to side but listened intently as Neve described her day's transcribing.

'And what about you?' Neve asked, when she'd said all there was to say about the literary estate of a minor poet. 'You said you were a writer?'

True, Edward had said he was a writer, but his writing largely consisted of blog posts about the Kennedy assassination. As he talked, he got more and more agitated until he finally admitted that he'd had a manic episode three months ago and was currently living with his parents and temping on the days he could actually get out of bed.

At least there was plenty to talk about, Neve thought, as she tried to steer the conversation away from Virginia Woolf, Sylvia Plath and other famous suicides. Max, whom she'd been trying really hard not to think about, had asked her what she'd be bringing to her first relationship other than an exit strategy, but as she patiently answered Edward's questions on Freudian analysis, Neve realised that if she went out with him, she might be able to effect some positive change in his life. Besides, he was looking at her with something approaching reverence as she described the difference between psychoanalysis and psychotherapy. No one had ever looked at her like that before.

He wasn't so bad-looking, Neve reasoned, as Edward walked with her to Tesco Metro so she could buy some skimmed milk before she cycled home. Rose from work would call him 'a fixer-upper' and if he got rid of the ponytail of lank hair and stopped sweating so much, he could be quite attractive, and it wasn't as if she was giving Angelina Jolie any sleepless nights. Besides, going out with Edward would mean that she never had to walk 'the green mile' with pounding heart and a flat metallic taste in her mouth to meet any more prospective dates.

'So, Neve, I think you're wonderful,' Edward breathed as they stood outside Tesco's. 'Do you think you might want to see me again?'

'That would be lovely,' Neve said decisively, and she was just wondering if now the second date was locked down, it would be all right to give Edward her phone number, when he raised one hand to cup her cheek.

It was a prelude to a kiss that never happened, because one touch from Edward's hot clammy hand *on her face* had Neve shuddering violently. It felt as if her skin was trying to crawl off her bones because even though her head had made a reasoned, rational decision and her heart was ambivalent, her body was absolutely, unequivocally repulsed.

They both pretended that it hadn't happened. Edward gave Neve his phone number, she promised that she'd call, and even though she had a tiny moment of shame when she got home and discovered that Edward had already sent her three messages to say that she was gorgeous and that he couldn't wait to see her again, her body shuddered again at the line, *Have a wonderful weekend, honey.* How could you date someone when you went into spasms of disgust just because they'd typed a casual endearment? You couldn't.

There were no dates on Saturday because Celia, Rose, Chloe and Chloe's flatmate had all decreed that anyone who went on an internet date on a Saturday night was a sad, desperate loser, making Neve a sad, desperate loser by association. Besides, Rose was hellbent on dragging Neve to a salsa club on the Charing Cross Road.

Rose was something of an enigma to Neve. She was in her forties, had worked at the Archive since she was eighteen and had never married, because she'd spent most of her adult life looking after her mother who had MS. Her mother had died five years ago and now Rose's social life, which rivalled Celia's, centred around meeting and ensnaring young men from South America, then discarding them a few weeks later when she got bored.

It was odd, because Rose looked exactly like a woman in her mid-forties who'd spent the best years of her life caring for an elderly parent. She was tall and buxom with a determined set to her face, which came in handy when Mr Freemont was being absolutely unbearable, and at work she favoured tailored separates and sensible shoes.

But on Saturday night she was transformed into a middle-aged sex kitten in a red sparkly dress that showed more cleavage than Neve thought fitting for a woman of Rose's age. Her mousy-brown hair had been swept up into a mass of ringlets and she was wearing skyscraper heels and a feral smile. Neve was wearing a black wrap dress, black cardigan and flats, though Rose forced her to remove her cardigan before the salsa lesson.

'You've got to show a bit of flesh,' she enthused, looking down at her own chest with satisfaction. 'I've got some body glitter in my bag. Really draws the eye to the breasts.'

Neve didn't want anyone's eyes on her breasts, which were heaving after an hour's salsa lesson – an experience which had confirmed all her worst suspicions that she had no sense of rhythm. While everyone went left, she went right, and she could only move her hips from side to side, rather than swivelling, circling and thrusting them like everyone else.

'You're doing great,' Rose called as she mamboed past Neve in the arms of a Chilean dishwasher called Esteban who looked like a young Antonio Banderas. Neve was left to tread on the toes of Jorge, who was very sweet about it, but as soon as the lesson ended and the more experienced dancers began to arrive, he kissed Neve's hand, made his excuses and left.

After a couple more dances, Neve was left on the sidelines – word had got out that she was a toe-stepper. She was relieved to rest her aching feet and slowly sip a lime and soda as she watched office workers from Croydon and minicab drivers from Edmonton sashay across the floor as if they had Latin blood flowing through their veins. Everyone was having a good time because it was Saturday night and for a few short hours, the trials and disappointments of the past week were forgotten. Saturday night was about drinking and dancing and flirting and shucking off whoever you had to be Monday to Friday.

Neve sat there in her basic black and wondered what was wrong with her. It was as if, once the pounds began to disappear, they'd taken her sense of fun with them. She'd been happy going to nightclubs with her friends when she was at Oxford and she could concentrate on having a good time (and minding everyone's coats and bags while they were dancing) because she didn't have to worry about trying to pull. Now she was desperate to be pulled, but she was still minding Rose's leopard-print fun-fur and matching bag while she did an energetic mambo. These were the wrong kind of thoughts to have at eleven thirty on a Saturday night sat in a dark corner of a heaving club as everyone else gyrated and whooped around you. Neve waited another five minutes for her sense of fun to make its presence felt, then she went to find Rose to tell her that she was going to catch the last tube.

As the tube pulled out of the station, Neve had to tense her facial muscles in an effort to stop glaring and grinding down on her back molars because the woman sitting opposite her was looking quite concerned. But really, the mores of modern dating were horrific and completely unjust.

It shouldn't be about numbers and carefully worded dating profiles and messages specifically designed to sell a version of yourself that didn't even remotely resemble the real thing. Even casual, no-strings affairs should be about romance, about connecting with someone, about eyes meeting in a crowded room, a shared smile across a dark club. But with the exception of poor, hapless Edward, there wasn't a single man she'd met that week who seemed to be searching for the one girl that made his heart go pitter-pitter. They just wanted a girl who was easy on the eye, untaxing on their frontal lobes and who'd drop her knickers in exchange for a glass of white wine.

All Neve needed was a fairly normal man to have a fairly normal relationship with, and she'd only met one of them in the last few weeks.

Neve pulled out her phone as soon as she got out of Finsbury Park station. She was going to do it right here, right now, before she even started walking home, because she knew that in those fifteen minutes she'd start thinking of all the reasons why she shouldn't and then she'd decide to sleep on it. Then by the morning, she'd have come up with a gargantuan number of obstacles and stumbling blocks and she'd prevaricate and procrastinate, then push it to the dusty corner of her mind where she put all the stuff that she didn't want to deal with. That dusty corner was already bursting at the seams.

Yes, she was going to do it now because she still hadn't got round to deleting Max's number from her phone. As usual, her subconscious was far ahead of her regular, bumbling conscious.

Max answered on the third ring, which was just as well as Neve had a feeling that she'd have chickened out by the fifth. 'Hello?' he said warily, as if he didn't like having an unknown number flash up on his screen.

'Max? It's Neve.' She turned around so she was huddled against the London Underground map, just like she'd been that night when he'd kissed her, and willed herself to carry on. 'Are you free to talk?'

'What? Who? I can't hear you,' Max shouted over what sounded like the noise of a Mardi Gras parade. 'Hang on!'

Neve hung on, counting silently in her head as she made a deal with herself that she'd hang up if she got to fifty.

'Sorry, who is it?' Max asked when she'd only got to thirty-seven.

'It's Neve,' she said again. 'Sorry for calling you this late on a Saturday night.'

'Ah, the night has barely begun,' Max drawled. 'So, how the devil are you?'

'Oh, I'm fine. Absolutely fine.' Neve realised she didn't know what to say. 'Congratulations! You've been the successful candidate for the position of my pancake boyfriend,' probably wasn't the right way to go. 'How are you?'

'I'm fine too,' Max said. 'So . . . what's up?'

You just have to construct one sentence of about ten words, Neve told herself. 'I was wondering if you'd like to go out on a date. With me,' she added, just in case Max wasn't clear on that point. 'If you're free. In the next week or so.'

Chapter Ten

Twelve hours later, Neve was walking down Crouch Hill towards Crouch End Broadway because Max was there having brunch in the Italian Food Hall and she had an open invitation to join him, after he'd taken pity on her complete inability to think of a time, venue and day for their date.

She was nervous, that was a given, but she wasn't coasting a tsunami of terror as she had before her other dates. At least with Max she knew what to expect, as much as she could with someone who was as mercurial as he was, and it was just one date. She was literally a veteran of 'just one date' by now and after she'd got that out of the way, she could get some organic olives from Waitrose and browse the shelves of the Oxfam bookshop and the stationery store, Neve told herself as she marched up to the Italian Food Hall at precisely five past twelve.

Neve peered through the window, trying to see beyond the deli counter to the seated area at the back. The damp air had smeared condensation on the window, making it hard to see, so Neve had no choice but to go in and wander through the tables and booths until she found Max – that is, if he'd actually turned up and hadn't just been playing a cruel trick on her.

There was a moment of dithering before Neve marched purposefully to the entrance – and then she stopped. At the side of the building was a canopied seating area completely deserted apart from one solitary figure who looked up from his newspaper and waved at her.

Neve waved back and now she was committed to clomping down the narrow walkway between the empty tables as Max got to his feet so he could lean forward and kiss her cheek when Neve reached his side. Neve bumped her nose against Max's chin as she tried to return the favour, while Max was aiming for her other cheek. She always forgot that Celia and her fashion friends did the double kiss and now she was flustered as she sat down and fussed with her bags.

'So, you and me on an actual date – who'd have thought it?' Max said lightly.

Neve smiled vaguely in response as she watched Max slip his BlackBerry *and* an iPhone into an inner pocket. It was the first time Neve had seen him in daylight or what passed for a murky kind of daylight, and there was something decidedly exotic about him. Maybe it was the slant of his cheekbones or the honey tinge to his skin. His hair was so dark that it was almost black and had some serious product in it to try and kill the curl. She'd forgotten how handsome he was; only his bloodshot, puffy eyes made Neve feel slightly less intimidated.

Before Max caught her staring, Neve picked up the laminated menu, which was difficult when she was wearing woolly gloves. She was about to ask why they were sitting outside when it occurred to her that maybe Max didn't want to be seen with her in a crowded public place.

'Are you ready to order?' Max asked, and Neve realised there was a waitress at her side.

She ordered a pot of tea and was going to send the waitress away when her stomach growled warningly. Normally she'd never dream of eating on a date or in front of anyone who wasn't immediate family, but Max watching her eat scrambled eggs on granary toast didn't even compare to their first half-clothed encounter.

The waitress left far too quickly for Neve's liking, so there was just Max gazing steadily at her and she hadn't said a single word to him since she sat down.

'Have you had a good week?' she asked shyly, painfully aware of how breathy and high-pitched her voice sounded and how she didn't want to take off her stupid woolly hat with the ear-flaps because she knew she'd have really shocking hat hair.

Max nodded. 'Been a bit of a nightmare, if you must know,' he sniffed. 'Trying to lock down the August cover. If there's one thing worse than dealing with the talent, it's dealing with the talent's agent, manager and publicist. Complete mare.'

Neve nodded in what she hoped was a sympathetic manner. She'd got the general gist of the conversation, Max had had a hard week, but the specifics eluded her. 'The talent? Is that someone's nickname in the entertainment industry?'

'No,' Max said slowly and rather condescendingly. 'It's how I describe a celebrity when I can't say their name because I've had to sign a confidentiality agreement.'

'Oh. I see.' Neve felt as if she'd been unfairly chastised for not knowing the machinations of the entertainment industry, but from the way Max winced as the clouds momentarily parted to allow a faint beam of sunlight through, she suspected he had a hangover and decided not to take it personally. 'Why are you working on the August cover when it's the beginning of March?'

'Hasn't Celia ever explained to you about lead times?' Neve shook her head and Max groaned theatrically. 'Well, get her to fill you in next time you see her. It's really hard having to explain these things to civilians.'

At least she was picking up some media buzzwords. Celebrities were called 'the talent' and lowly peasants like Neve were known as 'civilians'.

'I'll be sure to do that,' Neve said crisply, folding her arms because she was annoyed and absolutely freezing but she was damned if she was going to let Max know that. 'Silly old me, thinking that working on a fashion magazine was glamorous.'

'It is glamorous,' Max snapped. 'And *Skirt* isn't a fashion magazine. It's actually a luxury lifestyle title.' He paused as the waitress returned with a pot of tea for Neve and Max's triple espresso. 'Thank you, darling. I'm going to need another one of these in about ten minutes.'

Neve reluctantly removed a glove so she could pour herself a cup of tea and waited for Max to ask her how *her* week had been, but he was too busy knocking back his coffee in one swift gulp.

'So what glamorous things have you done this week?' she persisted and she didn't even care, but hearing Max jaw on about a lot of vapid celebrities had to be better than sitting there in tense and resentful silence. She couldn't believe that he'd agreed to go on a date with her, and had gone to all the trouble of actually turning up when he had zero interest in making even polite conversation.

'The usual. Launches, screenings, after-shows . . . Oh, and I went to the soft opening of Jamie Oliver's new restaurant,' Max said with markedly more enthusiasm than he'd shown up to now. 'Nigella and Sophie were both there – Sophie Dahl, that is. She dared me to nick the salt and pepper pots but that wasn't even the best thing that happened this week.'

It sounded pretty spectacular to Neve, who had a lot of time for Sophie Dahl and her struggles with her weight, though she was slightly shocked that she'd encourage Max in acts of petty larceny. 'It wasn't?'

'Didn't even come close,' Max said, resting his elbows on the table and giving her a swift and wicked smile. 'My publishers bought me a Mini Cooper, though Mandy sent hers back because she wanted them to paint it pink and put in a sunroof.'

'That would be a car?' Neve clarified because she wanted to make sure it wasn't more obscure media slang.

'Yup. *Penalties and Prada* was Tesco's bestselling fiction title last year and we just hit quarter of a million copies sold.' He smiled to himself. 'Of course, that doesn't include foreign sales.'

'Quarter of a million?' Neve echoed, and if she sounded appalled then she just couldn't help it.

'Why are you scrunching up your face like you're standing downwind of a sewage pipe?'

'Well, it's great that you got a new car and, well, at least it means that people are buying books, I suppose,' Neve hedged, but then she couldn't rein in these indignant words that needed to be spoken out loud. 'But really it says everything that's wrong about the publishing industry, that a quarter of a million people bought *and read* a sex and shopping novel that wasn't even written by one of those footballer girlfriends, and yet most of the shortlisted titles on the Orange Prize, which is an award for women writers, don't even sell ten thousand copies. It's just not right.'

'Well, it's probably because they're crap and go on about how shit it is to be an oppressed woman in a burqa in Iran or they're one of those worthy books about a young girl coming to terms with her burgeoning sexuality in a rural town some time in the past when it was all ration books and no TV,' Max rapped back at her.

Neve choked on her tea. Really choked on it so she spat drops of it on the paper tablecloth. 'Name me three books that were on the shortlist for last year's prize?' she hissed at him and didn't even wait for Max to answer because it would be a bloody long wait. 'You can't. I'm guessing you can't even name the winner.'

'Yeah, well, have you even read one of my books?'

'You mean one of Mandy McDonald's books, don't you?' Neve corrected.

'It's Mandy McIntyre, sweetheart, which you'd know if you read anything that was printed in this century.'

Neve had read lots of books that had been written in the current century, though she was currently hard-pressed to think of a single one. 'At least I read books,' she sneered, and she thought it might have been the first time that she'd ever sneered at anyone, but really, Max was the most objectionable person she'd ever met – so full of himself and obsessed with the shallow and superficial.

'It's probably why you work in some dusty old library, full of elderly lesbians with their cardigans buttoned all the way up to their necks as they read Agatha Christie novels and leer at your arse when they ask you to get books down from the top shelf,' Max announced scathingly as Neve spat tea over the tablecloth again.

'It's a literary archive and there's nothing wrong with wearing cardigans,' she all but shrieked, though that really was neither here nor there, but Neve never felt properly dressed without a cardigan, and yes, she usually did up all the buttons because she tended to feel the cold. 'And there's nothing wrong in being a lesbian, unless you're completely homophobic.'

'How dare you?' Max gasped. He certainly looked angry though he sounded as if he was ramping up the outrage for comic effect. 'I am not homophobic. Almost all of my male friends are gay and I love Lady Gaga.'

Neve snorted in derision and would have got up there and then, flouncing off to Waitrose, and maybe even swearing under her breath, but the waitress was back with a laden tray.

She was rewarded with a devastating smile from Max that made her flutter her eyelashes and shove her breasts in his face as she placed a full English breakfast, a basket of pastries and a pot of coffee in front of him. Almost as an afterthought, she put down Neve's plate.

'Sweetheart, you're a lifesaver,' Max said as he drizzled ketchup all over his eggs. 'Honestly, you keep spoiling me like this and we're going to have to make things official.'

The waitress giggled even though Max didn't even attempt to sound sincere, Neve thought to herself angrily, as she tugged off her other glove so she could eat her toast and eggs with a knife and fork. She'd been brought up properly, unlike Max who was shovelling baked beans on to a torn-off piece of toast.

It was hard to keep a grip on her cutlery when her fingers were turning blue. 'Why are we sitting outside anyway?' she asked.

To her surprise, Max smiled weakly and gestured under the table. 'I brought my wingman in case things got sticky, but I needn't have bothered as things have been going so *fantastically* well.'

'You brought your what?' Neve scooched back her chair so she could peer under the table. Curled around Max's chair legs was a stocky, tan-coloured dog that looked like a Rottweiler or a bull mastiff or another breed of devil dog that the *Daily Mail* was always trying to get banned. Neve gave the dog, and the bondage harness it was wearing, a wary look but she needn't have bothered. The dog glanced up, caught Neve's eye, and then huddled further under the chair with its front paws over its eyes. It was unbelievably cute but also rather a blow to Neve's ego.

'I don't think he likes me,' she said.

'Keith doesn't like anyone.'

'Your dog's called Keith? That's not a dog's name.'

Max shrugged helplessly. 'It's the only name he'll answer to. I tried out other noble and rugged names like Troy and Cassius, but he wasn't having it. Are you really too cold out here? You should have said something.'

Neve shook her head. 'I'll be all right as long as I warm my hands on the teapot every couple of minutes,' she said, because there wasn't much else she could say. They were meant to be brunching together and if Max had brought his dog, then they were going to have to brunch *al fresco*.

'It's just I try to spend a lot of time with Keith on the weekend. I have a dog-walker, but Keith gets left on his own during the week and he has serious abandonment issues.'

'He does?' Neve risked another look at Keith, who was still doing the whole see no evil thing.

'Well, he was a stray . . .' Max paused. 'You sure you want to hear this?'

'Of course I do. I always wanted a puppy when I was little but Celia had asthma so I made do with a goldfish. Goldfish are really boring pets,' Neve added, as she thought back to the many fish she'd owned and the many times she'd come downstairs in the morning to find their bloated, white-bellied corpses floating on top of the water.

'I didn't have any pets,' Max said. 'Though one time I stole my friend's guinea pig and took it home, which didn't go down well with my mum. She thought we had rats.'

Neve smiled and Max smiled back and it was such a relief not to be sniping at each other that Neve stopped fidgeting with the sugar bowl or pretending to read the menu or even calculating how long it would be before she could leave.

'So, you were going to tell me the root of Keith's abandonment issues,' Neve prompted. 'You don't think he'll get paranoid if we talk about him?'

'Paranoia is so far down the list of his emotional disorders that I think we'll be OK,' Max said with a grin, leaning back on his chair. 'So a couple of summers ago, my Broadband went wonky and I had to get an engineer around . . .'

Neve had finished her scrambled eggs and toast and was on her second pot of tea by the time Max had finished the heart-wrenching saga of Keith's early years. He'd followed the Broadband engineer into Max's flat. Max had assumed that Keith belonged to the engineer and it was a bit of a cheek for him to take his dog along on house calls, but the engineer had found Keith sitting on the doorstep and thought that he was Max's dog.

'I think he belonged to someone who'd gone on holiday and couldn't afford to have him kennelled so they just dumped him and hoped he'd be there when they got back,' Max said, reaching down to pat Keith. 'He was a bit beaten up, as if he'd got into a lot of fights, and when I took him to the animal shelter, they discovered these older scabs and scars as if his owners hadn't treated him very well.'

'So you didn't leave him at the shelter?' Neve asked.

'Oh, I did,' Max assured her. 'But I went back for him five minutes later. He had a skin condition and cowered and barked when anyone but me went near him and I couldn't see him being adopted any time soon, so I broke him out of there.'

Neve could feel everything in her turning to mush. 'Aw, poor Keith,' she cooed. 'Poor little pooch.'

It was a voice other women reserved for clucking at babies and kittens but Neve had yet to see a baby that didn't look like an angry, hairless old man, and ever since she'd been bitten by next door's cat when she was six and had to have a tetanus shot, she'd been a dog person. When her mother had corralled her into going to the Goddess Workshop to boost her self-esteem, there had been a lot of banging on about finding her happy place. It turned out that her happy place was a field of lolloping, rollicking Labrador puppies and, although she wasn't a crier, a particularly poignant episode of *It's Me or the Dog* could have her in pieces.

'Keith lives in the lap of luxury these days,' Max said sourly, his eyes crinkling up as if he was trying to suppress a smile. 'He's spoiled rotten.'

Neve felt it was only fair to revise her low opinion of Max. He couldn't be quite so feckless and shallow if he'd actually managed to make a commitment to another living being who obviously adored him if the snuffly noises from under the table were anything to go by.

'He deserves to be spoiled,' Neve insisted, and then she was sticking her head under the table so she could talk in that sickly voice again. 'You need lots of TLC, don't you? Yes, you do.'

Keith raised his head, and just as Neve expected him to

either bare his teeth or retreat so far under Max's chair that he came out the other side, he cautiously came a little closer to her outstretched hand and sniffed it.

'I don't believe it,' Max muttered, when he saw what was going on.

'He knows I'm a friend,' Neve said, gently rubbing the back of her hand against Keith's head. 'You're a lovely boy, aren't you?'

'Have you got some liver treats hidden up your sleeve?'

Neve shook her head. 'I don't normally carry liver treats on the off-chance that I might run into a skittish dog I want to befriend.'

'Keith usually hates strangers.' Max frowned, as he watched Keith nuzzle Neve's hand. 'You should feel very honoured.'

All in all, it was a good place for their disastrous date to end, Neve decided as she pulled her purse out of her bag and tried to catch the waitress's eye. 'Well, this has been, um . . . interesting, but I think . . .'

Max reached across the table to place his hand on top of hers to stop her from opening her purse. 'I'll get this,' he said firmly. His fingers were shockingly warm against her chilled skin. 'You're freezing!'

'Really, I'm fine,' Neve told him as she tried not to shiver, but it was less to do with the cold and more to do with Max's thumb rubbing against the tender place on the under-side of her wrist where her veins criss-crossed like lines on the tube map. 'Anyway, I really should be going.'

'Well, before you do, we should probably decide what we're going to do on our next date,' Max said. 'There's a fashion and film exhibition at the V&A that looks quite good.'

'Next date? We're not dating,' Neve spluttered. 'Why would you even think that?'

'Well, technically we've been on three dates now, so I think that we're having one of those pancake relationships that you're such an expert on. And you did phone up and ask me out, so why are you so surprised? What did *you* think we were doing?'

It was a really good question and one that Neve couldn't even begin to answer. 'I don't know. I'm not sure what . . .' She tried again. 'Really, why would you even be interested in that kind of arrangement with someone like me? Is it my novelty value?'

'Kind of, yeah,' Max admitted. He pouted slightly. 'I can tell that you don't like me that much and you're about the only person I've ever met who doesn't think I'm ace with added bits of aceness.' He treated Neve to an outrageous wink. 'You're going to be powerless to resist me in the end.'

Neve didn't have the guts to tell Max that she'd probably like him a lot more if he didn't come out with such arrogant twaddle. Obviously her face gave her away, because Max stopped holding her hand so he could wag a finger at her in admonition.

'You'll see. It's like the time everyone said that there was no way I could get Madonna for the cover of *Skirt*, but I spent a year wooing her publicist and then when the interview was set up, everyone said she'd be really difficult and I'd be lucky to get ten minutes.' Max smiled triumphantly. 'The interview lasted two hours and then we went clubbing. If Madonna loves me, then you will too.'

It was the first and only time that Neve had ever been compared to Madonna. It felt oddly insulting. She raised her eyebrows. 'Max, it's not that I don't like you – that is, I don't *not* like you – but I just can't see you in even a pancake relationship.'

Max flapped his hand in front of his face as if he was swatting a fly. 'Look, short of fucking some circus freaks and posting the video on YouTube, you name it, I've done it. At least twice. Having a relationship and not even a sexual one is so straight, it's practically perverted.'

Now Neve was definitely insulted. 'Well, I'm happy to be of service,' she snapped.

'Now don't go getting all huffy.' Max wagged his finger again. 'Let's face it, I'm the best offer you're going to get when it comes to pancake boyfriends. At least I'm not an estate agent and I don't have any suicidal tendencies. By the way, your sister really needs to remember that her voice carries from one end of the office to another.'

She was going to kill Celia. 'So, I had a few bad dates, but I just have to keep applying myself and I'm bound to have a good date eventually,' Neve said defensively.

'Applying yourself? Going on dates isn't meant to be such an ordeal.' Max pursed his lips. 'You're twenty-five, right? You are the oldest twenty-five year old I've ever met.'

'I can't help it if I'm mature for my age.' Though Neve preferred to think that she just had a very old soul. 'Maybe I should have spent a few years getting drunk and having lots of meaningless sex, but I didn't.'

'Look, are you absolutely certain that this Billy bloke is your one true love?' Max asked, as if the whole notion of William and even having a one true love wasn't to be taken seriously.

Neve immediately bristled. 'His name's William,' she reminded Max coldly. 'And yes – yes, he is – and you don't have to be so snarky about it.'

Max shrugged. 'I'm just saying that before you settle down with William, or whatever his name is, you should have some fun, and I am the god of having some fun.' Max was actually being serious, even though it was the most ridiculous thing Neve had ever heard anyone say. Then again, the whole point of all those excruciating first dates had been to inject a little fun and romance into her life, and both the fun and the romance had been sorely lacking. Sometimes Neve thought that fun should come with a bullet-pointed action plan and some handy diagrams.

'Well, when you put it like that, I suppose I can have

some fun,' Neve said brightly. Brightly was what she was aiming for, but the actual execution was more grimly determined, as something very important occurred to her. 'But I need you to promise that we are definitely not having sex.'

'No sex unless you absolutely beg me for it.' Max grinned at the acid-drop look on Neve's face. 'And I won't even use tongue when we're kissing. Not unless you do first.'

There were so many objectionable things about that statement that Neve didn't know where to begin, but while they were establishing some ground rules . . . 'I don't think we should hold hands either,' she blurted out.

'You don't?' Max asked mildly.

'Well, it's just we need to have some kind of reminder that this is a pancake relationship and not a proper one. So, if by some miracle, we were getting on really well and I went to hold your hand, I'd have to stop and remember that we don't hold hands because we're not a proper couple,' Neve babbled while Max just sat there and looked at her like she was having some kind of psychotic break. 'Don't you see? Not holding hands would be like a safety word.'

'What do you know about safety words?' Max drawled very slowly, and before Neve could take umbrage because being inexperienced didn't mean she was completely uninformed, he shrugged and said, 'Fine. No sex. No holding hands and we'll take the stuff in between sex and holding hands under advisement, OK?'

Neve nodded. 'Shall we just take this on a date-by-date basis?'

Max looked at her blankly. 'I suppose that would work.' He suddenly put his head in his hands and yawned. 'Sorry, don't know where Maria is with my next espresso. Haven't been to bed yet and I think my second wind has just upped and left.'

It was time to wrest some control back. Neve shoved her purse back in her bag and stood up. 'Well, I'm glad we've got that all cleared up,' she said officiously. 'I can usually do

Monday, Thursday and Friday evenings so, um . . . I'll call you.'

'Or I'll call you,' Max offered, but his voice was quiet and his eyelids were drooping down as if it was taking all his energy not to rest his head on the table and fall asleep right there.

'Right, well, I'm glad that's all sorted then.' Before there could be a painfully protracted goodbye, Neve crouched down to pet Keith, smiled tightly at Max and walked away.

PART TWO

Little By Little

Chapter Eleven

Neve had imagined that dating would be evening after evening in the pub making slightly forced conversation as they listened to each other's back stories but it wasn't like that at all. Or dating Max wasn't like that.

Max had such a full and varied social calendar that their dates doubled up as work events that he simply had to attend. Over the course of three weeks, he'd taken Neve dog-racing for the album launch of a band who all had moptop hairdos and mockney accents. There had been the swank first-night party of a photographic exhibition at the V&A, with waiters drifting past carrying laden trays of champagne and canapés. They'd been to the opening of a shop, which had featured burlesque dancers, a magician and a goody bag stuffed full of premium cosmetics, spa vouchers and a pair of cashmere pyjamas, which Neve had passed on to a grateful Chloe. There were film screenings, cocktail parties and band showcases, and Neve went to each one accompanied by Max and no fewer than twenty of his close personal friends.

Neve had never felt more out of her depth in this strange new world of press events and after-show parties and the party after the after-show party, and though she could hardly admit it to herself, she found comfort in the fact that Max kept his arm draped loosely around her shoulders most of the time. First they'd work the room; usually it took them an hour to do a full circuit because no sooner had they taken a step than they'd bump into someone Max knew and there'd be a flurry of air kisses, hugs and breathless compliments.

There was no earthly reason for the publicists or journalists or models, or actresses or reality TV stars to do anything more than smile vaguely in Neve's direction, but Max would take her arm to bring her forward from where she was cowering behind him to say, 'This is my very good friend, Neve.' Then he'd follow up the introduction with, 'Neve was just saying that she was thinking of taking a burlesque class.' Or, 'Help me out here. Neve insists that the film was just sub-par Tarantino.' Usually she'd been saying no such thing, but it got the conversation started; a conversation that she was part of, which was a novelty after all those years of sitting in a corner while her slimmer, prettier, less tongue-tied friends were being chatted up and having drinks bought for them.

After working the room, they'd sit down and within five minutes they'd be surrounded on all sides and Neve would sit there with the comfortable weight of Max's arm still around her and smile and nod and murmur, 'Really? Well, I never knew that,' as the conversation roared around her. It didn't matter that she never really joined in or that she didn't know the people they were talking about, because no one really listened to anyone else. It was a competition to talk the loudest, to say the most shocking thing, to brag about their latest work freebie and at the centre of it all, the sun around which everyone satellited, was Max.

Max's charm was so obvious, so in one's face, such an obvious mix of flirtation and flattery that Neve hadn't appreciated its subtle nuances before. That just by lowering his voice and staring at someone with a steady, unblinking gaze Max seemed to exert some kind of sexual thrall over people – male or female, gay or straight, it didn't matter. Then he'd touch them: tuck a stray lock of hair behind an ear, hook a finger into the strap of a dress where it had slipped off one tanned, toned shoulder and put it back in place, and suddenly he had a willing victim only too happy to do anything to please him.

Neve had even seen (though she really wished she hadn't) one of those male models that Celia was always harping on about drop his trousers to show everyone the results of his back, sack and crack wax after Max had drawled, 'Don't believe you had the stones to get it done, not when you cried like a baby when you were getting the world's smallest tattoo.'

All Neve could do was stay on her guard, ready to run shrieking into the night, in case Max directed the full force of his attention on to her. But apart from the arm around her shoulder and the constant endearments, he'd decided to use his power for her greater good.

The moment that Neve finally realised this, which was the same moment that she actually started to enjoy herself, was about two weeks into their pancake relationship. They were at the launch of an iPhone app (a concept that Neve had difficulty processing) and had spent the last ten minutes talking to an actress who Neve vaguely recognised from a BBC dramatisation of *The Mill on the Floss*. She was the official face of the app (again Neve was having immense difficulty understanding how some device on an iPhone could have an official face) and was desperate to be profiled in *Skirt*. Neve knew this because the other woman kept mentioning it every time she opened her mouth.

'I'm up for a part in the new Sam Mendes film and it would really help me out, Maxie,' she pouted. She looked even more beautiful when she pouted than when she was throwing her head back and laughing at every single thing Max said. 'And if you need a fashion angle, a friend and I are thinking of starting up a little accessories line.'

'Well, I'd love to but we're working on the August issue so it probably wouldn't be much help with Sam,' Max mused, idly stroking the top of Neve's arm. 'Don't get me wrong, you're gorgeous, but I need something a little bit more than gorgeous to convince my Editor.'

The woman licked her lips and stared meaningfully at Max. 'I'd be ever so grateful.'

'Ah, that's what they all say.' Max tugged on a strand of Neve's hair. 'What do *you* think?'

Neve looked doubtfully up at Max. What did she know about his criteria for choosing celebrities to shoot for *Skirt*? Especially actresses who didn't think there was anything morally wrong with coming on to a man who had his arm around another girl. 'I did like you in *The Mill on the Floss*,' she said diplomatically, 'but I don't understand this whole business of apps and what they do and how they're put on an iPhone.'

'You don't have an iPhone?' the actress breathed, her eyes widening in consternation. 'Oh my God. Wait here.'

'Am I going to get ejected because I don't have an iPhone?' Neve asked Max, who looked up to the ceiling and sighed because he knew she wasn't joking.

But the actress was back within two minutes with a publicist who presented a gold box to Neve with great ceremony and when she looked inside, there was a shiny black iPhone 'with the app already pre-installed on it'.

Neve had barely stuttered her thanks before the actress turned to Max. 'So?'

Max made her wait a good twenty seconds. 'Well, I guess I'll see what I can do.'

It was then that Neve understood that his charm and his connections were Max's social currency – he couldn't have one without the other. Then she had another startling revelation: Max was *her* social currency. It didn't matter that her party outfits consisted of a variety of shapeless black dresses, which were only slightly too big on her, but not so big that Neve felt as if she deserved to buy any clothes, or that she had a complete lack of conversational skills – she had Max.

After that, Neve stopped being terrified and began to

enjoy herself. It was like finding herself in the middle of an Evelyn Waugh novel, but one set in twenty-first-century London where the Bright Young Things all did something in the media and would tell Neve that she was a darling and 'my new very best friend' just for giving someone a spare tampon, or letting one of Max's mates have the condoms from her latest goody bag, because she certainly wasn't going to be needing them. And they all came back from their frequent trips to the loo with a hard, glittery look in their eyes and their chatter got louder and more animated. At first, Neve thought the constant bathroom breaks were due to the huge amount of free drinks they all consumed, until she was waiting in line for the Ladies with one of her new very best friends who asked if she wanted to do a line.

'A line of what?' Neve asked without thinking, because it was so outside her realm of experience that she hadn't ever expected to meet anyone who did Class A narcotics, much less be offered any herself.

'Shit, sorry,' the girl had said. 'Max mentioned something about you being in rehab for *years*. God, that must have sucked.'

'It was very tiresome,' Neve had agreed, and she couldn't even summon up the faintest whiff of indignation at how Max had found a way to explain her abstemious habits that didn't embarrass either of them.

Max's friends thought she had an interesting past and Max didn't suffer the ignominy of having a girlfriend who'd only drink one white-wine spritzer before she switched to lime and soda. It was win/win.

On the dot of midnight, Neve would always leave and Max would always offer to pay for a cab, before walking her to the tube station. 'Are you having fun yet?' he'd ask.

Neve would praise the goody bag or the canapés or the actor she'd talked to who'd done a season with the Royal Shakespeare Company and Max would shake his head and sigh.

'If you think that's fun, then you're not having fun yet,' he'd say, before asking the next question. 'But now you have to admit that I'm the most charming and likeable person you've ever met, aren't I?'

'You're growing on me,' Neve would say, which he was until he opened his mouth and his patented Max smarm oozed out. In the past three weeks, she'd seen him more than ten times and she didn't know him any better than when they'd started. She didn't know where he grew up (though he had a faint Northern accent) or what made him frightened. She didn't know where he stood on Europe or his thoughts on Fair Trade. All she ever got from Max was a loop of, 'You look gorgeous, we're on the list, baby, darling, sweetheart, let's go to the after-party,' and of course, 'Are you having fun yet?' It wasn't enough to form a friendship, let alone anything else, not by a long shot – but Neve could hardly tell Max that.

So he'd just sigh again, then he'd give Neve a quick peck on the side of her mouth, tell her he'd text her 'the deets of our next fun-filled date' and go back to the party to find a girl to spend the rest of the night with.

Neve often wondered what would happen if she suddenly declared that she'd had fun with a capital F and that Max was her new very best friend. She decided that either their pancake relationship would come to a very swift end because she was no longer a challenge, or that Max would move on to the next phase of his plan which involved Neve begging him to take her because she was desperate to know the feel of his hot, tight body against her naked flesh. Which was never, ever going to happen.

All in all though, dating Max was going better than Neve had expected until the night she was rumbled by Celia. It was a Thursday evening and they were attending the launch of a new ad campaign for . . . well, Neve wasn't sure but she understood that it was something to do with a high street fashion chain and some up-and-coming new designer. She was sitting in another VIP area on another red velvet sofa. Max had disappeared momentarily to discover why the free drinks weren't flowing like tapwater and Neve had actually found someone interesting to talk to – a middle-aged man who edited the lifestyle section of a Sunday paper and who had known Max since he was sixteen when he came down to London from Manchester to do two weeks' work experience at a teen magazine.

Jeremy had been the Editor of the teen magazine and hadn't thought much of Max when he arrived fresh off the train and brimming with boyish enthusiasm. 'He got in everyone's way,' he recalled. 'And if we had models come in for a casting, he'd turn bright red and start giggling.'

'Really?' Neve was hanging on to his every word.

'I could not wait for his fortnight to be up,' Jeremy said. 'Then came the fateful day that the Features Editor was struck down by a dodgy prawn sandwich, minutes before he was due to do an interview with this appalling boy band . . . what were they called? Never mind. Anyway, Max stepped up to the plate and wangled a confession from the lead singer that he'd shagged every single one of their backing dancers when he wasn't necking five Ecstasy tabs a night.'

'My goodness! Then what happened?'

'Well, I offered Max a job on the spot, obviously.' Jeremy smiled faintly. 'And a legend was born. I even gave him his own gossip column, which we called *Mad Max*. The funny thing was that, as soon as his contract was signed, there was no more red-faced giggling. Couldn't help but feel that I'd been played.'

Neve was practically sitting in Jeremy's lap by now. 'Do you think that Max might have tampered with the prawn sandwich?'

'Well, I wouldn't like to put money on it, but . . .'

Neve didn't get to hear Jeremy's theories on the dodgy prawn sandwich because all of a sudden she was hauled off the sofa by a strong determined hand belonging to her furious little sister.

'Neevy, what the hell are *you* doing here?' she demanded, dragging Neve across the room and into a secluded alcove. 'Why are you bothering Jeremy Hancock? What is going on?'

'I wasn't bothering him,' Neve insisted angrily. 'We were having a nice chat about the play on Radio Four this week and then we talked about Max.'

She thought that was quite a skilful way to lead into the inevitable conversation they were going to have but Celia exploded all over again. 'Why were you talking about Max? What are you doing all cosy in the VIP room when Grace and I had to wait for an hour to get in because the uppity girl on the door couldn't read the other uppity girl on the door's handwriting?'

'I'm sorry about that,' Neve said soothingly, but Celia's face was all scrunched up in an unsoothable manner. 'And we were talking about Max because well, um . . . I'm here with him. With Max. We've kind of been seeing a bit of each other.'

'Max! MAX! Oh my God, you have got to be fucking kidding me!'

'Don't swear,' Neve admonished, even though that always sent Celia into a defensive rage.

'Why? Why are you going out with him? How did it happen? Why didn't you tell me before?' Celia demanded, her face getting as red as her hair and Neve had to take Celia's hands and stroke them, because that always calmed her down, while she cobbled together a story about bumping into Max in Tesco's and going for a quick drink with him and how one thing had led to another.

'You don't know what he's like,' Celia said darkly, when Neve finished. 'There was this one time on a cover shoot and the actress was kicking off, then Max took her into the bathroom and they were in there for over an hour and

144

when she came out, she was all sweetness and light and kept groping him even when—'

'I don't want to hear it!' Neve said sharply. 'I know Max has a past but we're not serious. It's just pretend-dating to get me relationship-ready.'

'For the record, Neevy, I always thought that was a dumb idea but I never said anything because I was sure you wouldn't have the guts to go through with it.'

'Well, that's hardly fair . . .'

'And now you're pretend-dating with Max? Are you fricking crazy? And what about the other guys you dated? Suicidal Tendencies didn't seem so bad,' Celia said, boxing Neve against the wall by placing a hand on either side of her head. 'Your problem is that you're way too judgemental. You could easily have given one of those blokes another try, because seriously, Max is going to break your heart just for shits and giggles. It's what he does.'

'He's not going to break my heart,' Neve told her, pushing Celia's arms away. 'My heart belongs to William so there's no way Max can have any effect on it. And quite frankly, this is why I didn't tell you. It's none of your business, so stop talking about stuff that you don't know anything about.'

Celia took having her arms slapped away in a really bad humour. 'If you keep seeing that . . . that skank, then I'm telling Mum!'

'Don't even go there because there are things I could tell Mum about you that would make her brain leak out of her ears,' Neve snapped, even though she'd intended to walk away.

'Oh yeah, like what?'

'Like that you and Yuri smoke cannabis and you go out and get drunk all the time, and let's not even get on to the subject of your sex-life because it would take at least a week to fill Mum in on all *those* gory details.' Neve had been all set to fill Celia in on some of those gory details just in case she'd forgotten, say, about the time she'd pulled some bloke and had woken up the next morning to find his furious mother threatening to call the police because some strange woman had seduced her fifteen-year-old son, but she was interrupted by a pointed cough and turned round to see Max standing there.

'Don't wander off, sweetheart,' he said lightly. 'I had all sorts of horrible visions of someone slipping Roofies into your lime and soda. Come back to the table, because Jeremy wants to tell you in no uncertain terms that I had *nothing* to do with the dodgy prawn sandwich.'

'You do anything to hurt my sister and I don't care how high up the masthead you are, I'm going to kill you,' Celia growled, striding over so she could get up in Max's face. 'I swear.'

'Celia! I can look after myself,' Neve said furiously, as she tried to tug her away, but Max just smiled and kissed Celia's creased forehead.

'I promise when your sister's done with breaking my heart, you can have first dibs on what's left of me,' he said, putting an arm round her waist.

Celia huffed and Neve could see her opening her mouth to let loose a stream of vitriol, which never happened because Max's fingers skittered across her ribs and she burst out laughing instead.

'Don't do that,' she said, wriggling in vain to get free. 'You know I'm ticklish.'

Max held out his other hand to Neve. 'Come on, Neve. It'll do wonders for my rep to have a Slater sister on each arm.'

Neve had no choice but to become the other slice of bread in a Max sandwich. She smiled weakly at Celia who took advantage of the fact that Max was being greeted by someone across the room to hiss at Neve, 'You and me are not done talking about this.'

146

Chapter Twelve

Celia was still talking about it two days later.

'I can't believe you're going out on a Saturday night,' she moaned from her foetal position on Neve's bed. Not only was she crabby with PMS, but she was also mourning the loss of Yuri, who'd decided she might as well have a bash at dating the graphic designer she'd already slept with on the last five consecutive Saturday nights. 'Everybody's got something to do tonight except me.'

'You have something to do,' Neve pointed out as she took a swipe at her lashes with her mascara wand. 'You said you were going for dim sum in Soho, then Grace from work had booked a private room at a karaoke bar and if you were still upright after that, you were going clubbing.'

Celia glared at Neve's back. 'I meant everyone's going out with their boyfriends, except me. Even you!'

'You know you'll enjoy yourself once you're with your friends and you have a couple of drinks inside you,' Neve murmured, as she expertly twisted her hair up into a bun and started shoving in hairpins.

'Pull out some strands of hair so you don't look so virginal,' Celia ordered from her prone position. 'Unless there's something you want to tell me.'

'If I was doing something with Max, which I'm not and never, ever will, then you would be the very last person I'd tell. Actually, fourth from last,' Neve amended.

'Like, after Mum, Dad and Douglas? Thanks a lot!' Celia

gave Neve a serious once-over. 'You are doing something with him, I can tell. You're wearing a knee-length skirt. Not below the knee, but *on* the knee, and I can see the faintest shadow of cleavage. I rest my case.'

Neve turned back to the mirror for one last critical glance. She was bored stupid with the shapeless black dresses and had decided to branch out by wearing a black A-line skirt with red felt flowers embroidered along the hem and a black wrap top over a lace-edged camisole. There had been a moment when Neve thought she might wear the red tights that her mother had bought her, but then she remembered how they made her legs look like they belonged to Henry VIII, so she'd stuck with her trusty black opaques.

'But I look all right, don't I? I don't look . . . large or, like, larger.'

'You look gorgeous,' Celia insisted hotly. 'You don't know how lucky you are to have an actual waist. I look like a fucking fishing rod.'

'No, you don't!'

'Well, you don't look large. Not at all.' Celia sounded close to tears and she was paler than normal, which was a sure sign that her period was less than a day away.

'Why don't you stay in tonight?' Neve asked gently.

'I can't stay in on Saturday night!' Celia sounded even closer to tears as she scrambled off the bed. 'Look, I'm up. I'm ready to go. I'll walk to the station with you, but if you put on flats instead of heels, I'll smack you.'

They walked hand-in-hand down Stroud Green Road, Celia dragging her feet every step of the way. 'You know, it's not anything serious between Max and me, Seels. I'm in love with William and Max thinks the whole thing is an amusing diversion. It's just a game to him,' Neve said carefully.

'Max loves playing games,' Celia replied. 'I know that we all joke about what a gigantic whore he is, but he's pretty hard to resist when he's piling on the charm.'

'But I can see right through his charm. Please credit me

with some sense.' Neve put a hand on Celia's arm to still her. 'I already know that in a couple of weeks, Max is going to be so bored that he'll very sweetly and very suavely dump me, and that's fine. We have nothing in common and although I thought that maybe he had hidden depths, now I'm not so sure.'

'Then finish with him now instead of letting him drag you to all those parties,' Celia demanded. 'You *hate* going to parties.' She paused and looked at Neve more perceptively than Neve would have given her credit for. 'The weird thing is, on Thursday evening, you didn't look as if you were in a thousand agonies. Before I started screaming at you, you looked like you were having quite a good time. I mean, what's up with *that*?'

'You wouldn't understand,' Neve muttered, starting to walk again.

'Try me.'

'Do you remember Danny McGee from school?' Neve asked, though it was a rhetorical question, because everyone had known and loved Danny McGee. Even though Neve and Celia's older brother had been considered quite the heart-throb, compared to Danny with his dreamy blue eyes, cheeky grin and the adorable way he'd held his cigarettes between thumb and forefinger, Douglas might just as well have been Quasimodo. When Neve was fourteen, a girl in the year above had even tried to slit her wrists with a Bic safety razor because Danny had dumped her after two dates.

Celia was sighing rapturously. 'Danny McGee. I kissed your class photo every night for a year right in the spot where I could just about see half his fringe and one eye. Whatever happened to him?'

Neve had heard that he was in prison for burglary and ABH but that was beside the point. 'Well, do you also remember the two weeks that Mr Kent made Danny and me work together on an English project?'

'There was no working together, you did the entire thing yourself.'

'And for two weeks, no one picked on me, or teased me or called me that awful name all because Danny would stop and talk to me at school,' Neve said, slightly misty-eyed, even though Danny had only wanted to know if Neve had mastered the art of copying his handwriting.

'God, do I? I was so jealous and he never once came round to our house,' Celia said bitterly, as if she was still sore about it. 'So what's that got to do with you and Max and going to parties?'

'Well, Mum always forced me to go to those awful school discos no matter how much I cried and pretended that I had bacterial meningitis, and I'd spend the whole time I was there hiding in the school loos from Charlotte and her gang until it was time for Dad to pick me up.' Neve swallowed hard, because even after all this time it still hurt to dredge up these memories. 'I'd sit there for *hours* and imagine what it would be like to walk into the disco with Danny and how everyone would think I was cool and they'd actually come and talk to me and want to be my friend. When I walk into one of those parties with Max, it's everything I never had when I was at school, and I just wish that Charlotte were there to see it. So stop giving me such a hard time, Seels, because being Max's plus one makes up for a tiny, teeny bit of the utter misery that was my adolescence.'

Neve didn't want the tears to start trickling because her mascara would run, but Celia had no such compunction. She swiped at her eyes with her jacket sleeve before gathering Neve up in a swift, fierce hug. 'It's impossible to stay mad at you if you're going to say stuff like that,' she grumbled. 'OK, you have my blessing to carry on with this stupid arrangement with Max.'

'Thank you,' Neve said. 'And it really won't be for much longer, because all this partying is very hard work and I haven't had time to read a book in weeks. William and

I were talking about how we'd never read *Tristram Shandy* and we agreed to read two chapters a day, then email each other, and he's quite cross that I'm chapters and chapters behind.'

Celia gave Neve's hand a little squeeze. 'If that's what you and William get up to, then Max does actually seem like much better boyfriend material. At least he knows how to have a good time!'

'There are so many things wrong with that statement that I don't even know where to start,' Neve said with a sniff.

They'd reached the station by now and Neve came to a halt by the clock and watched Celia hunt for her Oyster card through various pockets and side compartments of her bag until she produced it with a triumphant air.

'I'd better get going,' she said. 'What time are you meeting Max?'

'Five thirty,' Neve said, glancing up at the clock. 'But he's always ten minutes late.'

'And you're not having conniptions about that?' Celia asked slyly.

'I understand that there has to be a certain degree of compromise involved in relationships. I reckon I won't sweat the small stuff like shoddy timekeeping so he can't really object tonight when I take half an hour to order dinner, then send it back because it's dripping with cream and butter.' Neve pinched Celia's arm who made a big show of squealing and ducking away, even though she was wearing a leather jacket and couldn't have felt a thing. 'Don't smirk at me!'

'You are so adorable,' Celia cooed, side-stepping away from Neve's hand, which was poised for another attack. 'I'm going. Now, be careful and don't do anything I wouldn't do!'

Neve assumed her primmest face, which just made Celia giggle harder as she walked to the station entrance, stopping to look back at Neve and wave before she disappeared.

It was five forty now and, right on time, she saw Max

hurrying under the bridge. Neve unfolded her arms so she didn't look as if she was standing there impatiently as Max caught her eye and started running towards her.

'Hello, gorgeous,' Max panted, as he reached Neve's side. He kissed her cheek, then the other one, his face cold against hers. 'Sorry I'm late. I swear, I think time speeds up the second I leave my flat.'

'I've only just seen Celia off,' Neve said, eyes downcast because the first five minutes still felt awkward and it took her time to warm up. When Max arrived, Neve was always struck anew by how handsome he was. Then she had to adjust all her notions about him and try to drown out the voice in her head that wanted to know what the hell he was doing with her.

Once she was composed enough to look at him, Neve saw that Max was wearing jeans and a houndstooth coat that looked like it had seen better days, though Neve knew that when he took it off there'd be a Marc Jacobs or Prada label stitched inside. He was looking her up and down too, a slight smile on his face. Then he took her arm and started trying to move her in the direction of the station entrance.

Neve didn't budge. 'Where do you think we're going?'

'You said you were taking me bowling,' Max said, looping his fingers round Neve's wrist to tug at her gently. 'We need to catch the tube.'

It had occurred to Neve after all the drama of Thursday night, that Max had planned all their dates up until then. She hadn't had much to do but worry about what to wear then turn up at the agreed time and place.

So when Max revealed that there was nothing on the social calendar for that Saturday, Neve had taken charge. Though when she'd suggested that maybe they could both have a night off so she could catch up on *Tristram Shandy*, Max had been appalled. 'I haven't stayed in on a Saturday night since I was about twelve and I'm not going to start now,' he'd said aghast, even more aghast than Celia had been, and for once he wasn't hamming it up for comic effect. 'I'll phone a few people. There has to be *something* going on somewhere.'

'We'll go bowling early in the evening and then we'll go out for dinner,' Neve had said firmly, because both those activities were reasonably cheap and she didn't get paid for another week. At the time, she was surprised that Max had agreed so quickly, but now as she watched his face crease in confusion, she realised that they had very different ideas about bowling.

'We don't need to get a tube,' she said, pointing at the huge grey and red building across the road. 'There's a massive bowling alley five seconds away.'

Max stared at the askew pins decorating the outside of the venue with furrowed brow. 'But I thought you meant we'd go to Bloomsbury Bowls or the All-Star Lanes, not . . .'

Not an ugly grey bowling alley that didn't have any kitsch retro features or a waitress service featuring girls with pin curls and little 1950s bowling dresses. 'It's really all right once you get inside,' Neve said weakly. 'Look, I just thought we could do something local for once.'

'Do they play really tinny disco music through the PA and have loads of ankle-biters getting in the way when you're trying to bowl?' Max asked.

'Are you sure you've never been there before?'

'I haven't, but it sounds a lot like the place in Didsbury where I had my tenth birthday party,' Max said. He took a deep breath. 'OK, let's do this. I can kick it with the common people.'

Taking Max bowling went better than Neve had dared hope. He'd winced theatrically when they'd got inside and seen hordes of kids, all hopped up on fizzy drinks, running around and shrieking. There'd also been some eye-rolling when Neve insisted the boy in charge of shoe rental sprayed foot deodorant in her bowling shoes before she could even think of putting them on. But then it had been all right because Neve was on home ground.

Bowling was a birthday tradition and a Bank Holiday tradition and also a bringing home a good school report tradition and even a 'Christ, Barry, the kids are driving me bloody mad, get them out the house,' tradition.

Neve knew how to input their names on to their electronic scoreboard even though the keys had rubbed off. She knew that they didn't want to get stuck with the furthest lane to the left because the wood was slightly warped and the balls all veered to the right, and she knew that it was always best to start off with one of the heavy green balls on her first bowl then move to a lighter orange ball to try and strike down the last remaining pins.

Yes, she was worried how her back view looked as she ran up the lane with a lumbering gait, but Max was far more concerned that she kept getting strikes than how big her bum looked or how the bowling shoes made her legs seem shorter and stockier than normal.

'Can't we get them to put the bumpers up?' he asked plaintively, as his balls kept rolling into the gutter. 'Like they have.' He gestured at the neighbouring lane.

'They have the bumpers up because they're tiny children,' Neve pointed out and Max pouted, and maybe if it was a different kind of relationship, she'd have leaned up and kissed the pout right off his face.

Instead, Neve deliberately sent her next two balls into the gutter because tamping down the competitive side of her nature was another compromise she was willing to make. She still won their two games easily, even though Max grabbed one of the bumpers to line up his last few balls, much to the screaming delight of the teenagers at the next lane. He just couldn't resist playing to a captive audience.

'Well, I truly sucked at that,' he announced, when they were back in their own unrented footwear and walking up

Stroud Green Road. 'But you . . . you have some serious moves.'

'If it makes you feel any better, I broke three nails,' Neve said, holding up a gloved hand.

'I could kiss them better if you like,' Max drawled, and it was a salient reminder that tonight it was just the two of them and she didn't really know how to handle his flirting when they didn't have at least ten of his sycophantic friends chaperoning them.

'Maybe later. If you're good,' she added, in what was meant to be an equally flirtatious manner, but sounded a little too schoolmarm for her liking. 'Very, very good.'

'And what if I've been very bad?' Max wanted to know and when Neve shot him a sideways glance, she could tell he was definitely teasing her.

'No pudding for you then,' she rapped back, tugging Max's sleeve because it was time to cross the road. 'Which is a pity, because the place I'm taking you to does a great tiramisu.'

'We're not going to the gastro pub, then?'

'The common people don't go to gastro pubs,' Neve said. 'They go to places like this.'

She stopped outside the huge Italian restaurant that had always provided post-bowling refreshment on all Slater family outings. Max peered inside with some trepidation as a waiter walked past holding a birthday cake ablaze with candles.

'Looks cool,' he said gamely. 'Wouldn't be so packed if the food was terrible, would it?'

Neve didn't have a chance to extol the virtues of the wood-fired oven, before the door was wrenched open and the owner, a wizened little man, his wrinkled face grinning from ear to ear, gathered her in his arms.

'Miss Neevy,' he said, pushing Neve back, so he could get a good look at her. 'You're wasting away. We fill you up with some pasta, huh?'

'Only a tiny bit of pasta,' Neve demurred. She could hear

Max sniggering behind her as Marco led them inside with a flourish.

'The best table in the house for Miss Neevy,' he shouted to no one in particular. 'You treat her badly, I get my boys to take you out back and chop you into little pieces,' he shot out of the side of his mouth at Max, as they were led to a table by the window.

'I'm very nice to her,' Max protested, then to Neve's mortification, he and Marco had a stand-off about who was going to pull out her chair.

Max won that battle but Marco made a big show of unfolding a snowy white napkin and placing it reverently on Neve's lap.

'I get you a bottle of wine on the house,' he insisted, ignoring Neve's frantic hand gestures. 'How's Barry and Margaret? They well, huh?'

'I'm sorry,' she hissed at Max, when Marco finally left after enquiring about the health of all of the Slater clan and asking Neve how 'the job at the library' was going. 'I didn't expect Marco to warn you off.'

'Well, you'd better smile and laugh at everything I say. I don't want to be chopped into tiny pieces,' Max hissed back, as he gazed around the room. 'What does it say on the back of the waiters' shirts?'

' "A nice-a place to stuffa your face".' Neve tried hard not to laugh. Max was all about opening-night parties at the V&A, air-kissing models and eating canapés made with crème fraiche. This really wasn't his scene. 'You hate it, don't you?' she asked, between giggles.

'I don't spend *all* my time eating mahi-mahi in minimalist restaurants in Soho. I can do beer and the pizza.' Max opened his menu. 'You've got the whole of Finsbury Park eating out of your hand, haven't you?'

'Finsbury Park till I die,' Neve said as solemnly as she could when it felt as if another round of giggles might unleash themselves.

'You've smudged your mascara,' Max pointed out, reaching across the table to brush his thumb against her cheek. Neve was used to the arm round her shoulders and the restrained kiss goodnight, but this was a whole new territory of touching, especially since, now that he'd brushed away any stray smuts, Max was still cupping her cheek. 'I like the side of you I'm seeing tonight.'

'What side is that, then?' Neve asked. She wanted to lean into Max's hand, and suddenly wished that it meant something real because it was so lovely to be *touched* as if she was something precious, but she forced herself to remain still.

'Pink-faced and giggly – makes your eyes look very blue,' Max said matter-of-factly, as if he wasn't just spinning her some line for once but it was the God's honest truth. Then he took his hand away. 'Now what should I have to eat? Pizza or pasta?'

'Well, the pizza's good,' said Neve, who could still feel the phantom touch of Max's fingers on her skin.

'Do you want to share some garlic bread as a starter?'

'Max! I need to tell you something,' Neve blurted out.

He looked up in surprise at her forceful tone. 'What?'

Neve rearranged her cutlery and adjusted the position of the salt and pepper pots. 'This is a really big deal for me, having dinner with you because . . . well, I have serious issues with food.' She sat back and waited for . . . she wasn't sure what exactly, but she had an image in her head of Max throwing his napkin down in disgust and walking out, singularly unimpressed by her confession.

'And how does that make you different from ninety-nine per cent of all other women?' he asked, tilting his chin so it seemed more like a challenge than a question.

'I'm just warning you, because I take ages to order and sometimes I have to send food back if they haven't followed my precise instructions.' Neve bit her lip. 'Celia says I'm an absolute pain when we go out for dinner.'

Max shrugged. 'I go out for lunch every day with people

who work in entertainment or fashion, and it's all egg-white omelettes and no carbs. Sometimes they even bring their own specially prepared meals and ask the chef to heat them up. Honestly, I've seen food issues and I bet yours don't even come close.'

This didn't make Neve feel better. It made her feel worse, because the people that Max was talking about were probably all size zero and got paid millions of pounds to maintain their figures while she wouldn't even be able to get her big toe into a size zero anything.

'Well, it makes me feel like a freak,' she admitted slowly. 'Like I shouldn't make so much of a fuss when I'm the size I am. People probably think I go home and stuff myself with cake.'

It was impossible to read Max's expression; his features were completely blank. 'I'm sure no one thinks that,' he said finally, with a look that was verging on exasperated. 'You just imagine that they do.'

'I've ruined everything, haven't I? I've been Weird Food Issues Girl and now you're all like, "God, would she just shut up because she's ruined my appetite and I just want to eat dinner then get the hell away from her."'

'My inner voice doesn't sound anything like that,' Max said as he picked up a packet of breadsticks. 'Now change the subject or I'm going to stab myself in the eye with one of these.'

Neve opened and closed her mouth a few more times, like a demented goldfish. Then she narrowed her eyes because Max had that challenging tilt to his chin again, like he thought she couldn't do it. 'OK, OK,' she said. 'I took Celia here for her birthday last year, and there was a mix-up with the cake, so I asked the waiters to improvise.'

Max was pouring them both a glass of wine and Neve paused to tell him to stop because she might just as well scarf down some packets of sugar. Then she thought better of it, snatched the glass he was holding out to her and took a few fortifying gulps. 'You have to know that Marco had the night off, that's a very important fact,' she said, picking up her thread again. 'So, we've finished the main course and I give the signal, then all the lights go off and all the waiters came to our table, singing "Happy Birthday" and holding something behind a menu.'

'And they'd shoved a candle in a piece of tiramisu?' Max interrupted. 'They always do that at these types of places.'

Neve glared him into silence. 'Not even close. They whipped away the menu and there on the plate were two profiteroles and a banana with a strawberry perched on one end in the shape of a . . .' She lowered her voice. 'It was shaped like a cock!'

Max had just taken a sip of wine, which he proceeded to spit down his shirt. 'Did you say what I think you just said?'

'I said cock,' Neve repeated; the giggles were back for another round. 'And all the waiters chanted, "Bite! Bite! Bite!" until Celia bent down and bit the strawberry off the banana.'

'Was she embarrassed?'

'As if! She absolutely loved it! *I* was embarrassed; all her friends thought it had been my idea.' Neve smiled as she remembered the look of horrified delight on Celia's face when her birthday dessert had been revealed, then she looked over at Max who was dabbing at the wine stain on his shirt with a napkin and started laughing all over again. 'I hope the change of subject was satisfactory?'

'My favourite part was when you said "cock".' Max grinned. 'Never thought I'd hear that word on your lips. Say it again.'

'I say all kinds of rude things once you get to know me,' Neve said, because she really wasn't *that* uptight. 'But I don't like to swear that much because I think it shows a lack of imagination. Just you wait until I drop the f-word. It will blow your mind.'

'I'm not going to be able to sleep tonight because I'll be so busy imagining all the various reasons why I might hear you say "fuck",' Max said, his voice on its most sultry setting, his leg rubbing against Neve's under the table. 'Yup, I see a cold shower in my immediate future.'

Neve's immediate reaction was to get hot and flustered and deny that the possibility would ever occur. She took another sip of wine and went with her second reaction. 'Now you come to mention it, I can think of a few reasons why I might want to say it in your hearing too,' she said tartly, moving her leg back so she could kick Max's shin, just hard enough that he choked on his breadstick.

'Touché,' he said softly, and when he smiled at Neve it was so genuine, maybe even a little bashful because of the way she'd beaten him at his own game, that she couldn't help but smile back. And just like that, they were in a happier place where Max wasn't trying to be challenging or seductive or catch her off-guard and Neve could relax.

They were still in that happy place even when Neve ordered three lonely pieces of spinach and ricotta ravioli for her starter, asked for the grilled swordfish without the new potatoes for her main course and sent back her green salad because it had a drizzle of olive oil on it, which she hadn't asked for, and not a trace of balsamic vinegar, which she had.

It was the lack of carbs and the one and a half glasses of white wine that made Neve stumble when they left the restaurant. Max's arm wrapped round her waist in an instant.

'I'm not used to wearing heels,' she moaned. 'They hurt and they're patriarchal signifiers designed to cripple women and stop them from taking big strides through life.'

'Why are you wearing them, then?' Max asked. He still had his arm round her waist though she was able to walk by herself now she'd got over the headrush. Walking with an unsteady gait, but able to do it unaided.

'Well, they're very pretty and they make my ankles look

slender,' Neve said, snuggling against Max because there was a vicious wind whipping down the street.

'You have no head for alcohol,' Max told her. 'You're a cheap date.'

They'd actually split the bill. Neve had insisted it was her treat but Max had insisted that he'd eaten and drunk twice as much as she had and was taking the leftovers home with him.

They arrived at her garden gate far too soon for Neve's liking, because Max was letting her go and already she was shivering without his warm body against hers. 'Do you want to come in for a coffee?' she asked. 'And when I say coffee, I do mean just coffee.'

This time it was Max who hesitated. 'I should really get home for Keith,' he said eventually. 'He needs his last walk.'

Neve was instantly suspicious. Poor Keith seemed to manage just fine when Max was out until all hours in his quest for female companionship. 'If I'd asked you in for "coffee"' – she put air quotes round the word – 'would your answer still be no?'

'Ouch! You're just full of surprises tonight, aren't you, sweetheart?' Max said, his eyes gleaming in the glow of the streetlight. He took hold of her chin, so he could drop a light kiss on her mouth.

Neve was expecting her one contractually obligated, perfunctory kiss, but Max brushed her lips with delicate, light butterfly kisses that felt like a warm-up act. Then he slowed right down, kissed her longer, kissed her a little bit deeper – and just as Neve leaned forward to capture his mouth, because how could she *not*, he stepped back.

'Well, I really should be going,' he said affably, as if that was quite enough Neve-baiting for one evening. 'I'll call you soon.'

He didn't even wait for a reply but was hurrying away, while Neve stood there in dismay.

'Un-bloody-believable,' she muttered, as she unlatched

the gate and stomped up the path. It wasn't meant to be *that* kind of relationship, but Max had said quite specifically that there would be kissing. Maybe he didn't want to kiss her properly because he didn't find her that attractive. And what was the point of being in a fake relationship if your fake boyfriend didn't find you that attractive? There was no . . .

'Neve! Wait up!'

She turned round to see Max coming down the path, slightly red-faced and panting. 'What do you want?' she asked warily, because she'd just made a really convincing argument in her head for ending this. Perhaps Max was thinking the same thing.

'I forgot to ask, did you have fun tonight?'

He was impossible and it was starting to seem quite . . . endearing. 'Almost,' Neve said truthfully.

Max nodded. 'And are you ready to admit that I'm the most likeable, charming person you've ever met?'

'Never! I'll say the f-word before I say that,' Neve told him, pretty sure that Max wouldn't take offence. Well, not too much.

He came to a halt at the bottom of the four steep steps that led up to the front door but didn't go any further. 'I am actually going home now, which means I won't spend most of tomorrow sleeping off my hangover, so I'll be free in the afternoon if you want to get together?'

Neve stayed on the doorstep. 'Is there some launch thing or opening-night gala going on?'

'No, nothing like that. Look, why don't you come round mine and I'll cook you dinner?' Max was already backing away as if there was nothing untoward or unusual about his suggestion. 'I'll see you at five.'

There were many good reasons why Neve was not going to turn up on Max's doorstep like a sacrifical lamb, but all she could come up with at such short notice was, 'But I don't have your address.'

'You're going to have to do much better than that,' Max said, with that sneery little smile Neve hated. 'I'll email you, even attach a Google map.'

'I'm not sure, I'm very busy tomorrow,' Neve prevaricated, which wasn't a lie, although all her social engagements would be over by four at the latest.

'Oh, right, so if you weren't "busy",' Max mocked her with her own air quotes, 'would your answer still be no? You were the one who invited me in for coffee ten minutes ago.'

'But I did actually mean a cup of coffee!'

'Yeah, and I actually mean dinner.' Max gave her a prim look, which Neve recognised instantly, because she usually saw it reflected back at her when she was looking in a mirror. 'I do have some self-control and I'm pretty sure you can be alone in my flat for three hours or so without me committing all sorts of depraved acts on your unwilling flesh.'

When he put it like that, Neve was appalled. Max made it sound as if she thought she was so ravishing that he wouldn't be able to resist her. She was also beginning to wonder just how unwilling her flesh really was when she was longing for something a lot more passionate when it came to their goodbye kisses. 'I'm sorry, Max,' she said contritely. 'I'd love to come for dinner.'

Max didn't look at all convinced by her apology and Neve stood on her doorstep, feeling slightly shaky and untethered now she didn't have the moral high ground. Then she saw his shoulders relax and a wicked grin spread slowly across his face. 'OK, I'll see you tomorrow then. And as long as you remember your safety word, everything will be fine.'

Chapter Thirteen

It had been an unexpectedly lovely day. Neve had gone to bed at a very respectable eleven o'clock and had been woken eight hours later by the early spring sunshine worming its way through the gap in her curtains. She'd caught up on *Tristram Shandy*, then spent an hour on the phone with Philip to see if he understood a word of it and to get some crib notes for when she spoke to William later that evening.

Then she'd cycled over to Kenwood to meet Gustav and trail behind him as he ran around Hampstead Heath in preparation for the half-marathon he was doing in a couple of weeks' time. Neve had been all set to go home and put in a few hours on the next chapter of her Lucy Keener biography when Chloe had phoned and invited Neve to brunch as she'd ended up staying over at a friend's in Muswell Hill after a raucous party.

Neve always felt like it was a real treat to see Chloe outside of work, proof that they were proper friends and not just thrown together by a mutual dislike of Mr Freemont and cross-referencing. It was also a real treat to be able to talk about Max with someone who wasn't Celia.

'Well, he's very pretty,' was Chloe's summing-up of Max when Neve showed her the photo he'd insisted she take on her new iPhone. 'You want to watch out for the pretty ones, Neevy. They know they don't have to try too hard.'

'He's actually been trying a lot harder than I thought he would,' Neve said in surprise as she thought about how well-behaved Max had been the night before. He'd kept the salacious remarks to a minimum, and been a really good sport about bowling and cheap pizza. 'It's odd, really. I know he thinks I'm a bit of a rarity because I'm the only woman he's ever met who's fairly immune to his charms, but he hasn't tried anything.' She bit her lip. 'It's probably because he doesn't fancy me.'

Chloe gave Neve a long-suffering look. 'I've got a beast of a hangover so I haven't got the energy to try and persuade you that you're completely fanciable.' She studied Max's photo again, then started scrolling through Neve's pictures of her new best ever friends. 'Men that look like this don't do anything they don't want to do. Compared to his usual type of girl, you must seem like a breath of fresh air. I bet he can't wait to try and corrupt you.'

'Really, he's not like that,' Neve protested. 'He's hardly even kissed me and we did agree that kissing was allowed.'

'Define hardly even kissing,' Chloe demanded, and Neve was forced to describe the very lacklustre kisses she'd been getting and how last night she thought they were finally progressing when Max had stopped.

'Is it weird that I want Max to kiss me when I'm in love with William?' she asked worriedly.

'Is William remaining a kiss-free zone too?' Even with a debilitating hangover, Chloe hadn't lost the ability to arch her right eyebrow. 'No? Well, then, go for it. No point in having a pretty pretend boyfriend and remaining kiss-free. He's probably waiting for you to give him a signal that he won't offend your maidenly sensibilities if he really goes for it.'

'Shut up,' Neve said without any rancour because the memory of Max when he was really going for it made her feel a little light-headed.

'When I was first going out with Andrew, way, way back, we'd spend hours snogging on his bed with the door open so his mum could hear if anything was being unzipped or unbuttoned and rush in with glasses of Ribena.' Chloe sighed longingly. 'I really miss that. I even miss the glasses of Ribena.' She looked over Neve's head. 'I think that guy is trying to get your attention.'

Neve looked around, her eyes widening in horror as she saw Douglas coming towards their table with a thin-lipped Charlotte bringing up the rear. Charlotte was wearing a dove-grey Juicy Couture tracksuit tucked into grey Ugg boots (no faux Primark ones for her) and the general impression was that of a storm cloud coming Neve's way, if storm clouds liked to accessorise with copious amounts of fake tan, gold jewellery and eyelash extensions.

'Mind if we join you?' Douglas asked, already sitting down. 'It's just there's a half-hour wait for the next table.'

Charlotte was forced to sit down next to Neve, who tried to scooch her chair as far away as possible, while Douglas introduced himself to Chloe who said she could see the family resemblance, which was a lie because Douglas, like Celia, favoured the Celtic side of the family and was generally considered to be the looker of the Slater clan.

Neve gulped down the rest of her peppermint tea as Chloe and Douglas chattered quite happily about the medicinal benefits of a fry-up on a hangover, even Charlotte chiming in with a completely inane remark about how she couldn't stand fried tomatoes. 'We have to go now,' Neve said, managing to extricate herself, her bag and her coat from the back of her chair without once touching Charlotte.

'I thought she'd look like a Gorgon,' Chloe remarked as they walked back along Muswell Hill Broadway. 'Sulky as a crow, but nothing Medusa-like about her. It was a bit of an anti-climax.'

'Next time she's screaming at me, I'll be sure to make a recording on my phone,' Neve snapped, her good humour completely gone, especially when she realised that it was too late to go back home and change before presenting herself at Max's front door.

There was nothing for it but to turn up in what she was wearing: jeans, a long-sleeved thermal, a crumpled summer dress over them and one of her ubiquitous cardigans, her hair scraped back in a ponytail to keep it off her face when she was cycling, and her tattiest pair of Converses. It didn't help matters that her mother phoned while Neve was in the off-licence trying to find a decent bottle of red wine for under a fiver.

Ten minutes later, Neve was standing outside a large terraced Victorian house on a wide tree-lined avenue behind Crouch End Broadway and trying to get her mother off the phone. Margaret Slater had supposedly called because she'd read an article in the *Sunday Mirror* about binge-drinking and wanted to know exactly how many units Celia got through in a week, but now she was gently haranguing Neve because she'd just spoken to Douglas 'and he said that you didn't even say hello to *her*'.

'She didn't say hello to me first,' Neve said indignantly. 'I can't believe you're telling me off about this.' Especially as her mother didn't know the half of it, or even a quarter of just how badly Charlotte had bullied her at school. And she certainly wasn't going to admit that nine years later, she was still letting Charlotte get away with it. 'It's not like you're a fully paid-up member of her fan club.'

'Well, I still think that Douglas rushed into things, but what's done is done and when they have children . . .'

'She's pregnant?' Neve stilled in horror. 'Oh God, no!'

'Well, not yet but they've been married nearly three years and she's not getting any younger.'

Charlotte was five months older than Neve, but this didn't seem like the right moment to bring that up, not when she was contemplating the awful idea that there might be a genetic replica of Charlotte roaming the earth before too long. 'Can we not talk about this now, Mum? I'm actually at a friend's house,' Neve said, as the front door suddenly swung open to reveal Max standing there in jeans, a Clash T-shirt and a quizzical expression.

'I saw you come up the path five minutes ago,' he said.

Neve pointed at her phone and mouthed the words 'my mother' at him.

'I'm just saying, Neevy, I know she can be very difficult and I know there was all that business when you were at school, but you have to live together and it would be much easier if you just let things lie.'

'But why should I be the one who has to—'

'It's up to you to take the high road because her mother – well, you know I don't like to speak ill of people, but that family, they're as common as muck. She always says that her father lives abroad, but I wouldn't be surprised if he was in prison.'

'I'll think about it,' Neve gritted, as Max hefted her bike up his steps and wheeled it inside. 'Will you just stop going on about it, please?'

It was another three, very long minutes before her mother hung up and Neve felt crumpled and frazzled and excruciatingly embarrassed because Max had been standing there listening to her bleat, 'Mum? Mum, I really have to go now,' in a never-ending loop.

'Sorry about that,' she said, and more because she was in need of comfort than because of anything Chloe had said earlier, Neve waited until Max had shut the front door behind her, then reached up to brush her lips against his cheek and give him a quick clumsy hug. 'I brought wine,' she added, thrusting the bottle at him.

'Poor Neevy,' Max cooed. 'Were you just being told off?'

'No. Well, kind of, in between being lectured about the dangers of binge-drinking.' Neve scowled as she tried to run her fingers through her hair and remembered that she hadn't even had time to free it from its constricting ponytail. 'Is my bike OK there?'

Max had propped her bike against the hall wall, and as

there had been five buzzers on the intercom, it stood to reason that there was going to be at least one other resident who objected to its presence. Probably not as loudly as Charlotte, but even so.

'Oh, it's fine,' Max assured her. He gestured to the stairs. 'Second floor. Come on, Keith's been beside himself all afternoon.'

She followed Max up the stairs, riveted by the sight of his long, lean legs and the tiny strip of skin exposed between T-shirt and jeans when they got to the top floor and he reached up to unlock his front door. Then he was brusquely pushed to one side as Keith scurried out into the hall to greet them, circled Neve a couple of times, then bounded up a flight of stairs painted bright blue and looked back at them expectantly.

'I think Keith wants to give you the guided tour,' Max said, helping Neve out of her coat. 'I'll be up in a minute.'

The stairs took a sharp turn into a narrow hallway, which opened out into a huge living room. Neve stood there for a moment and looked around as she got her bearings. The bright blue floorboards took some getting used to so she averted her gaze to the pictures on the bright white walls; Andy Warhol's *Marilyn Monroe* hung above the fireplace and on the opposite wall staring back at her was Her Majesty the Queen, with *Never Mind the Bollocks Here's the Sex Pistols* emblazoned across her face. There was a black leather sofa and armchairs, a glass coffee table, an interesting art installation-cum-floorlight that looked like the DNA strand for the double helix, six speakers mounted at different points along the walls, a huge telly and a stack of electronic *things* underneath it. She was in the domain of a modern bachelor.

Where she had books, books and yet more books, Max's shelves had proper vinyl records and CDs. There were piles of magazines neatly catalogued and just one set of book-shelves, which was where Neve headed. She hadn't expected Max to share her taste in literature – there weren't many men who bid aggressively on eBay for out-of-print Virago Modern Classics – but she was astounded to discover that he had no books. Well, he had coffee-table books bearing the names of fashion designers and photographers, but there were absolutely no novels apart from three lurid, glittery paperbacks. With some trepidation, Neve pulled one of them from the shelf: *Goals and Gucci* by Mandy McIntyre. Wasn't that the name of Max's pet WAG? Neve gave an excited little squeal and opened the book . . .

It was a good day to go shopping, Brandy Ballantyne thought to herself as she scooped up the keys to her Golf GTI and—

Max's hand smacked down on the page. 'Nuh-huh, you want to read it, then you do it on your own time. I'm not having you stand there and snigger over my prose style.'

Neve tried to hold on to the book as Max gently but firmly prised her fingers away. 'I wouldn't do that.'

'You'll hate it,' Max said, placing all three books on the tallest shelf so Neve couldn't get to them without a ladder. 'But if you like, after dinner, I'll turn the lights down low and read the dirty bits to you.'

Neve vowed to herself that first thing tomorrow she'd buy all three books on Amazon so she could see just how Max's dirty bits differed from the dirty bits in her grandmother's romance novels which were stashed in a plastic crate under her bed. At the tender age of thirteen she'd been shocked at just how filthy they were but since then, she'd read every single one at least twice, but not even Celia knew about that. 'Let's leave your dirty bits out of it,' she said as she wandered across the room to the mantelpiece, Max hot on her heels as she looked at the black-and-white framed photos.

Ooh! There was Max with Sarah Jessica Parker. And there was Max being kissed on the cheek by Lady Gaga and there was Max again, this time cuddling up to Kate Moss.

'Who's this?' Neve asked, picking up the one colour

photo, which featured Max with a middle-aged couple and two blonde girls in their twenties, all five of them proudly wearing Snuggies and paper hats and sitting in a row on a long sofa, wrapping-paper strewn everywhere. 'Is this your mum and dad? I didn't know you had sisters.'

'God, I should have Neve-proofed the flat before you came round,' Max said, snatching the photo away and putting it back on the mantelpiece. 'Nope, not my family. I just borrow them for major public holidays.'

Neve tried to peer past Max's shoulder. 'Seriously, who are they?'

'It's the McIntyres, which you'd know if you ever read a tabloid newspaper.'

'You didn't spend Christmas with your family?' she ventured timidly, because although Max had had a ringside seat to hear her mother berating her (and had probably heard every word because her mother was incapable of talking quietly), he was flaring his nostrils and beetling his brow and generally giving the impression that Neve was going somewhere he didn't want her to go.

'You know how secretly you think I'm a bastard?' He didn't even wait for Neve to deny that she'd ever thought such a heinous thing, but just flashed her a knowing smile. 'Well, technically I am. Never met my father, my mum's dead so I usually crash someone else's Christmas dinner.'

'Oh Max, I'm so sorry about your mum.' Neve took a hesitant step forward with the vague idea that Max might need another clumsy hug, but he folded his arms.

'No big deal, Neevy. Happened years ago and anyway, friends are the new family, blah blah blah.' He tilted his head. 'Are you hungry?'

She was always hungry. 'What are you making?'

Max looked more edgy than when they'd been discussing his lack of immediate family. 'Why don't you tell me what you can and can't eat?'

'Actually it's Treat Sunday. No gym and I can eat carbs

after six.' There was more to Treat Sunday than just those edited highlights but they'd do for now.

'So if I made you a jacket potato with steak and salad that would be OK?' Max asked doubtfully.

'If the potato has really crispy skin that wouldn't just be OK, it would be sheer, utter ecstasy.' Neve closed her eyes at the thought of it, and when she opened them again, Max was giving her a look that she imagined was a perfect mirror of her own heated features. 'Sorry, I get very excited at the thought of my weekly potato.'

'You really are an odd girl,' Max said, as if that was a good thing. 'Now that you've rooted through all my personal belongings, it's time for you to watch me slave over a hot stove.'

Chapter Fourteen

Neve perched on a stool in Max's red and green kitchen and watched him prepare her meal. Though watching became supervising as she had to keep pointing out that even though it was Treat Sunday, the steaks had to be grilled rather than put in a frying pan with butter. And that balsamic vinegar made a much better salad dressing than olive oil, and would the jacket potatoes still get crispy if he cooked them in the microwave?

Once Max was following her precise instructions, Neve allowed herself to sit back and just *watch* as he chopped tomatoes and washed rocket leaves and turned steaks with a little smile on his face. He'd put his iPod into a speaker dock and he moved around the kitchen in time to the music, looking up every now and again at Neve, who was sitting with her legs off the ground to avoid Keith who had silvery trails of drool hanging from his mouth and was intent on trying to wipe them off on her jeans.

She'd been so het up about being alone with Max in his flat, but actually he seemed less threatening on his home turf than when he was prowling across a crowded VIP room. Neve always thought of Max as someone who was supremely comfortable in his own skin, but now watching him tap out a drumbeat with a knife handle against his chopping board, she felt like she was getting a glimpse of the real Max that was buried so deep beneath the glitter and the free champagne and the air kisses, that she hadn't even realised he existed.

They ate at the little table in the kitchen. Max put tealights in shot glasses because he said that he didn't want Neve to see the mess he'd made of the salad, but as they started to eat, bumping knees under the little table, the candlelight turned salad and steak at five thirty on a Sunday afternoon into a romantic meal for two. Apart from when Max banished Keith to his basket in the hall because he kept nudging Neve with a paw and dribbling over her leg.

It was all Neve could do not to let out little whimpers of delight as she ate the last piece of her very crunchy potato skin, then sat back with a contented little sigh and patted her tummy. 'The memory of that potato will keep me going until next Sunday.'

'It was nothing,' Max insisted, but he looked very pleased as he mopped up the last of the steak juice with a piece of bread. 'This is one of my b-list meals. Thai green curry – that's my signature dish. What's yours?'

'Probably steamed fish.' Neve grimaced at the thought of the spartan meal she had on Monday evenings to make up for the excesses of Treat Sunday. 'I can do roasts and casseroles but nothing fancy. It wasn't until I left home that I realised that bolognese sauce didn't start life in a jar.'

'The only cooking lesson I ever got from my mum was "there's the Pot Noodle, there's the kettle, get on with it",' Max said lightly, and Neve smiled but resisted the urge to prod further – not when they were having such a nice time.

'My mum's such a terrible cook that I think a Pot Noodle would have been preferable to her idiosyncratic take on a sausage casserole.'

'Please, you have *never* eaten a Pot Noodle.' Max pushed back his chair so he could start clearing the table. 'No, you just sit there and look pretty. You're my guest,' he said, when Neve picked up the salad bowl.

She did feel pretty sitting there with the top two buttons

of her dress undone and her face flushed from the wine and because Max had turned up the central heating when she'd handed him a wooden spoon and he'd felt her cold fingers.

Max was rooting around in the fridge. When he straightened up, he was holding something behind his back. 'Now I know you probably won't eat pudding, but it's more about the actual spectacle, than the eating.'

'What is it?'

'Something I made earlier,' he said cryptically as he rummaged through a cupboard. He pulled out something that looked like an old-fashioned Thermos flask with a nozzle, which didn't give Neve any clues. Max had a frightening amount of gadgetry in his kitchen.

'What is that and what are you going to do with it?' she asked, as Max plonked it down on the table.

'Wait and see,' he admonished, patting her shoulder as he walked past to fetch the dessert he'd just got out of the fridge. 'Crème brûlée,' he announced grandly, putting a little ramekin down in front of her and sprinkling the top with brown sugar.

Neve looked down at it with undisguised interest. Although she preferred the chocolate-based desserts, the rules of Treat Sunday would allow her three good spoonfuls because she had cycled miles around north London earlier that day and she still had to cycle home . . .

'What are you doing?' she yelped when Max picked up the fiddly Thermos gizmo and made fire come out of the nozzle.

'Just watch – it's the coolest thing.' Max picked up her ramekin and scorched the top of the crème brûlée until the sugar caramelised. 'Give it a moment to set and then we can crack the top at the same time.'

'Oh my goodness,' Neve breathed as Max performed the same pyrotechnic trick with his own ramekin. 'Be careful with that thing!'

Max blew out the flame that licked across the top of the

brûlée and sat down. 'I know you can't eat any, but that's my party trick.' He beamed at her. 'I set our pudding on fire with my blowtorch! You have to admit, that was pretty cool.'

'It was very cool, though I feared for my eyelashes.' Neve prodded the top with her spoon to test its hardness and all the time she was thinking that as she'd been moaning to Chloe about Max and the nefarious games he was supposedly playing, Max had been making her crème brûlée.

Because it wasn't just Max carefully measuring out sugar and separating egg yolks, it was Max thinking about her. It was Max trying to impress her. And the whole thing with Max making fire? That was the metrosexual equivalent of hunting down a wild animal, then dragging it back to his cave for the approval of his cavewoman.

It wasn't crème brûlée. Not at all. It was Max trying to seduce her. So why wasn't he getting on with the seduction?

Neve was out of her chair, and before Max even had time to look up, she was half on his lap, half crouching down to smother his face with kisses.

Max tried to speak but there was nothing he could say that Neve wanted to hear, not when she wanted his kisses and he was still withholding. His mouth barely moved against hers, his hands on her shoulders to keep her at a distance and stop Neve from pressing herself against him, while she wanted something harder and fiercer and more passionate.

'God, why won't you kiss me properly?' she demanded, pulling herself away and standing up so she could loom over Max with her hands on her hips. Also, crouching down had been hell on her knees.

'Because I don't want you having a panic attack halfway through.' Max looked up at her, no trace of teasing on his face. 'You'd better be sure that this is what you want.'

'Either we're doing this for real or there's no point in doing this at all,' Neve snapped. 'God, this is a disaster. We don't fit together. I never know if you're joking or not, and you certainly don't know that I want to be kissed – really kissed – and if you don't want to do th—'

Her garbled speech was stopped abruptly when Max stood up and kissed the words right out of her mouth. Proper kisses that made her aching knees buckle just a little bit.

Neve had a sense memory of that first night on her sofa because these kisses were just as heated, but it wasn't the same because this time when Max cupped her breast and bottom, she pressed herself into his hands. These weren't kisses that were going to lead to sex, she had made her feelings about that perfectly clear; they were kisses for the sake of kissing. Which was fine with her.

They only broke apart when Keith barked and scrabbled at the closed kitchen door. He came bounding into the room, then stopped and looked at them suspiciously, his ears cocked.

After Keith was fed and they'd done the washing up, they reconvened to the sofa where Max fed her exactly three spoonfuls of crème brûlée and then they kissed again.

The first kisses had been a little desperate but now they were slow and deep, and sometimes they didn't even kiss but just lay on the sofa holding each other. Then Max would shift, so he could undo the third button on Neve's dress to reveal a little more of her thermal vest, or she'd lazily run her finger along the soft underside of his arm and they'd kiss again. Even though Max's living room was painted white and blue, Neve felt as if she was cocooned in a warm, red glow.

'I'm not too heavy for you?' she murmured in one of the not-kissing moments.

'For the fifth time, no,' Max said, smoothing the hair back from her face so he could kiss the tip of her nose. He glanced over her head. 'It's getting late. Will you stay over if I promise not to breach your thermals?'

Neve craned her neck to see the clock on the mantelpiece. It was nearly ten. William had said he'd call at nine.

'I should go,' she said half-heartedly. The thought of leaving Max's toasty warm flat wasn't that appealing. Neither was the cold bike ride home, and for a moment she thought about staying and kissing Max a little while longer, but then she thought of William at the other end of the phone. The pleasure in his voice when he said hello and the throaty way he'd laugh if Neve said anything even remotely funny and how they could just talk and talk for hours and . . . and talking to William on the phone was even better than staying where she was and kissing Max some more. Which was no slight on Max's kissing skills – in Neve's limited experience Max seemed to be an expert kisser – but in a contest between kissing Max and talking to William, William was always going to emerge the victor.

'Just to sleep,' Max clarified, sitting up with a little groan and swinging his long legs to the floor. 'You said you needed to get some practice in sleeping with someone else, didn't you?'

'I did,' Neve said slowly. Now she wasn't sure about that because there had been moments when they were kissing that she'd had the urge to rip off her many layers of clothing, tug away Max's T-shirt and do more than kiss. What if she felt that urge again when they were in bed together? And she wasn't sure how she felt about sharing a bed with Max when he'd made it perfectly clear that he was going to sleep with other women while they were dating. One whiff of someone else's perfume on his pillow would ruin everything. 'Have you ever shared a bed with a woman and not, hmmm, you know, had relations with them?'

Max gave the matter some thought. 'Well, no, but I'm ready to give it a try if you are.'

'It's not that I don't want to sleep with you, but we've

only just got the kissing thing ironed out and I have to go home now because there's stuff I need to do.' There was no point in lying about it, Max knew William was the whole reason why they were doing this, but Neve made sure she was sitting right at the other end of Max's sofa before she said, 'Actually, I'm expecting a call from William.'

'Fine, go home and coo sweet nothings down the phone to William,' Max drawled diffidently. 'Don't sleep with me, it's your loss.'

'Well, it's not as if sleeping with me is going to be that exciting when I'm sure you do all sorts of far more thrilling things when you're in bed with your other women.' Neve could only begin to imagine the lurid sex games Max played with his legions of other girls, which had to be much more fun and a lot more exotic than kissing a girl wearing a thermal vest, but his spine was set in a tense straight line like he wasn't too happy about Neve cycling off into the night. He probably wasn't used to being rejected. 'And it's not like I'm going home to sleep with William, though it would be hard to do that when he's in California and I'm not.' Neve willed herself to stop talking because she was rambling and also she didn't like to think of William in that way – their bond was so much more spiritual than that.

'I don't fuck a different woman every night,' Max snapped. 'Or every other night, for that matter. I do have some control over my dick.'

Neve winced at Max's harsh language. 'I know, I know,' she said hurriedly, although she hadn't known any such thing. They'd been having such a lovely time, not to mention stellar kissing, and now it was all going horribly wrong and she didn't know why or how to make it right again.

'Well, you'd better go then,' Max said, standing up and stretching. And just as Neve thought that the whole situation and their pretend relationship was irrevocably broken, he held out a hand so he could pull her up from the sofa. 'We'll take a raincheck on sleeping together.'

'Maybe next Sunday, you and Keith could come round to mine and I'll cook you dinner?' Neve suggested tentatively, as she hunted for her shoes. 'I'm not that great a cook and there won't be any blowtorches involved . . . Perhaps we could try the sleepover thing then, once I've had time to get used to it, if you still want to.'

'I still want to,' Max said slowly. 'I'm all about expanding your relationship knowledge, as long as you promise never to call it a sleepover again.'

'I suppose it does sound a little teenage . . .' Neve stopped and gave Max a shaky smile. 'So, we're OK? You're still all right with doing this whole relationship thing?'

Max smiled back. 'A pancake relationship. Quite frankly, I wouldn't want any other kind.'

Chapter Fifteen

Being properly kissed and being in an improper relationship put Neve in such a cheery mood over the next few days that it didn't matter when Charlotte started banging on the ceiling like she had a sixth sense about these things and knew the exact moment that Neve had fired up Microsoft Word to work on the next chapter of her Lucy Keener biography. Or that William hated *Tristram Shandy* too but still insisted that they finish reading it.

'But Neve, you can't start a book and leave it halfway through,' he'd said implacably. 'It's almost as bad as turning down the corner of the page, instead of using a bookmark.'

It also didn't matter that Gustav was exceedingly crabby because he'd pulled a thigh muscle and had to have a week off from training for his half-marathon and had decided to use the time to lecture Neve on the perils of pancake relationships.

'I thought you were saving yourself for William, your one true love,' he said sourly, as Neve huffed and puffed on a gym mat as she worked her core muscles. 'It shows no commitment to your romantic goals. I hope you're not going to take the same fickle attitude to your fitness goals.'

'It shows a total commitment to my romantic goals,' Neve panted, stopping her stomach crunches, only to start them again when Gustav pointed a finger in the direction of her domed belly. 'Going out with Max is like your marathon training. William is my finishing line.'

That made Gustav even stroppier. He had to go and get an ice-pack for his injured thigh and when he returned, he made Neve spend ten minutes lying on the floor doing scissor kicks. But scissor kicks did not destroy her; they just built muscle, which burned fat so it was all good.

Neve's good mood wasn't even punctured by the strange atmosphere at work. Every time she went into the kitchen, Chloe and Rose were already in there having a fierce, whispered conversation that stopped immediately when Neve asked if the kettle was on. The annual Board of Trustees' meeting was imminent, which always made everyone jumpy, as their thoughts turned first to lack of funding, then to pay cuts and four-day weeks and even redundancy. Neve was sure it wouldn't come to that, since funding always turned up at the eleventh hour and, for once in her life, she wasn't going to worry about the stuff she couldn't control.

What mattered was that things with Max were going smoothly and if she could be successful in a fake relationship, then a real relationship with William would be a breeze, a walk in the park, like falling off a log.

Neve would never admit it to Max, because he'd never stop crowing about it, but she was definitely having fun.

Though at two o'clock the next Sunday afternoon Neve was feeling less fun-filled and more frazzled. She had a beef casserole on a low simmer, a pore-minimising mask on her face, which was making her skin itch, and even though she'd changed her sheets midweek, she remade her bed swapping floral sprigs for a candy stripe, which was the manliest bedlinen she could find in her airing cupboard. Then she tore through her pyjama drawer for something suitable to sleep in. She'd never realised just how many dowdy, plaid pyjama bottoms she'd accumulated. Neve even contemplated phoning Celia to ask if polka dots were sexier than tartan but Celia was probably still in bed, and even if she did manage to answer the phone, she'd want to know exactly why Neve was having a sleepwear style crisis and that was a conversation that Neve didn't want to have.

There was a ring on the bell at precisely three o'clock as Neve was furiously dabbing powder on her face. The mask may have minimised her pores but had left the rest of her red and blotchy, and as she tiptoed down the stairs at great speed to answer the door, she realised she was still wearing her strictly 'round the house' jeans with the saggy knees and stretched-out waistband instead of her 'can just about walk in them' jeans. It was too late to go back and change now.

Neve took a deep, centring breath, then opened the door with a fixed smile, which turned into a grin of sheer delight when Keith leaped up to lick her hands and wag his stumpy tail.

'Hello, my precious little boy,' Neve clucked, taking his front paws in her hands so they could do a little two-step.

'And hello to you too,' Max said, stepping past them and shutting the door with his foot as he was laden down with two holdalls, a carrier bag, a bunch of flowers and a dog bed.

'So you and Keith are definitely staying over, then?' Neve let go of Keith's paws, so she could assess the sheer amount of stuff Max deemed essential for sleeping over. Even though she'd spent most of the morning panicking about bedlinen and sleepwear, she'd half-hoped that Max would have some good reason why he couldn't spend the night.

'I thought Keith could act as a chaperone but his requirements for an overnight stay rival any Hollywood celebrity,' Max complained, as he started up the stairs. 'Dog bed, special blanket, a selection of his favourite toys and he'll only drink and eat out of his own bowls. I even had to bring some smoked salmon paté to disguise the taste of his worming tablets and vitamins.'

'You're a very high-maintenance doggy,' Neve told Keith, who was making progress very slow by climbing a stair then stopping and looking round to make sure that Neve and Max were still behind him. 'I've got you some lovely doggy treats.'

'Please don't talk to him in that creepy voice. He's a dog, not a five year old with learning difficulties.'

'No pudding for you, mister,' Neve snapped, bumping Max with her hip as they reached her landing. She waited until he'd retrieved the dog bed, which had fallen to the floor, then gestured at the open door. 'Just go through, you know where everything is.'

She winced at the reminder of that awful, drunken night – but then again, if it hadn't been for that awful, drunken night then Max wouldn't be dropping his bags on the floor so he could take her in his arms.

'Hey,' he whispered, kissing the blotchiest patch of skin across her left cheekbone.

'Hey yourself,' Neve said, then they were kissing in her tiny hall with the door still wide open and Keith bashing his head against their shins.

It was absolutely perfect – or it was until Neve heard a loud thumping sound, followed by a door crashing back on its hinges and the thud, thud, thud of footsteps. Keith started barking and chasing around in circles as Neve tried to wriggle out of Max's arms because . . .

'For fuck's sake! What the fuck is going on up there?'

Charlotte was still on the half-landing between their two floors, foot raised to complete the climb to Neve's flat when she stopped and stared, her mouth hanging open.

Neve could feel her heart pounding and her face firing up so it would be impossible to tell where the blushing started and the blotching stopped. She took a step backwards and blundered into Max, while she willed herself to stay calm. She had back-up and she had a fierce-looking dog who flattened his ears and growled when Charlotte decided to climb another stair.

Charlotte hurriedly backed away to the safety of the

landing. 'Could you keep the noise down?' she asked politely, as if the screaming harridan of thirty seconds ago had just been an hallucination. 'I have a headache.'

'I'm so sorry,' Max purred, taking his hands off Neve's shoulders so he could come forward and give Charlotte a good telling-off because it was what boyfriends did when they met their girlfriends' arch nemeses. 'Keith, stop that!'

Keith let out a volley of defiant barks, then slunk behind Max's legs.

'I'm sorry,' Max repeated. 'All my fault. I don't think we've been introduced. I'm Neve's special friend and I can't believe she forgot to tell me that there's another gorgeous Slater sister walking the earth.'

Neve contemplated shoving Max head first down the stairs, but settled for a thousand silent curse words as she glared at his back. Charlotte tossed her hair back and made a horrible sound, half giggle and half simper. 'I'm only a Slater by marriage,' she said conspiratorially, as if confessing to some terrible crime. She gave Max a long look, eyes narrowed, as if he was a huge uncut diamond and she was trying to estimate how many carats he was worth. 'I'm Charlotte, Neve's sister-in-law.'

It was probably the first time that Charlotte had ever admitted they were tenuously related. Neve twitched with anger. Charlotte had obviously decided that Max was heterosexual, handsome and wasted on Neve because she flicked her long, shiny, stupid hair back from her face again, then stuck out her chest in her stupid Juicy Couture track-suit. Celia and Yuri had once tried to guess how many Juicy Couture tracksuits Charlotte owned, but they'd given up once they'd hit double figures.

'Why are all the beautiful ones already taken?' Max sighed. 'At least tell me that your marriage is on the rocks and there's a chance you might rebound into the arms of another man.'

'Oh, there's every chance,' Charlotte said, looking at

Neve, which was why she probably stopped giggling, simpering and sticking her breasts out and sounded more like her usual, sullen self. Then she gave Keith another anxious glance, even though he was now lying on Neve's doormat and scratching behind his ear. 'Is that a Rottweiler?'

'No, *he's* not,' Neve said indignantly. 'He's a Staffordshire Bull Terrier.'

Neve jumping into the fray reminded Charlotte why she was there in the first place. 'Well, just try not to bang about so much. Honestly, it's like having an *elephant* living above me.'

And with that parting shot, Charlotte went back to her lair, swinging her hips more than was strictly necessary.

'You never said anything about a sister-in-law,' Max remarked, and Neve realised she was so tense that it felt as if her bones would shatter. 'She's quite cute once you get past the orange tan and the hair extensions.'

'Oh, I can think of a few other ways to describe her,' Neve said bitterly, slamming the front door shut. 'I know you feel obligated to flirt with anyone and anything that crosses your path, but I wish that sometimes you could be a bit more discerning.'

'Oh, Neevy, so I flirt. It's what I do. Don't tell me you're jealous,' Max said teasingly. 'OK, chatting up your sister-in-law was a bit close to home, but I was only having a bit of fun.'

'Did you not hear her shouting at me?' Neve asked Max. 'If you had the willpower to hold off the charm for five seconds, it might have occurred to you that she doesn't like me and I certainly don't like her.'

From the puzzled expression on Max's face, it was clear that he was hard-wired to charm whatever the circumstances. 'Well, yeah,' he muttered. 'I suppose she was giving you a hard time. Does she do that a lot?'

'She's been doing that for ever,' Neve said, as she walked

towards the kitchen. 'I was at school with her and she made my life a living hell every day for five years. I'm going to put the kettle on, do you want a drink?'

'Coffee, please.' Max sat down on a chair and scooped up Keith. 'What did she do to you?'

Neve didn't answer at first. She was carefully spooning fresh ground coffee beans into the cafetière she'd bought in honour of Max's visit. Normally she made do with a jar of Kenco, but Max seemed to run on multiple tiny cups of espresso.

'Neve? What did she do?' Max prompted gently.

'What didn't she do?' Neve said bitterly, all set to launch into a blistering rant about the times that Charlotte and her cronies had followed her home from school, calling her names and throwing stones at her, and when she'd finally reached the safety of her house, the back of her blazer was always studded with globs of spit. There were the times they'd cornered her in the showers at school, until Neve had persuaded her mum to write her a note to excuse her from games. There was even the time that Charlotte had come over to Neve in the school canteen, poured a whole can of Diet Coke over her packed lunch and said, 'If you swapped your full-fat Coke for this, maybe you wouldn't be such a porker.'

Neve had spent most Sunday evenings throwing up and crying at the thought of school the next morning and the new tortures that Charlotte had had a whole weekend to devise. But now she wasn't going to cry because she'd already wasted too many tears on Charlotte in her life. 'She had this nickname for me,' she said finally. 'I think it's probably the only flash of genius Charlotte's ever had. She used to call me "Heave". And then everyone at school called me Heave. Once even Miss Harris, our games teacher, said it, though she pretended she hadn't.'

'Did she call you that because . . . because . . . of the way you looked, or . . . ?' Max was treading carefully, trying to pick his way through a minefield of words, and really there was no easy way to say it so Neve said it for him.

'I was fat, or fatter,' Neve said baldly. 'And the beauty of that nickname was that it meant all things to all people. Like, I was so fat that I made people want to be sick or that I should have made myself sick instead of digesting huge amounts of food or I was so fat that I huffed when I walked or I was so fat that I'd have made a great end member of a tug-of-war team. Take your pick.'

'But you're not the same person any more,' Max said. 'So why do you still let her get to you?'

'I don't know.' Neve pushed down on the cafetière. 'She always manages to make me feel as if I'm fifteen again, and it doesn't matter how much weight I lose, the fat me is still lurking just below the surface and Charlotte always makes her rise to the top.'

She placed a cup of coffee in front of Max and let him put Keith on the floor so he could take her hand and trace patterns on her palm with his thumb, even though she didn't really want to be touched. 'I promise I'll never flirt with her again,' he said earnestly. 'God, it must have been a shock when she started dating your brother.'

'I was at university and Mum didn't tell me because she thought it wouldn't last. Douglas's girlfriends never stuck around for long, but Charlotte – boy, did she stick.' She could still remember coming home after Finals and bumping into Charlotte sneaking out of Douglas's room at the same time that Neve was heading to the kitchen for a snack. Neither of them had said a word, though Neve could still feel the sickening jolt her heart had given.

Then there had been other things to worry about, and when Douglas and Charlotte had gone to Vegas and got married, Neve had simply been expected to deal with the fact that her adolescent tormenter was living one floor below her and sharing her surname.

Max didn't say anything, he just kept stroking her palm,

and when Neve made a move to tug her hand away, he refused to let go.

'We were never going to become best friends,' Neve said, 'but I'd have accepted her apology, except she's never once said sorry. Hasn't even hinted at anything that comes close to sorry, and her tactics might have become a bit more psychological but she's still bullying me and I let her because I'm weak and ineffectual and—'

'Bollocks,' Max said. 'You wouldn't be my pancake girl-friend if you were a loser.'

She didn't want to, but Neve was smiling. 'Excuse me? I think you'll find that I was the originator of the whole pan-cake relationship concept. Stop bogarting it.'

'How do you even know what "bogart" means?' Max asked. 'If you tell me that you smoke spliffs, my entire belief system will collapse.'

'I might smoke spliffs for all you know.' Except she never had, not at university and certainly not now, because she'd seen Celia and Yuri rampaging through her fridge when they had an attack of the munchies and that was something that Neve and her hips could do without.

'But you don't?' Max gave her a plaintive look, brow creased with consternation.

'I don't,' Neve confirmed. 'I just read a lot.' And it wasn't as if the nasty encounter with Charlotte, or the subsequent emotional fall-out, had been forgotten but Neve had moved past it because Max had skilfully steered her away from the rocks. She wished she knew how he did it; it would come in very handy the next time Celia was having an existential crisis or Philip was having relationship problems.

Before she turned her attention back to her beef casserole, which had been neglected in all the excitement, Neve dropped an impulsive kiss on the top of Max's head just to say thank you. Then she waited until he'd stopped looking at her in surprise, to surreptitiously wipe her lips free of hair gunk.

*

Neve was a little subdued during dinner and Max was so uncharacteristically polite, praising the tenderness of the beef in the casserole, complimenting her on the daring choice of fennel and asking for seconds, that Neve wondered if it was some new game of his. He even insisted on helping to clear the table and do the dishes and kissed her every time she handed him a plate or a bowl to dry.

'What do you want to do now?' Max asked after the last teaspoon had been put away. 'I thought we could pencil in another session on the sofa.'

'Well, the sofa does feature quite highly in my plans for the evening,' Neve agreed. 'I'm going to initiate you into the rituals of Treat Sunday.'

Max raised his eyebrows. 'I thought Treat Sunday was just about eating complex carbohydrates after six.'

'It's so much more than that,' Neve sighed. 'If you go into the living room, there's a cupboard under the bookshelf next to my desk. Because you're the guest, you get to pick.'

Neve waited until she could hear him rummaging before she started to gather her supplies. When she walked into the lounge, Max was on his knees and rifling through her DVD collection. 'I think you have every romcom ever made. You even have silent films!' he added, waving a copy of *My Best Girl*, made in 1927 and starring Mary Pickford, as proof.

'It's a classic,' Neve said mildly, placing the laden tray she'd brought in on the coffee table.

'I'm not watching anything with Meg Ryan in it.' Max's voice was muffled as he reached into the furthest corner of the cupboard and ran his finger along the spines. 'OK, do you fancy Katharine Hepburn and Cary Grant in *Bringing Up Baby*?'

'Always.' Neve curled up on the sofa and held her breath as Max closed the tray on the DVD player and turned round. He stared at the contents of the tray and then at Neve, who shrugged her shoulders. 'It's Treat Sunday,' she said, by way of explanation.

'I think I love Treat Sunday,' Max said, sitting down next to her. 'Am I allowed to put my feet on the coffee table?'

'Only if you take your shoes off first. Also, I have complete jurisdiction over the remote control and I don't mind you talking during the film, but I don't want any commentary about what I'm eating or how I'm eating it,' Neve finished in her strictest voice.

Max poured himself a glass of wine from the bottle Neve had brought in but didn't touch anything else on the tray. '*How* you're going to eat it?'

'That's what I said,' Neve clarified, handing Max a huge bag of Thai Spicy Bites and a Snickers bar. 'That's yours.' Aziz in the convenience store had assured her they were very masculine snacks and, as an added bonus, she didn't like either of them, so she wouldn't be tempted to steal any.

'Thanks, but I've got all this and you've only got a tube of Smarties and a bag of Hula Hoops,' Max protested, as Neve tipped the Smarties into a tiny china bowl.

'Did you not hear the part where I said that you weren't allowed to comment on my snack choices?' Neve tore open her bag of Hula Hoops and spilled them into a slightly larger china bowl.

Max didn't say another word, though he polished off his Thai Spicy Bites and Snickers in fifteen minutes, whereas an hour into the film, Neve was still delicately picking her way through the contents of her china bowls.

She always started with the Hula Hoops, letting them sit saltily in her mouth; only when they were just about to lose their crunch did she start chewing. Then, when Neve was halfway through the potato portion of her treats, she moved on to the Smarties.

Those she ate according to colour. Brown, green, blue, purple, pink, red, yellow and the orange ones for last because they had their own unique flavour. She'd pop a

Smartie into her mouth and suck long enough that she could bite off the candy shell but leave the chocolate centre intact. Then she'd suck on the chocolate until there was nothing left.

When she was halfway through the Smarties, in the gap between the purple and pink, Neve would stop snacking for ten minutes, just to prove that she could. She'd count the time off on her watch and when the ten minutes were up, she'd pop a pink Smartie into her mouth.

After the Smarties were finished, it was back to the Hula Hoops. The whole process took at least an hour, usually more. Either way, the credits were rolling as Neve finished crunching the last Hula Hoop, her eyes closed as she savoured the salty, potato-ey bliss that would have to last her a whole week.

When she opened her eyes it was to find Max staring at her as if she was a jigsaw piece that just wouldn't fit. 'You can't say anything,' she warned him. 'That was the rule.'

'I'm not going to say anything. Besides, there are no words.' Neve was about to bristle and get all defensive when she saw the way Max was looking at her, even though she'd just taken an hour to eat a tube of Smarties and a bag of Hula Hoops and she was wearing her 'just around the house' jeans. 'Why are you looking at me like that?' she asked, because she'd done absolutely nothing to warrant the speculative gleam in Max's eyes or the way his tongue kept moistening his bottom lip. 'Shall I make coffee?'

'Not in the mood for coffee,' Max said, pulling Neve closer before she even realised what was happening. 'Come here, you.'

So there was kissing. Kissing without thinking, so all the doubting voices in Neve's head were quiet and when Max undid each button on her tunic dress, she didn't mind because he kissed each inch of skin that he uncovered.

Max's shirt came off too and the T-shirt he wore underneath so Neve could gently rake her fingers through the fuzz of hair that disappeared below his waistband and though she toyed with the buckle of his belt because she liked the way that Max sucked in a breath every time she did it, her hands didn't stray any further.

His hands did though. They stroked the curve of her denim-covered hips and when they were lying face to face on the sofa, Max lifted Neve's leg so it was hitched over his and their bodies were fitted flush together. Neve didn't know where the urge to grind and shimmy and press against Max came from but it felt so good in a maddening, frustrating way that she gave into it.

'We need to stop now,' Max suddenly whispered urgently in her ear. 'Stop!'

Neve momentarily stopped kissing Max's clenched jaw. He was hard against her belly. 'Stop for just a minute or stop altogether?' she asked. Her voice sounded thick and heavy, probably because her brain and her blood and her limbs felt thick and heavy too.

Max eased back two centimetres. 'Unless you're ready for at least third base, we have to stop 'cause I need to . . . y'know, let my blood flow in the direction of my head again.'

Neve didn't really want to stop, but you could only kiss for so long with your top unbuttoned and with your kissing partner's erection prodding against you before the kissing became something else. She smoothed back Max's hair, and when he gritted his teeth, she made a mental note to Google *unrelieved erection + pain*.

She slid off the sofa, careful not to touch Max because every time she did, his nostrils flared. Max rolled over on to his back and now that the kissing had ended and the mood was shifting, standing there with her top unbuttoned and the waistband of her sagging jeans halfway down her hips seemed to matter quite a bit. Neve turned around and quickly buttoned herself up.

Max sat up very slowly as if he was getting over major

surgery. 'I need to take Keith for his last walk. Can I borrow your keys?'

Max hobbled to the hall. Keith, who was stiff from sleeping so long under Neve's desk, hobbled after him. Neve fished her spare set of keys out of a kitchen drawer and dropped them in Max's outstretched hand.

It was a watershed moment in their funny relationship but Neve had other things on her mind. 'If I was up for having sex, which I'm not, but if I was, would you want to? With me?'

'This isn't just an involuntary reaction I get from eating too many Thai Spicy Bites,' Max said grumpily, bending down to clip on Keith's lead. 'Of course I want to do more than kiss you, but you're saving yourself for your one true love and I'm trying to prove I'm more than just a fucktoy.'

'Don't say that,' Neve said reflexively, because she was never, ever going to *fuck* someone. 'Making love' sounded much nicer – poetic, even. 'And I was just checking.'

'I would say I was sorry for snapping, but as you're partly responsible for my current agony, I'm not going to.' Considering he was talking about his erection, it was sort of sweet that Max looked like a sulky little boy who'd just been bawled out for throwing stones. 'I'll see you in about fifteen minutes,' he added, with slightly less petulance.

Chapter Sixteen

As soon as she heard the street door close, Neve sped into action. Although she was perfectly clean, she had the world's quickest shower as she waited for the kettle to boil. She filled her hot-water bottle while swilling mouthwash. She hauled her sleepwear on to her still damp body and quickly spritzed her bed with lavender room mist as she shoved the hot-water bottle under the covers. Then she went through the pile of books on her nightstand, ruthlessly weeding out anything that might look like a romance novel to the uneducated eye.

Neve spent the last five minutes willing her night cream to absorb quicker as she tried to arrange her hair into an artless ponytail. She heard a key turn in the lock just as she decided that she was satisfied with attempt number nine and gave herself a quick look in the bathroom mirror; her night cream had almost sunk in, giving her a dewy look, and strands of silky dark hair framed a face that would have looked much better if she wasn't gnawing on her bottom lip.

She hurried out into the hall to greet the wanderers. Max looked as if he was in much better spirits; he was smiling for one thing, the smile getting wider as he caught sight of Neve.

'You look so sweet,' he said in what sounded suspiciously like the male version of her Keith-inspired coo.

'No, I don't,' Neve protested. Sweet was not what she'd been aiming for. She tugged at the lace-edged cuffs of her long-sleeved thermal vest, then reached down to pat Keith. 'Where's Keith going to sleep? With us?'

'In the hall. He's not allowed to sleep in the bedroom. He'll spend all night trying to get on the bed.'

'But what's wrong with that?' Neve had been looking forward to Keith sleeping at the bottom of the bed, preferably on her feet because they got very cold at night.

Max shook his head. 'I've spent a long time establishing some boundaries with him. Don't undo all my good work.'

She watched Max settle Keith down in his dog bed with a ragged blanket over him and a threadbare soft toy tucked between his front paws. Then there was the water bowl and a plug-in nightlight because Keith didn't like the dark, and Neve began to wonder just where Keith's boundaries were.

'I'm going to bed,' she said, when it became obvious that Max intended to stay with Keith until he was asleep.

Neve had spent five minutes with a hand mirror to judge her best angle when she was lying down and another ten minutes reading before Max put in an appearance.

'So you sleep on the right-hand side,' he remarked, as if it was a question that had been bugging him for ages. 'I sleep on the left, so that works.'

Usually she slept in the dead centre of the bed but that seemed like a very spinsterish thing to admit, so Neve put down her book and fluffed the pillows next to her so they'd be at optimum plumpness for Max. You could fault her for a lot of things, she thought, but she was a very considerate hostess.

Max sat down on the edge of the bed and bounced experimentally. 'Firm mattress,' he remarked. 'I do like a bed without much give to it.'

Neve could actually feel her blood pressure start to rise. Sleeping with Max on her candy-striped bedlinen had seemed like a good idea in theory, but the actual reality of Max in her bedroom again felt threatening and thrilling all at the same time. It didn't help that he was talking in a low, suggestive voice and had a smirky little smile on his face like he couldn't help but go into seductive mode when he was in a room with a bed in it.

Max was unlacing his Doc Marten boots and Neve quickly picked up her book again. This was all such new territory for her, but she tried to affect an ease that she didn't really feel.

'What are you reading?' Max pulled off his socks and wiggled his long toes. He had nice feet for a man; at least they weren't too hairy.

Neve lifted up her copy of *Rebecca* by Daphne du Maurier so Max could read the title, then gestured at the carefully edited pile of books on her bedside table. 'You're welcome to borrow one.'

Shirt half-unbuttoned, Max reached across the bed, inadvertently pinning Neve to the mattress, as he glanced through the pile. 'Oh, I've always wanted to read this,' he said, as Neve tried to look over his shoulder.

'How have you never read *The Catcher in the Rye*?' she wanted to shriek but settled for a simple, 'I think you'll really like that.'

Neve wished Max would finish getting undressed and get into bed so they could negotiate the next step of their relationship, but instead he was looking doubtfully at her copy of *Mansfield Park*. Which was just wrong because . . .

'If you haven't read any Jane Austen, don't start with that one,' she said with great force. 'Fanny Price doesn't work as well as a modern heroine as Elizabeth Bennet does.'

Max put down the book quickly, as if it was coated in something toxic. 'Well, maybe I'll try *Catcher in the Rye* and work my way up to Jane Austen.' He shifted back so Neve no longer had a dead weight on her legs, and smacked the book against his palm. 'I promise I won't crease the spine.'

'Of course, *Catcher in the Rye* is Salinger's most well-known novel, but personally I much prefer his stories about the Glass family,' Neve heard herself say in the prissiest voice she'd ever managed, as if her mouth was stuffed full of plums. 'I think *Franny and Zooey* has the edge over *Raise High the Roof Beam, Carpenters*, but it's very hard to evaluate Salinger's oeuvre as a whole, when it mostly consists of novellas and short stories.'

'Right. I'll be sure to remember that,' Max murmured, and then he stopped talking because he was pulling his shirt and T-shirt off in one easy movement, so watching the muscles in his back undulate was much more interesting than J. D. Salinger. Max was wiry without being weedy, his muscles defined without bulging like Gustav's did – so that Neve always wondered if he might bust out of the tight Lycra tops he favoured. She held her book to her face and peeked over the top as Max started on his belt buckle, biceps flexing as he pulled the leather free from his jeans.

Neve gulped. 'One could argue that the only available texts we have from Salinger are technically juvenilia, and that his subsequent reclusion was an attempt to create his own legend rather than admit that he couldn't live up to the promise of his earlier work.' She just couldn't stop talking. Neve winced as she heard her voice getting shriller and shriller, but there was nothing she could do about it. 'It's not unprecedented. After all, Rimbaud abandoned all his literary endeavours by the time he was twenty-one.'

Max shot her a slow, lazy smile. 'Neevy?'

'What?'

'I haven't got a clue what you're talking about,' Max informed her kindly. 'No need to be nervous. We're just going to sleep in the same bed. Think of me as a lanky teddy bear.'

That was actually good advice, or it would have been if the sound of Max's zipper going down hadn't derailed Neve completely. It struck her how ridiculous this all was. There was a man undressing in her girly pink bedroom, not made any less girly or pink by the fact there was a man undressing in it.

'Did you bring pyjamas?' she croaked, as Max kicked off

his jeans and stood there in his boxer trunks, unconcernedly scratching his chest.

'Never wear them,' he assured her, and Neve knew for certain that if he wanted to sleep naked next to her, then she was calling the whole thing off. She was not ready for full frontal nudity and sometimes she didn't think she ever would be.

She'd been the only clothed member of a naked family and it had been awful. When she was a child, Friday afternoons had been particularly harrowing. As soon as her father got in from work, she was sent out for five portions of haddock and chips. By the time she got back, her dad was sitting in the kitchen in his paisley Y-fronts sipping from a bottle of beer. Neve hadn't even possessed a swimming costume until she was five and had staged a mutiny on a Margate beach until her father had been dispatched to Woolworth's to buy her a Barbie bikini, even though she'd really wanted a one-piece.

All through her childhood, Neve had wished that her mother had been like the other Catholic mothers of her Sunday School pals. The kind of mothers who promised brimstone and fire if their daughters dared to wear skirts above the knee or painted their toenails. But no, she had a Catholic mother who said things like, 'Sure, if everything that God created is beautiful and God created your body, then your body's beautiful.'

But Neve had known that her body wasn't beautiful. By the age of five, she could tell that her body was rounder and chubbier than the bodies of her friends. She had a pot belly and her thighs looked as if they had elastic bands digging into them when she sat down.

'OK, this is your five-second warning,' Max announced. Neve looked up at him tremulously as he stood over her. It was best to keep looking up, at his face, and not anywhere else, though at least he'd kept his boxer trunks on. 'I'm just about to get into your bed.'

199

The covers were pulled back and Neve forced herself to remain perfectly still as Max slid into bed beside her and gave a tiny blissful sigh as he connected with her posture-paedic mattress and memory foam pillows. He slowly stretched out, then frowned.

'Is that a hot-water bottle?'

'Yes, yes it is,' Neve said hurriedly, snagging it between her feet and dragging it over to her side.

Max propped the pillows behind his head so he could sit up and survey his resting place for the night. 'Don't you think it's a bit warm under all these covers?' He lifted the eiderdown so he could confirm that there was a duvet underneath it. 'It's almost the official start of British Summer Time.'

Neve levered herself up from her recumbent position. 'But I still have to have the central heating on all day and there's ground frost and I really feel the cold.'

'There isn't any cold *to* feel,' Max said. 'Let's get rid of the top quilt.'

Neve decided it was time for action, not words. Even though she'd resolved that there would be no touching of any kind, she reached for the back of Max's neck with one of her icy paws.

'Fuck! Don't do that!' Max yelped, as Neve snatched her hand back and shoved it under the duvet and the quilt, which was staying exactly where it was. 'God, I didn't think you could be so mean.'

'Don't be such a baby,' Neve said, reaching up to kiss Max's cheek to take the sting out of her words. He made a big show of flinching, as if he expected her lips to be the same sub-zero temperature as her hands.

'Hey! Keep to your side of the bed,' he said, snuggling down under the covers. 'I won't be able to sleep if I'm worried that you're going to jump my bones.'

Neve had been thinking the exact same thing, but when Max said it out loud, she couldn't help but feel a little bit rejected. Of course she didn't want him to jump her bones, but she wanted him to *want* to, except only when they were fully clothed and not in bed together. Despite his manwhore reputation, Max seemed remarkably on-message about just sleeping together. He'd been happy enough to kiss her, but maybe he only fancied her in a kissable way or maybe she was really bad at kissing and he didn't have the heart to tell her, or . . . No! She wasn't going to think of any more 'or's and get so stressed out that she wouldn't be able to sleep.

'OK, fine, no kissing.' Neve rolled over on to her side, making sure there was at least a metre between them. 'Goodnight.' She snapped off the light, without even asking Max if he was ready to go to sleep, but it was her bed, so it was her rules.

They lay there in silence for a while. Neve concentrated on not exhaling too loudly in case Max thought she was a mouthbreather. Her fit of pique had shoved her right to the edge of the mattress, so if she made any sudden moves, she was going to end up on the floor, and there was a big draughty gap because Max had one end of the duvet and she had the other, and basically sleeping with someone else was awful and Neve was beginning to understand why some married people slept in twin beds, or even separate bedrooms. It wasn't because they were prudish; it was because they valued a good night's sleep.

'Are you sulking?' Max asked suddenly.

'No,' Neve said sulkily. 'It's just you're hogging the covers and there's this gap and . . .'

Neve was hoping that Max would relinquish his right to the quilt, but he slid across the bed and wrapped one arm around her. It was like being enveloped by a gigantic hot-water bottle. 'I know I called off the kissing but we can still cuddle,' he whispered in her ear, which tickled because she'd reached that stage where everything was irritating her. His arm moved lower and she jerked away in alarm.

'Don't touch my stomach! It's the one bit of me that

I don't like people touching,' she amended at a less ear-perforating volume.

'OK, you need to relax because you're not going to get any sleep and I can't either when you're sending out distress signals,' Max said, moving his arm so it wasn't pressed against her belly, but higher up and brushing the underside of her breasts, but it wasn't as if she could complain about that now she'd played the tummy card. 'Just pretend I'm Celia.'

'You don't talk as much as Celia,' Neve offered. 'And she's much more bony than you, always poking me with her elbows.'

'At least that's something.' Max's thumb was rhythmically stroking a tiny patch of skin on her arm not covered by the sleeve of her thermal top and that did feel quite nice, almost comforting. Neve shut her eyes and concentrated on breathing in through her nose and out through her mouth. But *not* too loudly.

It was the heat that woke Neve up. She lay there for a second listening to the hiss and crackle but unable to place it, then she sat up and threw back the covers in one jerky movement as she realised the flat was on fire!

The heat almost drove her back when she opened her bedroom door. Neve fought her way through thick smoke that caught at her throat, and went into the living room where bright orange flames were licking over the walls and streaking over the furniture. Fortunately, there was a clear path to her desk and she took it.

Her mind was running on two tracks. She knew she had to ring for the fire brigade, but at the moment saving her Lucy Keener biography was far more important. OK, there wasn't much of a biography to save, but Neve was still switching on her computer and rooting through her drawers for a disc and, oh, there was *How To Write A Book In Fifteen Minutes Every Day*, which she'd borrowed from Philip – he'd kill her if it burned to a crisp.

The flames were creeping ever closer and Neve danced on the spot now because the wood under her bare feet was blisteringly hot. Her eyes were watering, she was coughing and choking and her sodding computer was taking forever to boot up. Finally, there was her Virginia Woolf screensaver. Neve scrabbled for the disc, all fingers and thumbs as she tried to open the disc tray.

'Why are you bothering to do that?' a voice said in her ear, and she turned round to see Max right behind her. 'You know you haven't got anything worth saving there.'

'I've got five and a half chapters and notes,' Neve said, as she started dragging the files on to the disc. 'Don't you think you should be doing something useful like calling 999 or trying to smash open a window?'

'Well, I would but I've got a very important launch party to attend,' Max said blithely just as 'DISC ERROR!' flashed up on the screen.

'Bloody hell!'

'You'll wish you were in hell, Neve, if any of my Juicy Couture tracksuits get burned!' Now, Charlotte was standing there, hands on hips, screaming at her. 'This is all your fault! I bet you decided to bake a pie in the middle of the night because you can't go an hour without stuffing your gob.'

'I didn't,' Neve protested, flinging open drawers to find another disc. 'It wasn't me, it must be an electrical fault.'

'This is so like Neve, don't you think?' Charlotte faded away in a puff of smoke, to be replaced by Chloe and Rose talking in insinuating whispers. 'You know, she always turns on all three bars of the heater in her office.'

'You're right, she does. Someone should tell Mr Freemont that she's frittering away our funding on her own personal comfort and causing a fire risk.'

'But my heater has a sticker on it to say it's been safety checked,' Neve protested, as she rooted through a stack of envelopes for an elusive blank disc.

'I told you that you needed to replace the batteries in the smoke alarm every six months.' Great, now her dad was there to give her a hard time – and in his paisley Y-fronts too. 'I thought you were meant to be the clever one.'

'People! You're not helping. Either make your way to an exit or help me find a disc but really, I can't deal with the constant criticism right now.' There was a huge crash as one of her bookcases gave up under the onslaught of the flames and Neve held her hands to her face in horror. All her out-of-print Virago Modern Classics gone!

'Poor Neve,' said a much more sympathetic voice and she looked up to see William standing there with that soft, warm smile he always had for her. 'I hope my copy of *Writing and Difference* wasn't on that shelf because I could never love someone who treated books in such a cavalier fashion. Especially books that were on loan.'

'But it's not my fault. I didn't start the fire.' It was now just Neve and William, and the biography was still stuck on her computer and they were almost engulfed in flames but that wasn't important. 'Hey, William, do you notice anything different about me?'

William squinted through the smoke. 'Hard to say. Have you changed your hair?'

'Well, I grew out my fringe . . . No! What else is different about me?'

'I suppose you've lost a bit of weight, and not before time, but you're still too fat for me, Neve. I could never love someone who wasn't a size ten,' William told her sadly, then he became shrouded in smoke and fire and disappeared from Neve's sight.

She let the disc she'd just found fall to the floor, and really – what was the point of trying to save the biography or—

Hang on! William was in California, so there was no way he'd just suddenly appear in her flat. How would he have got in anyway? And her computer wallpaper was a picture of two Schnauzer puppies wearing tracksuit tops, not Virginia Woolf.

For the second time, Neve woke up. Properly woke up and this time the flat wasn't on fire. But she could see why her subconscious might have thought so, because it felt as if *she* was being boiled from the inside out.

The ends of her artless ponytail were sticking to the back of her neck and her skin was soaked in sweat. Neve didn't think she'd ever been this hot, not even that time when the air conditioning was broken at the gym; she'd been unable to grab a portable fan and she'd been on level ten of the fat-burn programme on the elliptical machine.

Really, it was no wonder that she was overheating when she was sharing her bed with Max. He was always warm to the touch but snuggled down (and snoring heavily) under her winter-weight duvet and quilt, and with a hot-water added to the mix, he was emitting enough thermo-nuclear rays to launch a weapon of mass destruction.

'Oh God, get off me!' Neve hissed, pushing Max's arm off her. He didn't even stir, just grunted and rolled over, leaving the covers bunched between them. With an annoyed growl, Neve sat up so she could tug off her socks. Then she burrowed under the covers for the hot-water bottle, which she threw on the floor, along with the top quilt. It felt less like being in a burning building and more like baling out of a leaky boat.

Neve flopped down again, covers off, and tried to achieve some inner calm, until she felt her skin become clammy with cold. She pulled the duvet around her and shut her eyes, even though she had the irrational urge to check the lounge just to make sure that it wasn't on fire. But that was stupid because she'd definitely turned the oven off after dinner. At least, she *thought* she'd turned the oven off. She lay there for long moments listening to Max snuffling away like a pig foraging for truffles, but as long as she had the duvet around her and the quilt between them, then she didn't have to suffer his almighty body heat.

She started to drift off, and she was in that soft, peaceful place between sleep and not-quite-sleep, when a heavy arm snaked under her duvet and a fiery hot hand clamped over her breast.

'What is the matter with you?' Neve snapped, using elbows and arms and legs to shove Max over to his side of the bed. It was just as well she was used to lifting weights. 'Get off me!'

In the dim light, she saw Max's eyes flicker open, then they closed again and he went back to sleep.

She was never going to get back to sleep, Neve knew that for a fact. But if she got out of bed, she was admitting defeat. She was admitting that she wasn't able to – or ready to – sleep with someone else, and sleeping with someone else was a prerequisite for a relationship. She was staying put even if it meant not sleeping for the entire night.

Half an hour later, as Neve was silently reciting as much of T. S. Eliot's *The Wasteland* as she could remember, Max rolled over, curved himself against her side and began to breathe hot air on her neck.

'Max? Can you move?' she whispered, and when there was no reply, not even a pause in the moist exhalations hitting her neck, Neve pushed back with her hips in an effort to dislodge him.

This time she got an immediate reaction. Max ground his pelvis against her bottom and Neve could feel his cock hardening, which was an interesting sensation but not really the point right now.

'Max!' she repeated with more feeling and volume. 'You're too heavy. Will you please get off me?'

Neve lay there for a few sweaty moments trying to think cool thoughts of blizzards and snowstorms and how her freezer really needed defrosting, but they weren't working, not when she could feel a trickle of sweat run down her cleavage. She was just debating the pros and cons of pinching Max really hard on his arm, maybe even using her nails, when she heard a buzzing sound.

Before she even had a chance to discover what it was or where it was coming from, Max was rolling off her with an emphatic grunt. Neve gave a grateful sigh of relief and stretched out her cramping limbs, only to realise that the buzzing noise was getting louder and louder as Max sat up and reached down to retrieve his BlackBerry from his jeans.

Neve didn't know who she should be more annoyed with – whoever had the temerity to be calling people past midnight on a Sunday, or Max who slept through poking and pushing and pleas, but woke in a nanosecond at the distant trill of his BlackBerry.

He was having a tense and heated discussion with someone in a monotone, which was completely unnecessary when she was awake and likely to stay that way for quite some time.

Neve sat up and snapped on her bedside light so Max would be able to get the full effect of her most ferocious frown. He didn't seem that bothered by it. Sure, he grimaced apologetically, but then he went back to his whispered conversation.

'It's OK, Max,' Neve hissed, even though it really, really wasn't. 'I'm up. I'm awake. You might as well stop whispering.'

'I really am so sorry about this,' he breathed, his hand over the mouthpiece. 'Been trying to get hold of this publicist for weeks.'

Neve decided that an extravagant eye-roll was answer enough, but Max had already turned away from her. They were going to be having serious words once Max was off the phone with Jennifer Aniston's people or whoever it was.

'Well, yes, I can sign something that says we won't ask her about Brad or Angelina,' Max was saying, and Neve's eyes widened as she realised that she wasn't that far off the mark. Imagine! A really famous Hollywood star's press person phoning Max while he was in her humble Finsbury Park flat. 'Yes, I do understand that I'm asking for one day out of her entire life, but I know she'd be very happy with the shoot. Armani are lending us dresses that they haven't loaned out to anyone else and— no, that's quite all right. Yeah, call me back in ten minutes.'

There was no point in giving Max a hard time when the person on the other end of the phone was giving him a much harder time. 'I'm not going to yell at you,' Neve said, as Max finished the call and turned back to her with a wary look. 'Well, in my head I'm yelling at you, but I understand that it's not your fault and you had to take the call.'

'I'm sorry,' Max said quickly. 'I know it's not really up there with sorting out peace in the Middle East, but as far as the person I've just spoken to is concerned, making sure that their client is kept happy is far more important than that.' He put his head in his hands. 'God, I really hate that publicist.'

Neve rubbed Max's back and hoped that he could tell that these were comfort touches and not the touches of a girl who was going to jump his bones. 'I'm sure everything will get sorted out,' she said, though she wasn't sure that it would, but it seemed the right thing to say. The smooth skin of Max's back was still blazing hot.

'To completely change the subject, when you've slept with other girls have any of them happened to mention that there's something seriously wrong with your internal thermostat?' she ventured, because now was as good a time as any to broach this subject.

'Have they what about my what?' Max no longer had his head in his hands, but was staring at Neve like she'd confessed to wetting the bed.

'You're really hot. Like, temperature hot,' she clarified when Max grinned as if she'd been passing judgement on his sex appeal. 'And when you go to sleep, you get hotter and hotter and you drape yourself over me, and I feel as if I'm being boiled alive, like a lobster.'

'Are you accusing me of being a snuggler?' Max asked, folding his arms.

'No, I'm not accusing and that wasn't the part that I wanted you to focus on,' Neve said. She reached out to touch Max's arm. 'Could you – I don't know, is there anything you can do . . .'

'To make myself a little less hot? It's not really something I have much control over, but you could wear fewer clothes in bed.' Max nodded at Neve's long-sleeved thermal top. 'Maybe wear short sleeves and lose the socks.'

'I have already lost the socks and the hot-water bottle and quilt: if I lose anything else then I'll be *cold*!' Neve protested and they were at an impasse. Of all the problems Neve had imagined coming between them, their incompatible body temperatures hadn't been one of them. It was just as well she hadn't started with Max's other annoying nocturnal habit of feeling her up in his sleep. 'We could sleep with a pillow between us.'

'That defeats the whole purpose of sleeping together.'

'Well, I'm not doing much sleeping when you're in the same bed as me.' Neve held up her hands. 'I can't see a way past this.'

Max was saved from having to reply when his BlackBerry rang. He looked at it helplessly. 'I have to get this.'

'I know you do,' Neve said, already halfway out of bed. 'I'm not mad at you, I'm really not, but I'm going to sleep on the sofa.'

Chapter Seventeen

It turned out that Neve's dream was alarmingly prophetic. The next day when she switched on her computer there was an email from her father (*In town mid-April, is your shower still leaking?*) and an imperious summons from the Archive's Board of Trustees, reminding Neve that the AGM was the following week and her attendance was mandatory.

And because bad luck always came in at least threes, there was also a letter from William on the doorstep, which was usually a cause for joyous celebration, except he'd skipped all the flowery reminiscences of their Oxford days for a very abrupt three sentences.

Have to be brief as I have a lecture in half an hour. Have you sent the Carr's Water Biscuits and the Sainsbury's Red Label teabags, as previously requested? Would very much appreciate it if you could ASAP.

There wasn't even a mention of Neve's last letter to him, which had taken her hours to write and had painstakingly compared their friendship to the relationship between the literary theorist Lou Andreas-Salome and the poet Rainer Maria Rilke, complete with quotations.

It put Neve in such a foul mood that she actually snapped at Mr Freemont when he told her off for getting back from lunch late because she'd had to queue for ages in Sainsbury's to buy the biscuits and teabags that William loved more than life itself – certainly more than he loved her.

Snapping at Mr Freemont was not a good tactical move when the AGM was so close, there were no funds coming in and no minor literary figures had had the decency to die recently. Neve had nothing to archive or transcribe, which normally would be all the incentive she needed to spend a couple of peaceful hours at the British Library, but she had an awful sense of foreboding that her name was top of the list of employees to be fired. What other reason could there be for Chloe and Rose to be avoiding her? Even Philip had joined their cabal, and whenever Neve happened upon the three of them whispering in the kitchen or in Rose's office, they'd immediately start talking in unnecessarily loud voices about whose turn it was to make tea or the ungodly stench Our Lady of the Blessed Hankie had left in the ladies' loos.

Neve took advantage of the downtime by working on her Lucy Keener biography so at least she looked busy when Mr Freemont did his hourly sweep of the offices, but on the inside, she was in torment.

Her mother was no help at all on Neve's work-related woes. 'I don't know why you still work at that library, they pay you a pittance,' she railed when Neve tried to talk to her about it. 'Have you thought any more about the Civil Service? Shall I put it into Google for you?'

Even an unexpected phone call from William to thank her for the speedy delivery of teabags and water biscuits failed to raise Neve's spirits. Usually, she could talk to William about work problems and he never once called her a librarian, but this time he was less than sympathetic.

'You're wasted there,' he said baldly, after Neve had spent twenty minutes detailing her latest conspiracy theory, which was that Chloe and Rose were going to stage a coup d'état, take down Mr Freemont, install Chloe as the Head Archivist, sack Neve for skiving off at the British Library and split her salary between the two of them. 'It was a good part-time job while you were studying for your MA, but it's not a career.'

'But I like working there,' Neve protested. 'Or I did, until I became a victim of Chloe's naked ambition.'

'This is a sign that you're meant to do a PhD. Then you can begin undergraduate teaching in your second year, and once you've finished your thesis, you'll be a shoo-in for a lecturer's position at a good redbrick university. We both know that you will sooner or later, Neve, so why not make it sooner?'

Neve didn't know any such thing. She was not cut out for teaching and, short of chopping off both arms and legs and her ears while she was at it, she couldn't think of anything that would make her less employable than spending five years writing a thesis about . . . God, she didn't even want to think about having to write a thesis on anything.

'Please, William, don't give me such a hard time about this,' Neve pleaded. 'Do you think I should send my CV to Senate House and the British Library? But the thing is, I know that Rose is really tight with the admin staff at both places, and they might say something to her.'

'You can't give up so easily,' William insisted with a touch of exasperation that Neve had never heard from him before, though she was exasperated herself at how whiny she sounded. 'It's one thing to leave of your own accord to pursue a PhD, but you can't go down without a fight. Don't be a quitter. It's not an attractive quality.'

In a horrible twist of irony, Max had said almost the same words to her when he'd woken up on the Monday after the sleepless Sunday night before. When she'd said that there was no point in a repeat of their disastrous attempt to sleep together, he'd told her, 'Nobody likes a quitter, Neve. It's not like I got much sleep either, with you tossing and turning and sighing every five minutes, but I'm prepared to stick it out.'

Neve could only silently gasp at the injustice of it all and she was still riled up about it a week later when they tried again. At least this time, there were no phone calls from LA publicists and she'd jettisoned the top quilt and the hot-water bottle, and had worn a short-sleeved T-shirt. To no avail. Within ten minutes of turning out the light, Max was fast asleep, snoring and doing a really good impression of an octopus – a very hot, very amorous octopus, which kept nudging her with its erection.

Unlike Neve, Max woke up in a sunny mood and even stayed for breakfast, though the previous Monday he'd left within ten minutes of getting up. Max's good humour didn't last long, however; his top lip curled until it was the same shape as the banana that Neve presented him with, along with a bowl of unsweetened muesli and soya milk.

'This is breakfast?' he asked incredulously. 'Can't I have toast?'

'Well, this is *your* breakfast,' Neve corrected him. 'I always work out on an empty stomach on Monday mornings and I don't have any bread in the house. Sorry.'

Neve didn't know it was possible to eat muesli resentfully, but Max managed it. She didn't want to start the new week on such a sour note, even though the thought of the Board of Trustees' meeting on Wednesday afternoon made her stomach clench. Which was another good reason not to eat breakfast; she wasn't sure she'd be able to keep anything down.

'Actually this muesli isn't too bad,' Max suddenly announced. 'As long as I make sure there are at least two raisins in every spoonful. And I can have coffee, can't I? You wouldn't deprive me of coffee.'

Three cups of espresso later, Max was restored to his usual vaguely chipper self and ready to leave. Neve walked with him and Keith to the bottom of the road, her mind already on her workout and what she'd say to Rose and Chloe, and even Philip, if she actually found some reserves of courage and confronted them about their whisper campaign. It was blatantly obvious that the three of them were planning to throw her under the bus to keep their own jobs. After all, there had been that time when Rose caught her sticking a personal letter in the post tray and . . .

'. . . and maybe during the week isn't such a good idea but we should have another crack at it next Sunday.'

Neve realised that Max was talking to her about something important, judging by his serious expression. Even Keith was gazing up at her solemnly.

'A crack at what?'

'Sleeping together!' Max jostled her arm. 'If we can't sleep together without you disappearing into the living room halfway through the night, then this relationship is doomed.'

'Pancake relationship,' Neve reminded him.

'Whatever! Do you know what an achievement it is for me to share a bed with a woman that I haven't had carnal knowledge of? And get up at six thirty without a word of complaint?' He nudged Neve's arm and gave her that cheeky smile that he seemed to think could get him out of any amount of hot water. 'I feel like I've grown as a person.'

'It would only be an achievement if I was your proper girlfriend and you actually wanted to have carnal knowledge of me but you managed to hold yourself back,' Neve bit out. 'But I'm not and you don't.'

'Christ! You can't have it both ways, Neve! You're the one who's saving it for that William bloke and I'm the one who's allowed a few kissing and groping rights before I have to stop.' Max scowled at her. 'And you are starting to sound like a proper girlfriend. You've got the nagging part down perfectly.'

'I've had no sleep,' Neve growled, and she didn't think she'd ever growled at anyone before. 'Have you any idea how hard it is to do a two-hour workout on no sleep?'

'I don't know and I don't care.'

They'd both stopped walking, all the better to stand still and glare at each other. Neve didn't know how long they stood there, but in the end she gave a tiny, defeated sigh. 'I haven't got time for this. Gustav will be furious if I'm late.'

She expected Max to rap out another 'What*ever*!' Instead, he took her chin in one hand. 'Are you all right?' he wanted to know. 'Is something bothering you, apart from our complete failure to sleep together?'

Neve hadn't told Max about the AGM and her fears of being sacked for gross misconduct. He never asked her about her work and was already on record as stating that the Archive was the last bastion of tweed-wearing lesbians and a far cry from his world of wall-to-wall parties and celebrity wrangling. And she certainly couldn't tell him that she and William had had their first ever argument.

'It's nothing. Just really dull work stuff. I'd tell you but it would render you catatonic,' she muttered, turning her head so Max had to let his hand fall away. 'I have to go. I'll call you in the week.'

Then she hurried away, because Gustav really was going to be furious with her if she didn't get a move on.

As she was about to cross over the road, some impulse made Neve turn around, if only to see Max and Keith walking in the opposite direction. But Max was still standing where she'd left him, and when he caught Neve's eye, instead of raising his hand and waving like a normal person, Max just stood there watching her so Neve had no option but to start walking again, her cheeks a fiery red as if she'd been caught doing something completely awful.

It was the kind of situation that was so out of Neve's remit that she longed to be able to talk to Chloe and ask her advice, which wasn't an option any more.

When she got home from work that evening she found a note from Charlotte shoved under her door. *Whn r u going 2 do smthng abt yr bike. Is totes in way. Won't tell u again!!!!!!!!!!!!!!* For a brief moment, a faint smile appeared on Neve's face and for an even briefer moment, she contemplated knocking on Charlotte's door to ask for relationship advice, if only because Charlotte's head might actually explode.

Anyway, even if Charlotte wasn't Charlotte, with pure evil running through her veins instead of blood, she was hardly an expert on relationships. Lately, she and Douglas kept having the same fight over and over again.

'Fucking shut up!'

'No, *you* fucking shut up!'

There was always Celia, but if Neve intimated that all was not right in pancake paradise, Celia would come up with fifty different variations on 'I told you so,' and she'd be unbelievably smug about it too. So when Neve went down to Celia and Yuri's flat the night before the AGM to pack Celia's suitcase because she was flying to Berlin to shoot fashion for *Skirt*, she resolved to keep her mouth shut.

It wasn't hard. Celia was far more interested in how many outfit options she'd need for five days, and while Neve diligently folded clothes and made sure all of Celia's many bottles and jars of beauty gloop were screwed tightly shut, Celia was on her iPhone checking the weather in Berlin, then she had to call Grace to find out how many outfits she was packing, and all that Neve had left to do was ball Celia's socks and put them in her shoes, when Celia finally deigned to speak to her.

'So, hey, meant to ask you if you're planning on dumping Max in the next couple of days?' she asked hopefully.

Neve's head shot up from her silent contemplation of Celia's suitcase. 'Why? Has he said something?'

Celia didn't notice Neve's distress as she was standing in front of the mirror in just pants and a T-shirt with a platform sandal on one foot and a peep-toe shoe boot on the other. 'Do I dare risk an open toe?' she mused, before she turned back to Neve. 'It's just it's his birthday this weekend and Grace says that if you're still faux dating, I should chip in more money for the Fashion Department's present. So, are you?'

As far as Neve knew she was, but if Max hadn't even told her it was his birthday then she didn't imagine she'd be faux dating for much longer. 'I suppose,' she said, without much enthusiasm.

'OK. Can you lend me fifty quid then?'

Neve tossed a balled-up pair of socks at Celia, which missed their target by a good few metres. 'No, I can't! It's three days until I get paid and I'm broke.' And now she had to buy a birthday present for Max too.

'But it's three days till I get paid too and I earn less money than you,' Celia pointed out.

It was hard to believe when Neve was barely earning fourteen thousand a year before tax that Celia had actually found a job that paid even less. 'But you don't have to pay rent or a mortgage.'

'Well, neither do you,' Celia sniffed. 'Come on, don't be tight.'

'I'm not being tight,' Neve said indignantly. 'You'd have loads of money if you didn't fritter it away on shoe boots and hot pants . . .'

'They're called short shorts, Grandma.'

'Well, I'm paying off two student loans and I have gym fees and Gustav fees – and have you any idea how much I spend a week on organic fruit and vegetables?' Neve demanded. 'I'm not lending you any more money. You never, ever pay me back.'

It was a fair point, because by Neve's reckoning, Celia owed her well over a thousand pounds, but it was something neither of them mentioned. Apart from now, because Neve was in a foul mood and Celia was the only person she dared take it out on.

'Snippy, much?' Celia kicked off her shoe boot and stood on one leg in her platform heel, but still managed to convey huge amounts of pathos. 'If you're not going to lend me money, then it would really help if you could dump Max so I only have to put in twenty quid.'

Neve hadn't considered it before, but dumping Max would be a solution to one of the many problems that was

217

weighing down on her. 'Well, I'll think about it,' she said and wasn't even attempting to be funny, but Celia grinned and pretended to check the calendar on her phone.

'Nuh-huh, Neevy! You said you'd date him for two months and you've still got another four weeks to go.' She gave her sister a stern look. 'You know what they say about quitters, don't you?'

Chapter Eighteen

Rose had ordered sandwiches from Pret A Manger for the AGM. They were arranged on platters in the Reading Room (the Archive was closed to visitors in honour of such an auspicious occasion) along with a tray of tired-looking fruit. Neve paused in the doorway and looked at the sandwiches in dismay – Rose knew she could only eat wraps because they had fewer carbs. She knew and she obviously didn't care because she already thought of Neve as an ex-colleague.

'Don't just stand there, Neevy,' Chloe grumbled from behind her. 'Move!'

The five Trustees always sat on the window side of the long table that ran the length of the room, and the Archive staff would cram themselves in along the other side. But it wasn't quite as simple as that, because no one wanted to get stuck next to Mr Freemont. Not just because he was grumpiness incarnate, but because he had severe odour issues, which was little wonder when he'd worn the same pair of grey trousers, grey shirt and maroon cardigan every day for the entire three years that Neve had worked at the Archive. Come rain, come shine, come blizzard, come heat-wave, Mr Freemont never deviated from his outfit and never took it off either, if the stench that emanated from him was anything to go by.

So choosing a seat for the AGM, or any meeting that Mr Freemont attended, was like a game of musical chairs. The rest of the staff jostled, side-stepped and, in the case of Chloe, body-checked, in their efforts to secure a chair as far away from Mr Freemont as possible. Right now, they were shuffling restlessly from foot to foot by the reception desk as they waited for Mr Freemont to enter the room and take his seat.

At five to one exactly, he bustled into the room, paused for one, suspense-filled moment, then purposefully strode to a chair exactly halfway down the table – but didn't sit down.

'Don't just stand there,' he demanded querulously of his staff. 'Sit!'

No one moved, apart from Neve who took a timid step forward.

'Don't do it, Neve,' Philip hissed in her ear but she ignored him because she was mad at him, and by inching herself ahead of the staff she was in prime position to gallop to the other end of the table when Mr Freemont sat down exactly level with the tray of sandwiches, which were positioned left of centre, just like he did every year.

Neve allowed herself a faint smile of triumph as Rose was almost sent flying by one of the part-time PhD students and lost precious seconds so she had no choice but to sit next to Mr Freemont, her face turned the other way and utter loathing oozing from her every pore.

After fifteen minutes of desultory chit-chat and eating those sandwiches that they were positive that Mr Freemont hadn't touched with his smelly fingers (it was an absolute, unequivocal certainty that he didn't wash his hands after he peed), the five Trustees trooped in.

There was the old man who'd fall asleep within the first five minutes. Behind him was the crusty Professor of Medieval History at University College London, who always wanted to know why they didn't archive any material written before the 1700s. Neve rather liked the dishevelled woman from the Arts Council but she didn't like Jacob

Morrison, literary super-agent, with his sharp suits, air of superiority and the way he always looked right through her. Bringing up the rear was the Chairwoman of the Board, Harriet Fitzwilliam-White, whose father had founded the Archive and generally regarded the staff as not mentally competent enough to protect his legacy. Last year, Neve thought that she and Rose might actually come to blows over the thorny topic of upgrading from Windows '98.

It was impossible for Neve to slump on her hard-backed chair like everyone else as the meeting started. She was far too anxious to slump and was mentally rehearsing the impassioned speech she'd give in defence of her work ethic when the moment arose.

The moment was taking a long time to arise. Instead, they spent a laborious hour going over the minutes of the last AGM, before moving on to the other items on the agenda.

It was the same as it ever was. The only good news was that they'd secured some funding from a couple of small bequests and a grant from a bunch of book-loving do-gooders – but it didn't seem like *much* funding. Certainly not enough to maintain four full-time members of staff, assorted part-timers and keep them in Post-it notes and teabags. Not that anyone else seemed particularly bothered, though it was hard to tell. When Neve scanned the assembled faces she was met with glazed eyes.

Mr Freemont was the only Archive employee who actually spoke, as he pedantically explained his criteria for choosing their latest acquisitions and mooted the possibility of having a more stringent vetting procedure for allowing access to the Archive. He'd had a real bee in his bonnet ever since he caught Our Lady of the Blessed Hankie popping a mint humbug into her mouth while she was in the Reading Room.

'. . . even though I'd like to draw your attention to the sign at Reception, which clearly states that all food and drink is strictly forbidden.'

Neve was starting to feel less anxious now and more like she might actually die from sheer boredom. She stifled a yawn and caught the eye of Mary Vickers from the Arts Council, who smiled at her.

'Well, that's certainly given us all something to think about, George,' Jacob Morrison suddenly said, cutting Mr Freemont off mid-rant. 'Shall we move on to Any Other Business now?'

'I hadn't finished,' Mr Freemont reminded them. 'I also wanted to talk about the umbrella-stand in—'

'Please, George, I would like to get out of here some time before midnight,' Mary Vickers said, with a rueful little smile, as if she was riveted by the conversation but had another very important engagement.

Mr Freemont settled back on his chair with an aggrieved huff and Neve gripped the edge of the table because Any Other Business could mean anything. Maybe Rose had also discovered that she sometimes faxed her mum in Spain when no one else was around; that was probably grounds for instant dismissal.

'So, Any Other Business?' Harriet Fitzwilliam-White looked around the table without much enthusiasm.

'Yes. Rose and I would like to discuss something,' Chloe said, actually daring to stand up. 'We have a proposal to take the Archive into the twenty-first century and bring in new revenue too.'

'I thought we'd talked about this, Chloe,' Mr Freemont snapped, spraying breadcrumbs across the table because he was in the middle of stuffing down the last prawn-cocktail sandwich. 'And I made my thoughts perfectly clear.'

'Yes, you did,' Chloe said evenly, looking directly at Jacob Morrison as she spoke, and Neve noticed that Chloe was wearing a much darker lipstick than she normally did and a smart grey dress and nipped-in jacket that was an upgrade on her usual jeans and jumper. 'But maybe I wasn't being perfectly clear, as you didn't seem to grasp the concept of bringing in our own revenue streams so we're not reliant on donations.'

'That's certainly something I'd like to hear,' Jacob Morrison said, lounging back on his chair. 'Who doesn't love a new revenue stream?'

'It won't take long,' Rose said crisply. 'I made a PowerPoint presentation.'

There was a faint murmur rising up. Neve still wasn't completely on board, as she had a horrible feeling that one way of bringing in a new revenue stream was by getting rid of her and using her annual salary of fourteen thousand, three hundred and forty-seven pounds (before tax) to secure some hot literary collection. She also hadn't known that the Archive possessed a computer that was capable of producing a PowerPoint presentation without crashing.

Everyone else seemed a lot more excited as Chloe started to talk and Rose pressed buttons on an ancient laptop. Their plan was to start digitising the Archive and introducing subscription charges, as well as joining up with other literary archives and academic libraries to create a database of dead people's writings. Apparently there were all sorts of organisations queuing up to fund such an innovative project.

It actually sounded do-able, though Neve could see a lot of scanning in her near future, if she got to keep her job. Maybe they'd want to hire some computer whiz kid, she thought, as she looked down the table and saw Mr Freemont's head sinking lower and lower in defeat, which made the three greasy strands of hair that he combed over his ghostly white bald pate even more prominent.

She couldn't help but feel sorry for him, and not for the first time either. Yes, he smelled awful and he was cantankerous, curmudgeonly and also rather misogynistic because he always tried to turn down any new acquisitions from women writers, but Neve knew what it was like not to fit in. She doubted that Mr Freemont had ever fitted in anywhere in his life, so it was no wonder that he'd turned his back on personal hygiene and good social skills.

Chloe and Rose had finished their presentation and shared a small, smug smile as absolutely everyone, except Neve and Mr Freemont, fired questions at them, which was absolutely unheard-of in an AGM. Usually you only spoke when you were spoken to and spent the rest of the time avoiding eye-contact.

Jacob Morrison had whipped out his BlackBerry and was pencilling in a meeting with Chloe, Rose and Harriet Fitzwilliam-White to discuss the matter further. Chloe was beaming, Rose was serene in her victory and Mr Freemont kept opening his mouth, only to close it again, as he realised that digitising the Archive was going to happen whether he liked it or not. Neve saw Philip give her a surreptitious thumbs-up, and light finally dawned: Mr Freemont was the one being thrown under the bus, not her.

Neve fidgeted in her chair, keen for the meeting to end now so she could beetle to the safety of the back office in the basement and avoid Mr Freemont, preferably for the rest of the year, because he was going to be in a *filthy* mood after this.

'There was one other thing we wanted to discuss,' Rose announced, once the hubbub had died down. 'It's about Neve.'

Everyone turned to look at her, including old Mr Granville, who hadn't been able to sleep in all the excitement.

Neve felt a blush scorching her cheeks, which was odd when the rest of her had suddenly gone icy cold. 'Look, if it's about that letter,' she stumbled, 'the thing is . . . there was a queue at the Post Office and—'

'It's about Neve,' Rose repeated, glaring Neve into silence, 'and a woman called Lucy Keener who died a couple of years ago. She never had anything published . . .'

'Actually she did have two poems in *Time and Tide*,' Neve interrupted, then lapsed into silence when Alice, one of the part-timers sitting next to her, gave her thigh a warning pinch.

'Which is probably why Mr Freemont didn't feel that there was a place for her literary estate in the Archive,' Rose continued smoothly, as if Neve hadn't spoken. 'While this is perfectly understandable, we think that decision should be reviewed.'

'It's something we all feel very strongly about, thanks to Neve, who has tirelessly championed Lucy Keener,' Philip said, as soon as Rose had got to the end of her sentence, and Neve wondered if they'd actually rehearsed this, because, as Chloe started talking about how much everyone had loved reading *Dancing on the Edge of the World*, it was coming across as very polished.

She sat there in frozen silence as, one by one, the other members of staff chimed in with the Lucy love. She didn't know whether to be mad at them for going behind her back or getting up so she could hug each and every one of them. She'd never have had the guts to plead Lucy's case before the Trustees.

'And Neve has even started writing a biography of Lucy Keener,' Philip finished proudly. 'Haven't you, Neevy?'

'Well, I wouldn't call it a biography,' she mumbled, head bent so she could stare at Mr Freemont's trail of bread-crumbs. 'It started off as a timeline of Lucy's life as I tried to collate her correspondence with her diaries and it kind of, well . . . it just sort of happened.' She frowned and came to a grinding and agonising halt.

There was silence, then someone coughed and Neve looked up to see Mary Vickers giving her an encouraging smile and she even had Jacob Morrison's full attention, which wasn't necessarily a good thing.

'So, Neve, can you tell us a little bit about the mysterious and unpublished Lucy Keener?' he asked.

She stammered out the first few chronological facts about Lucy, then paused. This wasn't hard, they weren't asking her to find the square root of something, and she owed it to herself and God, she owed it to Lucy Keener most of all, not to screw this up. And after Neve thought that, the rest was easy.

Neve didn't know how long she talked, though at one point, the part-timers left and Rose got up to turn on the lights, but eventually when she could hear that her voice was growing hoarse, she tried to wrap it up.

'. . . and she was ashamed of Charles for betraying his country and working for the KGB, but she also felt partly responsible because she'd introduced him to Socialism. When he left his wife and family and defected to Russia, she went with him . . . it was the only way that they could ever be together. But she was horrified by what she saw over there and she came back to England two years later to find herself completely ostracised, not just for defecting but because she'd run away with a married man, a member of the Establishment who'd turned traitor, and it destroyed her. She didn't write anything for thirty years, then she started again. Her last poems and short stories, they're just . . . well, they're kind of heart-breaking.'

There was another silence when Neve stopped and swallowed hard because she hadn't thought she'd get so emotional and choked up talking about Lucy. She smiled weakly and waited for someone to say something.

'This Lucy Keener, she certainly seems to have had quite an effect on you,' Harriet Fitzwilliam-White said to Neve. It was the first time she'd ever spoken to Neve. 'I can remember when Charles Holden defected; the papers hinted that there might be a woman involved, but they never named her.'

'Well, the family of Laura Holden, Charles's wife, were very well connected and they tried to keep as many details out of the press as possible,' Neve explained. 'It was bad enough that Charles was a traitor, without being an adulterer too.'

'I should probably read this novel then,' Jacob Morrison said, although he didn't sound overly keen at the prospect.

'You can't.' Mr Freemont had been silent all this time, though periodically his tongue would slide out of his mouth so he could moisten his chapped lips. 'Neve was under strict instructions to send everything pertaining to Lucy Keener back to the solicitor administering her estate.'

'George, I think it's fairly obvious that everything pertaining to Lucy Keener *wasn't* sent anywhere,' Mary Vickers said gently. She seemed highly amused by it all. 'It's very exciting. Maybe Ms Slater has discovered a new literary star.'

'So, Neve, do you have a copy of this novel?' Jacob Morrison asked, and for the life of her, Neve didn't know whether still being in possession of all of Lucy's papers was a good thing or a sackable thing. She threw Chloe an imploring look.

'It's being stored off-site,' Chloe said, which sounded a lot better than admitting it was in an archive box in Neve's spare room. 'You'll want to see the first few chapters of the biography Neevy's written too. Absolutely unputdownable.'

'Why don't you just bang me out a synopsis instead? No more than two pages,' Jacob suggested, reaching into the inner pocket of his suit jacket to extract a business card. 'You can include it with a copy of the manuscript of er, *Dancing on the Edge of the World*, is it?'

Neve stretched across to take the card and said thank you and smiled and nodded, but she knew that Jacob had only asked her to write a synopsis to be polite, in much the same way that he'd probably read the first page of *Dancing on the Edge of the World* and decide that it had no literary merit. He was a super-agent with a couple of Man Booker Prize winners on his client roster and at least three sex-and-shopping novelists who were always on the bestseller lists. He wouldn't 'get' the novel and Neve almost didn't want to send him the manuscript because she felt fiercely protective of Lucy – which had to be the reason why the universe (or Lucy's solicitor) had entrusted her literary estate to Neve.

The meeting was finally wrapping up. Neve was painfully aware of Mr Freemont's squinty eyes resting first on her and then on Chloe as Harriet Fitzwilliam-White thanked them all for attending, as if they'd had any choice in the matter. Then the Trustees were getting up, Jacob Morrison slipping Chloe another one of his cards as he walked past her.

Chloe, Rose, Mr Freemont and Neve sat there listening to the sound of five pairs of feet tramping over the parquet flooring in the foyer. Mr Freemont waited until they heard the door close behind them, then turned to Neve, his weak chin wobbling in fury. 'Well, I would never have expected that from *you*, Miss Slater,' he hissed, as Neve cowered back in her chair. She'd known that she'd bear the brunt of Mr Freemont's anger. He wouldn't dare start on Rose or Chloe, because they didn't even pretend to respect his authority. 'I expressly ordered you to return those papers. What you've done . . . well, it's theft.'

'Oh no, it isn't, George,' Rose snapped, as Chloe took advantage of the distraction to slip out of the room. 'It's not at all like theft. It's a pity you don't spend less time writing me memos about my excessive use of Post-it notes and spend more time thinking of ways to generate new business.'

'We're not about generating new business; we're about protecting a literary heritage,' Mr Freemont snapped back. Once they got on to this particular subject, they'd be going at it for hours, so Neve felt perfectly justified in jumping up and racing for the door with a muttered, 'Sorry,' flung over her shoulder.

'I want a word with you!' she squeaked furiously at Chloe who was hurrying down the stairs that led to the basement. 'Stop right there!'

Chloe didn't stop, but waited for Neve at the bottom of the steps, hands on her hips and an innocent expression on her face. 'It's all right, Neevy,' she said demurely. 'No need to thank me.'

'I should thank you for completely blind-siding me?' Neve protested. 'A warning would have been nice.'

'Well, see, I did think about it, but Rose and Philip said you'd pretend that you were OK with it, then you'd have a panic attack five minutes before we went into the meeting and chicken out,' Chloe revealed.

'I wouldn't do that,' Neve said, frowning as she thought about it. 'Except, I would totally do that.'

'Not telling you was a kindness,' Chloe went on, tucking her arm into Neve's. 'And it worked out all right in the end, didn't it?'

'I don't think that Jacob Morrison is going to like Lucy's writing. There's hardly any sex in the novel.'

'Apart from that bit in the alley during the blackout,' Chloe reminded her as they entered the kitchen, because it went without saying that they both needed a restorative cup of tea. 'That was seriously hot without even mentioning specific body parts. Anyway, he's only one agent . . .'

'A super-agent!'

'Yes, but if he doesn't get it, then someone else will.' Chloe filled the kettle. 'And that someone else will want to represent you too, as Lucy Keener's official biographer.'

'I'm not an official anything. Honestly, I only started writing it just to see if I could.' Neve shook her head. 'I just . . . it's not about me, Lucy *deserves* to be published.'

'So, what did I miss?' asked Philip from the doorway, because he'd scarpered from the meeting with the rest of the part-time staff an hour before it had ended.

As Neve took over the tea-making, Chloe started to fill him in on the details just as Rose bustled in, pink-cheeked and irritated from having words with Mr Freemont. 'That horrible little man,' she said to no one in particular. 'When will he put us all out of our misery and take early retirement?'

It was a rhetorical question that came up at least once every day, so no one even bothered to reply. Besides, Neve had a question of her own.

'So, why didn't you tell me about digitising the Archive? And you made a PowerPoint presentation,' she added accusingly. 'I could have helped.'

Philip put his arm round her stiff shoulders. 'Two words: Secret Santa!'

Neve wriggled out from under Philip's arm, because the three of them were laughing. At her, not with her. Because there was nothing about the Secret Santa affair of last year that Neve found remotely amusing. 'I didn't mean to tell Alice that you were her Secret Santa but she knew that I knew and she wouldn't stop pestering me about it. And then she told me that she'd got Chloe . . .' Neve shoved her hands into her hair, dislodging the pins that were holding her bun in place. 'None of it was my fault. It was everybody else's fault for telling me who they'd got. I cracked under the pressure.'

'Which is why we didn't tell you about Operation Digital,' Rose said. 'Thirty minutes and you'd have confessed everything to Freemont.'

'Not thirty minutes,' Neve grumbled.

'You'd have maybe held out for a day,' Chloe conceded. 'Come on, Neevy, we didn't tell you for your own good.'

'It was horrible. I knew something was up and I thought that you were going to tell the Trustees to fire me to save some money,' Neve admitted, and as she heard herself say the words out loud, she realised how highly unlikely that scenario would have been.

Philip shook his head. 'Why would you think something like that?'

'Yeah, why would you?' Chloe pulled a hurt face. 'I'm actually quite offended that you did. You're one of my best friends, Neve!'

Neve squirmed helplessly. 'I'm sorry, but all that

whispering in corners brought out the worst in me. I'm very prone to paranoia when people won't make eye-contact with me.'

Rose was certainly making eye-contact with Neve; eye-contact that conveyed disappointment and disbelief. 'I think it's time you went on another Goddess Workshop, because the first one obviously didn't take.'

Chloe had other ideas. 'You know what?' she said, putting down her mug on the draining board. 'Tea isn't going to cut it. Let's go down the pub.'

Chapter Nineteen

An hour after she'd got home, Neve was sitting fully clothed in her bath, laptop on her knees and a towel wedged under the door so Charlotte wouldn't be able to hear her as she started typing her synopsis.

And though Neve didn't want to jinx herself, it was going very well. She'd written her name and the working title of the biography: *Falling off the Edge of the World* without pausing. She'd even managed a whole paragraph explaining why she was writing a biography about a woman that no one had ever heard of, and now she was staring at a crack in the ceiling and trying to decide if Jacob Morrison needed to know the name of the grammar school that Lucy had attended.

Neve looked at Lucy's diaries neatly stacked on her bathroom stool, and was just hoping that inspiration would leap up and seize her by the throat, when her phone rang.

She snatched it up and answered it within two rings because it was just the kind of noise that usually sent Charlotte into a frenzy.

'Hello?' she whispered.

'Angelface, it's Max. How are you?'

Now that the AGM was over and Neve felt more in control of that aspect of her life, she also felt better equipped to deal with Max. She wasn't sure she had the guts to dump him, but she wasn't going to take any nonsense either. Or she was going to try really hard not to take any nonsense. 'I'm fine,' she said quietly. 'How are *you*?'

'All the better for hearing your voice, gorgeous.' Max's voice sounded as if it had been oiled and Neve knew him well enough to know that when he was tossing endearments around like confetti at a wedding, it could mean only one thing.

'If you want a favour from me, then just come right out and ask me, and if it's something I want to do, then I'll do it,' she told him.

Neve heard Max's swift intake of breath. 'Oh, so I'm not allowed to compliment you now, is that it?'

She didn't have the energy for this, not after such an emotionally draining day and two glasses of Pinot Grigio without even a hint of spritz about them. 'Max, I don't want to have a fight but is there something you need from me?'

Max paused and Neve swore to herself that if the next words out of his mouth were in any way combative, she'd pull the plug on their pancake relationship there and then, she really would. Or she'd send him an email once he'd rung off.

'Well, yeah, there was this teensy little favour I wanted to ask you,' Max said finally, and despite her earlier statement, Neve was instantly suspicious. Now that Max had spat it out, she remembered that when people wanted a favour from her, it usually involved Celia borrowing money or Rose trying to stick her with a load of filing. 'OK, ask away,' she said, trying to sound enthusiastic.

'My dog-sitter's just called and he won't take Keith while I'm in LA because he says that Keith terrorises his Cocker Spaniel, though I think it's the other way round,' Max burst out indignantly. 'Christ, the dog's called Aloysius. It automatically makes you want to terrorise him. And yeah, Keith barks at other dogs but it's a nervous bark and he'd never—'

'Do you want *me* to take Keith?' Neve interrupted eagerly. 'I'd love to!'

'Derek says he'll still walk him during the day but you'd have to give him a key and I know it's asking a lot . . .'

'Max, it's no problem. I'd love to have a little doggy flatmate.'

'You're using the creepy voice again,' Max reminded her sternly. 'Look, are you sure you don't mind?'

'Not at all,' Neve assured him. 'Keith might even keep Charlotte at bay. I don't think she can tell a nervous bark from a bark that says, "If you don't stop screaming at Neve, I'm going to rip out your jugular."'

'Not that Keith would ever rip out anyone's jugular.'

'Of course he wouldn't, but Charlotte doesn't know that. And he can come over on Sunday with you and settle in and I can take him running with me. He'd love that.'

'I can't put him in kennels for a week, he'd have a nervous breakdown.'

'Well, you don't have to,' Neve said. 'Honestly, you must have known I'd say yes.'

'Honestly? After Monday, I thought you might tell me to fuck off.'

Neve heard a noise from the flat below and froze for a second. The front door slammed and she held her breath, but the sound of footsteps was getting fainter, instead of reaching a crescendo as they approached her landing. Even so, she lowered her voice. 'I wouldn't have done that, and not even because I don't say that word.'

'Well, you might have told me to fuck off really politely,' Max chuckled. 'Why do you keep whispering? Are you with someone?'

'I'm at home,' Neve said, still in a whisper. 'I think Charlotte's just gone out but she and Douglas have been rowing all week and it makes her really trigger-happy with the broom so I'm doing some work in the bathroom. That way, she can only hear me if she goes to the loo.'

'Sweetheart, this is no way to live,' Max said gently. 'You can't let her get to you.'

The way that Max called her 'sweetheart', not in his usual careless, almost mocking way, but as if the word encapsulated exactly how he felt about her, made Neve's throat ache. 'I know. It's just now we're locked into this cycle and I don't know how to break it.'

'Bit like you and me and these stupid arguments we keep having, isn't it?' Max said, and it was the last thing Neve expected him to say. 'Look, Neevy, I talk a good game, but most of it is bullshit and you shouldn't take it to heart so much.' Over the phone, with the really good acoustics of her tiled bathroom, every sniff and snort and breath was amplified so Neve could hear the reticence in his voice. 'It's just you seemed really sad on Monday morning. Like you felt completely defeated. Am I making you that unhappy?'

Neve shook her head in disbelief. 'No. No! I mean, the sleeping together is getting me down and this whole dating experiment is much harder than I thought it would be, but that's not really why I was down on Monday.' She paused. 'There was a situation at work, but it's all better now.'

'What kind of situation?' Max asked.

'It's really sweet of you to ask, and I do appreciate it, but we both know that my job isn't the most interesting topic of conversation.'

'Neve, you're killing me just a little bit here,' Max groaned. 'Will you please tell me what evil has been going down at the Archive?'

Max was making an effort, even though Neve had already said that she'd be happy to dog-sit, and he hadn't called the Archive 'that library', so Neve decided to take him at his word. 'Well, we had our annual meeting with this Board of Trustees,' she began hesitantly, but she soon got into her stride and told Max all about the whispered conversations she'd kept breaking up and how she'd let her imagination and suspicions run wild. She told him about the coup d'état at the AGM. She even told him about the biography and how she was completely flummoxed at the thought of writing a two-page synopsis. 'I don't understand it,' she said at last. 'I've already written six chapters and now I get writer's block. Worse! I have writer's paralysis and it's not even as if I think that Jacob Morrison is going to like Lucy's novel, much less my amateur attempts at a biography, but I have to at least try. Oh God, I'm not sure I can do this.'

Max didn't say she could, despite all evidence to the contrary. And he didn't try and give her a 'buck up, kiddo' pep talk. He simply said, 'Why didn't you tell me any of this?'

'I don't know,' Neve admitted. 'I don't have a very interesting job and you think the Archive is populated by cardigan-wearing lesbians.'

'I can't decide if you have a low opinion of me or a low opinion of yourself.' Max sighed. 'Didn't I just tell you that most of the stuff that comes out of my mouth is utter crap?'

'I'm sorry,' Neve whispered. 'I wish I wasn't like this. I know it's tiresome and boring.'

'You're not boring, Neevy,' Max said, as if he really meant it. 'Synopses are an absolute bitch to write. I hate them. Just write everything down that you think you need to say, don't look at it for at least twenty-four hours, then start editing.'

'Oh! I used to do that when I was writing essay outlines at Oxford,' Neve said. 'That's a big help. Thank you.'

But Max wasn't done. 'You can tell me stuff, you know. I tell you stuff.'

Neve closed her eyes and when she opened them, she decided that if Max was going to be so forthcoming, then maybe she could be too. 'Max, we both know there's a lot of things that you don't tell me. Like, you didn't tell me that it's your birthday on Saturday. I had to find out from Celia.'

Max made a dismissive noise. 'Birthday shmirthday.'

'So, what's the plan for Saturday night?' Neve persisted.

'Don't be mad at me.'

The moment he said that, Neve could feel her hackles rise. 'Why would I be mad at you?' she asked, her eyes narrowing. 'What have you done?'

'Next Saturday . . . it's this thing . . . Mandy's booked a

table at the Ivy for me and her and our respective agents so we can talk about the next book.' He paused. 'Sorry, it was sorted ages ago.'

Neve was appalled. 'But it's a special day!' she exclaimed. 'You have to do something that isn't a business meeting disguised as a birthday dinner.'

'Well, then she's going to drag me off clubbing and it's not my actual birthday until Sunday but I have to fly out to LA the next day . . .'

'We could go bowling. Celia and I always go bowling on our birthdays.'

'Please, God, no. Never again,' Max said faintly. 'Have you forgotten how much I sucked at bowling?'

'But if you did want to do something on your actual birthday with me . . .' Neve trailed off as she realised how presumptuous she was being. 'I know you've got to get up early on Monday but you have to come round to my place to drop off Keith and I . . . I could cook you your favourite meal, anything you want, as long as it doesn't involve making pasta from scratch. I'll even cook something heaving with butter and cream and lard.'

'Can I have roast chicken with roast potatoes, and can you make proper Yorkshire puddings?' Max sounded wistful. 'I'd like that.'

'Of course I can. I have Yorkshire blood running through my veins,' Neve declared, though she was pretty sure that she didn't even own a mixing bowl. 'And you get to pick the DVD and it doesn't have to be a chick flick. Honestly, I'll watch a mafia film or something really violent by Quentin Tarantino that's full of popular culture references that I absolutely won't get.'

'You've got yourself a deal then,' Max said, and Neve was sure he was smiling. She was also sure that it was probably time to wrap things up.

'Well, I suppose . . .'

'Neevy? I don't know if I've mentioned it but Mandy's

237

getting married in Manchester in a couple of weeks' time and I think you should come with me. It's a Thursday to Monday deal so I don't know if it would be a problem taking the time off work.' She heard him swallow. 'What do you think?'

'Who's she getting married to? Oh! It's a footballer. Darren Somebody.'

'How can you not know this stuff?' Max asked in an exasperated voice. 'Do you read the newspapers?'

'I don't have to,' Neve said defensively. 'My specialist area is British literature between the wars, and the papers are full of depressing stuff about the economy and terrorism that I don't need to know. Why is it a whole weekend?'

'They're getting married on the Saturday, after all the guests have relinquished cameras and phones because they've sold the rights to *Voila* magazine, but there's a cocktail party on the Thursday evening and Mandy's really nice and her family have been really good to me and I want you to meet them.'

'As what, your girlfriend?' Neve stopped. 'They're not going to believe that I'm your girlfriend.'

'Why wouldn't they?' Max demanded.

'Because of the way I look and well, because of the way I dress and because I haven't got much to talk about that isn't British literature between the wars.'

'I thought I was the one who talked utter crap,' Max said very tersely. 'Are you going to come to the wedding with me?'

'Can I think about it?'

'No, you have to decide right here, right now,' Max insisted.

'That's not fair!'

'If I give you time to think about it, you'll come up with a hundred lame reasons why you can't go. And you never know, Neve, if you do come, you might have fun. You were meant to be having more fun, remember?' It was just as well that Max delivered that insightful glimpse into her psyche with his most playful tone so it was impossible to take offence, which was a pity, because a WAG wedding would be sheer hell.

'I seem to recall that I did have some fun once in 2005.' She hoped that cracking a joke during these fraught negotiations might make Max soften.

'What's the worst that could happen?' he demanded. 'You get to drink free champagne and mix with some Premier Division footballers and their wives and girlfriends. That's not so bad.'

'The worst that could happen is that I'll walk in there with you and they'll all think I'm a badly dressed, dull as mud, fat *blimp*.' It was the constant voice nagging in her ear, and Neve couldn't believe that she'd said the words out loud, though from Max's bitten-off groan, she probably had. 'For example.'

'You have the lowest self-esteem of anyone I've ever met,' Max said quietly. 'It'll be a fun weekend where we get all gussied up and spend seventy-two hours mocking everyone and everything in sight. It's very hard to mock when you're flying solo.'

That did sound like fun. Sort of. 'Does it really mean that much to you that I'm there for mocking duties?'

'I wouldn't have asked otherwise. I could have taken one of the *Skirt* girls or, y'know, picked someone up in a club in Manchester on Friday night,' Max revealed, and Neve felt something that might have been her heart plummet. 'But I don't want to do that. Not just because I'm sick of doing that but because I want to go with you.'

The non-specified internal organ hoisted itself up to its proper resting place. 'But I have nothing to wear!'

Max laughed. 'You really are starting to sound like a proper girlfriend. Wear that dress you had on the first night we met.'

'But it's black. Isn't it bad luck to wear black to a

wedding?' Not that she'd said she was going for definite.

'They're having a black and white theme, probably so Mandy can really stand out in a pink wedding dress, or leopardprint. She does love her leopardprint,' Max mused. 'And they're putting us up at Malmaison and I'm going to drive up there so you'll be delivered door to door and—'

'It's all right, you can stop with the hard sell,' Neve sighed. 'I'll come. I'll mock. I'll wear something black.'

'Well, OK, then. Actually I thought I'd have a harder time persuading you,' Max said with another chuckle. 'So, we're sorted then?'

Neve murmured her agreement and stared stonily at her laptop, which she'd have to fire back up once she was off the phone.

'And we'll have one last crack at sleeping together on Sunday and if you still can't get the hang of it, we'll leave it.'

The relief that Neve felt almost rivalled the relief from earlier that afternoon when she'd realised that her friends still liked her and she still had a job. 'Well, at least we're very good at the kissing part,' she said. 'I think I've got the hang of that.'

'Gold star every time,' Max said. 'And remember, you can tell me about anything that's bugging you and as long as it's not about the carb content in whatever I'm eating, there'll be no judgement.'

'Well, that goes the same for you,' Neve replied, her voice wobbling slightly because she was touched beyond all measure. 'Even work stuff. Well, especially work stuff because I'm an impartial third party.'

There was silence, but it wasn't awkward. It seemed to Neve that it was charged with something deep and significant but she didn't know exactly what it was until Max said, 'I think we're having a moment, aren't we?'

'We totally are,' she agreed. Then she spotted a book in the pile on the floor that was the answer to all her immediate problems. 'Sorry, Max, but I think the moment's over. I've just found my inspiration.'

'Well, I guess they're called moments because they don't last very long. Get back to work and I'll see you Sunday.'

Neve finished the call and reached for the book she'd spotted, then she reopened her laptop and began to type.

As she moved through the rest of the week, Neve felt a vague, nagging discontent, as if she'd forgotten to turn off the oven or had misplaced her keys. Work, workouts, working and then reworking the synopsis – instead of feeling as if she had a safe, comfortable little routine, it was starting to seem as if Neve was stagnating, standing still rather than moving forward. The only bright spot was sending *Dancing on the Edge of the World* and a copy of her synopsis (after it had been approved by Chloe, Rose and Philip) off to Jacob Morrison. As Neve handed the Special Delivery package over to a Post Office employee, she vowed that once it was out of sight, she was going to do her darnedest to make sure it was out of mind too.

Then there was the prospect of a Max-less Saturday night, which felt downright wrong. Max *was* Saturday night and had been for the last few weeks, but when Neve finished her afternoon workout with Gustav and she told him she didn't have any plans, he invited her out for dinner with him and his boyfriend Harry, which was always a treat.

Not only was it a novelty to see Gustav in casualwear, even if it was all black like his gym clothes, but Neve adored Harry, six foot four inches of strapping jovial Australian who always told Gustav off when it was obvious that he was mentally calculating how he'd make Neve work off the calories in every mouthful of food she ate.

But the best thing about going out with Gustav and Harry was that Harry would always get Gustav drunk (which wasn't hard, since he had even less tolerance for alcohol than Neve did) and Gustav was a very giggly drunk. By the time Harry's pudding arrived with three spoons, Gustav's head was on Neve's shoulder and he kept patting her breast in an avuncular manner, even though Neve kept telling him not to.

'If I wasn't homosexual, I'd love you even more than I do, Neve,' he said, nuzzling against her neck. 'You remind me of my mother.'

'Aw honey, you must feel so proud,' Harry said between guffaws, as Neve tried to make sure that Gustav didn't dribble down her dress, which was dry-clean only.

'Gustav, if you don't get off me, I'm going to eat all of Harry's chocolate fudge cake,' Neve said warningly, but Gustav just snuffled happily.

'You always smell nice,' he remarked. 'Even when you're very sweaty.'

'I think it's time to get this lightweight home,' Harry said, and Gustav smiled slyly at Neve.

'I love Harry too,' he confided. 'He has a huge penis.'

Neve was still laughing as she helped Harry to put Gustav in the back of a taxi. 'I'm going to remember this conversation and bring it up every time you try to make me do jumping jacks,' she said to Gustav as he lolled on the seat and blew her kisses until the cab pulled away.

She was left standing in the middle of Old Compton Street at nine on a Saturday night, and even though she knew that Charlotte was in Brighton for a hen weekend, Neve didn't feel like going home.

If she'd been with Max he'd have come up with half a dozen places to go or things to see, but Max didn't have the monopoly on having fun, Neve decided as she walked down the escalator at Leicester Square tube station and in an audacious move headed for the southbound platform. Chloe's band, The Fuck Puppets, were playing in Brixton, and even though Neve tried to avoid screechy guitars and south London at all costs, she could stick both of them out for a couple of hours.

'Oh my God, did you get stopped at Border Control?' Chloe asked tartly, when she discovered Neve queuing to get in. Then she gave Neve a sudden, fierce hug. 'Let me stick your name on the guest-list.'

Simply turning up at a gig (a gig!) in a spur-of-the-moment, off-the-cuff, completely spontaneous way gave Neve a giddy thrill at her own daring, which carried her through the rest of the evening, even though The Fuck Puppets were very screechy and someone spilled their drink over her. The audience was a strange mix of emo-kids and young academics, and Neve didn't just cling to her colleagues from the Archive as she'd planned to, but bumped into a couple of people she knew from Oxford and managed to strike up a conversation with a man whom she recognised from the British Library, who was also obsessed with Our Lady of the Blessed Hankie who made guest appearances there too. He even made interested noises about going for a coffee the next time their paths crossed in the Humanities Reading Room. It wasn't a date because he had really bad halitosis and she had Max, but it still put a small, proud smile on Neve's face, which was still there when she got home at a scarcely believable two thirty in the morning.

Chapter Twenty

Neve wasn't smiling when she opened the front door the next afternoon and found Max leaning against the wall all puffy-eyed, pale-faced and unshaven.

'You're two hours late and you look awful,' Neve said, as she crouched down to pet Keith.

'I feel awful,' Max moaned. 'I have a fucking monumental hangover and I thought the fresh air might make me feel better, but actually it made me want to die.'

'I have no sympathy for you. It's entirely self-inflicted.' Neve stepped aside to let him stagger through the door. 'It's as well that I've only just put the chicken on,' she added, flushing slightly because the only reason the chicken was late going into the oven was because she'd spent two hours failing to make Yorkshire puddings from scratch and then William had emailed her unexpectedly from Rhode Island where he was giving a paper and needed help sourcing some quotations.

'Not sure I can keep anything down right now,' Max said, as he collapsed on the bottom stair. 'When will I learn not to mix grape and grain?'

All the good work of their last telephone conversation was rapidly unravelling, Neve thought as she bit down on an angry tirade about the organic, free-range chicken that she'd just stuffed and trussed.

'I might be able to manage a small cup of espresso,' Max said pitifully, just as the door to the ground-floor flat opened and Celia stuck her head through the gap.

'Keep the noise down,' she snapped. 'I have a hangover and jet lag and I don't need to hear you two having a lover's tiff.'

'We aren't,' Neve rapped back. 'And you can't have jet lag from a two-hour flight from Berlin.'

'Actually, you can.' Celia stopped to sniff the air. 'Hmmm, something smells good. Is it chicken? Is there enough for me?'

'No,' Max said from the stairs, as he lifted his head to give Celia a baleful glare. 'It's my special birthday tea. No presents, no admittance.'

'Are you going to let him talk to me like that?' Celia demanded of her sister. 'Can you bring me down a plate when it's ready? Lots of potatoes and . . . Fuck! What the fuck is that and why is it growling at me?'

Keith had been hiding behind Max, but now he'd rested his snout on Max's shoulder to see where the noise was coming from. Because it was coming from a tall girl with sticky-up hair and ghostly white skin, it was a perfectly normal reaction to flatten your ears and growl.

'It's Keith, Max's dog,' Neve explained, rushing over to pet Keith, who even bared his teeth at her, until she held out her hand to show she didn't have any concealed weapons. 'He's growling because you're giving off a really hostile vibe. He's more scared of you than you are of him.'

'People always say that about dogs, right before the dog rips their arm off,' Celia insisted, inching away from Keith who refused to stop growling. 'I'm going back to bed now. You can text me when you're just about to come down with my dinner.'

Neve and Max both winced as Celia slammed her door.

'Can you manage the stairs?' Neve asked tartly, as she stepped past Max. 'Or I could throw down a blanket and a couple of pillows?'

'I'll be all right,' Max said bravely. 'I just need to lie down.'

It was Max's birthday and he was perfectly entitled to

spend it nursing a hangover, but Neve had planned all sorts of treats for him and blown half her weekly budget in the process, so she felt rather aggrieved that all he wanted to do was collapse face down on her sofa when he got to her flat.

'Coffee,' he mumbled. 'I need coffee.'

Neve took her sweet time making coffee, especially as there was another email from William waiting for her. *You're an angel and a lifesaver*, she read, as she waited for the kettle to boil. *I don't know what I'd do without you and I hope I'm never in a position to find out.*

William really was a prize among men, compared to Max who'd managed the difficult task of rolling on to his back while she'd been out of the room, and now had his sneakers resting on her favourite cushion.

'Have you got the energy to pour the coffee yourself or do you need me to do it for you?' Neve enquired peevishly as she put the cafetière and a mug down on the coffee table.

Max sat up and ran a hand through his unkempt hair. 'You're not allowed to be snippy with me today, not when you haven't even said happy birthday.'

Neve capitulated immediately. 'I'm sorry. Happy birthday.' She took a step closer so she could gingerly ruffle Max's hair. 'Would you like some paracetamol?'

'Rather have the first of my birthday·kisses,' Max said, tugging Neve half on to his lap so he could kiss her soundly, his tongue sliding into her mouth, one hand shaping her breast, thumb rubbing against her nipple, which obediently peaked on Max's command.

The ancient sofa creaked in protest as Max pulled Neve down so she was squashed between the cushions and his hot, hard body. 'I need to put the potatoes in the oven,' she said breathlessly, after what felt like hours of long, sweet kisses. Max had unbuttoned her cardigan slowly so he could mouth her breasts through her dress and now the material was clinging damply to her and her breasts felt swollen and full. 'Do you still need those paracetamol?'

Max smiled and he looked so sleek and sexy, his face inches from hers, that Neve could hardly believe he was hers to have and to hold for the next few weeks. 'It turns out that your kisses cure hangovers, Neevy.'

She blushed and his smile got wider, more wicked, the way it always did when he was teasing her. 'So, that's a no then?' she asked, slapping away a hand that was creeping towards her breast again. 'I'm going to put the potatoes on.'

Yet another email had come in from William and Neve felt an unfamiliar twinge of shame. There was William, the one true heir to her heart, and there was Max, who'd be the first to admit that he wasn't steadfast or reliable or ready for anything other than a good time. They had two separate places in her life, but it seemed wrong and wholly inappropriate to still be light-headed and sore from Max's kisses while she quickly replied to William's message asking her if she'd listened to a Radio Four podcast on Christina Rossetti.

Max was slumbering on the sofa, Keith was slumbering in a patch of sun by the bay windows, so Neve could get on with chopping vegetables and polishing glasses and reliving the heated memory of every single one of Max's kisses. Then when she started to feel guilty, she'd switch to trying to remember every word of William's phone call to her.

After she'd texted Celia to say that she'd bring down her dinner in ten minutes, Neve went into the living room to wake up Max. She'd been planning to poke him in the ribs with her oven-gloved hand, but he looked so sweet and defenceless for once that she found herself dropping a gentle kiss on his mouth.

By the time he opened bleary eyes, she was standing in the doorway. 'Dinner will be ready in five,' she said, just as there was a peremptory rap on the door. 'That's probably Celia demanding food.'

It was Celia, and standing behind her was Douglas who held a Tesco's carrier bag aloft. 'Hurry up and let us in,' Celia said, trying to barge past Neve who stood her ground. 'I'm so hungry that my stomach thinks my throat's been cut.'

'You all right, sis?' Douglas grunted, giving Celia an almighty shove so Neve had no choice but to stand aside and let them in.

'Hey, Neve, tell your sister to piss off,' Max said as he entered the fray, and her tiny hall was suddenly full of three very tall people and one stocky dog who kept banging against everyone's shins.

'I'm Douglas, Neve's older brother,' Douglas said, completely ignoring Neve so he could step round her and give Max and Keith the once-over. 'I guess you're the boyfriend and that's the devil dog.'

Max didn't say anything at first and he would be well within his rights as both alleged boyfriend and owner of the alleged devil dog to shut Douglas right down – and the perfect birthday Sunday that Neve had diligently planned would be completely derailed.

Neve let out the breath she was holding when Max mustered up a friendly smile and held out his hand so Douglas had no choice but to shake it. 'I'm Max, this is Keith, but I'm sure Celia's already told you that.'

Neve didn't think she'd ever glared so hard as she was glaring at Celia at that moment. 'I said I'd make you up a plate and bring it down to you. What part of that didn't you understand?'

'Well, yeah, but Max said if I had presents then I could come for tea . . .'

'That wasn't exactly what I said!'

'And then I bumped into Dougie, and Charlotte's away and he's been tormented by the smell of your chicken for the last hour,' Celia babbled.

'Come on, Neve, it's been ages since we had a family dinner,' Douglas said. 'And I chipped in with the present.'

'It had better be a fantastic present,' Neve grumbled, herding her siblings into the kitchen. She caught hold of the back of Max's jumper as he passed her. 'I'm so sorry about this,' she hissed in his ear. 'I'm going to make them up two really small plates and send them packing.'

'It's cool. I can pump them for embarrassing stories about when you were little,' Max said, brushing his lips against her cheek. 'And I get more presents so it's all good.'

It wasn't all good, it was very, very bad, Neve thought as she tried to put the finishing touches to the dinner with everyone getting in her way. Max had to shut Keith in the lounge because he wouldn't stop growling and Douglas had to go down to his flat for another chair, which Neve wanted to disinfect with her anti-bacterial gel because it probably had Charlotte germs all over it, but finally the three of them were sitting elbow-to-elbow, knee-to-knee round her tiny kitchen table.

Neve plonked the chicken down on the table, then stood there with arms folded. 'Give Max his presents, then I'll feed you,' she commanded.

The Tesco's bag was handed over and Max pulled out two bottles of Cava (which Neve knew were in a two for five pounds promotion), a small box of Quality Street and a pair of Homer Simpson socks.

'My God, have you no shame?'

'Look, it was four o'clock on a Sunday afternoon, so our present-buying options were severely limited.' Celia held her hands up like little paws. 'Food. Now? Please?'

'OK, OK,' Neve sighed, picking up the bread-knife, which was going to have to do time as a carving-knife too. 'But I'm really annoyed with the pair of you.' She wasn't even continuing her snit for comedic effect, either – she was going to have to sacrifice her three roast potatoes for the greater good, and there was still barely enough to go round. Plus she'd spent more on the organic chicken than she usually paid for a pair of shoes, and she'd wanted to eke it out for at least a couple of lunches and an evening meal.

Neve flopped down on her chair, a sibling on either side of her and Max sitting opposite, and began to dish up the vegetables, ignoring Celia's protests that she was allergic to broccoli and carrots.

It wasn't the Sunday dinner Neve had planned, and she hadn't even bothered to light the candles she'd bought and she was damned if she was opening the bottle of champagne that was chilling in the fridge. Everything had been ruined.

Neve half-heartedly speared a carrot with her fork and pretended to listen as Celia over-shared about the tattoo artist she'd hooked up with in Berlin, but mostly she tried to eavesdrop on Max and Douglas's conversation in case Dougie started questioning Max's intentions towards his sister. Not that Neve thought that was likely. Douglas was never that concerned about what she did and didn't get up to.

It was astonishing even to see Douglas sitting at her kitchen table eating off her mis-matched crockery, because usually they just passed each other in the hall and he'd say, 'You all right, sis?' and be on his way before she could answer. When Neve really thought about it, the only serious conversation they'd ever had was when he'd got back from Vegas, after being married to Charlotte by an Elvis impersonator.

'For fuck's sakes, all that stuff happened years ago,' Douglas had shouted after Neve had spent ten rambling minutes explaining how hurt she was that he'd decided to make Charlotte his bride. 'Your problem is that you dwell on stuff too much. You wanna put down the books once in a while and get out of the house.'

But it was easy enough for Douglas to say. He'd always been popular, always been smiley and happy and so good-looking that when they'd been little, people had always stopped her mother on the street to exclaim over his angelic features. Celia's pointy features were echoed on Douglas's face in a killer pair of cheekbones but he had the blunter Slater nose and chin to offset them. He'd also inherited the height from their mother's side of the family and his hair was such a dark auburn that no one could ever taunt him with ginger jokes, and even if they had, Douglas would have just laughed and joined in because he was like that, Neve thought, inwardly squirming at just how mean she was being.

On the plus side, he'd never, ever, *ever* said anything derogatory to her face about her weight, and when they were little and her dad had shouted, and she'd cried (which had happened a lot because her father had a quick temper and she'd been a real cry-baby), Douglas had always gone and stolen chocolate digestives out of the biscuit tin to cheer her up. Besides, it couldn't be easy being married to Charlotte and being responsible for the London office of Slater & Son, General Builders. According to her dad, who'd told her mum, who'd passed it on to Celia, who couldn't wait to tell Neve, Douglas was making a complete mess of it and they'd asked Uncle George to come down from Sheffield to keep an eye on things.

He really wasn't so bad, Neve decided, and as if Douglas could read her mind, he stopped banging on about his predictions for Arsenal in the FA Cup, so he could catch her eye and give her the thumbs-up. 'Fantastic grub. I suppose your bloke isn't too bad either.'

'Well, *I* like him,' Neve said mildly, and Max smiled at her as if it was a private joke and only they knew the punch-line.

'You're very quiet,' he said to her. 'You OK?'

'Oh, Neve can never get a word in edgeways with me and Dougie,' Celia said. 'It's even worse when Mum's here too – that woman does not stop talking. Dad says he needs earplugs when the three of us are together.'

'Yeah, but Dad can go days without saying more than ten words. Do you remember the time we went to Morecambe?' Douglas asked Celia.

She rolled her eyes. 'God, yes! I still think we should have reported him to ChildLine.'

'What happened when you went to Morecambe?' Max asked and now it was Neve's turn to roll her eyes.

'It's one of those stories that's really boring unless you were there. And actually, I was there and it wasn't *that* funny.'

'Yeah, that's because Dad let you stay in the car,' Douglas reminded her, as he turned to Max. 'So, we're going on holiday to Morecambe, all packed into the Ford Mondeo, all really excited. Neve's sat between me and Seels with about fifty books . . .'

'She was deep into her *Chalet School* phase at the time . . .'

'And Celia and I are doing kid stuff in the back, like playing I Spy and counting up all the black and white cars and . . .'

'You two fought from the minute you got in the car,' Neve said, interrupting this little trip down memory lane, which was losing a lot in translation. 'And Mum kept turning around every five seconds to scream, "If you two don't stop right now, I'm coming back there and knocking . . ."'

'" . . . your bloody heads together",' the three of them said in unison.

'And what were you doing while all this was going on?' Max asked, nudging Neve's foot with his toe.

'I was trying to read *Eustacia Goes to the Chalet School* even though Celia kept smacking me in the face with her ballet Barbie.'

Celia tried to look repentant as she gnawed on a chicken bone. 'In my defence, I was only six but anyway, Dad was so fed up with us that when we made him stop at a service station . . .'

'Though he'd had to stop at every service station because as soon as our mum gets in the car and the engine starts running, she says she feels it right in her bladder,' Douglas explained, though Neve was certain that their mother didn't want that kind of information revealed over Sunday roast – or at any other time. 'So me and Seels get out the car because anything's better than staying *in* the car but Neve won't budge because she's all up in the Chalet School – and when we get back to the car it isn't there! What do you think about that, then?'

'Um, I don't know,' Max said. 'Did you get turned round when you left the service station?'

'Not even!' Celia sniffed. 'Dad only drove off without us. We had to wait there for an hour and it was in the prehistoric era before mobile phones so we couldn't call and Mum was just about to dial 999 from a payphone because she thought they'd been kidnapped, when Dad pulled up and said that he wasn't going to let us back in until we promised to shut up.'

'Except it was only twenty minutes,' Neve said. 'Half an hour tops. And he only drove to the other side of the service station.'

'I can't believe you let Dad just drive off like that,' Douglas said, because even after seventeen years he wouldn't let it go.

'But I didn't even realise you weren't there,' Neve explained for the hundredth time. 'I'd got to the chapter where they were caught in a blizzard and had to stay in a mountain hut; it was riveting.'

'Tell Max what you and Dad did when you finally got your nose out of the Chalet School,' Celia ordered and Neve thought she was being a bit heavy-handed with the righteous indignation but Max was grinning, his eyes darting to each of them in turn as they spoke.

'We had egg, chips and beans and a Cornetto for afters and he read the paper and I read my book and neither of us said a blessed word to each other,' Neve recalled with relish. 'Good times, my friends, good times.'

'While we had to make do with some soggy cheese and pickle sandwiches,' Douglas said. 'And when we got back in the car, I think we managed to stay quiet for, hmmm, five minutes.'

'More like two minutes,' Neve said dryly. She looked at the remains of the chicken; if she was really lucky she might be able to make soup from the carcass. 'Everyone done?'

There were empty plates all round, except for one solitary and exceedingly crispy roast potato sitting on Max's plate. Celia was already reaching for it. 'If you're not going to eat that, can I have it?' she asked, fork poised.

'No,' Max said, slapping her hand as she made a dive for it. 'It's Neve's.'

Neve could see Douglas and Celia exchanging raised eyebrows and a smirk as Max handed over his treasure, so she shut her eyes to enjoy her tiny moment of carbo-riffic bliss without them ruining it.

'Thank you,' she said, when she was done. There was pudding, and it couldn't be shared between three, but to her surprise, Neve realised that she didn't want to kick Douglas and Celia out just yet. Though it pained her to admit it, it had been lovely to have a family dinner and Max wouldn't be opening the second bottle of Cava if he wanted them to go.

'So, I have a question to ask about your sister,' he announced as he expertly popped the cork. There was a twinkle in his eye that Neve didn't trust at all but she was sure it couldn't be anything too embarrassing. She'd led such a blameless life.

'Like, what?' Douglas wanted to know, bristling slightly as if he might have to defend Neve's honour, which was sweet and very unexpected.

'Like, have you ever heard her say the f-word? That's what she calls it,' Max explained, as Celia snorted with laughter. 'She can't even bring herself to say it as she explains why she won't say it.'

'Oh, stop it!' Neve tried to swipe at Max with her oven mitt but he was too far away. 'I told you, I don't like swearing.'

'It's true; she really doesn't swear that much,' Celia said, shaking her head as if she couldn't understand why anyone would have a problem with frequent cursing. 'I mark it on the calendar if she says "bloody".'

'I'm not *that* bad!'

'Except for that one time, of course.' Douglas leaned back in his chair and smiled smugly.

'What time?' Neve asked crossly as she tried to give Max a look that said, 'Can you believe this?' though from the eager expression on his face, he wanted to believe it more than anything.

'The time you were back from Oxford and working all hours on some essay *thing* and I get woken up by you screaming, "Fuck you! You fucking useless excuse for a fucking computer!"'

Celia sat up straight and gasped: 'I'd forgotten all about that! The Day That Neve Swore – they're going to make it a public holiday.'

'What was I meant to do? The computer just died on me and I hadn't backed anything up.' Neve covered her burning face with the oven mitt. 'There were extenuating circumstances.'

'Don't suppose either of you caught this on tape, did you?'

'No birthday presents . . .' she growled at him warningly, even though Max was too busy clutching his sides to pay any attention.

'It's not on tape,' Celia said sadly. 'Though the memory lives on in our hearts. There were quite a few more "fucks" after that first outburst. Mum was all for getting Father Slattery to do an exorcism because she thought Neve was possessed.'

'I can't believe you've been holding out on me all this time,' Max said between giggles. All the sharp angles of his face were softened and he looked at least ten years younger. 'Come on, Neve, just say it. Say the f-word. It's my birthday!'

Neve scrunched up her face as if she was seriously weighing up the consequences of dropping the f-bomb, while the three of them looked at her expectantly. 'It's never going to happen,' she said at last. 'Swearing is neither big nor clever and I'm not going to bow to peer pressure.'

'Oh, you always do this.' Celia jumped up so she could pretend to throttle her, while Neve tried to swat her away until the fake strangulation turned into a hug. 'Just as well I love you, you little non-swearing freak of nature.' Celia rested her chin on top of Neve's head and looked at Max. 'So, what about you, Birthday Boy? You got any embarrassing childhood stories to share?'

'None that I'm going to tell you,' Max said, pushing his plate away. 'I'm an only child so there aren't any witnesses.' He gave Neve and Celia, then Douglas, a long, hard look. 'It's cool that you three are so close.'

'Those two are thick as thieves, but there's no way I'd want to hang out with my little sisters,' Douglas announced cheerfully. 'And you two never used to be so tight until Celia buggered off to New York.'

'True,' Celia conceded, letting go of Neve so she could start clearing the table, which was a Celia first. 'But I was so upset and pissed off when I left and Neve had been in Oxford for three years so I didn't feel like I knew her that well, but then . . . Do you remember those emails you sent me, Neevy? They were so sweet, then you flew out to New York and we had so much fun that week.'

It was obvious that there was backstory but Max didn't start firing questions in all directions. He just waited until Celia had turned back from the sink, tilted his head and simply said in a voice that was as warm as honey in the sun, 'New York?'

Neve could see why Max interviewed celebrities for a living. The combination of head tilt and soft voice was a lethal combination that made you want to sit down as close as possible to that sympathetic gaze and unburden.

Well, it would have done if Neve hadn't tried to repress all the painful memories of what had made Celia bugger off to New York.

But Celia wasn't made of such stern stuff. Neve finished clearing the table, did the washing up, put the dishes away, made coffee and Celia and Douglas were still regaling Max with the sorry saga of the last Sunday lunch they'd had en famille.

It had been a gorgeous, golden day; the French doors wide open so a light breeze blew into the dining room. It was also meant to be a happy day to celebrate Neve's First from Oxford, Celia's A-level results and Douglas taking over the family business. All three Slater children taking big steps out into the world.

Except it had also been the week that Celia had spectacularly failed all her A-levels because instead of revising, she'd been sneaking out of the house to meet her friends and chat up boys. Douglas had fouled up a huge contract from the local council and got arrested for being drunk and disorderly when he'd gone out to drown his sorrows. So the Sunday lunch, where their parents planned to make the big announcement that their three responsible, adult children were getting a flat apiece in their grandmother's house while their parents took early retirement and split their time between Yorkshire and the new place they'd bought in Malaga, had come at the end of a week of arguments, tears and slammed doors.

Neve had spent most of the week in her room steadily re-reading all her Jane Austen novels (such a joy to read for pleasure now that her Finals were over), crying because William had flown out to California days before and eating her way through packets of chocolate fingers dipped in vanilla ice cream. But she'd had a ringside seat at the dining table, when her father staggered back from the Hat and Fan drunk.

Her mother hadn't even had time to put down an

over-cooked lamb joint on the table before he'd torn into Celia and Douglas. 'The pair of you make me sick,' he'd shouted, his face red raw with anger and alcohol as he kept banging the electric carving-knife on the table to make his point. 'If it was up to me you'd be out on your ear.'

Douglas had shouted right back, Celia had cried, her mother had kept saying, 'Barry, that's enough! Barry, will you just stop!' and Neve had just sat there waiting for it all to be over so she could barricade herself in her room and disappear to a world where there was never any shouting, just barbed remarks from behind fans at Regimental Balls.

'It was awful,' Celia was saying. 'But that's the thing with Dad. He's so quiet and he bottles stuff up, then he just explodes. He was really sorry about it afterwards, sent a huge bunch of flowers over to Auntie Catherine's house in New Jersey. Must have cost him a packet.'

Douglas picked up the thread. 'Yeah, he slept it off, then he took me to the pub to say he was sorry and give me this speech about manning up and accepting responsibility. I preferred it when he was shouting at me.'

'And what about you?' Max asked Neve, who was sitting there silently, hands curled around a mug of peppermint tea. 'Did you escape all this paternal wrath?'

'Kind of. Well, no, not really,' Neve said quietly.

'At least he didn't shout at you,' Douglas said, as if that had made it better. It hadn't. It had made it worse.

Because Neve had been sitting there, tuning in and then tuning out as the row raged on and maybe she'd even been feeling a little superior because she'd been awarded a First and been accepted on to her MA course with funding from the British Academy. Those were achievements that any parent would be proud of.

Yes, she'd definitely been feeling a little superior and then relieved, as her father stopped shouting, sank down in his chair and put a hand to his ruddy forehead and . . .

'He said to me, "As for you, I can hardly bear to look at

you. You're eating yourself to death."' When her father had said it, the words had been underpinned by a flat, resigned anger that was far more terrifying than anything he'd directed at Celia and Douglas, but after years of practice, Neve could repeat the words without any emotion, her face a perfect blank. Max, however, managed to look outraged and appalled and sympathetic on her behalf.

'He shouldn't have said that. He had no right . . .'

'He had every right,' Neve retorted sharply. 'It was the truth and he did me a favour. Yes, it hurt and yes, it was a shock, but it was a shock I needed. So here I am at just over twelve stone.'

'Really? You don't look like you weigh that much,' Douglas said, earning himself a slap from Celia and an anguished, 'Don't tell Charlotte how much I weigh,' from Neve. 'Well, she doesn't. And Dad did do her a favour. He did all of us a favour. Neevy isn't fat any more, Seels found her work ethic and I made an honest woman out of Charlie.'

'Take more than that to make an honest woman out of *her*,' Celia muttered darkly, and maybe the snide remarks and the picking of old scabs that should have been left to heal was just as much a part of having dinner with your family as all the giggling over long-ago trips to the seaside. She turned to Max, who hadn't taken his eyes off Neve though she refused to look at him. 'Despite what Neve might have told you, Dad isn't so bad.'

'I know it might be hard for you to understand, Brat, but Neve and I have lots to talk about that doesn't involve you or your family,' Max said, and Neve still didn't understand how he could say something really obnoxious but do it in such a light, playful tone that people didn't take offence.

Celia certainly didn't. She just nodded and said, 'Well, Neve doesn't like to talk about it because then she'd have to admit that she hasn't spoken to Dad since it happened.'

'That's not true!' Neve said, uncurling her hands from

around her cup, so she could place them flat on the table. 'I am speaking to him. I see him and Mum when they come into town. Honestly, the stuff you come out with sometimes.'

'You don't speak to him,' Celia insisted. 'Mum says that he emails you all the time . . .'

'Only to ask if anything needs fixing around the flat, which it doesn't.'

'And you always call her on her mobile, rather than the landline because Dad always answers that phone.'

'Yeah, and all he ever used to say was "I'll pass you over to your ma,"' Neve said furiously. 'I'm not *not* speaking to him. He could always call me, but he doesn't, and even if he did, he hardly says anything anyway.'

'What*ever*,' Celia drawled, leaning back in her chair, so she could meet Neve's glare with one of her own. 'You're both as stubborn as each other. That's what Mum says.'

'Yeah, she does,' Douglas agreed, and if Neve was as stubborn as her father, which she wasn't, then Douglas and Celia were just like her mother and never stopped talking about things that were best left unsaid.

There was a tense stand-off as the three of them sat with narrowed eyes and folded arms until Max coughed. 'Well, I guess there are some benefits to being an only child.'

'Sorry, mate.' Douglas patted Max on the back. 'Sisters! Worse than having a wife.'

'How is dear Charlotte?' Celia asked sweetly, then launched into an account of how they'd been having their usual 'Fucking shut up', 'No, you fucking shut up', row a couple of evenings ago, when Yuri had opened the front door of their flat to scream up the stairs, 'Why don't both of you fucking shut up?'

'Charlie's not so bad,' Douglas said stoutly but without much conviction, and when Celia opened her mouth to contradict that statement, he scraped his chair back and stood up. 'Well, this has been great, but I should probably get going.'

Neve stood up too so Douglas could give her an awkward one-armed hug. 'I'd say thanks for coming but I don't remember actually inviting you.'

Douglas just grinned. 'Great dinner, Neevy. We should do this again some time. Maybe you and Max, me and Charlie . . .'

Celia made a great show of choking on her last sip of coffee. 'You do know that dear, sweet Charlotte absolutely terrorises Neve?' she spluttered, but Douglas was already striding out of the kitchen, saying, 'Come on, Seels, I'll let you take me to the pub and buy me a drink.'

Grumbling, Celia got to her feet too. 'I'll leave you two lovebirds alone so you can do whatever it is you do when you're alone,' she said with a theatrical wink that made Max laugh and Neve hustle her towards the front door.

'You really are a brat,' Neve said with one hand at the small of Celia's back to keep her in forward motion. She opened the door and pushed Celia through it. 'I'll talk to you tomorrow.'

'Can we do something tomorrow night, just the two of us? Even if it's just one of your foul steamed haddock and rice combos and a DVD?' Celia pleaded. 'You never have time for me any more.'

That wasn't strictly true but Neve was only too happy to agree, with one proviso. 'As long as you realise that I'm going to lecture you for at least ten minutes about things we say in polite company and things we don't.'

'I'm counting on it,' Celia grinned. 'You go back to Max and make some pancakes.'

Celia thudded down the stairs and Neve shut the door and walked slowly back to the kitchen so she could talk some more about stuff she really didn't want to talk about.

Chapter Twenty-one

Max was still sitting in the kitchen and as Neve walked past him with a weak smile on her way to finish the last of the clearing up, he caught her round the waist and tried to pull her on to his lap.

'Are you crazy? I'm too heavy,' Neve insisted, as she tried to get free. 'I'll break your legs.'

'Don't be daft,' Max said, hoisting her up and stretching his legs out so there was no way that Neve could rest her feet on the floor and ease the pressure on his thighbones. 'Look at me, Neve. Please.'

Unwillingly, she lifted her head so she and Max were nose to nose. 'What?'

'Thank you for my lovely birthday dinner,' he said in a perfectly serious voice and Neve couldn't see even the flickeringest flicker of amusement in his eyes.

'It wasn't lovely,' she groused, ducking her head again. 'Celia and Douglas ruined everything and you had shop-bought Yorkshire puddings because my batter kept going lumpy. It was a rubbish birthday dinner.'

'God, don't be such a Debbie Downer,' Max said sharply.

'Can I get off your lap now, because I don't think it's very comfortable for either of us?'

'No,' Max said, and he put one hand on her chin so he could keep her still as he kissed her for just long enough that Neve happily began to kiss him back, but not nearly long enough before he was pulling away and Neve was sighing just a little. 'You promised me presents before we got invaded,' he reminded her.

'Yes! God, that feels like days ago.' Neve jumped off Max's lap, relieved that he didn't immediately start rubbing his legs as if he was trying to coax the circulation back, and pulled a star-patterned gift bag out from behind the kitchen bin. 'Happy Birthday,' she said, shoving it at Max.

Max didn't just dive in, but pulled out each package and piled them on the table, so he could read his card first, which just wished him a happy birthday, though Neve had put a cross after her name, which may or may not have been a kiss.

Then he opened the largest parcel first, while Neve busied herself at the kitchen counter preparing the next part of his birthday surprise, while his attention was elsewhere.

'You know, I've really been getting into *The Catcher in the Rye* and I wanted to read his other stuff,' Max said, tapping J. D. Salinger's three other books with one finger. 'What should I open next?'

'The little one,' Neve muttered over her shoulder, and when Max's head was bent over the tiniest of his presents, she took the opportunity to get a couple of packets down from a cupboard.

'I've been meaning to get one of these for ages!' Max exclaimed, when he pulled out a little gizmo that would turn his iPod into a voice recorder. Neve glanced at Max to make sure that he looked genuinely thrilled and wasn't faking his enthusiasm, as he started unwrapping the last present and unearthed a tiny espresso cup with a picture of Keith printed on it. 'Oh, this is hysterical.'

'I had some pictures of him on my phone and I put them on a disc and took them to this photo place . . . Do you really like them, Max?'

'I love them. All of them,' he said, picking up the espresso cup and holding it up for closer inspection. 'You've caught his "bitch, please" expression perfectly.'

'I never know what to buy other people 'cause the best present that anyone could ever get me is a book token,' Neve explained, twisting her hands nervously. 'I can take everything back, except the cup. You're stuck with that, I'm afraid.'

'Neve! I said I liked them and I do. Can we have a time-out on the self-criticism for the rest of the evening?'

'Not the rest of the evening. I can do about half an hour and then force of habit takes over,' Neve admitted. 'So, did you bring a DVD?'

'Yeah, I thought you might enjoy watching my Bruce Lee boxed set.'

'Bruce Lee?' Neve knew perfectly well who Bruce Lee was and having to watch kung-fu movies for the next few hours was really pushing the birthday indulgence further than she'd ever intended. 'A boxed set? How many films would that be?'

'You can relax. I left it at home.' Max stood up and Neve planted herself firmly in front of the worktop, arms stretched out on either side of her so she could hide all evidence of the next item on her birthday agenda. 'What's going on behind you?'

Neve lifted one leg and planted her foot on Max's knee to keep him at bay. 'Not another step or you'll ruin the surprise,' she ordered. 'Go into the living room and pick a DVD and I'll be in in ten minutes.'

Max tried to peer over her shoulder. 'This surprise – is it bigger than a bread-bin?'

'That *is* my bread-bin!'

'But you don't eat bread, Neve,' Max said, and he took a step forward so Neve was forced to tense her leg, and thank God for all those stomach crunches, to ward him off. 'OK, OK, I'm going!'

Twelve minutes later, Neve nudged open the door to the living room with her toe, as she had the bottle of champagne and the box of Quality Street wedged under one arm, two glasses in her left hand and in the other a miniature chocolate cake with one forlorn candle stuck in it.

'I would sing "Happy Birthday" but I can't hold a tune,' she said, carefully placing her attempt at home-baking on the coffee table in front of Max. 'But you still have to blow out the candle and make a wish.'

'How did you make chocolate cake in ten minutes and why is it in a mug?' Max stared warily at Neve's humble offering. 'Is it meant to ooze?'

'It's not oozing, it's molten,' Neve said, sitting down next to him. 'I got the recipe from Rose at work. You make it in a mug in the microwave. She says it's perfectly edible. Go on, blow out the candle.'

Max closed his eyes and blew out the candle, then stayed motionless, lids lowered for a moment as if he wasn't just wasting his birthday wish on a frivolous request that Manchester United won the Premiership but wanted the wish to count for something. 'Don't you want to know what I wished for?' he asked Neve when he opened his eyes.

'It won't come true if you tell me,' she said lightly, struggling to ease the cork out of the champagne bottle. 'So, what did you want to watch?'

'Thought we might play a game instead,' he said, holding up a familiar dark green box. 'Found this on the bottom shelf of your DVD cupboard . . . if you tilt the glass, the champagne won't froth like that.'

Neve finished pouring champagne into the 50p champagne flutes she'd got from the discount store and waited until Max had drunk a good half of his in two swift swallows. 'The thing is, you might find it hard to believe but I can be very competitive and I have an astonishing vocabulary from years spent having no life and reading a lot – and well, if you play Scrabble with me, I'll totally kick your arse.'

Max was about to eat his first bite of molten mug cake but

he paused with the spoon halfway to his mouth. 'You're gonna kick my arse?'

'Until it's black and blue and you won't be able to sit down for a week.' That sounded very arrogant. 'Really, Max, Mum stopped me from playing when I was thirteen after I got a score of four hundred and twenty-seven, and when I was at Oxford, I used to play with two Linguistics post-grads and an English don.'

'Well, my little pancake girlfriend, I played Scrabble against Carol Vorderman for a *Guardian* feature and I kicked *her* arse because Scrabble has got nothing to do with vocabulary; it's logic and tactics,' Max informed her loftily, taking a huge bite of the cake.

For a second, Neve hoped that it was as foul-tasting as she suspected just to get Max back for that snide little speech, but he just licked the back of the spoon thoughtfully. 'This is surprisingly more-ish, do you want some?'

'I think I'll pass.'

'Well, you're not getting out of Scrabble that easily.' Max leaned back against the cushions, the mug cradled to his chest, and propped his feet up on the table so he could poke the Scrabble box nearer to Neve. 'Come on, set 'em up. Unless you're too scared.'

'Max, I have all the two-letter words memorised, and as for Carol Vorderman – well, she might be good at maths but there was a reason why she wasn't in Dictionary Corner on *Countdown* so I'm not surprised you beat her at Scrabble.'

'Fighting talk.' Max rapped his knuckles gently against Neve's head, which made her furious. 'I'll remind you of that little speech once I'm done making you eat every single one of those high-scoring words you seem to think you're so good at.'

'Right, that does it.' Neve snatched up the box and practically tore off the lid, so she could bang the board down on the coffee table.

'You can't be that good at Scrabble if you keep your

letters in a crumpled paper bag,' Max noted, actually daring to nudge her arm with his foot. Neve knew he was only doing it to get a rise out of her, but God, it was working.

'Game on, Pancake Boy,' she snarled, throwing a letter rack at Max, which just made him laugh. 'And don't think I'm going to let you win just because it's your birthday.'

It was the most fun Neve had ever had playing Scrabble. It might even have been the most fun she had ever had. For every obscure word she tried to play in the highest scoring place, Max would put down three tiles to make three different words and block off huge sections of the board.

Every time she tried to flounce or throw a strop because 'you're going against the whole spirit of the game', Max would pop another Quality Street into her mouth because, as he said, 'It is Treat Sunday and you only had one roast potato.'

When there were no more Quality Street left and they'd drunk all the champagne, he stopped each one of her snits with a slow, devastating kiss so there were long pauses between each round.

It was a point of honour to Neve that she won in the most satisfying way possible; finally getting to use her 'q' on a triple word score by turning Max's 'hogs' into 'quahogs' and waving the *Oxford English Dictionary* in his face when he dared to challenge her.

Then it was her turn to kiss the sulk off Max's face until they were entwined on the sofa. Max's hands had disappeared under her cardigan and dress, and Neve had been happy to curl her fingers around Max's belt buckle but he was so hard and she was so curious that she slowly worked his belt free so she could slip her hand into his jeans and explore the twitching length of him through his boxer shorts.

It still felt weird to be touching an erect penis, but the good kind of weird that was doing as much for Neve as Max's fingers slipping into the cups of her bra so he could rub her nipples, his tongue and teeth worrying at a pulse point on her neck. And soon having that cloth barrier between his cock and her fingers wasn't reassuring but irritating. Neve skimmed her hand down and for one shocking moment she had him, hot and smooth and throbbing in her hand, until Max arched away from her.

'Don't do that,' he gasped, head thrown back, eyes closed, and Neve thought he'd never looked quite so pretty as he did right then in soft lamplight, so the planes of his chest and the tense lines of his face had a ghostly glow. 'Time to stop.'

Neve didn't want to stop because she was half-drunk on champagne and chocolate and Scrabble victory. Which had to be the reason for the strange, compelling urge to peel away her clothes, not caring what horrors they uncovered, and beg Max to finish what they'd started.

Instead she lay on the sofa and tried to get her breath back as Max zipped up his hoodie all the way to his chin, so she wouldn't be driven into any further frenzies of lust by the sight of even a centimetre of his skin.

'I'm going to walk Keith,' Max announced unnecessarily because he always had to walk Keith when things had got hot and heavy between them. It was part of their Sunday-night routine.

Neve was sitting up in bed with teeth brushed, hair pony-tailed and an absolute certainty that she was in for another sleepless night as Max slipped out of his jeans and dived under her duvet.

'It's freezing in here,' he complained, grabbing great handfuls of quilt, which Neve attempted to grab back. 'Is the heating on the blink?'

'No, but I turned off the radiator and I've had the windows open all day, there are no hot-water bottles and I'm wearing my summer pyjamas.' Neve huddled closer to him. 'Any time you want to start doing a good impersonation of a thermo-nuclear blast is fine by me.'

'Get away from me,' Max said, shoving Neve to the other side of the mattress. 'It's like sharing a bed with a block of ice.'

'Well, it's colder for me than it is for you.' Neve huddled down under the duvet, too cold to even read a couple of chapters of *The School at the Chalet* (inspired by Douglas and Celia's reminiscences of her Chalet School phase) because it would mean exposing her arms to the elements. She'd just have to think warm thoughts instead.

Ten minutes later she was still freezing cold and wide awake. So awake that every time she closed her eyes, they opened of their own accord. Neve thought that Max might be asleep because he was still and quiet, though not deeply enough asleep to have started snoring, when he suddenly rolled over and she had every deliciously warm inch of him spooning against her.

'I suppose you can put your feet on me if you like.'

Neve immediately pressed the soles of her feet against his shins with a blissful sigh. 'That's better.'

Max pressed a kiss to her shoulder, his arms tight but tense around her as if he was worried she might shatter into tiny pieces. 'You can tell me if I'm way out of line, but you shouldn't let this thing with your dad drag on.'

She'd been relieved that Max hadn't mentioned anything dad-related after Celia had left, because deep down Neve knew that it was true; she wasn't speaking to her dad. Or rather she was *not* not speaking to him in her usual passive-aggressive fashion. 'I know,' she said softly, hoping that was enough to satisfy Max and end the conversation.

'What he said was unfair and hurtful, I get that, but there's going to be a time when it will be too late to make up with him because he's not there any more.' Max kissed her shoulder again almost as if he knew Neve was debating the quickest way to remove herself from the conversation, even if it meant hurling herself out of bed. 'Then what he said and how he said it won't be important any more. What will be important are all the things you never got to say.'

She didn't want to escape any more but turned over so she could hold Max instead of being held. Neve wriggled in his embrace until she could trace patterns on his face in the dark with her fingers. 'If your mum was still around, what would you want to say to her?' she whispered, and it felt like the bravest thing she'd ever done; hoping she was worthy enough that Max would let her share some of his pain.

He didn't answer at first, but let her smooth out the worry lines that had appeared on his face. 'I don't know . . . probably I wouldn't even say that I missed her or that I loved her, I'd just make her a cup of tea and ask her about her day and what she thought of last night's *Coronation Street*.' He made a small indistinct noise and for one moment that made Neve's heart hurt, he rested his forehead on her shoulder. 'I suppose the things that you always take for granted, that you don't even notice, are what you miss the most.'

Neve held on tight to Max's stiff body. 'It's OK to miss her, you know.'

'She was always so angry. Angry at my dad for pissing off. Angry at me because she had this fantasy that she'd have had an amazing, fulfilling life if she wasn't lumbered with a kid.' Max rubbed at his eyes and swallowed hard. 'It wasn't so bad when my nan was alive but after she died, my mum got even more depressed. Moving to London when I was sixteen was the best thing that ever happened. But if I'd known she only had another two years left, I'd have stayed. I should have been there for her.'

'But you couldn't have known that, Max, and on some level, she must have had some peace in knowing that you were independent and could look after yourself.' Neve didn't know what else to say to make him feel better so she kissed him. It was a clumsy kiss and they bumped noses, but that made Max smile against her lips and Neve could feel the tension slowly leaving his body like air escaping from a puncture.

'So, I'm just saying, you should make up with your dad,' Max said. 'Because I don't want you to have to live with this kind of regret. It's a pain in the arse.'

'Well, I'll talk to my mum,' Neve decided because there were benefits to having a mother who wanted to know everyone else's business. 'See how the land lies.' She tried to shrug, which was surprisingly hard when you were cuddling someone. 'The silly thing is that I'm *glad* that he said it. I needed to hear it, but I wish it hadn't been from him.'

She turned over because now it was Max's turn to hold her. She didn't even tell him off for splaying one hand over her belly. 'It sounded to me as if you and your dad used to be close,' he prompted.

And they had been. They'd shared . . . silence and it had been golden. 'When I was at Oxford, he'd visit and take me out to lunch,' Neve said falteringly. 'We'd go to this restaurant on the river and I'd read a novel and Dad would read a *Which Guide* and we'd not say a word, but we were still there together. It was the only time that I ever felt really comfortable just being me, as if he loved me and didn't judge me, so when he said what he did in the way that he did, I felt so betrayed.'

Max didn't try and kiss the hurt away or hold her tighter, but kept stroking her belly in slow, concentric circles. They lay there silently until he cleared his throat. 'When I'm interviewing someone and I go quiet, it usually encourages them to keep talking.'

Neve choked out a giggle. 'Sorry, I'm done with my paternal signifier issues for now.'

'Only you could use those big, wordy words at this time of night,' Max grumbled, shifting slightly so Neve could put her feet back on his shins. 'God, all these confessions have really taken it out of me.'

'Me too. We should go to sleep,' Neve murmured. She should have been exhausted because it had been one hell of a day, but Max's hand had slipped under her T-shirt and she could feel the warmth of his palm on the bare flesh of her stomach. All those urges from earlier had only been dozing and now they'd woken up and were pleading with her to do something. Something like arching against Max or unclipping her bra so she could surreptitiously rub her breasts against his arm.

'Yes, sleep,' Max slurred, as if he was already halfway there and didn't realise that his thumb was looped into the waistband of her pyjamas.

If she'd been cold before, now Neve was burning hot. She closed her eyes, but that made the urges worse, as if her senses were heightened and all that she was were the nerve-endings beneath Max's hand.

Neve could have screamed in frustration when Max's hand moved up instead of down, but actually that was OK because his fingertips grazed the underside of her breast. She breathed in sharply.

'Sorry,' Max mumbled sleepily, as if he didn't even know what he was doing, when Neve wanted him to know exactly what he was doing and to do it more and harder and just *there* . . . 'Why do you sleep in a bra?'

'I'll take it off,' Neve said quickly, fumbling with one hand to release the catch. 'And it's all right – what you were doing. I mean, you can carry on doing it if you want. I don't mind.'

'Doing what?'

Neve managed to get her bra straps down her arms, then pulled the bra through the armhole of her T-shirt. 'You were touching me *here*,' she said, and she placed Max's hand on her bare breast because the urges won out over bashful modesty. No contest.

Max tried to pull his hand away, but the rub of his palm against her aching nipple was all the incentive Neve needed to keep a tight grip on his wrist.

'I thought we agreed that we weren't going to do this,' Max said, and his voice didn't sound thick with sleep any more but as if he was so wired that he was clenching his jaw to stop his teeth from chattering.

'No, we said we weren't going to have sex but I don't want that, I just want you to touch me,' Neve explained, pushing herself into Max's motionless hand in case he needed a practical demonstration as well. 'And I'm really tense and I *know* I'm not going to be able to sleep.'

'So, I'm just performing a public service?'

'Personal service,' Neve corrected, and she could let go of Max's wrist because his hand was moving now: shaping, pressing, and each touch of his fingers had her arching back against him so Neve wasn't that shocked when she could feel his cock hardening against her.

'Anywhere else you want me to touch you?' Max's voice had thickened again, not with tiredness but something else.

Neve didn't even have to think about it. 'Here,' she said, grabbing Max's hand again so she could slide it down her belly and, there really was no point in prolonging her agony, into her pyjama bottoms.

This time she released his wrist straight away because Max was already cupping her pussy, testing how wet she was with the tip of one finger, then sliding it inside her so he could thrust shallowly, as she tightened around him in shocked delight.

'Like that?' he asked hoarsely. 'Do you like that?'

'Yes!' Neve gasped, reaching around awkwardly to try and touch him. She was surprised to encounter bare skin and hipbone and her knuckles kept brushing against his cock until Max tugged her pyjama bottoms down to her knees and they could start moving together.

Max had found the perfect combination of thumb rubbing against her clit, his finger moving inside her and Neve could *hear* what his other hand was doing behind her. Had never heard that soft slapping sound before but she knew instinctively what it meant and wasn't surprised when Max suddenly groaned and she felt something warm and wet hit the small of her back.

It should have been gross, but Neve was more concerned with wrapping her hand round Max's wrist one final time so she could grind down on his hand and then she wasn't capable of doing anything. Her airless gasps sounded deafeningly loud as Neve screwed her eyes tight shut and felt as if she was freefalling through time and space until in that split second before she hit the ground, Max was there to catch her.

Afterwards, when they'd dabbed ineffectually at each other with tissues and were halfway decent, Neve let herself snuggle back into Max's arms. Not being able to sleep was the mootest of moot points, she thought, as she felt herself drifting off.

'Are you freaking out?' Max asked suddenly.

It was hard to speak when Neve felt as if she had syrup running through her veins and up into her brain. 'Not right now,' she yawned. 'Probably will in the morning.'

'Sometimes I worry that if I keep focusing on sexual gratification, I'll never be able to sustain a proper relationship. That's what my th— one of my friends keeps saying,' Max admitted. 'What do you think about that?'

Neve tried to give the matter the serious consideration it deserved. Then she gave up. 'I think you need to find some new friends.'

Chapter Twenty-two

Max's half of the bed was empty the next morning but the duvet had been tucked tight around Neve. She'd given Keith a walk and was just packing her gym bag, when she received a text from Max.

Thanks for my lovely birthday surprises. Especially the last one. Are you freaking out yet? he wanted to know, as if Neve being freaked out was her only rational response to what had happened the night before.

Truthfully, she was a little freaked out and a little embarrassed too. Or actually a *lot* embarrassed, but God, she was twenty-five and it turned out that she had needs that couldn't be satisfied by her own hand and a one-armed read of Anaïs Nin's *Delta of Venus* any more.

Sort of, she texted back, and was just about to hit send, when she decided that if Max was hinting at what she thought he was hinting at, then she needed to make her feelings crystal clear. *But I want to do it again and next time, I want to return the favour.*

She wasn't sure what time Max's flight was, but after ninety minutes of cardio and free weights, there was another text from him.

Can't wait, you naughty girl. Give Keith a kiss for me and have one for yourself.

Max had left a week's supply of foul-smelling dog food and two pages of instructions about doggie daycare. Neve had expected advice about dog-walking, worming tablets and the vet's emergency phone number, but it turned out that Max had a very dim view of her dog-sitting abilities:

- Do NOT let him in your bedroom.
- It also goes without saying that he is NOT to sleep on your bed.
- Do NOT let him in the bathroom. He'll try to drink out of the toilet bowl.
- Do NOT feed him at the table. He eats dog food not human food.
- And do NOT give him chocolate. I'm serious. Human chocolate can make dogs very ill. Have left a bag of liver treats instead.
- He doesn't like old men, especially if they have walking sticks or zimmer frames.
- He doesn't like balloons, carrier bags or kites.
- Also avoid small children.
- A small child trying to fly a kite, while holding a balloon and a carrier bag in their other hand would just about finish him off.

By the time Neve went to bed that night, Keith had stayed in the bathroom while she had a shower (and tried to get in the cubicle to drink the water), because he'd barked and scrabbled at the door so hard, she'd feared for her paintwork.

He'd also had a piece of steamed haddock from her plate because she hadn't been able to eat dinner without his nose in her crotch and his paw prodding her leg until she fed him.

Neve had secretly suspected that Keith wouldn't have so many emotional issues if Max refused to indulge him, but it turned out that she was the softest of soft touches, unable to wield any sort of discipline or say, 'No, Keith, you have to sleep in the lounge,' in an authoritative voice.

She'd lasted five minutes until the sound of Keith

whimpering and howling and generally giving the impression that he was being tortured had forced her into the living room to pick up his bed, and his toys and his water bowl. But if he had to sleep in her room, then he could do it in his own bed, Neve reasoned as she sat up, eyes fixed on Keith. Every time she took her gaze off him and tried to read, he'd dive out of his bed and start advancing towards her.

'Back to your basket, you wicked boy,' she'd say and he'd slink away, eyes downcast, only to be given away by the joyous wag of his stumpy tale, as if it was the best game ever.

It was inevitable – as soon as Neve turned out the light, there was a scrabble of claws on the wooden floor, then a dead weight landed on her feet. 'Bad dog,' she snapped, but they could both tell her heart wasn't in it. Besides, if Keith stayed at the bottom of the bed, he could double up as a hot-water bottle.

Keith had other ideas. He wriggled up the bed on his belly as if he was being stealthy and settled down next to Neve, batting his paws against her back until she was shoved right over and he could put his head on *her* pillow and pant hot doggy breath against her face.

'Celia was right,' Neve grumbled. 'You *are* a devil dog.'

Celia hadn't revised her opinion of Keith when she came round the next evening for Chinese food and sisterly support.

'I can't believe you let him sleep on your bed!' she exclaimed, with a horrified look at Keith, who was watching her every move as she shovelled chicken and cashew nuts into her mouth. 'He could have savaged you in your sleep and it's gross and unhygienic.'

'I did read somewhere that dog spit is cleaner than humans',' Neve countered, feeling a paw thump against her leg in agreement. It stayed there until she fed him one half of her steamed veggie dumpling. The only food Keith wouldn't eat was celery. 'Seels, let him have a bit of your egg roll and you'll have a friend for life.'

'I'm not giving him one of my bloody egg rolls.' Keith turned imploring eyes on her until she broke one in half and gingerly fed it to him. 'I thought he'd have one of my fingers,' she said in surprise and Neve smiled as Celia patted Keith's head and gave him the rest of her egg roll.

By the time Celia had worked her way through wonton soup, sweet and sour chicken, egg fried rice, prawn Foo Yung and the egg rolls with Keith's help, the two of them were becoming firm friends.

'If he's sick, you're clearing it up,' Neve told her.

'He's not so bad for a mangy, flea-bitten mutt who probably mauls toddlers when no one's looking,' Celia cooed, scratching Keith under his chin. It seemed that the creepy voice was buried deep in both their DNA. 'So, you've told me off about Sunday and I've bored you to tears about Yuri and that lame graphic designer, and I still say they won't last another week. I think it's time we bitched about Charlotte.'

'I'm not coming down to her level,' Neve said sanctimoniously, as she waited for the kettle to boil and squirted Fairy Liquid over the remains of Celia's egg fried rice so she wouldn't be tempted to eat it later.

'Yeah, you always say that but you always do once I've warmed you up.' Celia grinned and cracked her knuckles. 'Where to begin? She's got a new Juicy Couture tracksuit – powder blue. Wonder how much that cost Douglas?'

'She works, she probably paid for it herself,' Neve said, sitting back down and taking a sip of peppermint tea.

'How much do you think she gets paid for piling slap on the faces of her unwilling victims?' Celia sneered, because although she hated Charlotte for many valid reasons, most of her contempt was directed at Charlotte's choice of career, which largely consisted of standing behind a make-up counter and trying to interest shoppers in the new spring colours. 'She doesn't even work somewhere cool like

Selfridges. She works in a large branch of Boots, and those tracksuits don't come cheap.'

'They're tracksuits! How much could they cost?'

Celia gave Neve a pitying look. 'Try a hundred quid for the hoodie and about ninety for the bottoms.'

'Two hundred pounds for a tracksuit?' Neve nearly choked on her outrage. 'That's disgraceful! It's so typical of her to pay for the privilege of having the word *juicy* scrawled over her bottom.'

'There you go! I knew you couldn't hold out much longer. Now, what do you think about their latest row? Did you hear what Douglas called her?'

Neve hadn't, and before Celia could fill her in on the details, her phone rang. Nothing unusual in that but the way her stomach flip-flopped as she retrieved her phone from the worktop, because she thought it might be Max, was new territory.

'Hold that thought,' she said to Celia as she answered the call. 'Hello?'

'Is that Neve? Max's Neve?' asked a young woman with a lilting Mancunian accent.

'Er, yes, this is Neve,' she replied.

'Great! This is Mandy. He's told me all about you. Well, he didn't want to but I threatened to knock a half percentage point off his royalties and that worked like a charm. So, how are you?'

'I'm fine,' Neve said carefully. She didn't have a clue who the woman was, but she seemed to know Max very well. 'I'm sorry – Mandy . . . ?'

'Mandy McIntyre. Max said you weren't very up on your current affairs. And when I asked why, he said you'd recently come out of a convent 'cause you weren't ready to take Holy Orders, but I thought he was taking the piss. He usually is.'

Oh God, *that* Mandy! 'Oh yes, hi. Sorry about that, couldn't quite place the name,' Neve said, pulling an anguished face at Celia and mouthing 'Mandy McIntyre' as she pointed at her phone. 'He *was* taking the, um, piss. I haven't been in a convent, I just don't watch a lot of TV or read *heat* magazine.'

Celia was practically on her lap, face pressed against Neve's as she tried to listen in. 'What's she saying?' she hissed.

'What do you do with yourself if you don't watch telly?' was what Mandy was saying. 'We had a power cut last week and the Sky box didn't record *Glee* and I thought I was going to die. Anyway, you're probably wondering why I'm calling, though it's nice to get to know each other, isn't it?'

'Very nice,' Neve said, elbowing Celia who was jostling her so hard she was in danger of falling off the chair. 'Congratulations on the wedding. You must be very excited.'

'It's a total mare, if you must know,' Mandy sighed. 'But that's why I'm calling. Now has Max told you about the dress code, which is black and white? That's black *or* white but it can also be black *and* white. For instance, you could wear a white dress if it had a black floral pattern.'

Celia moaned like she was in pain, then stuffed as much of her hand as she could get into her mouth to mute the giggles.

'I think I'm going to wear black,' Neve mumbled. 'Um, is that all right?' Mandy seemed to be the sort of person who didn't like to get caught unawares.

'Black's fine and you'll need a sexy little number for the Friday when we're having a girls' night out. That's the other reason why I'm calling. Honestly, you put my head next to a sieve and you wouldn't be able to tell the difference.'

'Oh, I'm sure that's not true,' Neve simpered, as Celia pulled a face to let Neve know she was very unimpressed at her sister's lame attempts at conversation. 'But I'm not sure when we're coming up. It might be too late to go out on Friday night.' Or rather, she was going to make certain she wasn't available for a girls' night out with Mandy and her friends. Mandy seemed like comedy gold, but her WAG friends? It would be like going out with a gang of Charlottes.

'Well, I already told Max that you have to come up on the Thursday and that's a Mandy McIntyre order,' Mandy said without one jot of irony. 'So you need to get a lush frock 'cause we're going clubbing in town and we're having a spa day before that, so don't worry if there's no chance to top up your tan before you leave London. They do terrible tans down there anyway. I went to one place in Mayfair and I came out beige. You can have anything you like at the spa, as long as it's not a deep facial 'cause I don't want anyone looking blotchy in my wedding photos.'

'That's very kind of you, but—'

'Now, Neve, are you about to say no to me?'

'Well, it's just that—'

'Because the word "no" is not in my vocabulary, along with the words "can't" and "Victoria Beckham". So, even if you did say no, I wouldn't understand – and don't worry about the expense. It's a freebie 'cause I've already done a pre-wedding photo-shoot at the Spa for *Voila*, and one of the other girls had to drop out. See, my sister Kelly's best mate, Shelly, she was going out with one of Darren's team-mates until she copped off with someone from Chelsea *and* she got found out *and* she sold her story so I said to Kelly, "I don't care if she is your best mate . . ."'

Neve held the phone away even though she could still hear Mandy chirping happily about what she'd said to Kelly about Shelly. 'I'm going to kill Max,' she told Celia, who was flapping her hands and contorting her face into a terrible grimace as she tried to contain her mirth.

'. . . need you to sign a privacy agreement so you don't blab to the papers about anything that happens during the weekend.' Mandy paused – by this stage oxygen had to be getting scarce. 'I should have probably faxed that before I called but you've got a really nice voice and I'm sure you wouldn't go to the papers. I'm a really good judge of character about these things. I never liked Shelly; her eyes are too close together.'

Mandy stayed on the phone for another ten, very long minutes, then she had to ring back because she'd forgotten to get Neve's fax number. When she finally rang off and the phone stayed silent this time, Neve collapsed on the table. 'Oh my God, I'm going to be an honorary WAG for a whole weekend.'

'They're going to eat you alive,' Celia announced with grim satisfaction. 'I can't believe that you didn't tell me about this wedding. It sounds hysterical! And, more importantly, what are you going to wear?'

'That black vintage dress I wore to the *Skirt* party, which only fits if I wear foundation garments under it,' Neve muttered.

'Oh, you've lost loads more weight since then.'

'I haven't. I've lost four pounds and barely an inch off my hips,' Neve said, trying to resist Celia's attempts to pull her to her feet. 'And I'm meant to have – and I quote – "a va-va-voom number which shows off your girls" to go clubbing in. I can't do this.'

'Now, now, the word "can't" isn't in Mandy's vocabulary,' Celia teased, wedging a hand in Neve's armpit and hauling her up. 'You must have something halfway sexy in your wardrobe. Let's go and have a look.'

Celia was another person who had never heard the word 'no', Neve thought as she was dragged to her bedroom, then made to stand in front of her wardrobe while Celia rifled through the contents and provided a running commentary.

'Five black wrap dresses! Five! Why do you need five?' Celia threw them on the bed, as if she couldn't bear to look at them any more.

'Well, one has long sleeves, and one has kimono sleeves and that one has a satin edging at the waist, and—'

'How did you get a massive rip in this?' Celia had already

moved on and was holding up the black vintage frock Neve had worn the first time she'd met Max, taken him home and torn a huge frayed hole in the dress in her haste to properly lose her virginity.

Neve stared at the dress and blinked rapidly. 'Well,' she said slowly, 'I suppose I must have caught it on something?'

'Are you asking me or telling me?' Celia demanded sternly. 'Max didn't tear it off you in a fit of passion, did he?'

'No! God, why do you say these things?' Neve snatched the dress from Celia, tearing it even more in the process. 'Just concentrate on the problem at hand. Is this repairable?'

'No, you've torn it right across the skirt,' Celia said sulkily. 'You've ruined vintage. There's a word for people like you.'

If there was, then Neve didn't care to know what it was. She gestured at her sparse wardrobe. 'Will you please focus? In your professional opinion, is there anything here that's remotely suitable for a wedding or a night out on the town with a bunch of girls who are really into fake tan?'

Celia flung herself down on the bed and put her arms behind her head. 'This pancake relationship of yours . . . I mean, I thought you'd have broken up with him by now. It was only meant to be for a couple of months and you didn't sound like you were that happy with him this time last week. But then when we had dinner on Sunday you were being really sweet to him like you meant it and weren't just doing it to rack up some relationship points.'

Neve sighed and sat down on the bed because Celia was sounding very belligerent and it was clear that making over her sister's wardrobe was very low down on her list of immediate priorities. Also, Celia had unknowingly hit upon an uncomfortable truth; a few days ago the thought of dumping Max had seemed like the answer to several problems, or at least the problem of not being able to successfully sleep together, but now everything had changed. Not that she could tell Celia why everything had changed. No matter how many times Neve explained it to other people, the arrangement always sounded odd and callous. But when Neve wasn't explaining it and it just *was*, it was starting to feel natural. As if Neve was exactly where she needed to be, which was with Max.

'Well, he has grown on me in the last few days,' she admitted. 'And yes, I suppose in some ways it's sort of become a proper relationship, albeit with the understanding that it's not going to last beyond a certain point.'

'I'm still not convinced,' Celia decided, sitting up and wrapping her arms around her knees. 'I get that sometimes you might meet a guy and there's no way in hell he could ever be The One, but you still end up shagging him for a while. But to be with someone who knows that you're in love with another bloke . . . Max does know about William, doesn't he?'

'Of course he does,' Neve said huffily, because really, what kind of girl did Celia think she was?

'Well, I know why you're all about the pancakes, but what does Max get out of it? Apart from the pleasure of your charming company, which is beyond price,' Celia added quickly as she saw her sister's eyes flash.

That was a question that Neve still didn't have an adequate answer to, so she tried to shrug insouciantly. 'I don't know. You'd have to ask him.'

'Yeah, like he'd tell *me*.' Celia dragged herself off the bed so she could survey the sorry state of Neve's wardrobe. 'There is nothing here I can work with.'

'You don't think I could wear one of my wrap dresses to the wedding if I added some accessories?' Neve suggested.

'Er, unless it's a Diane von Furstenberg wrap dress in an on-trend graphic print, then no. You have nothing remotely sexy to wear clubbing either. I don't think any of your clothes have even sat next to sexy on the bus.' Celia put her hands on her hips. 'We'll have to go shopping.'

'Anything but that.' Neve squinched up her face in horror as if Celia had asked if she could pull out all of her toenails one by one. In fact, that would be preferable. 'I'm completely broke and I promised myself I wasn't going to buy any new clothes until I was a size ten.'

'But sweetie, you're going to a WAG wedding, you need a new frock.' Celia patted Neve's shoulder. 'Just to make your misery a hundred times worse, Mum's down for the weekend and I said I'd go shopping with her on Saturday. Except she thinks we're going to Oxford Street but actually I'm taking her to Westfield – it's *so* much cooler. You'll have to come too. I can't let you buy two statement dresses unsupervised.'

'I'm not going shopping with Mum and there's nothing you can say that will make me change my mind.' Neve tilted her chin defiantly.

'Well, a) I'm going to tell Mum that you refused to go shopping with her and let her wear you down with hourly phone calls demanding to know how she could have raised such a heartless daughter who doesn't want to spend quality bonding time with the woman who almost died giving birth to her. I should also warn you that she'll spend at least quarter of an hour reminding you that the midwife had never seen a baby with such a large head. And b) Grace is lending me her discount cards so I'll get between twenty and forty per cent off in all the shops we go to.' Celia smiled beatifically. 'But if your mind's made up, then fine.'

'Have I told you how much I hate you lately?'

'All the time and right back at you,' Celia replied, flopping down on the bed so she could put an arm around Neve's slumped shoulders. 'Now, if we have to spend a day with Mum, then we need to talk about all the things that we're absolutely *not* to talk about in her hearing.'

Chapter Twenty-three

Neve knew that she'd lost almost thirteen and a half stone. That her hips had gone down from sixty-one inches to forty-three inches. Her bras were now a 34DD and not a 52GG. Objectively, she knew that.

But subjectively, when she went shopping and was trying on clothes in a harshly lit changing room and could see all her flabby white flesh on display, she still felt like a Death Fat – was sure she looked like one too.

Even worse, clothes shopping with her mother was giving Neve a terrible sense of déjà *ew* back to those horrific August afternoons when they'd gone shopping for a new school uniform. By the time she was fourteen, Neve was too big to get into Marks & Spencer's largest school skirt and had to make do with a navy one from their plus-size collection instead. Then there was the year that she'd busted out of the regulation school blazer and her mother had got special permission to have her friend Agnes run one up in a cheap poly blend that hadn't looked even remotely like everyone else's blazers. Charlotte had just about exploded with spite when Neve had turned up for school wearing Agnes's best effort which didn't do up over her chest, had puckered seams and gave her electric shocks in the Physics lab.

Neve perched on the bench in the fitting room and tried to avert her gaze from her reflection because, really, did anyone look good under fluorescent striplight when they were wearing the sturdiest bra and knickers that money could buy? And what was taking Celia so long?

Neve had thought that Celia and their mother were on the same page as her – the page that had a picture of a nice black dress on it. But Celia had decided she was going to bully Neve into buying a black trouser suit 'with a fitted tuxedo-style jacket. You'll look just like Marlene Dietrich.'

As Neve had stared at her in disbelief because the only thing that would make her look like that lady was radical plastic surgery, liposuction and a different set of genetics, her mother had added her two-penn'orth.

'You can never go wrong with a smart pair of black slacks,' she'd informed Neve. 'And they'll come in useful for job interviews and court appearances. Oh, and funerals too.'

'Here you go,' said Celia's voice from behind the cubicle curtain, because Neve had trained her well enough to know she wasn't allowed into the hallowed space without express permission. 'Try these on.'

Two black trouser suits were thrust through the gap in the curtain, but because this was an upmarket high street chain that had delusions of grandeur, the curtains were billowy, swagged chintz.

'Celia, can you please get me some black dresses?' Neve called, but there was silence.

Without much enthusiasm, Neve hung up the suits. Why Celia had brought her a size fourteen, she didn't know, but she'd try on the size sixteen first just to show willing, and when the trousers got stuck on her child-bearing hips, she'd firmly insist that they moved on to black dresses.

The trousers slid easily over her bottom with the minimum of tugging, and Neve could even fasten them, but they gaped at the waist and were far too tight over her hips and thighs. Neve took the jacket off the hanger and tried it on over her bra, just to satisfy her curiosity. The jacket fitted at least; she could do up all of the buttons, but . . .

'How are you doing in there?' Her mother's strident tones carried through the curtain then, to Neve's horror, it was pulled back so her mother could march into the cubicle. 'Let's have a look at you.'

'The trousers don't fit,' Neve said, wrapping her arms round her waist defensively. 'Jacket's OK, I suppose.'

'Let me see.' Her mother forced Neve's arms down and then had the audacity to stick her hand in the waistband of the trousers. 'These are far too big for you.'

'They're too small. They're clinging to my bottom and my thighs.'

'Nonsense. They're too big and the jacket is bagging over your bosoms.'

'Mum! Get off me!' Neve tried to bat away her mother's hands, which were busy unbuttoning the jacket.

'I gave birth to this body and it was no picnic, believe me, and we're all girls together. Nothing to be embarrassed about.' Her mother had succeeded in getting the jacket undone. 'Oh, you're much smaller-busted than I would have thought.'

'What did I tell you?' Now Celia was pushing back the curtain so she could stare at Margaret Slater in horror. 'You don't come into the changing room uninvited. You don't offer an opinion, unless Neve's asked for it, and there is definitely no touching. Get your hands off her!'

'Really, I've never heard the like,' Mrs Slater grumbled, unhanding her eldest daughter. 'You've got nothing to be ashamed of, Neevy. Ah, there's hardly anything left of you.'

'There's plenty of me,' Neve snapped, buttoning up the jacket again and offering herself up for Celia's inspection.

'You need to go down a size,' her sister said. 'It's all too big.'

'Am I talking to myself? Yes, the trousers are too big on the waist but they're too tight on my gargantuan backside.'

'Please, just put on the size fourteen so we can compare and contrast because I'm losing the will to live here,' Celia begged.

'Fine, whatever.' Neve reached for the other suit, then

glared at her mother and sister in the mirror. If Margaret Slater didn't have a good twenty-five years on her youngest daughter, they could have been mistaken for twins. Same height, same build, same look of indignation on their faces, though Mrs Slater had started to go a few shades lighter on the Clairol colour chart, once the fiery red of her hair had started to fade. 'I don't need an audience, thank you very much.'

'Well, we're here now,' her mother said, dropping down on the cushioned bench. 'Lord, my feet are killing me. Now, this wedding – who do we know who's getting married?'

Neve grabbed the other suit and threw Celia a desperate look because when they'd drawn up their list of Things Not To Be Discussed In Front Of Mum, they'd also entered into a pact to provide a diversion if their mother wouldn't let something go. Not letting something go was Margaret Slater's *raison d'être*.

'We've already told you, Ma, it's a friend of one of Neve's friends that you don't know,' Celia said quickly. 'Anyway, have I told you that Dougie and Charlotte are fighting all the time? Looks like we might have the first divorce in the family before too long.'

'Hmmmph. When I think of all the lovely girls he courted and he gets married to *her*.' Mrs Slater pursed her lips and looked up to the heavens. 'I really should ask Father Slattery to drop in on them. But then *she's* not Catholic, is she?'

'She's really not, Mum,' Celia said piously, though she hadn't been to Mass in ages and it would take a good day in the Confessional and a week of Hail Marys and performing Acts of Contrition before she was absolved from all her sins. 'That's what happens when you marry out of the faith.'

As diversions went this one was a sure-fire, guaranteed winner so that Neve could change suits secure in the knowledge that her mother was busy expostulating over the godless masses who were responsible for everything terrible from knife crime to swine flu.

Neve yanked on the trousers and pulled them up to mid-thigh where they'd refuse to budge. Except there was more than enough room to pull them all the way up, though it was futile as she'd never be able to get them to do up.

'Celia, I think you must have picked up two size sixteens,' Neve said, as she slid the zipper all the way up. 'I mean, they're still too big on the waist and too tight on the thighs. But the jacket seems smaller. Is the jacket *too* small?'

'Let me have a look,' Celia said, and then in complete contravention of the no touching rule, she dug a hand into the back of Neve's waistband so she could look at the label. 'Nope, it's a size fourteen. And they're not too tight; they're meant to fall from the widest part of your leg, which they do, and they're flat-fitted to your stomach.' She turned Neve round so she could tweak and tug at the jacket. 'The size sixteen was far too boxy. See how this nips you in at the waist.'

'But I can't be in a size fourteen pair of trousers. My hips are forty-three inches. Size fourteens are forty-two inches.' Neve shook her head. 'Are you sure they're not too tight?'

'Of course they're not,' Mrs Slater cried, pushing Celia out of the way so she could start poking and prodding at Neve too. 'You've got a proper shape, my girl. Not like Celia, she's built like a stick. They *are* too long in the leg, but a court shoe with a medium-sized heel will sort that out.'

'*Stick?* I got my lack of curves from you, Ma,' Celia hissed. 'And you're not buying any court shoes on my watch. But I think you are ready for a three-inch heel. Don't worry, we'll get you something with a T-bar.'

'I can't believe I'm in size fourteen trousers,' Neve murmured dazedly, craning her neck to see what her bottom looked like. She honestly couldn't tell if the trouser suit looked good on her or not. All she knew was that it was a size fourteen and that meant she had to have it. 'What shall I wear underneath the jacket?'

'You know, most women would wear nothing

underneath the jacket, but I know you're not most women,' Celia said quickly, as Neve's eyes widened in horror. 'I hung some stuff up outside.'

There was a pretty chiffon blouse decorated with a smudgy cherry-blossom print with a shirred waistband and cuffs that Neve loved, and a dress that Celia had selected in case Neve had proved intractable on the whole trouser-suit thing. It was made of oyster-coloured satin with a black lace overlay and featured a shawl collar, three-quarter-length sleeves, cinched waist and a full skirt that swooshed around Neve's legs as she walked. It was the prettiest dress Neve had ever worn and now she was wavering because it would do just as well as the trouser suit for the wedding. Even better, it had rendered her mother speechless.

'Oh, Neevy,' she sighed because the speechlessness only ever lasted a minute. 'You look lovely. You really have got a cracking bust.'

'Could this be my clubbing dress?' she asked Celia hopefully.

'Only if the club is from the 1940s,' Celia said exasperatedly. She lowered her voice. 'It looks gorgeous but it's not WAG friendly and you'll get much more use out of the trouser suit. Anyway, I picked something out for clubbing and I want you to try it on with an open mind, which I know might be a real stretch for you.'

'Why?' Neve asked suspiciously. 'What's wrong with it?'

'Nothing!' Celia said, sticking an arm through the curtain. 'It's just not your usual style, which I have to say is a little safe.'

'I have classic style,' Neve told her, though she knew that really she didn't have much style at all. As long as her hips, thighs, belly and upper arms were covered, then she declared her outfits a success. But she could be open-minded – hadn't the trouser suit proved that? 'Oh my God, I am not wearing that! No way. It has sequins all over it.'

The dress Celia was holding up was short and covered in

silver paillettes. The only thing going for it was the long sleeves, which was the only reason why Neve let her mother and sister cajole her into trying it on.

Neve looked at her reflection in the mirror, but all she could see were starbursts in front of her eyes from the sequins, and her meaty legs. 'It's too short. I look like mutton dressed as lamb. I have nothing to wear with it and it just looks stupid and ridiculous and unflattering. No!'

'It's a fricking A-line shift dress. That's like, the most flattering cut in the world and you can wear it with leggings . . .'

'Leggings?' Neve echoed. 'I don't *do* leggings.'

'Mutton dressed as lamb! You're only twenty-five,' Mrs Slater added. 'That's a nice little dress for the discothèque and it leaves something to the imagination. Some of these girls – they might just as well leave the house in their undies.'

Neve looked at herself in the mirror again. She was flushed with irritation, and when she forced her eyes downwards, her body covered in sequins didn't match her anxious face. And good God, her legs looked *huge*.

'I look horrible,' she said flatly.

That should have been that, except Celia exploded, though Neve didn't think it was so much to do with her as with the prolonged exposure to their mother. 'Why can't you see what we see when we look at you?' she demanded, clamping her hands down on Neve's shoulders so she couldn't turn away from the mirror. 'You look gorgeous and sexy! Or you would if you lost the mardy face. Christ, Neve!'

'Now, there's no need to take the Lord's name in vain . . .'

'That dress is a size fourteen! You're a size fourteen. By no stretch of the imagination do you look fat in anything, unless you were trying stuff on in Chanel and, quite frankly, in that world size six is morbidly obese.'

'You're not helping, Celia,' Neve gritted. It was just a silly spangly dress and Neve couldn't understand why her sister was behaving as if it was a matter of life and death. 'Look, I'll get something with a few sequins on it for my clubbing outfit. Maybe round the hem or the cuffs or something.'

Celia folded her arms and planted herself bodily in front of the curtain. 'You are having that dress.'

'Celia, I'm an adult woman who's quite capable of making her own decisions, so you can stand there and give me fight-face for as long as you like, it won't do any good.'

'I'm buying the dress for you,' Celia insisted belligerently, as if she was offering to take Neve round the back and give her a good slapping.

It was time to call in the big guns. 'Mum! Tell her!'

Mrs Slater pulled herself to her feet. 'Celia, you're not buying the dress for Neve. I'm buying both dresses and the suit. Now where do we go to get these shoes you were talk-ing about?'

Celia could usually be cowed by a stern voice and a steely glare but she was just a second-generation copy. Mrs Slater was the real deal and she refused to listen to Neve's im-passioned pleas about how she didn't want the sequined dress and she could buy the trouser suit now and put the other dress on her credit card.

'You'll let me buy them for you and you'll bloody well like it,' Mrs Slater finally shouted when they reached the till. 'Now wait outside because you're not so old that I won't take you over my knee and smack some sense into you.'

Neve was mortified. Even Celia, who'd been about to say something, closed her mouth with an audible snap.

'Thank you, Mum,' Neve said meekly when Mrs Slater emerged with a stiff cardboard bag. 'I do appreciate it.'

'Well, I can't remember the last time I went shopping with you, Neevy, and it's a treat not to have to go to Evans. Now, shoes.'

They found the perfect pair of black suede shoes in Office with not one, but two straps and a solid enough heel that Neve decided she'd probably be able to walk in them with the aid of a cushioned inner sole. 'So, we're done, yes?' she asked eagerly, after taking possession of another carrier bag. 'Shall we stop and get a coffee?'

'I need to go to Marks and get some towels. They don't have very fluffy towels on the Continent and this might be some fancy shopping centre, but I ask you, how can you have a shopping centre in the middle of London without a John Lewis?' Mrs Slater shook her head.

'I say we do towels, then stop and get a drink,' Neve said firmly. 'Chloe from work said there was a nice coffee shop up on the balcony.'

'As long as there's somewhere to sit. I wouldn't wish my bunions on my worst enemy.' Mrs Slater adjusted the shoulder strap on her bag. 'Which way is Marks?'

Celia smiled winsomely. 'Can we go to Topshop because you haven't got me a present yet and the new Kate Moss collection has just come in?'

'I'm not getting you a present,' Mrs Slater said sharply. 'I haven't been shopping with Neve since she left school and Neve never rings me to say that the electricity's about to get cut off because you and that other little madam can't pay the bill. And Neve never rings me because she's got no money to top up her Oyster card and can't get into work. I think you've had plenty out of me and your father over the years.'

'Mum, Celia doesn't make much money,' Neve said, putting a calming hand on each of their arms because they were both bristling and she didn't want them to come to blows in the middle of Westfield. 'Fashion jobs are very low paid.'

'They really are,' Celia gasped. 'And London is the most expensive city in the world. Apart from, like, Tokyo.'

'But you don't have to pay rent or a mortgage every month,' Mrs Slater said crossly. 'That was the whole point of giving you a flat. And if it's not you, it's Douglas on the phone wanting a handout. But does Neve ever call? No. And do you know why?'

'Because she never goes out and she lives on steamed fish and brown rice,' Celia said sulkily. 'No offence, Neevy.'

'Well, I'm taking offence. I was trying to stick up for you!'

'The reason Neve never asks for money is because she has a monthly budget and she sticks to it even though she gets a pittance from that library and she graduated with first-class honours from Oxford too!'

'Is that meant to be a dig because I didn't do a degree in the end? Jesus, when are you going to let that drop?'

'You could have retaken your A-levels but you swanned off to New York without even leaving a note . . .'

Neve sank down on the nearest bench. Celia and her mother would be at it for hours now they'd started. She pulled her phone out of her bag to check her messages and as she'd half expected there was a text message from Max; they were getting to be a daily occurrence.

Can't stop thinking about all the rude things I want to do to you. How's Keith? How are you? How's Lucy? Max x

Duly noted, Neve texted back, because flirty texting wasn't really her forte. *Keith is fine, he sends his love. Lucy's fine too. Hope those LA publicists are behaving themselves. Neve x*

Even though she hadn't heard anything from Jacob Morrison, Neve was still diligently working on Lucy's biography. During the last week, it had become a habit to try and write at least five hundred words of an evening. Neve put her new work ethic down to having Keith in residence, as the last time Charlotte had come up the stairs to scream at Neve, Keith had done a really good impersonation of an attack dog.

'I don't care what life was like when you were my age! I bet the only reason people got married that young was so they could have sex.'

The argument was still raging on. Neve scooched down to the end of the bench so the people who were rubbernecking wouldn't know she was related to the two red-headed, red-faced women shouting at each other.

'Better to get married young than be out gallivanting every night and dropping your knickers left, right and centre. I'm just saying, Celia, a few nights in would do you a world of good. All that drinking and pre-marital sex, no wonder you're so short-tempered. We never have to worry about Neve. She's always been such a good girl.'

Neve really wished her mother would leave her out of this. Celia obviously felt the same way, because her face reached the very zenith of redness as she stabbed an accusing finger in her sister's direction. 'She's got a boyfriend,' she shrieked. 'Who she's using for sex practice because she's in love with someone else. Sorry, Ma, but your good girl's gone bad.'

'You horrible little cow,' Neve said, her voice murderously low, while her mother was rendered non-verbal for the second time that day.

'Whatever,' Celia drawled, but Neve could tell that she already regretted her outburst because the delivery of Celia's all-time favourite word lacked its usual jauntiness. 'I'm finished with the mother/daughter bonding!'

Celia scattered a gang of teenage girls like skittles as she stomped right through them. Neve was left with her mother, who was staring at her as if she'd suddenly started displaying the signs of stigmata.

'It's not as bad as Celia made out,' Neve offered feebly. 'I didn't tell you about him because . . .'

'Towels. Marks & Spencers,' her mother said mechanically, as if that was the only thing she could focus on because focusing on Neve's sex-life would make her head cave in.

Her mother kept up a steady stream of chatter all the way to Marks, pausing briefly to buy two sets of towels in a peach colour that would complement the autumnal shades in the guest bathroom of the villa in Spain, then she talked all the way back to Finsbury Park.

Neve now knew all about her father's cholesterol levels

('much lower since he's taken over the cooking, though I still think you can't have a sauce without some butter and cream in it'), the silent suffering of her Auntie Catherine in New Jersey who was a slave to her Irritable Bowel Syndrome and her mother's sketchy view of what she did all day.

'Does this library of yours stock DVDs?' she asked, as she opened the front door of their old house, which had now been converted into two flats. Her parents had rented out the ground floor to a family of Jehovah's Witnesses, and though her mother had plenty to say about people who turned their nose up at blood transfusions, apparently they were very good tenants who always paid the rent on time. 'You know, Neevy, you're too over-qualified to be directing people to the larger-print books. Have you thought about becoming a teacher?'

'It's not that kind of library, Mum,' Neve said, following her mother up the stairs. They'd had this conversation countless times, but as far as her mother was concerned, libraries were where she went to take out romance novels, that she begrudged paying £6.99 for. 'It's a literary archive. And I don't think I'm cut out for teaching.' It would be sheer hell having to sit in a room full of cocky teenagers who'd much rather be texting other cocky teenagers than respecting Neve's authority and listening to what she had to say about the Post-Modern novel.

'Well, it's worth bearing in mind,' Mrs Slater said, as she eased off her shoes. 'Oh, Neve, you might get a job in a nice private school. That would be lovely. They have very high standards, no hoodies . . .'

'I'll put the kettle on, shall I?' Neve interrupted quickly. These little pep talks also made her painfully aware of the gaping chasm between her actual reality and her mother's expectations.

They had their tea in the living room, which had once been her parents' bedroom. Like the guest room in the

Spanish villa, it was decorated in her mother's favourite autumnal shades: rust-coloured carpet, brown velvet sofa and armchairs and a pair of bright orange curtains that hurt Neve's eyes if she looked at them too long.

'You sure you won't have a biscuit?' her mother asked her again. 'Just one won't hurt. Go on, treat yourself.'

They were her favourite plain chocolate digestives that Neve had used to devour by the packet, but she shook her head and went back to nibbling on the protein bar she'd found at the bottom of her handbag.

Mrs Slater looked wildly around the room and Neve knew that she was searching desperately for something to say that would mean they didn't have to talk about her sexual escapades. Not that *that* was something she wanted to talk about with her mother, damn Celia.

'Did I tell you about Auntie Catherine's IBS—?'

'Mum, let's get this over with,' Neve interrupted calmly, though she was feeling distinctly uncalm. 'I am seeing someone and he's very nice but it's not serious, which is why I never told you about him.'

'And why isn't it serious?' her mother demanded, little spots of colour appearing along her cheekbones. 'You're a gorgeous girl. He should be madly in love with you.'

Neve never knew who this beautiful, whip-smart girl was that her mother talked about but she wished she was more like her. 'He's not in love with me and I'm not in love with him. That's why it's not serious, because, well, I happen to be in love with someone else. With William,' she added recklessly, because just saying his name felt like tempting fate. Though as she said it, Neve realised with a little pang of guilt that she'd barely thought about William all day. Which was weird and wrong, when not so long ago, he was her first thought as she got out of bed and, before she could even brush her teeth, she was tiptoeing down the stairs to see if there was an airmail envelope waiting for her.

Her mother, though, didn't seem to have spent any time

thinking about William. 'Who's William? Is he one of your friends from the library?'

'It's an archive . . . William! William from Oxford, who drove me down that time I'd left my essay behind and he stayed for tea.' Mrs Slater was still obviously scrolling through her memory banks. 'And he came round after Christmas in my second year and you made him a turkey sandwich and he bought you a brandy on Graduation Day, when you said you were really nervous because none of the other mothers were wearing a hat and you needed something to calm your nerves.'

'Oh, *that* William.'

'Why are you saying it like that?' Neve put down her mug. 'He was always perfectly nice to you.'

'Well, yes. Yes, he was. Had lovely manners.' Her mother paused delicately, which was very unlike her. 'Don't you think, well, that he's a little out of your league?'

'What's that meant to mean? Five minutes ago you were telling me that I was gorgeous. Yes, I know William's really handsome but we connect on a much deeper level than just the aesthetical.'

'Don't you start using those long words on me.' Her mother was looking around the room again as if she wished that she'd changed the habits of a lifetime and selected her words with more care. 'You're a very pretty girl, Neve, but men like that don't go for women like you. And it's got nothing to do with looks, it's about where you come from.'

'I come from Finsbury Park, William grew up in Fulham – what's that got to do with the price of milk?'

'He's posh and you're not. I know you speak nicely and I don't know how, considering your father sounds as if he was brought up in a coalmine, and that awful school you went to, but you're working class and that William . . . well, what do his parents do for a living?'

Neve longed to tell her mother that owning two houses in London, a cottage in Yorkshire and a villa in Spain meant that her parents were now firmly entrenched in the middle classes, whether they liked it or not, but she knew her mother would just counter-attack with the miners' strike and the potato famine and not being ashamed of your roots.

'His father's a lawyer,' Neve admitted, though she wasn't going to elaborate any further and reveal that he was actually a QC. 'And his mum's a doctor.'

'Well, there you are then. And I bet he went to a fancy private school and they eat cheese after their tea instead of a dessert like normal people.' Her mother smiled grimly. 'It would never work.'

'Well, I don't eat dessert,' Neve reminded her tetchily. 'So I'm sure William and I will be just fine.'

'If you and that William are going to be just fine, then why are you messing around with another man? What's his name anyway?'

For what felt like the gazillionth time, Neve explained, though her mother knew only too well that she had no relationship experience. 'I just want things with William to be perfect and so going out with Max is like revising before a big exam.'

'You . . . really . . . what on earth?' Her mother opened and closed her mouth, her eyes flickering from side to side. 'Have you not got an ounce of common sense? I've never heard such nonsense. Relationships aren't something you can prepare for and there's no such thing as a perfect one. They're a lot of hard work,' Mrs Slater said baldly. 'The first year your father and I were married we did nothing but argue. I even threw the butter dish at him once.'

The mention of her father gave Neve another painful twinge as she remembered what she'd pencilled in for discussion next. 'I know they're hard work,' she gritted. 'But most girls my age have a lot more experience in how to make them succeed.'

'I didn't think you were interested in that sort of thing,'

her mother said, curling her lip. 'We all thought you took after your Great-Aunt Sinead.'

Neve was appalled. 'She's a nun while I was just hugely fat. Chalk and cheese. Nothing in common with Great-Aunt Sinead *at all*, though she's a very nice lady.' She was actually horrible and mean, and Celia always said she'd be a lot less horrible and mean if she'd ever had a good shag and a couple of shots of Jack Daniel's.

'I just hope you're being *safe*.' Her mother winced as she said the word. 'In the bedroom department.'

'That's really nothing for you to worry about, Mum,' Neve said quickly.

'I know you children think I'm old-fashioned but you don't want to throw away the most precious gift you can give a man, ideally your husband, because you're being pressurised into it by this Max or even that William. Once you've given it away, you can't get it back.'

Even a year ago, when she was still a size twenty and despairing that she'd ever see a size eighteen tag in the back of her clothes, Neve would have agreed with her mother. But the more she moved towards that mythical size ten and the reality of being in a relationship, her precious gift felt like one more obstacle that she had to rid herself of. Besides, most men she knew would rather have an iPad or a plasma TV than the precious gift of her maidenhood.

'I know that, Mum,' she said, wondering how on earth she was going to change the subject.

'So you don't want to do anything with this Max that you might regret later on,' her mother persisted.

'It's not really about Max,' Neve said, because it wasn't. In the most clinical, calculated analysis of their pancake relationship, he was just a means to an end. And the end was . . . 'It's about William. I . . . well, I love him and I feel as if part of me is missing while he's not here. And when he comes back, everything will change. Everything will be better.'

301

'You said that about losing weight,' her mother reminded her in a sharp voice to match the sharp look she was giving her. 'Aren't things already better?'

'Of course they are, but they'll be even better when I'm a size ten, and then William and I will be together and everything will be perfect.' Neve had this picture in her head now of a green field studded with wild flowers, the remains of a picnic laid out on a rug and William in a white shirt, his blond hair falling in his eyes as he lay on the grass, his voice a soothing soft murmur as he spoke. She was somewhere in that scene in a pretty size ten summer dress, but try as she might, Neve just couldn't imagine that, so she focused on William and smiled as she said to her mother, 'William's my soulmate.'

'Honestly, Neevy, you sound like a lovestruck teenager. I should have stopped you reading so much and made you get more fresh air when you were little.' Her mother didn't even try to make it sound like a joke. 'I just hope you know what you're doing.'

'I do,' Neve said and she did, until she had to explain her actions to people who weren't her or Max and then it all seemed vague and undefined. 'Look, anyway, that's really not what I wanted to talk to you about. I wanted to talk about Dad.'

It came to something when changing the subject to the non-relationship she had with her father was a welcome relief. Her mother didn't seem to think so. 'And what would you want to be saying about him?'

'Well, Seels and Dougie have this crazy idea that I'm not talking to Dad because I'm angry with him. About what he said. You know, that time.'

She couldn't manage whole sentences but her mother nodded as if she understood and wasn't that surprised that Neve was bringing it up.

'*Are* you angry with him?' There was something to be said for the way Margaret Slater didn't bother with niceties and just got straight to the point.

'I think I was,' Neve said slowly. 'At first. I thought he hated me. That I disgusted him.' She swallowed hard, the tears not so far away again.

'Your father adores you, always has done, always will,' her mother stated forcefully. 'Between you and me, you're his favourite and he's still in pieces about what he said that day. He wishes he'd never said it.'

'But he did say it and he's never tried to talk to me about it or say that he was sorry, because if he had . . .' Neve had to stop because her voice was thickening.

'Oh, come here, you silly girl.' Mrs Slater patted the sofa next to her and twenty-five was far too old to cuddle up against your mum, but Neve was getting up from her chair so she could curl up next to her mother and rest her head on her very bony shoulder. 'You know what a stubborn old git your dad is because you're exactly the same. He can't talk about his feelings at the best of times, never mind coming out with an apology. He tries to show it in other ways.'

'With emails asking me if I need anything to be fixed around the flat?' Neve sniffed, wiping her nose with the back of her hand.

'Do you remember that awful row we had on the way back from Brent Cross that time? I told him that he was going the wrong way but he wouldn't listen to me, oh no, and we ended up in an awful traffic jam in Neasden and he was too busy shouting at me to pay any attention to what he was doing . . .'

'And he went into the back of that car, which belonged to an off-duty policeman. What's that got to do with anything?'

'I never got an apology but I did get a new kitchen a few months later,' her mother recalled fondly. 'I'd been on at him for *years* to do that.'

'He might be sorry but he still thought it, still said it. "I can't bring myself to look at you."' This time Neve couldn't

303

say it matter-of-factly, but choked it out as her mother shushed her and stroked her hair until she could get herself under control and struggle to sit upright.

'You feel better now?' Mrs Slater asked, rubbing Neve's back. 'He was drunk, he was angry with Celia and Dougie, but not with you, Neevy. And he should never have spoken to you like that but he was worried about you, we both were, and we should have sat down and talked to you about – well, maybe dropping a few pounds. You made this awful wheezing sound when you were going up the stairs.'

'That's the thing, Ma. He had to say it and I had to hear it so I could lose a lot more than a few pounds, but it still really hurt.'

'You never knew your grandmother because she died before you were even thought of, but she was a very large lady.' Her mother bit her lip, then decided to plough on. 'It's another thing your father doesn't like to talk about, but I think you need to hear this. She had heart problems and she caught diabetes . . .'

'You can't *catch* diabetes, Mum,' Neve corrected because she couldn't help herself when there was an incorrect use of a verb.

'Well, she *got* diabetes and she wouldn't change her diet and she lost the sight in one eye and had terrible problems with her teeth and feet. Had to have two of her toes amputated. Then she died of a heart attack when she was fifty-one with three children under eighteen left to look after themselves. That's no age to die, Neevy. And your Auntie Susan, well, she's going the same way. Your dad's side of the family, they run to fat.'

Neve had been horrified when Gustav insisted she went to the doctor's before they started her fitness programme, and her blood-sugar levels had been in high double figures, although now they never deviated from a very respectable four point eight. Yes, she'd known about Type 2 diabetes during her fat years, but it had never been enough of an incentive to stop herself from unwrapping another Twix.

'I'm disgustingly fit now, Mum,' Neve assured her. 'I mean, I know I'm still a bit overweight but I'm really healthy, and everything's working like it's supposed to be. No wheezing unless Gustav's made me do super-sets without any breaks.'

'Well, I don't know what super-sets are but your father's very proud of you, we both are. He often says you're the spitting image of his mother when she was younger. Last Christmas, he said it was like seeing a ghost walk in through the front door.' She patted Neve's arm. 'It would mean the world to him if you let him back into your life. What's the harm in letting him mend a leaking tap or something?'

'Well, I'll think about it.' Neve put her head back on her mother's shoulder. 'Thanks for telling me about Grandma Slater. At least I can see where Dad was coming from.'

'Your father says I talk too much, but it's not easy being married to a man who can go hours without saying anything but, "Shall I put the kettle on then, pet?" '

'But you wouldn't have him any other way, would you?' Neve asked curiously.

Her mother pulled a face and was taking far too long to come up with an answer for Neve's liking. 'Well, I wouldn't mind if he looked a bit more like Pierce Brosnan, but he'll do,' she snorted, and then she didn't say anything because she was too busy laughing like a hyena.

Chapter Twenty-four

There was a letter from William waiting for Neve on the day that Max was due back from LA.

Usually the sight of that pale blue envelope gave Neve a serious case of the happies, but that morning it gave her a nasty shock, as if someone had pushed a dog turd through the letterbox. Neve scooped it up and stuffed it in her pocket and it wasn't until lunch-time that she'd finally worked up enough courage to read it.

And in way she wished she hadn't, because it was the kind of letter that she'd always dreamed William would send her.

Dearest Neve
I wanted to ring you. I should have rung you, but sometimes it's easier to put my thoughts and feelings on paper, because when I try to say them out loud my words are clumsy and inadequate.

I realise that I've treated you appallingly these last few weeks. I'm hanging my head in shame and offering the most abject of apologies for the inexcusable crabbiness of my last letter. Though when I say letter, I actually mean my terse request for teabags and water biscuits. All I can say in my defence is that I'd had a terrible day that culminated in an argument with a visiting professor over a missing footnote, which meant I was hauled up in front of the Dean. All this and I was going through Sainsbury's Red Label withdrawal. But really that's an explanation rather than an excuse.

Then there was that infamous phone call when I should have offered you sympathy and understanding instead of hectoring you about your future at the Archive. I just wish, Neve, you could see how special you are. Your friends are fortunate to have you in their lives, as am I, and it saddens me when you fail to see your great potential. I know that you will achieve important things in your life but you need to know that too.

Ah, yes, there are so many other things I need to apologise for, aren't there? Like, shattering the calm of your Sunday with my endless requests for research help. And completely ignoring the letter you sent me with your thought-provoking comparison between our meeting of minds and Lou Andreas Salome and Rilke. After I'd read your letter properly, with a glass of Shiraz and a fervent wish that you were sitting there next to me, to debate the finer points of your argument, I came to the realisation that you're my intellectual soulmate. I have close friends in LA, people who mean a lot to me, but with you, Neve, it often feels as if we're sharing the same brain, unless we're talking about Miss Austen, of course! I've never met a woman with such an enquiring mind or such a vivid, elegant imagination. Ah, the places you will go . . .

I should be back in blessed Blighty by the middle of July and I'm longing to see you. I've so much to share with you that I think you'll need to block an entire fortnight out of your schedule (rest assured I haven't started pronouncing that word in the same way as my American colleagues) so we can get reacquainted.

Though I feel that I know you so deeply. How strange that the years and ocean between us have brought us closer together.

I have to go now. Did I tell you that some ex-pats and I have formed a cricket team? I fear I'm late for practice.
Much love
William
PS: Sorry to impose (yet again!) but could you possibly look up the enclosed references for me next time you're at the British Library and fax them to me? Number at the top of the page.

*

Neve put the letter down and sighed deeply. With William so far away and Max suddenly at the forefront of her life, she'd allowed herself to get sidetracked. William was the golden, glittering prize that was just within reach, so close she could almost touch it. It had been the horrible shock of her father's words that had galvanised Neve into taking the first wobbly steps on her weight-loss journey, but somehow the closer it got to William's return, the more her transformation became about William. It wasn't about losing weight so William would drop to his knees and declare, 'My God, Neevy, when did you get to be so beautiful?' it was about becoming the kind of woman she wanted to be. The kind of woman who deserved a golden, glittering prize because, damn it, she'd worked so hard and for so long that she was overdue her reward.

But when would she start to *feel* like a golden girl? Would it be the day she effortlessly zipped up a size ten dress or would it be when William came back and everything just fell into place? She had just over three months before he was in her life again and not just a voice on the phone or a copperplate script on airmail paper, and Neve didn't feel as if she was ready. God, her body certainly wasn't and she was still as awkward and self-conscious as she'd been the last time she'd seen William standing on the station platform as she'd forlornly waved at him from the window of the train.

Which was why she had Max. He was meant to be the goodtime guru; bringing the fun into her life and limbering her up for a real relationship. But they still had so much ground to cover and they hadn't even really cracked the sleeping-together thing yet. Inevitably, Neve's mind drifted to the dark of her bedroom and the sense memory of Max's hands on her, in her . . . and her stomach clenched with a deep, dark pleasure like it did every time she thought about it.

She had to learn to be more like Max, Neve decided as she cycled home. Max wasn't fixating on every aspect of their fake relationship and Max didn't have any problem in being with Neve and seeing other women. He'd probably slept with a different woman every night that he'd been away, and she doubted he was having any pangs of conscience over it. Just because Max roused these passions in her didn't mean anything deeply significant; she'd been virtually celibate all her life, was it any wonder she had all these new confusing feelings that she didn't know how to deal with?

What she did know, Neve thought, as she quickly changed into jeans and a smock top with an Art Noveau tulip pattern that Celia had said was very on-trend, was that she had to lighten up. All she and Max meant to each other was a no-strings, fun-filled fling, which they'd both walk away from with no regrets and no recriminations – but what she had with William was real. It was what her heart yearned for.

Then Neve heard two short rings of the doorbell and her stomach clenched again.

As soon as she opened her door, Keith was frantically wriggling past her legs so he could bound down the stairs with a series of high-pitched yelps, as if he instinctively knew who was visiting. Then he ran up and down the hall, barking all the while, until Neve opened the front door.

Neve barely had time to register Max standing there with a smile that made his entire face light up, because she was trying to make a grab for Keith's collar, but he hurled himself out of the door so he could pelt up the path, skid to a halt and race back. He did that several times, until finally on the last sprint back to the door he leaped up at Max, front paws skittering at his leather jacket, tongue frantically licking Max's hands.

Neve didn't think she'd ever seen such complete rapture. 'Hey, little fella, did you miss your old man?' Max asked throatily, squatting down so Keith could swipe his face with his big, pink tongue. Then he looked up at Neve, who was trying not to go all misty-eyed. 'Hello, angelface, did you miss me too?'

'Hi! Yes! It's really good to see you,' Neve said, trying to inject huge amounts of light-hearted perkiness into her voice. To her ears, she sounded kind of manic. 'My goodness, you've caught the sun.'

Max's skin had deepened to caramel and he looked entirely snackable. squatting there in jeans and his stripy jumper.

Keith had calmed down enough that Max could stand up, though the Staffie was glued to the heels of his Converses. 'It was really hot in LA,' Max said. 'Well, when I wasn't freezing my bits off in air-conditioned buildings. And everyone was so tanned and musclebound that I *have* to start running again now that it's getting warmer.'

'Well, we could go running together,' Neve suggested brightly. She hadn't stopped grinning and her cheeks were beginning to ache, and trying to keep some emotional distance was hard when just standing next to Max on her doorstep made her realise how much she had missed him. What's more, she'd forgotten how handsome he was, and when he smiled at her, all she wanted to do was smile back. 'I've got Keith's stuff ready for you.'

She stepped through the open door, expecting Max to follow her, but he stayed where he was. 'Neve? I need to tell you something.'

It sounded horribly ominous and the inane smile was wiped off her face instantly. 'Oh?'

At least now Max had crossed over the threshold and wasn't planning on delivering the bad news on the doorstep. But it did sound as if he was going to dump her there and then, which was fine. In fact, it would make things far less complicated, Neve tried to tell herself as Max sat down on the stairs and patted the space next to him.

Neve sat down and looked at Max anxiously. 'What's the matter?'

'Nothing's the matter,' Max assured her quickly, and he was gulping as if he was nervous – but then, if you'd never gone in for relationships before then you'd never had to end one either. 'Are you cool with what happened the night before I left?'

She could feel her cheeks heating up because it was one thing to text about it, but to talk about it . . . 'Well, yes. I mean, it was fun, wasn't it?' Neve could still feel the echo of that need which had clawed its way out of her with harsh, pained little cries as Max's fingers twisted and turned inside her, the palm of his hand grinding against her clit. Fun didn't come anywhere close to describing it. 'Um, are *you* not cool with it?'

'Oh, yeah,' Max drawled. 'Made me hard every time I thought about it and I've been thinking about it a lot.'

Neve put her hands to her cheeks, which felt like they were on fire. If she was about to be dumped, then Max was going about it in a very circulatory way. 'So, er, is that what you wanted to tell me?'

Max put his hand on her knee. Neve stared down at his long fingers resting on the dark blue denim of her jeans. 'It's just if we're going to do *that*, then I figured I'm not going to tart around and sleep with other women any more. It just seems *rude*, y'know?'

Max's statement had just made their complicated situation even more complicated, but Neve was almost gasping with relief. 'Right, well, good. If that's what you want.' She patted his hand nervously. 'I'm fine with doing *that*, or variations on *that*, but we're still agreed that we're not going to have sex, right? Because if you need to have sex, then I totally understand if you want to carry on with other women.'

Max sighed. Then he grinned. Then he sighed again. 'Do you know how many men would love to hear their girl-friends say that?'

'Pancake girlfriends,' Neve reminded him.

'Whatever.' Max's hand slowly and deliberately moved from her knee to her thigh. 'There are a hundred different ways we can get each other off without full-on sex.'

'Not hundreds, surely?' Neve frowned, then dug her elbow into Max's ribs because he wasn't even bothering to hide the fact that he was laughing at her. 'Four or five surely, then the rest are just variations on a theme.'

'So, we're agreed? Lots of fun sexy times, but no actual shagging?'

'And no hand-holding either,' Neve interjected because now she thought about it, agreeing not to hold Max's hand had been one of her better ideas. During the last few weeks, there had been countless opportunities where Neve could have taken Max's hand, but she always checked herself because holding hands was what proper couples did. And now that they were going to have 'fun sexy times', every time she checked herself it was a reminder that this wasn't for keeps. She wasn't in love with Max and, God knows, he wasn't in love with her, judging from the exasperated expression on his face at that moment.

'So, you're cool with me getting you off, but I still can't hold your hand?' he clarified with deep and heavy irony.

'Yes, and when you say it like that it sounds ridiculous.' Neve glared at him. 'Don't raise your eyebrows at me. OK, it *does* sound ridiculous but I need some boundaries. Boundaries are very good things; without them there's just chaos and uncertainty and confusion.'

'Your head must really hurt from all the unnecessary thinking you make it do,' Max said, standing up. 'So, I would help you up but I don't want you to think that I'm trying to cop a feel of your hand.'

Neve got up and started to climb the stairs. 'Don't be cranky with me, Max.'

'I'm not being cranky,' Max said, but it seemed to Neve that they stomped up the stairs in a tense silence.

'I just need to put the spare cans of dog food in the bag,' Neve said, once they were inside her flat. 'I won't be a second.'

'So, no holding hands . . .'

'I told you . . .'

'If I'm not allowed to hold your hand, am I still allowed to do this?' Max demanded, and just as Neve was about to ask what *this* was, he backed her up against the wall, hands around her wrists, and kissed her.

Neve tugged her hands free, not because it was almost too much like holding hands, but because as soon as Max bit down on her bottom lip she wanted to wrap her arms around him and kiss him back.

'Now, are you allowed to tell me that you've missed me or is that against the rules too?' Max asked, once they'd had to stop kissing, as Keith was barking furiously because if anyone was meant to be getting Max's undivided attention, it was him.

'I'm sorry,' Neve said. 'Of course, I missed you and will you . . . do you want to stay for tea or do you have at least three product launches and a shop opening that you have to go to tonight?'

'I don't know. Depends what you're making.'

'I've got two salmon fillets and . . . oh, I see!' Neve pouted. 'Well, I certainly didn't miss you teasing me. Come into the kitchen and I'll put the kettle on.'

Neve went to take his hand and checked herself, noticeably pausing, because holding someone's hand after you'd kissed for ten minutes was such an automatic gesture and just proved that it was a line they shouldn't cross.

'You think too much,' Max said, as he watched Neve spoon coffee into the cafetière. 'I'm not leaving you on your own again – you have too much time to think and it doesn't lead to anything good.'

'What's going to happen next time you go to LA?'

'I'll have to take you with me,' Max said lightly, because it was a joke. It *had* to be a joke. 'There's nothing else for it.'

'I don't think I'm an LA kind of girl,' Neve said just as lightly, because she thought she might be starting to get the hang of light-hearted banter. 'But I want to hear all about it. How did the cover shoot go?'

They talked for hours. Over coffee, over dinner and then over the red wine Max bought when he took Keith for a walk.

Max was so good at painting pictures with his words that Neve was right there with him as he drove down Sunset Boulevard, the road lined with palm trees, then pulled into the sweeping driveway of the Polo Lounge where his hire car was parked by a valet wearing a pink polo-shirt. She could picture the minimalist photo studio where he'd waited for five hours for a B-list actress to arrive to be shot, and she could even see the obsequious expression on her publicist's face as he blatantly lied to Max about the reasons for his client's no-show.

There was no way her own week could even begin to measure up, but Neve told Max about the expedition to Westfield and Celia storming off in a huff, only to appear a few hours later laden with presents and a shame-faced apology. Neve even told him about the heart-to-heart with her mother and showed him the text message she'd sent to her dad later that evening.

'*Jennifer Aniston has a new film coming out,*' Max read out loud. '*Maybe we could see it when you're in London?* Is that secret code?'

'It's secret code for "I know that you're sorry and I'm sorry too".' Neve smiled at the perplexed look on Max's face. 'My dad loves Jennifer Aniston. I mean, he *really* loves her. Celia and I went halves on the boxed set of the entire ten seasons of *Friends* for his fiftieth birthday, and we're sure we saw him wiping away a tear when he opened it.'

Max patted Neve's feet, which were resting on his lap. 'So, did it work?'

Neve nodded and held out a hand for her phone, so she could scroll through her messages. 'He texted me back a minute later. *I'd like that. Will check cinema listings. All best, Dad.*'

She squirmed a little under Max's gaze. 'Look, we'll go and see the film, we'll talk about Jennifer Aniston's Oscar-worthy performance and what a home-wrecking tramp Angelina Jolie is, and everything will be all right.'

'It's that easy?' Max asked.

'It is if I want it to be. He's my dad and I can't change the way he is, so my only other choice is to just accept him with all his faults. That's what love is, isn't it?'

'So I'm told.' Max suddenly smiled wickedly. 'Just so you know, if we have a row and you're too chicken to apologise, text me and ask me if I want to go and see Angelina Jolie's new film, because she'll never be a home-wrecking tramp to me.'

Neve picked up a cushion and threw it at Max's head. 'We're Team Aniston in our family.'

'Say that again and I won't give you any presents.' Max pinched her big toe and held on tight as Neve tried to pull her foot away. 'I have a bag full of gifts but I could just leave them outside Oxfam tomorrow.'

'You brought me presents? My birthday isn't for ages.'

'They're to say thank you for looking after Keith and I thought that generally, if boyfriends went away, they came back with presents for their girlfriends. Even pancake girlfriends. That's not crossing any lines I didn't know about, is it?'

It wasn't. Especially when Max was pulling out a fancy cardboard bag with ribbon handles from the side of the sofa.

'I didn't mind looking after Keith,' Neve said, cringing ever so slightly because Keith had had her wrapped round his paws the entire week. Max held the bag up and shook it gently so it made a very promising rustling sound. 'Well, if you insist.'

Neve opened the bag, peered inside and pulled out a large box. 'Noise cancelling headphones; do they get rid of the background noise when I'm listening to my iPod?' she asked, taking out a huge pair of headphones that looked like doughnuts attached to a hair band.

'Well, they can, but they cancel out all background noise too, even if you're not listening to your iPod, so you won't have to sit in the bathtub any more.'

'But my fingers will still be making a terrible noise as I type and Charlotte will still bang on the ceiling with her broom handle.'

Max grinned. 'Yeah, but with these bad boys strapped to your head, you won't hear her.'

'How can such a thing be possible?' Neve held up the headphones. 'So, I could wear them in bed and they'd drown out the sound of your snores?'

'I do not snore!' Max hissed.

'Well, you do when you lie on your back,' Neve told him as Max shook his head in protest. 'I think this is the best present anyone's ever given me. Even better than when I got the *Oxford English Dictionary* for my twelfth birthday.'

'Aren't you going to open the rest of your presents?' Max's eyes were half closed as if present-giving was a tedious chore, but when Neve turned her attention back to the bag, he sat up and leaned forward so he didn't miss her reaction.

There was a pretty moss-green, velvet pouch to keep her Scrabble tiles safe, a box of gourmet low-carb, sugar-free chocolates, and then right at the bottom was a flat squidgy parcel wrapped in layers and layers of gossamer-soft tissue paper.

Neve felt Max suddenly tense up as she began to delicately peel back the gold embossed sticker that sealed up the parcel. There were so many pieces of tissue paper, each one a pale sherbet shade of pink, yellow, lilac or green, Neve felt as if she was playing a very posh version of Pass the Parcel, but when the last piece of tissue was swept away, there was no toy surprise just three neatly folded pieces of clothing that felt as smooth and fragile as silk beneath her fingers.

'I thought they might solve the sleepwear problem,' Max said in an oddly strained voice. 'Do you like them?'

Neve held up a slip in a dusky colour that wasn't quite pink and wasn't quite lavender but probably had an old-fashioned name like Ashes of Roses, delicate black lace stitched around the bodice and hem. There were two other slips still resting in their tissue nest; one a dull red that was miles away from the nasty, lurid red of cheap nylon underwear, the other a smudgy, inky blue, both of them adorned with cobwebs of black lace. In fact, slip was too prosaic a word for them; Neve really wanted to call them something French like peignoir or negligée.

'They're gorgeous,' she breathed reverently. They really were, but there was no way they were going to fit her.

'One of the assistants was about the same size as you – well, maybe a little larger, and she looked at the pictures of you on my phone.' Max swallowed nervously as Neve looked at him sceptically because fancy shops called . . . she looked at the logo on the gold sticker . . . called *Boudoir* did not have sales assistants who were about her size or maybe a little larger. 'You do like them, don't you?'

'Of course I do, they're lovely,' Neve was able to say truthfully, because even if they didn't fit her, she could very well have them framed and hung on her bedroom wall. 'You didn't have to get me presents, I liked having a four-legged room-mate.'

'I know he can be a pain in the arse and I felt guilty leaving all those instructions, but he seems happy.' Max looked down at Keith who was sprawled on the floor in front of them, licking enthusiastically at his undercarriage.

Neve thrust the bag of presents away and bit her lip. 'Max, I don't deserve any gifts. I was a *terrible* dog-sitter. Keith didn't respect my authority at all!'

Max didn't seem that surprised as Neve began to explain how she'd failed to obey his list. Neve could tell he was trying hard not to laugh as if he'd suspected all along that she would cave in immediately under the pressure of a paw prodding her leg or prolonged nocturnal whimpering. He only looked annoyed when Neve confessed that Celia had brought home a range of dog outfits from the *Skirt* offices and they'd dressed Keith up and taken photos.

'Christ, Neve,' he snapped. 'Thanks for violating him.'

'But he loved it,' she protested. 'The next evening he brought me one of the T-shirts in his mouth, as if he wanted to put it on again.'

She decided, on reflection, it was best not to tell Max that one of the outfits had been a tutu and that same night, she and Celia had let Keith sit on a kitchen chair so he could eat his freshly prepared lean steak mince at the table.

She also decided that for someone who was so keen on boundaries and lines that shouldn't be crossed, she wasn't very good at enforcing them.

'Just as well I've persuaded the dog-walker to take Keith again when we're away,' Max said, less sharply. 'At least he doesn't force Keith to dress up.'

There'd been no forcing about it, but Neve still hung her head. 'I'll never do it again,' she promised. 'And thank you for my presents, unless you're going to take them back now.'

'Well, I would, but those slips really aren't my colour,' Max said solemnly. 'Why don't you try one on while I take Keith out for his last walk, and if I like what I see then I might be persuaded not to donate your presents to Oxfam tomorrow.'

Neve could feel panic take a hard grip of her as Max stood up and nudged Keith gently out of slumber with his toe. 'They might not fit,' she offered nervously, but Max had already left the room and he couldn't have heard as the front door opened and he was gone.

It was actually their first mid-week sleepover but Neve didn't have time to worry about the significance of that. She quickly showered, slipped into one of the soft bras she slept in because her breasts were still too large to be unfettered, and eyed the midnight-blue slip with some trepidation. It had a size M tag neatly stitched to a side seam, and try as she might, she still felt like an L or even an XL on a bad day.

'Oh well, here goes absolutely nothing,' she muttered to herself and pulled it carefully over her head because she didn't want to tear the paper-thin fabric. Then she sucked in her tummy as far as she could, as if that was going to help, and let the silk fall. It *did* get stuck on her hips, but a gentle tug was all it took before the material was floating around her thighs and she was wearing a medium-sized slip.

Neve padded quickly to her bedroom and the full-length cheval glass, which had taken a whole afternoon to achieve the most flattering degree of tilt. Her tilting skills had to be truly spectacular because the girl staring back at her in the mirror looked rather splendid.

The slip was empire cut and fell in graceful folds from under her breasts, lovingly skimming over lumps and bumps to rest just above her knees. Neve pushed her breasts together with her arms to give herself a deep cleavage. Yes, she still had flabby upper arms and her shins were still sturdy and muscular, but the overall effect was actually . . .

'Hot,' said a purry voice behind her. 'You look unbelievably hot, Neevy. I knew it would fit you perfectly.'

'How did you know when I wasn't sure until I tried it on?' Neve asked Max's shadowy reflection.

'Well, I might not be allowed to look, but I'm allowed to touch, aren't I?' When Neve leaned back, she could feel the solid wall of his chest against her spine as his hands shaped her waist, then slid up to cup her breasts.

Neve watched as the girl in the mirror obligingly slanted her head back so Max could kiss her neck as his thumbs rubbed against her nipples, which were suddenly hard and aching.

They looked . . . no, *she* looked sexy for the first time in her life. She turned within the circle of his arms, so she could reach up on tiptoe and press fierce kisses against his mouth.

'Thank you for my presents,' she murmured against his lips. She didn't just look sexy, she felt sexy too with Max hard against her because she'd made him that way. It was her turn to touch, pulling his T-shirt out of the way so her palms could graze over hot, dry skin and the tiny trickle of hair that she followed down and down and down. Max sucked in a breath, which allowed Neve enough room to slip her hands down his jeans and feel him getting harder as she traced the outline of his cock. 'Do you want your present now?'

It was a corny line but Max didn't call her on it, because he was bucking into her hands, knees banging against her legs. 'Yes,' he whispered against her neck. 'Yes.'

And really it would have been a perfect time to take his hand to lead him over to the bed. For a moment Neve wondered if she should invoke a new sub-clause to the hand-holding rule, but it would have killed the mood. Pushing him backwards worked just as well.

Max let her push him down on to the bed, his eyes burning bright in the lamp-light, as Neve straddled him, careful to rest her weight on her knees and her hands as she leaned down to kiss him; tiny nibbles of her lips, her tongue darting out, then retreating every time Max tried to kiss her back.

'What's got into you tonight?' he asked, as Neve dragged him upright by his collar so she could yank his T-shirt over his head.

'I think this slip has magical powers,' Neve said with a grin and she did feel different. She looked hot; he'd said it twice and she felt hot too. It didn't seem to matter that her experience was sorely lacking because her blood was bubbling in her veins and every inch of skin felt newly sensitised, and there was this pulsing in her clit, which made her act purely on instinct. 'Now, I know I said I'd got you a present but I need to unwrap it. Is that all right with you?'

Max nodded. 'Fine with me.'

'I thought you'd say that.' Even her voice sounded different; a little dark, a little desperate as she settled back on her haunches and dealt with Max's belt and buttons with fingers that didn't falter.

Max's cock was hard and wet-tipped, lying almost flat against his stomach. Neve ran her finger up the large vein that ran underneath it. 'Does it hurt when you're like this?'

Max shut his eyes. 'Yeah. Kind of. But it's a good kind of hurt.'

Neve was there to put him out of his agony. She took hold of his dick with a firm grip and moved her hand up and down, gauging how well she was doing from the way Max threw his head back and arched off the bed.

'Is there anything in particular you like?'

She didn't think Max had heard her until his eyes snapped open. 'Give me your hand,' he demanded in a raspy voice and when Neve complied, he seized her wrist, held her hand up to his mouth and ran his tongue along her palm. It made her shiver. And when his tongue darted between her fingers, she shifted her legs so she was straddling one of his thighs and could grind against him. 'Now hold me tighter than you were,' Max said, putting her hand back on his cock, his fingers covering hers and squeezing. 'And you can do it harder and faster.'

They worked together to bring him off, and when his hand fell away and he was oozing pre-cum over her fingers, Neve leaned forward in a cat-like stretch and took him in her mouth. She didn't even attempt to do anything fancy; just tightened her lips around him and continued to move her hand along his shaft.

Max's hands tangled in her hair as if he didn't know whether to pull her closer or pull her away and he was saying her name over and over again in a rising chant, until he said, 'I'm going to come,' as if it was a warning.

Neve hollowed her cheeks and that was all it took.

It was like getting a mouthful of water when she was

321

swimming. Except the water tasted a little salty, a little bitter but not so foul that she wanted to gag. She placed one final kiss on the tip of Max's half-hard cock, then sat back on her heels and wiped the back of her hand across her mouth.

'Was that OK?'

Max didn't say anything, just stretched his arms above his head so Neve could see the frantic rise and fall of his chest. 'Where did you learn to do that?' he finally asked. With what looked like great effort, he managed to raise his head. 'You haven't been practising on anyone else, have you?'

'Hardly,' Neve snorted. 'I did what I always do when I need information.'

'You took out a book on blow-job technique from the British Library? They shouldn't have books like that in there!'

'I wasn't sure if I should be looking in Social Sciences or Humanities. That was embarrassing, let me tell you.'

'Neve, please. You've just let me come in your mouth and right now I don't even remember my own name. I can't tell whether you're joking.'

'I Googled it,' Neve sighed. She crawled up the bed and curled herself around Max, smoothed back his damp hair and kissed his ear, the side of his neck. 'You've still got your jeans on.'

They were bunched around his knees because there hadn't been time to take off his socks and sneakers. Neve shuffled to the foot of the bed and removed the offending items then kissed her way back up Max's prone body, circling her tongue around each flat nipple, but he didn't stir and when she lay down next to him again, his eyes were closed.

'Max? Are you asleep?'

There was no answer and while Neve was pleased that she'd proved to be such a quick learner in the art of oral thanks to the article *A Gay Guy's Guide To Giving Head* that she'd found online, she hoped that Max would find his second wind soon. Because the article hadn't said anything about how arousing it was to give, not just receive, and now she was wet and wanting. She was also seriously contemplating taking matters into her own hands. Would Max want to watch? Would she let him?

'I've never seen anyone look so pleased with themselves.' Max had found the energy to open one eye.

'Well, I wouldn't say I was pleased exactly,' Neve said meaningfully, looking at him from under her lashes and hoping he could take a hint.

'Smug, then?' Max suggested sleepily.

'I think it was a respectable first effort.' Neve snuggled closer, so she could hitch a leg over his and run a hand down his chest casually, as if it was a simple, affectionate caress that just happened to bring her fingers into contact with his cock, which looked as sleepy as the rest of him.

Still, there was no harm in trying, Neve thought, and prodded it gently with the tip of her index finger to see if it had a bit of life left in it. 'God, don't!' Max winced. 'Have you any idea how sensitive a dick is after a man comes?'

Neve snatched her hand away. 'I'm sorry! I was just . . . I wanted to . . .' She flopped back down on her side of the bed. 'It doesn't matter.'

'Wanted to what?'

'Nothing,' Neve said firmly, because the moment Max was asleep she was going to the bathroom with her copy of *The Pearl*, though actually she was rapidly cooling off. 'Go to sleep.'

Max gave a happy grunt and settled back down. He was asleep in an instant, Neve could tell because his limbs slackened and there was a steady up down, up down of his chest. She sat up and swung her legs over the edge of the bed, but before her feet could make contact with the floor, Max's arm suddenly wrapped around her waist and hauled her back.

'Where do you think you're going?' he asked in a voice

that didn't sound the least bit sleep-fogged any more.

'To the loo . . . what are you doing?' Neve yelped, as Max flipped her over and pinned her arms above her head.

'Payback,' he replied succinctly, letting go of her wrists because they both knew she'd keep her arms exactly where he wanted them. 'Time for you to get yours.'

All it took was one hot hand sliding up her thigh and one hot kiss pressed against the flesh that Max had just un-covered to have Neve back in the moment. The moment where she wanted to writhe and arch into the touch of Max's clever fingers and mouth.

'Any chance you might take this off?' he asked, as he settled himself on his stomach between her thighs and tugged at her slip.

'Not a cat's chance in hell,' Neve murmured, reaching over to snap off the bedside light for good measure.

'I can't see what I'm doing,' Max protested, his breath ghosting against the wet lips of her pussy. And when Neve let out an impatient moan, his tongue darted out to taste the sticky glaze that coated her. 'Oh, well. Guess I'll have to feel my way.'

PART THREE

Some Of Your Lovin'

Chapter Twenty-five

Neve slept the whole night with Max's arm tight round her, and she wasn't too hot or too cold. She was perfect. Just perfect. She hadn't slept so well in months.

She only opened her eyes when she felt Max stir and kiss the back of her neck.

'What time is it?' she mumbled.

'Nearly seven,' Max said. 'I have to walk Keith and I've got two pieces of copy to file before we go to Manchester on Thursday. I need to get up.'

Neve was so comfy that she clamped her arm over his when Max tried to loosen his grip on her waist. 'Don't go. Keith will let you know when he wants to go out. He's better than an alarm clock.'

'I should . . . well, I suppose ten minutes won't make much difference.'

The sun was streaming in through a chink in the curtains and Neve felt as if the whole room was bathed in light and that it was a precursor to what was going to be a glorious day, even if she had to spend most of it in a windowless basement transcribing tapes from a dead academic who'd had a very boring sideline in botanical studies.

Max ran his fingers through her hair. She could feel him tugging on the strands, holding them up to the light. 'You've got strands of auburn in your hair. Never noticed that before. How long have we got?'

'You said we were good for at least another ten minutes.'

'No, I meant: how long before Mr California isn't in California any more?'

Neve rolled over because this sudden change in topic felt like the sort of thing that should be discussed face to face. 'His name's William,' she said softly. 'And in his last letter, he mentioned July. Mid-July.'

'It's the middle of April now,' Max said, as Neve stroked the little freckle that sat high up on his cheekbone. 'That's three months and I want us to make the most of them. Will you promise me that you'll stop obsessing about what this all means and just, y'know, live in the moment?'

Living in the moment was something that Neve had always shied away from, in much the same way that she studiously avoided tapered trousers and anything deep-fried, but she found herself nodding in agreement. 'I'd like that. Still not holding your hand though.'

Max smiled so sweetly that Neve could have got a sugar high just from the curve of his lips. 'I wouldn't expect anything less,' he said, inching forward, even though they were almost nose to nose as it was. 'How about we seal it with a kiss instead?'

'Let me brush my teeth,' Neve started to protest. 'Although I suppose not brushing my teeth would fall under the category of "living in the moment".'

'I can handle a bit of morning mouth,' Max said, the smile still there as he kissed her.

Neve thought the sleepy, soft, early-morning kisses might morph into something more urgent as their bodies strained towards each other and hands began to explore, until there was a scrabbling at her bedroom door, followed by a pitiful and urgent whimpering.

With a cardigan over her nightie, Neve saw Max and Keith out. Despite the sun, there was still a bite to the air and she stood on the doorstep trying not to shiver as they made arrangements for the journey to Manchester.

'I'll pick you up at eleven sharp on Thursday morning

after I've dropped Keith off at the dog-sitter,' Max said. 'Bill and Jean are having cocktails in the hotel bar from eight. Should leave us enough time to get there and get ready. Is that all right?'

Neve wasn't sure her limited wardrobe could stretch to cocktails on Thursday night too, but she nodded. 'I suppose this is goodbye until Thursday then?'

Max smiled glumly. 'Roll on Thursday when I'll have six thousand words of copy written and filed.' His shoulders slumped. 'I'd better buy industrial quantities of coffee on the way home.'

'I get through an awful lot of peppermint tea when I'm working on my Lucy chapters,' Neve said. 'I mean, it's not even in the same league as your stuff which people actually read, but well, I have a very vague idea of what you're going through.'

'You know, what with us both being authors, I'll give you permission to read my WAG novels if you let me have a look at this biography you're working on,' Max offered casually.

Neve bit her lip. 'I don't know. I'm not sure what I've written is fit for public consumption, but maybe I should read your novels before Thursday. As research, so I know what to expect before the wedding.'

'It will be fine, Neevy. Everyone will be so shocked that I've turned up with a nice girl who says please and thank you, that they'll fall on you with grateful cries.'

'I still think I'll pop into Waterstone's on the way to work and buy your books,' Neve decided. 'Just so I can pick up some tips.'

'Nope, I absolutely forbid it,' Max stated forcefully. 'I'm not showing you mine, if you won't show me yours.'

Neve grinned. 'That's not how it worked last night,' and then she wasn't grinning because she had to take a moment to remember how Max had worked blind to make her beg and plead and moan.

'Don't change the subject,' Max said, even as he dared to

lift his hand and rub his thumb over her nipple as Neve squirmed away from him, because they were on her doorstep, in broad daylight! 'You have to give me your word you won't read them?'

'But you were really peeved when I said I hadn't read them!'

'That was before we really got to know each other and I don't want you to lose that smidgen of respect you have for me by reading my ghost-written drivel,' Max said and it was such a silly, un-Max-like thing to say that Neve cupped his face as a prelude to giving him one last kiss when there was a bark and a pointed cough from behind Max and Neve opened her eyes to see Gustav standing there, his face impassive. Gustav's face was usually impassive so that didn't mean anything, but Neve could tell from the particularly pronounced lockjaw that he was less than happy.

'Are you ready to run laps round the park before work?' he asked tonelessly, though it was pretty clear from Neve's current state of deshabille (she'd always longed to be in a state of deshabille, but not like this), that she wasn't.

Max pulled a face at Neve before he turned round to hold out one hand to Gustav and calm Keith with the other, because he was straining at the leash and growling. It seemed that Austrian personal trainers in head-to-toe black Lycra were yet another thing that yanked his chain.

'I'm Max,' he said casually. 'Neve's boyfriend. You must be Gustav.'

'Yes, I suppose I must be,' Gustav said in that same flat tone, but at least he shook Max's offered hand.

Neve could tell from the pained look on Max's face that Gustav had his puny writer's fingers in a crushing grip. She glared at Gustav, who glared back but released Max, who hurried down the garden path with a rushed goodbye and a limp wave from the hand that had almost been broken.

*

330

'Why are you so angry with me? You know that I've been seeing someone,' Neve panted an hour later as Gustav had her doing press-ups in Finsbury Park itself. Proper press-ups, not girl press-ups, *on grass*, even though she'd complained that it was covered in dog pee and worse.

'You said it was casual. That he was like a crêpe – and stop arching your back,' Gustav said sourly. 'You never said you were sleeping with him.'

Neve was sure she'd done twenty press-ups by now and her back was killing her. 'Please, Gustav. Stomach crunches, side planks, anything . . . I can't do any more.'

'Crunches, then. Two months ago I would never hear you say "I can't" and you would never have forgotten a training session.'

'You never usually make me do proper press-ups,' Neve hissed through gritted teeth as she started her crunches. 'Look, I'm committed to this. You know I am. I have to drop the last two dress sizes in three months.'

'It's easy to say that but I see this all the time. My clients form attachments,' Gustav curled his mouth around the word as if it tasted bitter, 'and they start neglecting their fitness. They go out for candle-lit meals all the time and they put on weight. That boyfriend of yours looks very out of condition. He'll be a bad influence on you.'

'I've told you a million times, Max isn't really a proper boyfriend and honestly, Gustav, do you think I've come this far only to slide back into old habits?' Neve insisted breathlessly because apart from a few glasses of wine, she hadn't deviated from her diet. 'Anyway, Max is going to start running again now that the weather's getting warmer.'

It was one of the worst things she could have said, short of admitting that she'd been drinking liquid lard. Gustav had plenty to say about fair-weather runners, and when Neve told him that she wouldn't be able to make her Saturday session because she was going away, she thought his jaw would break, he was clenching it so tightly.

'But you never miss a Saturday session,' Gustav gritted. 'They're our special time. I always think of new and exciting things for us to do.'

He did, though Neve would never class exercises with kettle bells or skipping ropes as exciting. 'Don't your other clients have to skip the odd session because of their personal commitments?'

'You're not like my other clients,' Gustav said, and Neve knew that he meant it as a compliment, but having seen some of Gustav's other clients, all successful, glamorous, high-flying types, she suspected that they probably had to cancel personal training sessions because they were jetting off for a weekend skiing in Gstaad or a fortnight in St Barts. Whereas Neve never jetted off anywhere because she was dependable, predictable and, until Max had come along, didn't really have much in the way of a social life.

Celia also seemed a little put out that Neve was going through with her audacious scheme to leave the Greater London area for the weekend.

'But what if I have some kind of emergency this weekend and I need you and you're not here?' she demanded, when she came upstairs the following evening to borrow some milk and found Neve trying on her trouser suit to make sure her hips hadn't expanded since she bought it.

'You could phone me,' Neve suggested as she twisted round to see what her bottom looked like in the mirror and caught sight of Celia's pained face. 'Seels, you knew I was going to this stupid WAG wedding because you were with me when I got the summons from Mandy McIntyre and I know you haven't forgotten one excruciating second of our shopping trip for wedding outfits.'

Celia threw herself down on Neve's bed and actually flailed her limbs in frustration. 'Yeah, but I never thought you'd actually go through with it.' She folded her arms and stared at the ceiling. 'I bet you any money that on Thursday morning, you bottle it.'

'No, I won't!' Neve snapped, even though she had half hoped that Mandy's fiancé might be one of those footballers who couldn't keep it in his trousers and would be exposed by the tabloids as a serial love rat and that the wedding would be called off, but no such luck.

Her only other hope was that either she or Max went down with something icky and intestinal like the novovirus, but every time she'd spoken to him on the phone, all his usual studied cool and nonchalance had disappeared as he babbled on about getting his Dior Pour Homme suit dry-cleaned and asking if Neve had any preferences for what music she'd like to listen to in the car.

No, she couldn't bail out when Max was so excited about the wedding. Not just because it was going to be crammed full of celebrities, but because he seemed to be an honorary member of the wedding party. Mandy and Darren had even asked him to help write their vows, and Mandy had also made Max load up his iPod with Northern Soul classics because she didn't trust the DJ they'd booked for the reception. For someone who didn't do relationships, Max seemed very excited about seeing Mandy and Darren plight their troth. 'Though I don't think I'll mention "plighting their troth" in the vows,' he'd said to Neve. 'Isn't a troth something that pigs eat from?'

It wasn't just the thought of turning up with Max and having the McIntyres and the attendant WAGs wonder what the hell he was doing with her that had Neve in such a panic. No, she was also freaking out about the havoc the wedding would wreak on her routine. What if she couldn't work out for the entire four days they were in Manchester? And what if the hotel didn't have unsweetened muesli on their breakfast menu but the regular kind that was stuffed full of sugar, and what if she couldn't sleep without her memory foam pillow? These were silly things to be panicking about, Neve knew that, but she was a creature of habit and that habit was being sorely tested by the wedding.

It was almost a relief to have an email from Jacob Morrison waiting for her when she got into work on Wednesday morning. At least it would be something different to worry about.

```
Dear Neve
Sorry I've taken so long to get back to you.
I read Dancing on the Edge of the World last
night - actually I stayed up until three
because I couldn't put it down.
   I think you've discovered something very
special here. I love Lucy's voice; her dry
humour and the way she can write with such a
depth of feeling without ever veering into
sentimentality. Could you phone my assistant
and arrange to courier over Lucy's short
stories and poems?
   I also read your synopsis and would like to
see what you've written so far.
Best wishes
Jacob
```

It was impossible to tell whether he'd liked the synopsis or not. Neve dared to hope that the very fact that Jacob was asking to see what she'd written was a good thing. Or else he just wanted to confirm his suspicions that she could barely string a sentence together.

Neve completely abandoned any thoughts about transcribing, but every time Mr Freemont poked his head round the door of her office and saw her working so diligently, he gave her a tight smile (he was still smarting over his smackdown at the AGM) and left her alone to try and sprinkle some magic dust on her prose.

Neve spent the rest of the day and a good portion of the night, too, prodding and poking at her six and a half chapters, interrupted only by regular emails from Chloe who kept sending her links to increasingly preposterous tabloid stories about the wedding, though Neve doubted that Her Majesty the Queen had really granted Mandy McIntyre permission to have swans swimming in specially built lily ponds in the middle of the dancefloor at the reception.

The courier arrived at ten on Thursday morning to pick up two laden Jiffy bags while Neve was still unshowered and in her pyjamas. There hadn't even been time to go to New Look in a lunch-hour to find a suitable dress for bar-hopping with the WAGs, so Neve had no choice but to stuff the silver-sequined shift dress into her weekend bag. It was either that or one of her black wrap dresses, and Celia had made her feelings about them perfectly clear. Besides, it was already eleven twenty and Max was leaning on the door-bell. Neve decided she'd try the sequined horror on again once she'd bought some heavy-duty body-shaping tights to see if it was as bad as she remembered.

'That reminds me, do you think we'll have time to go to a Marks & Spencer when we get to Manchester?' she asked Max as he slid into the driver's seat of the bright red Mini Cooper he'd been given by his publisher.

'We can make time,' Max promised. He shot her a side-ways glance. 'You look a little bit terrified. You're not going to hurl yourself from the car if I stop at a red light, are you?'

Neve nodded. 'Thinking about it.' With the rush to do her best by Lucy, there hadn't been time to have any more panic attacks about the wedding, but now Neve was free to work herself up into a state of near hysteria about spa days and clubbing with Mandy and her WAG friends who she'd have nothing in common with – and what if the robes at the Spa didn't fit her, and—

'You've gone really pale,' Max noted. 'You don't get travel sick, do you?'

'It's not that,' Neve said, winding down the window to get some fresh air. 'I just don't want to show you up.'

'Well, that's not going to happen, as long as you don't tell anyone that your brother supports Arsenal. Is that a smile?'

'Might be,' Neve agreed, and she let her hand rest on Max's knee for a moment because she'd missed touching him. Which was ridiculous because she'd only seen him three days before. Maybe it was because she'd always tamped down any sexual longing and now her body wanted to make up for lost time. And then some.

Max looked down at her hand, still on his knee. 'I've come up with a song which is absolutely guaranteed to get rid of your nerves,' he announced proudly. 'Do you want to hear it?'

'I didn't know you could sing.'

'Well, I can't, but I think that will just add to my performance. Are you ready for this?'

There wasn't enough time in the world to prepare Neve for Max's out-of-tune rendition of 'It's a Nice Day for a Wag Wedding'. His loud, toneless voice was almost as bad as her reedy, high-pitched singing, because after she'd stopped laughing, Neve couldn't resist joining in.

By the time they passed Birmingham, they were happily and randomly adding the word WAG to any song they could think of, when Neve was suddenly inspired and began to warble, 'With her Fendi bag/She's my wonderWAG.'

Max had to cut through two lines of traffic, pull over on the hard shoulder, rest his head on the steering wheel and get himself under control before he crashed the car. His shoulders shook violently as he tried to rein in the giggles. Every time he stopped, Neve would think of another line to torture him with, 'And all the clothes we have to wear are skintight/And if we didn't tan so much we'd be lilywhite.'

'No more,' he begged, his voice hoarse from laughing, as he started up the engine again.

They arrived in Manchester just after four, leaving the good weather behind them as they joined the M6. Malmaison Manchester was an elegant redbrick building – just round the corner from a large Marks & Spencer, Neve was pleased to note. Once they'd braved the paparazzi that were lurking outside, much to Neve's disbelief, they then had their reservation details, wedding invites and ID approved at two different security checkpoints. Only then were they allowed to approach the reception desk. Another security guard escorted them to the lift, and finally Max and Neve were shown into their junior suite. The huge space was sleek and modern, all cool white with icy blue accents and striped wallpaper, which made Neve's vision blur if she stared at it for too long. Max had already opened his laptop and was checking the wi-fi access, as Neve peeked into the black and gold bathroom and stared in awe at the huge shower and the sunken bathtub, which was the last word in decadence.

'This is amazing,' Neve said, as she walked back into the bedroom. 'I've never stayed anywhere like this. In fact, I don't think I've stayed in a proper hotel before.'

'But this is only a junior suite. It's not that amazing,' Max protested. 'And what do you mean, you've never stayed in a hotel before?'

'Well, I stayed in bed and breakfasts when we went on holiday when I was little, and when I went to New York, I slept on Celia's sofa.'

'What about when you go away on holiday now?' Max asked.

'Well, for some reason spending two weeks on a beach in Corfu has never really appealed to me.'

'I'm not big on vacations either. They're not much fun when you live on your own and then you go on holiday on your own and you end up cruising bars to find someone . . .' Max came to an abrupt halt as he realised that he was heading steadily for the door marked TMI. 'Maybe we could sneak in a week's holiday between now and July?'

'I've always wanted to go to France,' Neve blurted out, her heart thudding excitedly. In all her stress about the WAG-sponsored weekend, there hadn't been one moment of angst devoted to spending three nights in a hotel room with Max. On the contrary, Neve had even attempted her first, very amateur bikini wax half an hour before Max had arrived to pick her up. She smiled at Max, who grinned back at her. 'Right now though, I really want to go to Marks & Spencer.'

Max checked the time. 'It's half four now, so we could have a really late lunch or an early dinner, but we'll still have a couple of hours to kill before cocktails.' He struck a pensive pose, finger resting on his chin. 'What would you like to do in this big, comfy room with a big, comfy bed in it?'

'I need to have a bath and wash my hair,' Neve said innocently, as she slipped her jacket back on. 'And it takes me for ever, ten minutes at least, to do my make-up. That still leaves us an hour with nothing to do.'

'An hour and a half,' Max decided, as he ushered Neve out of the room. 'Can't turn up at eight exactly. That's ninety minutes, Neve.'

Neve waited until the lift doors were just about to open before she turned to Max, 'I could always give you another blow job if you wanted. Just to kill the time.'

Chapter Twenty-six

In the end, Neve only had time for a quick shower and made do with some dry shampoo and five minutes for her make-up. The moment that she'd slid between the covers of that big, comfy bed and collided with Max who was already hot and hard, time had seemed to slow down, then speed up, and it wasn't until she was coming down from her second orgasm that she happened to catch sight of the clock and discovered it was already eight o'clock.

'We're not fashionably late,' she said to Max, as she screwed the top back on her mascara. 'We're just plain late.'

Max shrugged. 'It was worth it. Next time I'm going to persuade you to take off your slip at some point.'

'Good luck with that,' Neve said tartly, because yes, she'd come a long way but letting that last barrier fall away . . . she didn't think she'd ever be that brave. She took a step back to peer at herself in the mirror, tilting back and forth so the skirt of her black lace and oyster satin dress fluttered around her.

Her new black suede, three-inch Mary-Janes were already making her toes want to curl up and die, but paired with black opaque tights, they made her legs look longer and leaner, and the dress gave Neve a decent cleavage and a smaller waist. But it was more than just the agreeable reflection that Neve saw in the mirror, it was Max sitting on the bed, watching her watch herself, with nothing but appreciation, his eyes lingerering on her breasts.

'You look beautiful,' he said quietly, as they descended in the lift to the bar.

Neve stole one last look at her hastily assembled up-do in the mirrored walls of the elevator and nervously patted a stray tendril of hair. 'I need to find something else to do with my hair that isn't a messy ponytail or a messy bun,' she murmured. 'But thank you,' she added, when she saw a flicker of irritation on Max's face, because the one thing he didn't have any patience with was her self-deprecation. 'And you look pretty spiffy yourself, but I still think you should have worn the suit trousers as well as the suit jacket. And maybe some shoes that weren't made by Converse.'

Max looked down at his Levis and sneakers. 'But these are my good jeans and my least scuffed Converses,' he protested. He protested even more when Neve pulled her comb out of her bag and tugged it through his hair.

'For someone who won't hold my hand, you're clutching my arm really tightly,' he whispered once they'd given their names to yet another security person and were walking towards the bar.

Neve could hardly hear him over the pounding of her heart and the hum of conversation and laughter that got louder and louder as they approached the open doors at the end of the corridor. Neve had a vague impression of a very upmarket bordello; red lights descended from the ceiling and illuminated tiny tables and leather armchairs decorated with huge metal studs that swept in a gentle arc around the huge room.

'Clutching your arm very tightly isn't a bit like holding your hand,' Neve whispered back, her voice high-pitched and squeaky, and they were getting closer now and she wanted to dig her heels into the thick carpet, or even better, turn and run back to the safety of their junior suite. Instead she leaned against Max, trying to leech some of his calm, and put one foot in front of the other, until they were in the bar and fighting their way through the crowd.

The faces were all a blur and all Neve could focus on was the black wool sleeve of his jacket, as she kept a death grip on Max. She tried to shrink in on herself to navigate the narrow path between the press of people, head down, and it was only when she found herself staring at a pair of tasselled loafers and pink polished toenails peeking out of a pair of open-toed gold sandals that she realised they'd come to a halt.

'Neve, I'd like you to meet Bill and Jean, Mandy's parents. This is Neve, my . . . girlfriend,' she heard Max say and his hand was covering hers, which was still on his arm and she forced herself to look up.

'It's very nice to meet you,' she said automatically, as her parents had drummed into her from an early age, and smiled weakly at them.

Bill had thinning, snowy-white hair brushed back from a weather-beaten face and was tugging at the collar of his pink dress shirt with one hand while the thick fingers of his other hand were clutched round a delicate flute of champagne. He looked as if he'd be more comfortable in jeans and a T-shirt with a can of lager to hold.

'Now, Max has told us all about you, but he never mentioned how gorgeous you are. Look at that skin,' Jean said, and she actually raised a hand and pinched Neve's cheek, just like Granny Annie had used to do, though Granny Annie could never have got away with wearing a white trouser suit and a black sequined camisole, unlike Jean McIntyre with her big blonde hair and glossy pink lips, which were stretched in a warm, welcoming smile. 'Smooth as a baby's bum. She's got a degree from Oxford as well, Bill.'

'Surely a clever girl like you could do better than this little sod,' Bill said, with a nod in Max's direction, his barrel-like chest shaking with laughter. Then he wrapped an arm around Max so he could ruffle his hair, while Max squirmed and rolled his eyes. 'This boy is the son I never had and never wanted. Hope you're not going to break his heart.'

'Well, I'll try not to,' Neve said helplessly, and they were both still smiling at her so she smiled back and racked her brains for something else to say.

'So, Bill, Neve's dad is in the building trade too,' Max said once he'd been released, and as Bill immediately started firing questions at her, Neve shot Max a grateful look.

After they'd discussed the impact the credit crunch had had on new builds, Neve mentioned that her father owned a builder's yard in Sheffield and it turned out that Jean's sister lived in Brincliffe, just down the road from Neve's cousin, Linda, and ten minutes had gone past.

Neve was still nervous. Her fingers tapped against Max's arm, but she wasn't paralysed by fear any more and when Jean suddenly gasped and said, 'We'd better go and find our Mandy. She's dying to meet you. You stay here, Max, and tell Bill about when you met that Paris Hilton,' Neve was able to let go of Max's arm and let Jean lead her through the crowd.

It was a very slow process because every time they took a step, Jean would introduce her to someone that Neve dimly recognised from *Coronation Street* or the old issues of *Now* and *OK!* that she'd borrowed from Rose so she could swot up on her WAGs.

'This is so kind of you,' she said to Jean, as they reached the back of the room and the crowd began to thin out. 'I mean, taking the time to introduce me to everyone when you must have so many people that you need to talk to.'

Jean patted her hand. 'Don't you worry about it, pet. Could tell you were terrified as soon as I clapped eyes on you. Between you and me, I'd give my right arm to be back at home with a nice mug of tea and a box of fondant fancies. Now, where has that girl got to?'

They didn't find Mandy McIntyre because she found them. One moment Neve was gawping at a man across the room who looked a lot like Thierry Henri (and even *she* knew who he was), the next there was an ear-splitting squawk and someone was throwing their arms round her.

'Neve? You're Max's Neve, right?'

Neve could neither confirm nor deny this as her mouth was pressed against Mandy's neck and she was almost asphyxiated from inhaling great whiffs of Gucci's Envy.

'Mandy! Let the poor girl go. You're smothering her.'

Neve was thrust away by two strong hands as Mandy said, 'Let's have a proper look at you, then.'

All Neve could see was tanned, tanned skin, blonde, blonde hair and the shortest, tightest, stretchiest white dress in the world, until her eyes reached Mandy's face. Once you stripped away the tan and the highlights and the bandage dress, even the bright blue contact lenses, Mandy McIntyre was what her mother would call homely looking. Her mascara-encrusted eyes were small and she had a snub nose and a short top lip, but there was something so unthreatening and achievable about the way she looked, that Neve totally understood why she earned millions of pounds from endorsing supermarket chains, starring in workout videos, lending her name to a range of home tanning products and pretending to write books about an ordinary girl living in an extraordinary world.

'I knew Max would go for a boho girl. You're so arty and cool,' Mandy declared so sincerely that even Neve was convinced for a few blissful seconds. 'I'd love to work the opaque tights but I think, well, what was the point in getting fake baked? Then I spend the whole evening freezing my arse off.'

And that was the other thing that had made Mandy McIntyre a multi-millionairess: within five minutes of being introduced, eight out of ten people thought she was the nicest person they'd ever met.

Neve was no exception. For the second time that evening she held hands with someone who wasn't Max and let Mandy lead her around the bar like a little lapdog to be patted and petted. In fact, she did meet Mandy's Shih Tzu, Gucci, who was being held by Mandy's fiancé. Darren Stretton was gangling, tongue-tied and didn't have that much to say for someone whose right foot was insured for £2 million. Neve did manage to establish that he was 'over the moon about getting married to our Mandy'. He and Mandy shared a long, affectionate look, which was interrupted by the arrival of Darren's team-mates, who all shook Neve's hand politely and didn't seem that bothered that she could barely stammer her way through the introductions. As it was, she wished, like she'd never wished for anything, that Douglas, Celia and especially Charlotte were here to see her surrounded on all sides by eleven men wearing shades, designer suits and buckets of expensive cologne. 'You see?' she'd say. 'There is some cool in me, after all.'

Except, Neve wasn't being cool. She was gawking and blushing like a twelve-year-old girl at a Jonas Brothers' concert and it was a relief when Mandy took her hand and dragged her over to meet her gran and her great-aunt and Wendy, who used to live next door before the McIntyres moved to Alderley Edge.

Neve was trying to politely defend herself against allegations that everything in London was horribly expensive, which served Londoners right for being so up themselves, when Mandy took her hand again. 'I want Neve to meet the girls,' she explained, yanking a grateful Neve away. 'Sorry about that. My nan will only go as far south as the Trafford Centre, and then she moans and groans about the state of the loos. Now, let's go and find the girls and you haven't even had a drink. There should be some champagne knocking about but I need to ask someone how many calories there are in a glass.'

'Seventy-five,' Neve said, without even having to think about it.

'God, you're so smart,' Mandy trilled, leading Neve to a raised seating area at the back of the bar. 'Here are the girls.

344

Neve, this is my sister, Kelly, and my best friend, Tasha, and my other best friend, Chelsy, and Emma, who's also my best friend and Lauren, who's my best friend *and* my PA. This is Neve – Max's Neve.'

Mandy's five best friends were arranged on a black leather sofa and two armchairs. They looked Neve up and down, with faces that weren't completely unfriendly, but weren't exactly welcoming either. Neve knew that all her worst fears had been confirmed: Kelly, Tasha, Chelsy, Emma and Lauren were cut from exactly the same cloth as Charlotte.

They were all tanned with long, flicky, super-shiny hair, and the only thing smaller than their skirts were the teeny tiny clutch bags adorned in gilt hardware and logos that even Neve could recognise: Gucci, Louis Vuitton and yes, Fendi, except that didn't seem quite so funny now when she was standing in front of them wearing a big foofy dress that was more Mother of the Bride than arty, cool Girlfriend of the Bride's ghost-writer.

'I'm going to get some champagne. Come on, guys, budge up,' Mandy demanded and Kelly, Tasha and Chelsy (or was it Emma?) grudgingly shifted so there was a tiny gap on the sofa that wasn't going to accommodate Neve's forty-three-inch hips.

'It's OK,' she mumbled, perching uncomfortably on the arm of the sofa and hoping that she wasn't sticking her bottom in someone's face. 'I can sit here.'

'So, you and Max, then?' Kelly queried, tossing her long, streaked hair away from her face. Neve counted at least five different tones in her highlights and marvelled at the sheer level of grooming on display. It must take them *hours* to get ready. 'How long have you been hooking up?'

Was hooking up the same as dating? Neve wasn't sure. 'Well, we've been seeing each other for just over two months.'

'What? Speak up. I can hardly hear you.'

Neve repeated herself at a volume that had to qualify as a

bellow and the five of them nodded and conferred amongst themselves. 'When did Max hook up with Shelly then? Wasn't that long ago, was it?'

'Well, it was after Ricky but before Bryan. And she was with Ricky for Christmas but Bryan took her away to the Seychelles for Valentine's Day, so it must have been January.' They all looked at Neve who had no option but to sit there with a frozen face while they thought it appropriate to discuss exactly when Max had been having sex with some other girl who wasn't her.

'You can say what you like about Shelly but she's really gorgeous and she always pulls the fittest blokes,' Kelly piped up in defence of her morally-lacking friend who'd been kicked out of the wedding party for shagging the wrong kind of footballer, then selling her story to the tabloids. 'I always thought she and Max would be perfect together.' She gave Neve another searching look, which verged on incredulous. 'How did you and Max meet anyway?'

'Through my sister,' Neve bit out, accepting a glass of champagne from Mandy, who'd hopefully come to her defence.

'Neve is the smartest girl I've ever met,' Mandy informed her friends, who looked singularly unimpressed. 'She's got a degree from Oxford and Max says she's got more books than anyone he's ever known *and* she knew how many calories there are in a glass of champagne without having to look it up on her iPhone first.'

That last point was greeted with murmurs of approval as Mandy pressed on. 'You have to be extra nice to Neve 'cause she doesn't know anyone except Max,' she announced, plonking herself down in the gap between her sister and Tasha. 'So, Neve, what are you doing tomorrow morning?'

Mentally girding myself for the prospect of having to spend an afternoon at a spa with your friends, Neve wanted to say, but she just flailed her hands and spilled champagne down the front of her dress. 'Um, I don't know. Max said something about . . .'

'He's got to have a meeting with my agent about our next book,' Mandy told her sweetly. 'So you're coming to our last bridal boot-camp session. We're doing it in the grounds of the Country Club where the spa is and it's where we're having the reception. It's dead gorgeous. I really wanted to get married in a castle but we couldn't find a nice one that was near Manchester and I was *gutted* but then my dad said—'

'Mandy! We've been doing bridal boot camp for months. *She* probably won't be able to keep up with us,' Chelsy interrupted. 'Do you really want to have to go at half speed for the last boot camp when you still need to lose another two pounds before Saturday?'

Mandy bit her lip and Neve could see her hesitation. Her innate goodwill was being sorely tested by the demands of fitting into a designer wedding dress.

'It's all right,' Neve said quickly. 'I can just do my usual workout in the hotel gym.'

'You work out?' Kelly's sculpted eyebrows disappeared into her fringe. 'Really?'

'Well, yes, a few times a week but not in a group, with a trainer, and I don't—'

'That's perfect then,' Mandy sighed in relief. 'Neve can do the bridal boot camp and hang out with us all day.' She stood up. 'I have to go and rescue Darren. I think Gucci's being traumatised by all the noise.'

Neve watched her walk away with dismay. She craned her neck to see if she could spot Max in the crowd and was wondering if now would be a good time to make her excuses when Lauren tapped her on the knee.

'I need to talk to you about your spa treatments,' she said brusquely, as she held up her iPhone. 'I've got you down for a pampering facial, a leg wax, but the waxer's got an extra half-hour free so she said she'd do your bikini line too.'

'Oh, that's very nice, but—'

'But I need to check whether you want a luxury pedicure or a medi-pedi?' Lauren looked expectantly at Neve.

'Um, what's a medi-pedi?'

'You don't know what a medi-pedi is?'

The five of them looked appalled. Outraged, even, as if there was no point in owning a lot of books if you didn't even know what a medi-pedi was.

'A luxury pedicure will be fine,' Neve said woodenly, and it was silly and she was over-reacting because she'd had much worse treatment from much meaner girls than this, but she could feel her bottom lip trembling and she had to stop herself from blinking, because the next time she blinked, she knew the first tears would start to trickle down her face.

'Then we're heading back to town to get our hair and faces done but they haven't got time to do anything more than give us a wash and blow dry and—'

'That's fine. I have to go now and find Max.' Neve was already getting up and almost falling off her heels in the process. 'It was very nice to meet you all.' She didn't wait to hear what they had to say about that, but tripped down the three steps and frantically scanned the room for Max.

He was right where she'd left him, standing at the bar, and just seeing his lovely, easy smile as he talked to some-one was like coming home to a warm flat after walking through a snowstorm.

Neve began to fight her way through the crowd, all set to launch into a tirade about how vile Mandy's friends were and she was not, repeat not, boot-camping with them or Spa-ing with them either, come to that. If Max had to find a doctor who'd write her a sick-note, then so be it. But as she got nearer to Max, even using elbows when she really had to, Neve saw that he was still talking to Bill and Jean. Jean had her arm tucked through Max's, her head tilted to catch his every last word. Then when he got to the end of his speech, Bill clapped him on the back, maybe a little too hard, because Max rocked back on his heels, but it broke Neve's heart a little.

She was probably being too fanciful, that's what her mum would say, but looking from the outside in, it occurred to her that Bill and Jean really were Max's honorary parents, or as close as he had. This wasn't just a work event for him. He'd been invited by people who cared about him and she didn't want them to say, 'Lovely to see Max, but that sulky girlfriend of his was a real piece of work,' when they left on Monday morning.

There was nothing else to do but suck it up and get through tomorrow even if it killed her – she wouldn't put it past those horrible girls to put something toxic in her hot wax. What did those scary LA publicists say to Max when he was requesting shoot time with their celebrity clients? It was one day out of her entire life.

Max looked over, caught her eye and waved. He said something to Bill and Jean, who both smiled, and there was nothing else to do but paste a grin on her face and walk towards them.

Chapter Twenty-seven

'You have exactly the same look that Keith gets when I'm taking him to the vet,' Max remarked when he pulled up in front of the Alderley Edge Country Club, which was an ugly Victorian building that looked like a very ornate gingerbread house. 'I thought you liked working out.'

'I do,' Neve said, trying to mask the unease she felt as Max switched off the engine. She'd prayed that he'd crash the car somewhere along the A34; not badly enough that anybody got fatally injured, but she'd have been perfectly happy with a broken leg. 'I'm fine. I'm just tired.'

'Ah, so that's what's bothering you,' Max said knowingly as he nudged her arm. 'Make it up to you tonight, I promise.'

'Make what up to me? It's not that,' she sighed, as light finally dawned. The night before, she'd left Max in the bar to have 'one more for the road'. 'I don't expect *that* every night.'

It had been another two hours before he'd finally stumbled back to their room and woken her up by falling over his weekend bag. Then he'd staggered over to the bed and tried to start something, which he obviously had no intention of finishing because he was so drunk that he couldn't even take his own clothes off. Neve had pulled him out of bed, undressed him, helped him to brush his teeth, then left him to do the rest himself. He'd ended up spending the night on the sofa, because he hadn't been able to make it back to the bed.

'What's the matter then?' Max asked, a hand on Neve's chin to turn her face towards him. 'What are you so scared about?'

'I'm not scared of anything,' she declared shakily.

'You can't pull that crap with me any more. I know you too well now,' Max said, with just one squeeze of lemon juice in his voice. 'I know that Mandy's mates are, well, they're a bit ... you don't have much in common with them, but after they've jawed on about designer handbags and fake tans for a couple of hours, you can keep them entertained by telling them what a great boyfriend I am.'

'I think they're already up to date on that topic,' Neve said scathingly, and she hadn't wanted to pick a fight with Max, but the good intentions from the night before were wearing thin. 'I think your mutual friend, Shelly, hit the highlights for them.'

'Is that what this is all about? I never went out with Shelly.'

'So I heard.' Condescension dripped from every syllable and it wasn't just that picking a fight with Max was a great way to take her mind off the ordeal that lay ahead, it was also because of the amount of time Neve had spent last night thinking about the infamous Shelly. She only had a handful of facts to go on: she'd slept with Max as well as two Premier Division footballers, she was really gorgeous according to Kelly McIntyre, and she was a girl who had no problem with sharing details of her sex-life with the readers of the Sunday tabloids.

It was a pretty damning character assessment but Neve was already skipping ahead to fill in the blanks. Shelly obviously adhered to the WAG stereotype and was long of leg, large of breast, had shiny, blonde hair and orange skin best displayed in tiny dresses and Hoochie Mama heels.

In short, she was the polar opposite of Neve, which was humiliating enough, but not as humiliating as having to find out from those awful girls that Max had slept with Shelly.

'If Shelly's the kind of woman you'd prefer, then there's really not much point in either of us continuing with this little charade,' she told Max coldly. 'I'd hate to think that all the time you were with me, you were wishing you were with some other girl who—'

'You've got a fucking nerve!' Neve had never heard Max sound so angry and she really didn't like it. He turned to her. His face was pinched and tight, eyes blazing with sudden fury. 'The whole point of "this little charade" is because you're in love with some guy on the other side of the world, in case you'd forgotten. So, if I don't bring up your future, then why the hell are you bringing up my past? Why?'

'Well, because . . . you should have warned me that you'd slept with Mandy's friends,' Neve blustered, because when she'd decided to pick a fight, she'd imagined a one-sided fight, where she'd have an opportunity to vent all her frustration, while Max just sat there and took it. Though now that he was glaring at her and she could feel his anger stirring the air, she should have known that he wouldn't meekly sit there and take anything. 'It was mortifying.'

'Yeah, about as mortifying as knowing that every single one of those little moves that you've picked up on the internet are being neatly rated and catalogued in your head so by the time you get to use them on Mr California, they're perfect.' Max leaned towards her. Neve shrank back in alarm, but he was just opening her door. 'Get out.'

'You're not actually in a position to take the moral high ground here . . .'

'I was going to tell you to call me when you wanted picking up, even if you decided you'd had enough after an hour, but you know what, sweetheart? You can call a bloody cab.'

Neve released her seat belt with shaking fingers and scrambled out of the car. 'I wouldn't have to bring up your past if you'd been a bit more selective about the people that you've had sex with,' she hissed, before she slammed the door shut so hard that she could feel the reverberation all the way up her arm.

Max started the car and swung around in a fast, tight circle, gravel spraying up and hitting Neve in the face before she could step back. Crunching gears, he then took off at great speed down the sweeping driveway, lurching to the left to make room for a huge people-carrier coming the other way.

Picking a fight with Max hadn't made Neve feel any better. She still felt insecure, resentful and terrified, and she half expected Max to come back, tell her to get in the car, drive her to the station and put her on the first train back to London.

But he wasn't coming back and the people-carrier had now pulled up alongside her, the doors were sliding back and her companions for the day began to emerge, each one of them wearing a pink velour tracksuit. As Chelsy climbed out of the car, Neve saw *Team McIntyre* written on the back of her hoodie in diamanté and hoped that she wasn't going to be forced into bloody Shelly's bloody pink tracksuit.

Chelsy, Kelly, Lauren, Emma and Tasha all nodded coolly at Neve as they lined up, like a little reception committee for Mandy who was the last to disembark. Mandy at least looked pleased to see her as she jumped down from the car.

'Neve! So glad you could make it!' Mandy's hair was in two bunches that bobbed as she spoke, which was very distracting. 'Was that Max going the other way? He nearly ran us off the road – and the day before my wedding too.'

'He's late for an appointment in town,' Neve lied, her voice shrill with anxiety.

'Oh, you should have come with us,' Mandy said, tucking her arm into Neve's as they began to walk up the steps towards the entrance. 'We had to pick up Chelsy and Tasha from Malmaison – didn't anyone mention that last night?'

They hadn't and it might have saved Neve from fighting with Max in favour of being cold-shouldered by the pink-tracksuited hordes. She couldn't decide which would have been a lesser evil.

They dumped their bags in a cloakroom, then Neve watched as all six of them pulled out designer make-up bags from designer holdalls and began to retouch bronzer, mascara and lipgloss. Just how brutal was bridal boot camp if you could do it without smudging your make-up or your hair going frizzy Neve wondered, as she began her warm-up stretches. She always ended a workout with her hair and skin soaked in perspiration.

'How long do you work out for?' she asked Mandy as they left the cloakroom and walked through a set of French doors out on to a green lawn, which looked as if it was more used to a gentle game of croquet than a boot camp.

'We've got it up to three hours,' Mandy said cheerfully. 'But we take lots of rest breaks and the last hour is Pilates. Very gentle Pilates.' She looked Neve up and down, though for once Neve knew no fear. She sometimes thought that she'd quite like to live in her workout gear; it was comfortable and had such a high Lycra content that she always felt pleasantly contained. Even her breasts behaved themselves when they were encased in a racer-back sports bra *and* a crop top under a thin, long-sleeved T-shirt. Her ensemble also met with Mandy's approval because she was nodding happily. 'You didn't have to bring your own towel or water, Jacqui sorts that out.'

Neve was just about to ask who Jacqui was (just how many personal assistants did Mandy need?) when the French doors opened and a small, athletically built woman with a platinum blonde crew cut and a pugnacious face trotted out, followed by a trail of Country Club employees carrying crates of gym equipment and a huge coolbox.

'OK, ladies, line up and let's get stretching,' she shouted.

The WAGs quickly got into line and Neve found herself next to Kelly, who was already bending from the waist eagerly.

Neve tried to do everything that everyone else did at roughly the same time, though the WAGs had moved on to 'Step, touch, double arms,' while she was still getting to grips with 'step, touching'.

Jacqui jogged over and stared at Neve as she stepped and touched and windmilled her arms. 'You're not wearing pink,' she said accusingly. 'Who are you?'

'Oh, this is Neve and on the inside she's wearing pink,' Mandy said helpfully from further down the line. 'She's standing in for Shelly and it's OK, she works out all the time. Even her boyfriend says she does.'

Neve tried to smile but Jacqui was unmoved. 'Try to keep up,' she barked. 'Last boot-camp session, can't have any stragglers.'

'Actually, um, you know, I probably will hold you back,' Neve stammered. 'I'll go and run some laps while you do, er, what you do.' Then without waiting for permission to leave, she took off down the manicured lawn as if the hounds of hell were snapping at her heels.

When she reached the end of the lawn, Neve followed a gravel path at a gentle jog so she could take in the rolling green fields around her and look at the little folly on a tiny island in the middle of the lake. The air was fresh and clean and for the first time that day, her stomach didn't feel as if it was tied in huge, gnarly knots.

She gradually increased her speed and let her mind go blank so all she could feel were her lungs burning and the ache in her thighs so she had to push herself harder and harder. Each time Neve felt as if she couldn't go any further because her legs would collapse, she'd summon up another spurt of energy and force herself to do another lap around the lake. It was heavenly not to think, just to feel.

'Slow down, slow down,' said a voice and Neve realised that Jacqui had fallen into step alongside her. 'One more lap and I want you walking the last quarter.'

'OK,' Neve panted, and decreasing her speed felt as good

as stopping. 'Sorry . . . for running off . . . used to working out . . .'

'A lot harder than that bunch of lazy arses,' Jacqui said with a grin. 'Mandy's a good kid but they're all bloody useless. Come on. Slow it down, girl.'

Neve came to a halt and bent over, hands on her knees as she got her breath back. Jacqui ran back to where the WAGs were sprawled in a pastel-pink heap, as Neve stretched her hamstrings, then rejoined them.

She was paired with Chelsy, which did not fill her heart with joy. From the unhappy look on Chelsy's face, she felt the same way. Underneath her thick foundation, which was decidedly smeared by now, the other girl looked green as they stood opposite each other and began to pass a medicine ball.

Mostly Neve held the medicine ball because every time she tried to give it to Chelsy the other girl would shy away, her hands warding off any possible passing-type action. 'Give me a minute,' she kept gasping, until she bent over and began to dry heave.

'Are you all right?' Neve asked helplessly, because another human being was in pain and she couldn't stand idly by, even if that other human being had been unwelcoming and hostile. Gingerly she rubbed Chelsy's back.

'I think I'm going to puke and I've got a terrible stitch.'

'Left side or right?' Neve asked.

'Left.'

'OK, you need to raise your left arm in the air and lean on me with your right arm, hard as you can,' Neve ordered, as she helped Chelsy into an upright position. 'Harder than that. I'm pretty solid, I can take it.'

Eventually Chelsy straightened up. 'I think my hangover's kicking in,' she whispered conspiratorially with an anxious glance at Jacqui who was shouting at Emma for refusing to touch the medicine ball in case she broke her acrylic tips. 'I got absolutely hammered last night.'

For a moment Neve thought she had a stitch too because she felt a sharp twinge in her gut as she wondered if Chelsy had been getting hammered with Max. Maybe doing other things too, as well as getting hammered. Chelsy was really, really pretty and really, really pretty seemed to be just Max's type.

'Mandy thought I went home at midnight, but I snuck out with Billy, my hairdresser, and I ended up drinking mojitos in a club on Canal Street until three in the morning.' Chelsy bent over again. 'Wish I hadn't mentioned the mojitos.'

The stabbing pain disappeared as suddenly as it had arrived so Neve could trot over to the coolbox and grab a bottle of water for Chelsy. 'Don't gulp it, just little sips,' she said, unscrewing the cap and handing the bottle to the other girl.

By the time Chelsy felt up to passing the medicine ball, the workout was almost over. There were five minutes of cooling-down stretches, then Neve was surprised to see the WAGs converge on Jacqui to hug her and thank her for 'being an absolute mare'.

After that, they were led into a ballroom to do Pilates on a sprung floor that squeaked under Neve each time she shifted position. Usually she loved Pilates but she was finding it hard to concentrate on her core muscles and her breathing when her mind was on other things.

There was a collective sigh of relief when the class ended, and as the other girls gathered around the instructor, a softly spoken, serene woman who had nevertheless ruled the class with a steely grit that didn't tolerate whinging and complaining, Neve dived for the doors. She hurried for the stairs, took a wrong turn down a rabbit-warren of corridors, but eventually found the cloakroom. Neve was still rooting through her gym bag for her phone, when the other girls trooped in.

Not a single one of them looked groomed any more. The make-up had been sweated off, the pink velour was looking decidedly grubby, and each shiny strand of hair had been tied back; the overall effect was less threatening than before. Chelsy even smiled at Neve and touched her lightly on the arm. 'Thanks for looking out for me,' she said, as she opened her own locker. 'We're going to have a steam now, before we shower. Sweat out all those toxins.'

'Oh, I think I'll just have a shower,' Neve mumbled, averting her eyes as tracksuits began to get cast off. She never ever changed at the gym, or showered, or did anything that would mean that the other women in the changing room would see her body in all its stretchmarked, lumpy glory. There was absolutely no way she was going to strip off in front of six strangers who really didn't like her that much.

She could shower while they steamed, then be back in jeans and tunic top before they'd finished soaping up and rinsing off. Neve sat down on one of the cushioned benches that lined the room and studied her phone intently, even though there were no messages or missed calls from Max.

'Come on, Neve. We're all girls together,' Emma called out from the other side of the changing room. 'If a lardarse like me doesn't mind stripping off, then you've got no worries.'

'Yeah. My cellulite's been on the front cover of *heat*,' Mandy said happily, twisting round to look at the backs of her thighs in the mirrors. 'Do you think I have less cellulite than I did last week?'

'You call that cellulite? It looks like my arse is made out of orange peel!'

Neve stared at her trainers and let the body flaws one-upmanship float over her. She'd heard this talk countless times from countless other women with bodies that she'd kill for. It was just a bonding exercise, in the same way that men talked about football.

'Neve! Lose the trackie bottoms and come and have a steam,' Emma demanded. Neve could see her polished pink toenails heading in her direction and she swallowed hard.

'Really, I'm OK,' she bleated, as she saw two more pairs of naked feet coming over and she had three WAGs standing directly in front of her and a horrible flashback to the showers after PE lessons. They'd drag her into the steam room, while somebody else hid her clothes. She just *knew* it.

But Mandy wouldn't let them do that, she realised, just as Mandy muttered something about her wedding planner, put on a robe and disappeared out of the door.

Which left her staring resolutely at the floor and surrounded on all sides.

'Look, I know we've been giving you a hard time but we don't know you from Adam,' said Tasha, plonking herself down next to Neve. She, at least, was still fully clothed. 'And the thing is that Mandy's our friend.'

'I know that,' Neve said quietly, because what did they think? That she had some elaborate scheme in mind to steal Mandy away from them? 'She's been really nice to me, but—'

'Mandy *is* really nice,' Tasha agreed. 'She could have turned into a stuck-up cow with all the stuff that's happened to her in the last three years, but she's still the same old Mands. And people try to take advantage of her and we're her friends so we have to make sure that doesn't happen.'

'But I would never do that!' Neve gasped, indignation making her look up so all she could see was tanned flesh and nipples. 'I'm a nice person. Or I try to be.'

'Yeah, well, you seem all right,' Kelly said, and there was a murmur of agreement as though Neve had passed some test that she wasn't even aware that she'd been taking. 'But if you have a hidden camera and your best friend is on the showbiz desk of the *News of the World* . . .'

'One of my best friends is a forty-something gay man who's writing his PhD on Stephen Spender,' Neve protested. 'My sister works on *Skirt*, but she's not interested in anything other than fashion.'

'Oooh! Does she get free clothes?' Lauren asked.

'Not really, but sometimes she pretends that things got lost on photo-shoots and doesn't give them back.' Neve forced her shoulders down from around her ears. 'Look, I'm sure it can't be much fun having a new person foisted on you when it's the day before your best friend's wedding and you all just want to relax and have your Spa Day. I understand that and I'm going to have a shower and then I'll get a cab back to the hotel.'

'Don't be soft,' Tasha scoffed. 'Come and have a steam and tell us which celebs your sister's met.'

'I can't,' Neve insisted grimly and she was just going to have to come clean and tell them. 'Look, I used to be very large. Very, very large and I'm still large and I don't like—'

'How big were you?' Emma demanded boldly. ''Cause you're not much bigger than me.'

Neve blinked to clear her vision and then she looked at Emma, who was stripped down to bra and thong and was about two dress sizes smaller than Neve. 'I used to be twenty-five stone,' she admitted. 'And you're taller and slimmer than me and I'm much, much saggier than all of you.'

'Get away,' Emma snorted. 'Did you have a gastric bypass or a lap band?'

'Oh, I didn't have either. I just, you know, ate less and exercised more.'

'So, how much have you lost exactly?'

'How long did it take you?'

'I went on Atkins to get rid of the baby weight after I had our Keiran and I got so constipated. Did you low-carb it?'

The questions were flying thick and fast and Neve started looking beyond the fake tan and the manicures to Lauren's caesarean scar and Emma's lopsided breasts and Kelly pointed out that she had stretchmarks on her thighs and Tasha said that people came up to her on the street and asked her if she was anorexic.

Each one of them had something they hated about their bodies. Neve wasn't sure if that made her feel better or worse, but she stood up and began to take off her clothes even though it felt as if she was about to jump out of a light aircraft without a parachute. Or dive into shark-infested waters. Or charge naked into battle. She still wasn't going to charge naked into the steam room but she could compromise and wrap a towel around herself or something.

When Neve was finally down to her gutbuster knickers and racer-back bra and frantically snatching up a towel from the neatly folded stack on a counter, Kelly said, 'I don't know what you're complaining about. You look fine to me. It's just as well the bubbly should be arriving soon. You really need to chill out.'

It was a pity that the several glasses of champagne she'd had during the course of the afternoon hadn't supplied Neve with the necessary amount of Dutch courage she needed to face Max after her impersonation of a Billingsgate fishwife that morning. It also made dealing with the key card that opened the door very tricky.

Neve hoped that she could sidle stealthily into the room then just look at Max with her most hangdog expression (she had it on very good authority that it was imbued with the very essence of hangdog), so that Max would instantly forgive her and she wouldn't have to stammer through an abject apology. That was the plan. But after fumbling with the key card and rattling the handle, the door suddenly opened.

She looked up, expecting to see Max standing there but he'd simply left the door ajar. Neve had known that he was still mad at her because he'd switched his phone off and every time she'd called to apologise it had rolled straight to voicemail, but she hadn't imagined that he'd still be *this* mad. The only person she knew who could hold a grudge this long was, well . . . herself.

Neve stepped through the door, mentally preparing herself for the wintry look on Max's face and the barbed remarks that he'd had all day to work on, but he was sitting with his back to her at the small desk between the bed and the window, his fingers flying over his laptop keyboard.

At least she could get on with the big apology without any interruptions from the peanut gallery, she thought glumly.

'I'm sorry,' she said, because that was the best place to start. 'I'm sorry I was such a witch this morning and you were right, I was scared of spending the day with Mandy's friends 'cause they were very hostile last night and I took it out on you. And actually, they were really nice to me today. Well, not at first but we bonded eventually and it turned out that we had lots in common, though you wouldn't think that, would you?'

There was still no response from Max, but he'd stopped typing, which had to be a good sign. Frankly, Neve would take her victories where she could.

'Look, I'm sorry for what I said about that Shelly.' Neve edged nearer to Max. 'I know I've no right to make judgements about the people you were with before me, but you could have given me heads up about her, Max. You must have known that someone would mention that you and she had got together. That's why I was so angry.' She squinched up her face as she got to the really difficult part of the apology. 'Well, also I was angry because I felt jealous and I know it's ridiculous because we're not meant to have that kind of relationship, but when I think about the girls you were with before me, what they looked like, I know I don't measure up.'

Neve placed her hands on Max's shoulders and he flinched for a second. She tried to communicate everything she was feeling through her fingertips, and when that didn't seem to work, Neve began to knead the knots of tension she found. There was one, just below Max's neck, that was absolutely huge.

She leaned over so she could whisper into Max's ear, her voice low and urgent. 'You have to know that when I'm with you, I'm not thinking of William. Well, hardly ever. And the things that we've done, that I've done, I would *never* do them because I was trying them out on you so I could . . . could . . . hone my technique. That was really low, Max.'

There wasn't much left to say, especially as Max was still giving her the silent treatment. He was much better at sulking than she was. Neve always caved in as soon as Celia blurted out, 'I'm sorry,' with the appropriate amount of conviction.

'God, why are you still mad at me?' she demanded pitifully, straightening up and taking her hands off Max, because her soothing touch wasn't having any effect. 'I've tried to apologise, what more can I say?'

She was all set to give up and skulk in the bathroom until it was time to go out with the girls, when Max cleared his throat. 'You said you wanted to end it,' he reminded Neve in a voice that wasn't quite as Arctic as she'd been expecting.

'No, I said that there was no point in carrying on with this if . . . *if* I wasn't the type of girl you wanted to be with, and I've already told you why I said that. But if you want to call it quits, then just tell me,' Neve pleaded, but Max had retreated back into silence. He didn't so much as twitch a muscle. 'God, you're bloody impossible sometimes.'

She was in the middle of turning herself around in preparation for the most majestic flounce of her life when Max looped his arm around her waist and now it was his turn to pull Neve's stiff, resisting body nearer.

'I don't want it to be over,' he said, with enough sincerity that she almost believed him. And then he kissed the back of her arm, which was the only part of her that he could get his mouth on. 'And I'm sorry too. I should have told you about Shelly, but it's a bit of a sore point really.'

'Why is it a sore point?' Neve asked, and she wriggled a little in Max's hold just to let him know that he had to do better than that.

'I don't want to talk about it. It's in the past. I'm moving forward,' Max said mechanically, as if he'd learned the words by rote. 'I'm here with you and that's all that matters. Not what I did months ago with some other girl or you heading off into the sunset with Mr California in a few weeks' time. But right here, right now.'

Neve wound a lock of Max's sticky hair round her finger. 'It's not like this will end and the next day I'll be with William.' The truth was that she didn't know what it would be like, because she always skipped over the logistics and went straight to the happy ending. 'And I hope, whatever happens, that we'll still be friends. I like having you in my life, apart from when you're giving me an icy cold shoulder.'

Max pulled Neve closer, turned her around so he could rest his head on her breast. 'Was I really that bad? I'll have to try and warm you up,' he said, and it was so like Max to deflect an honest but painful discussion by getting sexy but even through two layers of clothing, Neve could feel his breath on her skin and her breasts felt fuller and heavier so she wanted to press them against Max's mouth and have him take the ache away. Instead she let him wrap his arms all the way around her and she kissed the top of his head, and when he tried to pull her on to his lap, she guessed they were friends again.

'You know, I live in fear of breaking your legs when you try to make me do that,' she told him, wriggling free of his arms so she could perch on the edge of the desk. 'So, what have you been doing all day?'

'Oh, I got some writing done,' Max said, leaning back and looking up at Neve properly for the first time since she'd walked through the door. 'Jesus Christ, Neevy, you look amazing!'

Neve remembered now that she didn't even remotely

resemble the girl he'd seen that morning with her hair scraped back and a moody expression on her face. After the Spa-ing was done, they'd been chauffeured to a swank Manchester salon to get their hair and make-up done for that evening. 'Really?' she asked. 'They tried coming at me with bronzer, which I resisted but I did wonder if it was still a bit too much.'

'No, it's just enough,' Max said, his gaze riveted to Neve's face as she fluttered sooty lashes at him. Whenever she'd tried to do smoky eyes, she'd ended up looking as if she hadn't slept for a month, but the make-up artist had showed her how to do it properly and made her go a hundred shades deeper than her usual rose-tinted lip salve, so she now had glossy red lips that made her want to pout, even when there wasn't that much to pout about.

She tried to angle herself up so she could see her reflection in the mirror opposite. 'I don't even look like me,' she said, because it would have been really arrogant to tell Max that actually she loved her present incarnation who was all eyes, cheekbones and pillowy lips.

'Yes, you do. You just look like a really high-maintenance version of you.' Max peered up at her. 'Your hair – it's so *big*.'

'I know!' Neve nodded happily. The hairdresser hadn't even wanted to blowdry, much less backcomb what he called her 'virgin hair', but he'd sexed up her usual ponytail by clipping a foam wedge to her crown and pulling her hair over it so she had a big bouffant that Neve hoped was more Audrey Hepburn in *Breakfast at Tiffany's* than Amy Winehouse. 'I think I'm at least two inches taller.'

'At least,' Max echoed. 'So, did you have a nice time in the end?'

Neve wasn't sure that they'd talked through things properly, but it was a relief to have that cold, pinched look on Max's face replaced by his usual easy grin and hear him laugh as she told him about working out with the WAGs and Mandy making her wedding planner strip off and come into the steam room so she could sweat out her toxins *and* lock down the final seating plan.

'And they finally told me what a medi-pedi is,' Neve said, reaching down to start unlacing her sneakers. 'A qualified podiatrist turned up with this thing that looked like a potato peeler and shaved all the hard skin off my feet as if they were two massive hunks of Parmesan cheese.'

'That's disgusting.'

'It was,' Neve agreed, tugging off her socks and nearly falling off the desk in the process. 'But feel how soft my feet are.'

She waggled her foot in Max's face as he reared back even though her feet were as fragrant and silky smooth as they were ever likely to be.

Max wasn't looking at her feet but her face again. 'Are you drunk?'

'Of course I'm not,' Neve scoffed, because she wasn't drunk. Although now the row was over and they were friends again, the sheer relief was making her feel light-headed. 'I had a leetle bit of champagne.' She tried to hold up her thumb and forefinger to illustrate the minuscule amount of champagne that she'd drunk, which wasn't as much as the others had knocked back, and she'd had some croutons with her chicken salad at lunch to mop up the alcohol, but now she was having difficulty in getting her thumb and forefinger to do what she wanted.

'What have those girls done to you?' Max shook his head. 'You are. You're pissed.'

'Maybe just a teensy bit merry,' Neve decided, clutching Max's arm so she could get down from the desk. 'But I'm only going to drink spritzers tonight and Mandy wants everyone tucked up in bed by eleven so we don't have hangovers tomorrow. She's very detail orientated.'

'You should eat something before you go out,' Max said firmly. 'Something laden with carbs to give you some ballast.'

Neve glanced at the clock on the nightstand. 'I haven't got time.' Max was dogging her footsteps as she went from wardrobe to bathroom. 'You're not going to be stuck in here writing all evening, are you?'

'I'm meeting Bill for a drink so we can work on his father-of-the-bride speech,' Max said, eyeing up the dress that was in Neve's hand. 'Don't suppose that has a zipper you might need a hand with?' he asked with a leer.

'No, it just goes on over my head so . . .' Neve put her hands on her hips and tried to look stern. 'You're not doing anything to me that will smudge my make-up or flatten my hair,' she said, shutting the bathroom door.

She'd just succeeded in carefully easing the dress on without dismantling her bouffant when Neve heard a banging on the door of their suite, then the sound of much shrieking and laughter.

Neve buckled her three-inch Mary-Janes, which seemed to be getting less comfortable the more she wore them, and was just about to step back, look at herself in the mirror and decide that silver-sequined shift dresses really weren't her thing, when the bathroom door crashed back on its hinges and the bathroom was invaded by skimpily dressed, bare-legged, shiny-haired, highly excitable women.

'Right, you'll do,' Kelly said. 'Let's get going. We've got a pink stretch limo waiting in a no parking zone behind the hotel, because the front is *crawling* with paps.'

Neve had to push Tasha and Lauren out of the way so she could get a good look at herself in the mirror. 'Does this look OK?' She tugged at the hem of the dress. 'I don't look fat?'

'You look gorgeous,' Emma said as she sprayed herself with a generous amount of Neve's Chanel No. 19. 'Lose the tights.'

Neve would lose her 60-denier, body-shaping opaque tights when they were ripped from her cold, dead legs. 'I don't think so,' she said. 'Maybe I should wear jeans and a nice little top. My sister Celia says—'

No one was interested in Celia's opinion that heels, jeans and a statement top could take a girl from day to evening and even cocktails. Tasha took Neve's arm and yanked her out of the bathroom. 'Just grab your phone,' she ordered.

'Purse . . .'

'You don't need a purse,' Lauren said pityingly. 'Dinner's paid for, limo's paid for, we're on six different guest-lists with bar tabs, what do you need money for?'

'Take your purse,' Max said, shouldering Emma out of the way. 'And call me if you want to bail out early and— Christ, that dress *is* a bit short.'

Neve looked down at her legs in dismay. 'My legs look sturdy even in body-shaping tights.'

'Of course they don't,' Max snapped, his face reddening when Emma openly laughed at his over-protective boyfriend routine. 'You look great, that's what I'm worried about.'

'Aw, sweet,' Tasha cooed. 'Don't worry, lover boy, we'll have her back by midnight. Or around midnight.'

'No, Mandy said we had to be back by eleven,' Neve reminded them. 'She was really particular about that.'

'Eleven, twelve, what's the diff?' Emma drawled, grabbing Neve's hand and pulling her towards the door. 'Will you get a move on?'

As she was hustled out of the door, she heard Max bark, 'I want her back in one piece.'

There was a collective cackle from the cheap seats. 'One piece was never part of the deal.'

Chapter Twenty-eight

Something diseased and furry had crawled into her mouth and expired while she slept. That was the only possible explanation as to why Neve had a rancid taste in her mouth and a heavy, viscous paste coating her teeth and tongue.

'I think I'm dying,' she groaned. The wretched state of her mouth was the least of it. There was a pounding in her head, echoed in the roiling of her gut, and her bones ached, her vital organs ached, her throat ached, even her hair follicles ached.

'You're not dying,' said a voice in her ear, which sounded like nails scraping down a blackboard, even though Max's voice had barely risen above a whisper. 'You've got a hangover.'

Neve had had hangovers before and they just made her feel a tiny bit nauseous and grouchy. This felt like the bastard child of bubonic plague and the ebola virus.

'Dying,' she reiterated, and now she realised that she was in bed, which had been a very comfy bed the last time she'd slept in it, but now it felt as if she was lying on a pile of rocks, and even though she had the quilt and Max's arm tucked around her, she was still cold and clammy. Neve tried to raise her head but her gaze collided with the stripy wallpaper and as well as searing her retinas, it was making her stomach heave. 'Sick. Going to be sick.'

'Sweetheart, I don't think so,' Max said, stroking the back of her neck with feather-soft fingers. 'You've already thrown up just about everything you've eaten in the last week.'

'Urgh . . .' Had she? The night before was a big gaping hole in her memory. 'What happened?'

'I don't know what happened but I got a phone call from the Head of Hotel Security at three in the morning asking me if I could identify a raving madwoman in a silver dress who couldn't remember her room number but insisted that someone called Max Pancake was sleeping there. They thought you might be a hack from the *Sunday Mirror* pretending to be absolutely spannered as a way of getting into the hotel.'

'Oh, no . . .'

'Yeah, apparently Ronaldo's staying in one of the penthouse suites and I saw Wayne and Coleen in the bar last night. Anyway, as you were staggering down the corridor, you told me very proudly that you'd lost your phone and you'd just eaten two pieces of KFC and a bag of chips.'

'KFC? Oh, God . . .'

'But I wouldn't worry about that because after you'd tried to persuade me to have my wicked way with you, you started throwing up and you didn't stop, not for hours. I thought you were going to sleep curled around the toilet at one point.'

'Goodness . . .'

The blanks Max was filling in weren't coming as a total surprise and Neve started to see a slideshow of images: being followed by a flashing, yelling pack of paparazzi everywhere they went, velvet ropes being unclipped, a tutorial from Kelly and Mandy on how to strut rather than walk, a table full of empty glasses and a clutch of bedraggled cocktail umbrellas.

There was the boy who wouldn't leave her alone at Dry Bar until Kelly mentioned that he played for Manchester United's youth team and was only fifteen. She remembered Mandy going at ten accompanied by two hulking

370

bodyguards, after making the girls solemnly promise that they'd leave the bar they were in no later than eleven. Obviously they'd still been raging well past eleven because Neve could now distinctly recall hitting Canal Street where she'd sung 'Don't Leave Me This Way' in a karaoke bar with Dolly Parton. A very masculine-looking Dolly Parton and . . .

'I think I danced on a podium. Why would I do that?'

'Please tell me there's photos.' Max's voice bubbled with barely contained laughter though it couldn't have been much fun for him, when she'd got back in such a drunken state.

'Sorry I got you out of bed,' Neve mumbled, carefully and slowly rolling over so she was lying on her back. The movement made the room and her stomach lurch alarmingly.

'I wasn't in bed. I was pacing the floor and worrying that you were dead in a ditch somewhere when you didn't answer your phone the first ten times that I called it.'

'Oh God. Alcohol bad. Very, very bad.'

'It is very bad but I think you'll live to drink another glass of champagne,' Max said, propping himself up on one elbow so he could look down at Neve who was lying with her eyes shut. 'You'll probably feel better once you've had a shower.'

'It will kill me.'

'No, it won't, it will just feel that way for the first five minutes,' Max said, sitting up, which made the bed move and Neve moan piteously. 'I'm going to ask Housekeeping to send someone up to sort out the bathroom and then you'll have to get up, because I hate to break it to you, Neve, but we're attending the Wedding of the Year in five hours.'

Neve tried to tell Max that she couldn't leave the bed, much less stand unaided for the foreseeable future, but he was already getting up. She could hear him pottering about the room, speaking in a low voice on the phone as she let herself drift in and out of sleep, barely stirring even when two chambermaids arrived to start work on the bathroom.

Maybe it was shame that forced her back to sleep, when she heard one of them say, 'We're going to need more bleach. A lot more bleach.'

The second time that Neve opened her eyes, she realised that she wasn't going to die. Not until she'd cleaned her teeth anyway. She threw back the covers and tried to pass on a message to her brain that she really wanted to move her legs.

'Hey! What are you doing? Let me help you.' Max was standing in the bathroom doorway and Neve could only gape at him in amazement.

'You're wearing a suit,' she pointed out with razor-sharp powers of deduction, because he was indeed wearing a black, slim-fitting, beautifully cut suit with a snowy-white shirt. Even his hair had been tamed into submission with what looked like an entire tub of Brylcreem. Only the toes of his red socks poking out from the bottom of his trousers jarred against the general dapperness of his ensemble. 'You look so smart.'

Max put his hands in his trouser pockets. 'I hate wearing a suit,' he scowled. 'I'm not putting on my tie until I hear the first notes of "The Wedding March".'

He moved over to the bed and gently levered Neve to a standing position. She swayed uncertainly for a moment, then decided that she could remain vertical, as long as Max kept hold of her arm. 'I need to clean my teeth,' she said, as they started the slow, perilous walk to the bathroom, passing a crumpled heap of silver sequins on the way.

At some time during last night's shenanigans Neve had stripped, or had been stripped, down to bra and knickers, but she still felt too wretched to care. Max hadn't been so traumatised by the sight of Neve's wobbly thighs, sagging paunch and all the other horrors that she usually kept hidden, that he'd done a runner. In fact, he was being incredibly sweet and patient as he carefully steered her to the bathroom as if she was made of spun glass.

'What you need is a really good fry-up,' he told Neve, grinning as she winced. 'But I'll order you some tea and toast to start with. You're still looking really peaky.'

Peaky was the greatest understatement of all time, Neve decided as she looked in the mirror while she brushed her teeth. The foam wedge was poking out of Medusa-like tendrils of hair and she had black eye make-up smeared around her eyes and running in sooty rivulets down her cheeks, where it mixed with the remains of her red lipstick.

She looked and felt a whole lot better after showering and washing her hair, apart from the bruising around her eyes, where she'd burst blood vessels from retching so violently.

'People are going to think I've been knocking you about,' Max said, when Neve emerged from the bathroom wrapped in a fluffy white robe and a towel wound turban-style around her head. 'We need to send out for some heavy-duty concealer.'

'Just in case you didn't hear me the first time, I want you to know that I'm never, ever drinking alcohol again,' Neve sniffed, pouring herself a cup of tea but avoiding the toast that had also arrived – she didn't feel ready for solids just yet. 'But thank you for taking care of me.'

She sat down on the sofa next to Max and took another slightly incredulous look at him. Yes, it wasn't a DT. He was wearing a suit. 'You look so spiffy.'

'Spiffy?' Max nearly spat out a mouthful of toast and jam. 'You're the only person I know who uses words that I've only read in books.'

Neve wrapped her fingers around her cup and took a cautious sip of tea. It tasted like the nectar of the gods, and when Max put his arm around her and she snuggled against him, head on his shoulder, she decided that her hangover wasn't terminal. She might just make it through the day intact and even manage to smile in the wedding photos.

'I want you to eat at least one piece of toast, then you're going to have to slap on the war paint,' Max murmured as if he could read her thoughts. 'Can't have you looking all pale and wan in the wedding photos, Mandy will kill you. And I want you fighting fit for mocking duties.'

Even given the fragile state of her health, Neve was looking forward to the wedding. Not just shamelessly gawping at the celebrities who'd be attending, or even hanging out with her gang of new best friends who'd promised to point out all the celebrities to her, but mostly she couldn't wait to spend the day with Max. He was in an insanely good mood and when Max was in an insanely good mood, cracking jokes, his eyes twinkling, he was such fun to be around.

'You're much better at mocking than I am,' Neve said.

Max bowed his head in acknowledgement of that indisputable fact. 'Oh, I don't know, Neevy, you do a nice line in an acidic quip. Now, eat a piece of toast like a good little girl.'

She was halfway through a piece of dry toast when Max's phone rang.

'It's Bill,' he said, looking at the caller display. 'Probably calling to ask if anyone's seen Kelly. God knows what time she got home last night.'

Neve's last memory of Kelly was seeing her doing tequila slammers in the karaoke bar so she pulled a dubious face, which made Max laugh as he answered the phone.

'Bill? How is the father of the bride this morning?' he asked cheerfully. 'Lovely day for a WA . . . white wedding.'

She was still draped over Max's shoulder so Neve could feel the exact moment that he tensed up, before he even said, 'Oh, right. Yeah, that does sound like a bit of a problem.'

Not wanting to eavesdrop, Neve stood up and, munching unenthusiastically on her toast, began to assemble her wedding outfit. She hoped that last night's KFC hadn't gone straight to her hips.

'No, it's OK. Of course I understand,' Max was saying in a tight, strained voice as if it, whatever *it* was, was not at all

OK. 'Well, you can tell Mandy to stop crying for starters. It's not the end of the world and she'll be gutted when she looks at the photos twenty years from now and she's got blood-shot eyes.'

Neve glanced over at Max who was sitting hunched over, elbows on his knees and a miserable look on his face. 'Really, Bill, it's fine. To tell you the truth, Neve's been sick all night – must have been something that she ate – and she's probably better off spending the day in bed.'

Something bad *had* happened, though Neve was foggy on the details. For a moment she wondered if either Mandy or Darren had called off the wedding, but that couldn't be it because there wouldn't still be wedding photos that Mandy had to look picture-perfect for. Maybe they'd over-booked the church or . . . oh God, she'd made such an exhibition of herself last night that they didn't want her anywhere near the wedding party in case she started knocking back the Veuve Cliquot again.

'Honestly, Bill, you don't have to do that. It's all good. Wish Mandy all the best for me and I'll talk to her when she gets back from St Barts, OK?'

Neve was just debating whether to unzip the garment bag and put on her trouser suit, when Max hung up.

'Well, you needn't bother with that,' he said. 'In fact, if you want to go back to bed, then I'm not going to stop you.'

'What's *happened*? Has the wedding been called off? Did I do something so terrible last night that they don't want—'

'You're not the problem, I am.' Max smiled thinly. 'I'm not allowed to go to the wedding.'

'But why?' Neve hung up the garment bag and tottered over to the sofa so she could take Max's hand and . . .

Max tutted and pulled away. 'No hand-holding, remember?' he snapped, and she knew he was upset and angry over the mysterious phone call and was taking it out on her because she was the only person in range, but it still hurt.

Neve sat down close to Max in the hope that she could emit rays of sympathy and support through her thick terry-towelling robe. 'Please tell me what happened.'

'Well, you don't sell the rights to your engagement, wedding and honeymoon for two million quid without signing a lengthy legal contract with lots of clauses,' Max explained, leaning back against the cushions as if he was totally at ease with the situation. It might have been more convincing if his voice wasn't catching on every other word as if it hurt to breathe. 'Turns out that journalists who aren't employed by *Voila* magazine are prohibited from attending the wedding . . .'

'But you're going as a friend!'

'. . . in any capacity, professional or otherwise,' Max parroted in a toneless voice. 'Mandy's agent had to go through the guest-list with the magazine's celebrity fixer this morning and all hell broke loose.'

'Well, it's morally reprehensible to auction off an access-all-areas pass to your wedding day anyway,' Neve said crossly, because even though she liked Mandy, she really did, she liked Max a whole lot more.

'No long words, Neevy, not right now.' Max smiled another one of those teeth-baring excuses for a smile. 'That little bitch. I've made her hundreds of thousands of pounds.'

'If I were you, I'd have nothing more to do with her. It's a shocking way to treat somebody.'

'Yes, it is, but then that little bitch has made *me* tens of thousands of pounds,' Max said bitterly. 'Well, at least we don't have to spend ages sitting in a draughty church and then choke down dry chicken in a cream sauce at the reception while Mandy mugs for the cameras.'

'I'm sorry,' Neve offered. It seemed an inadequate thing to say when Max was sitting there, his body so tightly wound that Neve was frightened to touch him, and an awful grimace instead of a smile on his face.

'Yeah, well, this whole weekend has been a complete

waste of petrol,' Max said, standing up. 'We might just as well head back to London.' He grabbed his leather jacket from the back of a chair. 'I need to clear my head. You can go back to bed for an hour, if you want.'

'Are you all right?' It was a dumb question. Neve knew that as soon as she'd said it. 'Well, of course you're not. I saw you with Bill and Jean on Thursday night and I could tell that you're more than Mandy's ghost-writer. You're part of the family, Max, so I—'

'No! I'm not part of the family,' Max said sharply, as he headed for the door. 'Sure, I'm fun to have around but that's part of the job. All it really comes down to is how much use I am to the McIntyre brand, and right now, I'm no fucking use at all.'

He slammed the door behind him and for one tense moment Neve thought the piece of toast was going to re-appear, but it didn't and she could sit on the sofa and burst into tears.

Neve wasn't a big crier but the excesses of the night before had left her feeling shaky and fragile. Mostly she was crying because Max was angry and hurt, and that made her feel angry and hurt by proxy, especially as she didn't know how to make him feel better. Even if she did, she wasn't sure that Max would let her come close enough to try.

If she hadn't lost her phone, which was probably being used to make a very long, very expensive call to an overseas number at that very moment, Neve knew there were any number of people she could call who'd offer her all sorts of advice: Celia, her mum, Philip, Chloe, Rose, even Gustav who, after lecturing her on the hidden calories in alcohol, would tell Neve to go for a long run, which would make her feel better. And she knew, like she knew the fat units, calorie content and number of carbs in over four hundred different types of food, that if she called her father, he'd drop everything to fetch her and bring her home.

She had all these people in her life and sure, Max knew

hundreds of people and he might call them his friends, but when it really came down to it, he had no one who was really there for him when he was hurting, except a Staffordshire Bull Terrier with severe boundary issues. And her. Max deserved to have a bigger support network than one girl and a dog.

When Max returned nearly two hours later, Neve's eyes were even more puffy than the last time he'd seen her, but she was pale, composed and had read her way through the *Guardian*, *CityLife*, the hotel information pack and guide to the local area, and watched an old episode of *Come Dine With Me* while she waited for him.

'You're dressed,' Max said, as he shut the door behind him. 'Are you packed too?'

'No.' There had been a long speech planned, but seeing Max walk through the door with the same cold, remote look on his face made it clear that this wasn't the time for long speeches. Instead, Neve got to her feet and hurled herself at Max.

He immediately went rigid, trying to squirm away as she wrapped her arms tight around him. 'What are you doing?'

'Shut up and let me hold you,' Neve mumbled, though she wasn't holding him so much as restraining him.

'I don't need to be held,' Max said stiffly. 'You're being stupid.' And to show Neve just how stupid she was being, he kept his arms by his sides and a long-suffering look on his face as she stroked his back and pecked at his cheeks with her lips.

It was like hugging a concrete girder and Neve wondered what she needed to do to get through to Max, because she was all out of ideas. 'I'm not just your pancake girlfriend, I'm your *friend*,' she told him fiercely. 'I'm going to care about you and worry about you and want you to be happy whether you like it or not. So you'd better get used to it, all right?'

Max's lips twisted as if he had a whole lot to say about

that and none of it good. Then he murmured something too quietly for Neve to hear.

'What was that?'

'Can you let go?' Max asked, still rigid in her embrace. It sounded horribly portentous – as if he was asking her to do more than drop her arms.

Neve loosened her grip, but kept her hands around Max's waist, because all of a sudden it seemed terribly important to keep a connection between them. 'What did you just say?'

Max wouldn't look at Neve but stared at a spot above her head. 'I said that you wouldn't want me as your friend, or anything else, if you knew what I was really like.'

'What *are* you really like?' Neve asked, though she was dreading the answer.

Max wrenched himself away from her then, as if he couldn't bear to be touched. He walked over to the window. 'I'm a fuck-up,' he said harshly. 'Everything in my life is fucked up, and the only reason that I'm in this fake relationship with you is because my therapist thought it would be a good idea.'

Finally, Neve had the explanation that she'd been searching for – the reason why someone like Max would want to be with someone like her, even if it was only just pretend. She was surprised to find that she wasn't that upset – it really didn't seem that important right then.

She sank down on a squashy leather cube that she'd been using as a footstool. 'What made you decide to see a therapist?'

'Because there's something wrong with me,' Max said, his voice distorted because he was gulping hard, but at least he was talking so Neve stayed where she was. 'I have this great job and a cool flat and I go out every night to these fantastic parties and meet all these famous, glamorous people and they're all my best mates but I feel empty inside. Like, none of it means anything and none of it's real.'

379

There was nothing Neve could say so she just 'hmmm-ed' to let Max know she was listening.

'And the reason why I shag around is because I can't bear to be on my own. My therapist says that I don't commit to any of the women I shag because I'm scared of intimacy, but the thing is, I don't know *how* to be intimate with anyone. And I'm only seeing my therapist because I slept with Shelly, and Mandy and Kelly were furious with me and Bill took me out for a chat, like he was my fucking father or something, and told me I needed to sort myself out because I was better than that.'

'You are,' Neve said quietly, as she tried to process Max's furious onslaught.

'And I shagged one of the interns at work and I didn't know she was engaged to the son of the MD and I nearly lost my job, and my Editor said if I didn't get some help then she'd have to fire me. So I'm "in therapy",' Max still had his back to Neve but she could see him air-quote, 'and she's trying to peel back my layers and get to the real person, but I don't think he exists. I'm just all style and absolutely no fucking substance.'

'Come on, you know that's not true.' Neve got to her feet and even took a couple of steps towards Max but she could see his shoulders shaking. He didn't sound as if he was crying, but he sounded as if he was close, and Neve instinctively knew that he was only holding it together because she was on the other side of the room. 'Look, I know you and I are only temporary, but the more I get to know you, the more I like you.'

Max coughed wetly. 'You say that because you're a nice girl and you're trying to make me feel better, I get that, but we're not real. The only real thing I had was the McIntyres and I let myself think that they cared about me and that I was the son they never had, but it was just bullshit.'

'No,' Neve said sharply, hesitation forgotten as she stumbled towards Max. 'That's not true. I've spent my entire life on the sidelines, just watching other people. I'm an expert people-watcher and when I saw you with Bill and Jean, it was obvious that they *do* care about you, and . . . well, so do I. I care about you too, Max.'

She wrapped her arms around him, rested her head against his shoulderblade and hugged him as hard as she could. This time Max didn't wriggle or squirm but seemed to relax back against her. 'I don't even know what caring looks like,' he muttered.

'Yes, you do,' Neve told him. 'Once you stopped making such a concerted effort with the flirting and the shmoozing, you've been nothing but kind and patient with me. I know I'm not the easiest of people to be around, but you've stuck it out and maybe it's because your therapist has told you to, but you committed to our fake relationship and you should be proud of that.'

Max patted Neve's hands, which were clasped over his midriff. 'I should be proud that I've managed to last two months in a fake relationship with a girl who's in love with someone else?'

It was impossible to continue having a conversation with Max's back so Neve twisted around so she was standing between him and the window and could look him right in his red-rimmed eyes. She'd been right about the tears. 'Yes, I'm in love with William and yes, he has my heart, but he doesn't have all of it.' She held up her thumb and forefinger. 'I'd say there's a tiny part of my heart that is yours alone.'

'You're just saying that,' Max insisted sulkily, as if he didn't want to be talked out of his downward spiral. 'I bet on the inside you're furious that I wasn't honest with you from the start.'

And maybe she was a little annoyed, but the truth was better than the version of the truth that Neve had been tormenting herself with: that Max saw her as nothing more than a challenge and that once she'd fallen for his consider-able charms, his work would be done.

'Well, you should have told me, but I can see why it was difficult for you to tell that kind of thing to a comparative stranger.' She shrugged and smiled. 'I'm glad you have told me, and whether you like it or not, I'm sticking around for a bit, so you're just going to have to put up with it, all right?'

Max pulled a face but then, unbelievably, a tiny glimmer of a smile appeared. It was maybe first cousin to a smile but it was as welcome as the first hint of sun after weeks of rain. 'All right,' he agreed.

'Glad to hear it.' And when Neve squeezed him extra tight, he squeaked in protest but then he was hugging her back. Max was a great hugger. Neve always felt like a tiny, fragile slip of a thing when his long arms were around her.

Neve's head was telling her to get out of there as fast as she could because the weight of responsibility was bearing down on her and she could just about look after herself, never mind anyone else. But the tiny piece of her heart that she'd just given to Max spoke louder and so she stayed right where she was.

'I've got a present for you,' Max said, when Neve finally, reluctantly, released him. He pulled a familiar-looking object out of his jacket pocket. 'Apparently you left it in the limo.'

'I thought I'd never see it again!' Neve exclaimed, snatching her phone and cradling it to her breast. She immediately started reading her text messages.

'You know, the room is paid for up until Monday morning,' Max said casually as Neve made the unhappy discovery that she'd taken a pouting, preening photo of herself in the mirror of a club toilet and had sent it to everyone in her address book, including her parents and Mr Freemont, with the message, *Do I look foxy or what?* 'If you wanted to stay?'

'Stay where?' Neve muttered distractedly, as she wondered whether she could bear to read the text messages she'd received in reply.

'In Manchester for the weekend, with me,' Max said uncertainly, as he stared down at his feet. 'We should be OK as long as we avoid Alderley Edge. I think *Voila* magazine has probably put up roadblocks anyway. I mean, unless I've completely ruined everything by over-sharing and behaving like a tool.'

Neve put down her phone because if they were going to stay until Monday, she could postpone worrying about her drunk texting until then. 'Don't be silly, you haven't ruined anything, and it *is* a nice room, although the stripy wallpaper is still making me feel bilious.'

'Shall we go out then?' Neve didn't know how to deal with this hesitant version of Max, who still seemed so flat and dejected, especially when he was giving her a tired, resigned look. 'I suppose you'd like to go to the Old Trafford Centre and do some shopping.'

'God, anything but that!' After last Saturday's shopping expedition, Neve was all shopped out until it was time to start thinking about Christmas. 'I've been reading a guide to Greater Manchester and apparently there are some local areas of outstanding beauty. Can't we go to one of them instead? Please? I think a long walk would clear both our heads.'

Max wouldn't tell Neve where they were going. Instead he zipped her up into his favourite red hoodie and drove them out of Manchester towards Ashton-under-Lyne.

It was a long time since Neve had been out of London and she'd forgotten that north of the Watford Gap could feel like another country. The scenery was wilder and more rugged than the fields and gardens of southern England, and even the place names – Rusholme, Cheadle Hulme, Wythenshawe – sounded exotic in a dark, satanic mills kind of way.

Max had been quiet and subdued for most of the journey but he suddenly grinned as he pulled into the car park of the Daisy Nook Country Park. 'I'm guessing that even a hangover won't put you off a long walk with river views?'

A long walk was exactly what she needed and Neve

hoped that Max would benefit from the endorphin rush too. The focal point of the park was the River Medway running through a wooded valley between Oldham and Ashton-under-Lyne. They stopped off at the Visitors Centre to get a map and headed for the Waterhouses Aqueduct, so they could walk along the footpath, which was eighty feet above the park.

Neve could feel the last remnants of her hangover float away in the breeze as she breathed in the clean air and knew that whenever she smelled that peaty top note, she'd always remember this weekend. They leaned over the wall to look down at the children paddling in the river below them. Although it was a sunny day in late April, there was still a chill that lurked just beneath the warmth of the sun – certainly not paddling weather, Neve thought, but the youth of Greater Manchester were obviously made of hardy stuff.

They barely spoke as they climbed down from the aqueduct and walked along the canal path. Every now and again, their arms brushed against each other and Neve wished that she'd never issued a decree against holding hands. The imaginary boundary that would be breached if they held hands didn't seem to matter so much any more, but she made do with Max's hoodie, which was soft and warm and smelled of Brylcreem so that it felt as if she was being hugged by him, even when he went on ahead to see if there was a café around the next bend.

After a couple of hours, the sky clouded over and the sun disappeared. The first fat drops of rain began to fall as soon as Max mentioned heading back to the car. Then the first fat drops suddenly became a sluicing torrent, forcing them to shelter under a canopy of trees.

'It's just a shower,' Max said hopefully, pulling Neve back by her hood as the rain slanted down on their feet. 'Probably.'

The rain stirred up the ground so everything smelled

earthy and ripe, and there was no sign that it would ever stop. Neve pulled out the map and squinted at it in the dim light. 'Can you remember exactly where you parked the car?'

'I think it was near Stannybrook Road?' Max made it sound like a question rather than a definite location. 'You think we should make a run for it?'

'You have any better ideas?'

Max didn't, so on Neve's count of three they started running. It was hard to read a map in a downpour, while running full pelt. They got lost twice and kept coming back to the lake in the centre of the park, until Max spotted a sign to the Visitors Centre and from there, they squelched back to the car, sneakers sodden and muddy.

'I can feel my jeans chafing every time I change gears,' Max moaned as he slowly edged on to the main road. 'And you're dripping over my car.'

'You're dripping over your car too,' Neve pointed out, reaching down to tug off her plimsolls and socks, so she could prop her feet up on the dashboard. 'You know what this rain means, don't you?'

'That we're going to die from bronchial pneumonia?'

'The wedding . . . I saw the marquee going up yesterday and Mandy showed me the spot by the lake where they were going to take the wedding photos.' Neve looked at Max from under her lashes and smiled. 'I'd say this rain was God's punishment for treating you so badly, wouldn't you?'

Chapter Twenty-nine

Max started stripping off his wet clothes before Neve had even got the door of their suite open. Neve left him struggling to free himself from a chokehold of wet cotton as she ran for the privacy of the bathroom. She knew that if she were a normal girl, she'd let him have a hot shower while she soaked in the tub. They could even have bathed together, but she wasn't a normal girl and so she couldn't blame Max for repeatedly banging on the bathroom door to ask how much longer she was going to be.

Eventually she relented and let him shower while she combed out her wet hair and slathered moisturiser on skin that still felt horribly dehydrated. Mostly though she surreptitiously stared at Max's reflection in the mirror as he stepped out of the shower and briskly dried himself off. She loved watching the flex of his biceps as he rubbed at his hair with a towel, and his long lean legs that led up to taut buttocks and the two delicious dimples just above them. She was just willing him to turn round so she could get a full frontal view too when she realised her mouth was hanging open and she was practically drooling.

Max did turn round then and catch her eye as she snatched up her moisturiser again and smeared a huge dollop on her face.

'You *did* look really foxy last night, to quote your text message,' he remarked casually.

'I sent it to *everyone*!'

'But I think you look prettier now wrapped in a towel with wet hair and gunk all over your face,' he continued softly. 'If you wanted to spend the rest of the weekend in a towel, well, that would be fine with me.'

'I'm not pretty,' Neve snorted, peering critically at the bruises around her eyes. 'You're seriously deluded, but I appreciate the sentiment.'

'You know, I think you're getting better at taking a compliment,' Max mused, flicking her with the edge of his towel and grinning when Neve squawked in outrage. 'You're pretty, Neve, just deal with it.'

Wrapped in a fluffy towelling robe, Neve left the bathroom and walked over to the huge floor-to-ceiling window that took up one wall. It was still raining, but now she was inside, Neve could appreciate how the rain made the streetlamps and headlights sparkle down on the street below.

'Shall I make reservations for the restaurant downstairs or do you want to go out?' Max asked, his hands settling around her waist.

It was Saturday night and they had the whole city laid out before them and . . . 'So, I need to put on clothes and dry my hair and leave our room?'

'Well, I don't care if you want to go out wearing a dressing-gown, but not everyone has my relaxed attitude to appropriate restaurant attire. We could always stay in and make a serious dent in the room-service bill.'

Neve twisted around. 'Do you mind? It's just I'm still achy and I have six blisters from those stupid shoes.' She had a whole list of other complaints but they were interrupted by the deafening rumble of her stomach. It seemed to last for ever and sounded a lot like thunder rolling across the sky.

'I had a huge lunch after I stormed off in a huff, but have you had anything since that piece of dry toast?' Max asked.

Neve shook her head. She was so used to not listening to her body when it was demanding food, on the hour, every hour, that she hadn't realised she was hungry. Ravenously, rapaciously, voraciously hungry. If Max wasn't holding her there was a good chance she'd drop to her knees and start gnawing on the legs of the coffee table.

'I want steak,' she announced. 'Steak so rare that it's dripping blood over the plate. And a salad, I suppose.'

'Let's assume that you threw up everything you ate yesterday and factor in your bridal boot camp and the long walk you had today, which ended with a sprint back to the car . . . well, I think you're functioning on minus five thousand calories and you could probably have some carbs without the world caving in.'

'Don't be an enabler, Max.'

'Don't be a diet bore, Neve.'

They compromised. Max would order an extra-large bowl of chips and Neve would eat some of them, because everyone knew that food eaten off someone else's plate had *at least* half the calories of regular food.

Although Max insisted that a bathrobe was fine for in-room dining, Neve decided to change into something a little less comfortable, especially as Max kept talking to her cleavage every time the belt began to loosen.

She was just pulling on her spare, unsodden jeans and the cherry-print blouse she'd been planning to wear with her wedding suit, when she heard a knock on the door and hurried out of the bathroom in time to see two waiters wheeling in a trolley with yes, plates obscured by huge silver domes just like they had in the movies.

In her attempt to get nearer to lift up a dome and swallow her fillet steak in one gulp, Neve kept getting in everyone's way because more staff were coming into the room laden down with gift boxes, ice buckets, a platter of chocolate-covered strawberries and a huge bouquet of roses and lilies.

'I know you said you wanted to put a huge dent into the room-service bill, but isn't this a little excessive?' she hissed at Max.

'But I only ordered dinner and a selection of DVDs,' he hissed back. Then he cleared his throat. 'Excuse me, but I think there's been a mix-up. I didn't order flowers or champagne or boxes of . . . *stuff.*'

'These arrived by courier while you were out, sir.' The most senior of the flunkies, judging by his age and the cut of his suit, handed Max an envelope. 'Have a good evening.'

'Who's it from?' Neve asked, as Max pulled out a sheet of notepaper and scanned the contents. 'What does it say?'

'Read it yourself.' Max thrust the paper at her and Neve looked down at the childish scrawl.

Dear Max and Neve
I'm so gutted that you weren't part of me and Dazza's big day.
Wish I'd never signed that stupid contract but two mill is two mill
and I promised my Nanna she could have a new kitchen.

Anyway, I wish you were here with us and I can't believe you
won't get to see me in my red Dolce & Gabanna wedding dress and
the leopardprint number they ran up for the evening reception.

But you can still toast me and Dazza, unless you totally hate me.
I hope you don't.
Lots of love
Mandy (McIntyre – but not for much longer!)

Max was looking boot-faced so rather than cooing over her new Clarins skincare products and his new watch, Neve told him to pick a DVD, while she ferried the plates over to the coffee table along with a bottle of champagne that she absolutely was not going to be drinking.

After demolishing her steak and salad and making major inroads into the chips, until Max was forced to slap her hand away so he could have some too, Neve reasoned that one glass of champagne wouldn't kill her. People were always extolling the benefits of having some hair of the dog that had bit you the night before.

Besides, it was easier to talk to Max with a drink inside

her, especially when there was still unfinished business between them and she had to tell him something that he didn't want to hear.

'Drink up,' she ordered, as she filled Max's glass, then took a cautious sip of her own champagne in case the taste triggered an horrific sense memory and she had to hotfoot it to the bathroom. It didn't. It actually tasted rather nice.

'So, was that note from Mandy hand-written?' she asked casually. 'It looked as if it was.'

'Well, the little hearts over the i's were a dead giveaway,' Max said, as he got up and began to load their empty plates on to the trolley. 'I'll just put this outside the door.'

His response wasn't exactly encouraging, but when he came back and sat down close enough so his thigh was pressed against hers, Neve persisted. 'I understand why you're angry with her, but I think it was really sweet that she took time out *on her wedding day* to get us presents.'

Max held up his hands in protest. 'It's not like she nipped down to Selfridges in between having her hair done and practising her vows.'

'Well, no, but she obviously spent enough time thinking about how upset you would be that she got someone else to organise the gifts and she wrote a note in between having her hair done and practising her vows.'

'Where exactly are you going with this, Neve?' Max asked, his voice cold and forbidding, but if he'd been that annoyed he wouldn't have tucked a lock of damp hair behind her ear.

'Just that she obviously feels genuinely upset about un-inviting you and you're much more than a little cog in the McIntyre branding machine.' Neve fixed him with her most flinty-eyed look, the one that could even get Celia to do the washing up. 'You should call and thank her and let her know that you're still friends. It will make you feel a whole lot better too.'

'I think she might be a little busy cutting the cake and

listening to Darren grunt his way through his speech,' Max said sullenly and he was pouting too. It was adorable.

'Well, leave a message then.' Neve stared at him without blinking, until Max gave in with a sigh and pulled out his phone.

'Waste of bloody time,' he muttered under his breath, but he rang the number and looked completely flummoxed when someone answered.

'Mandy? Why the hell are you answering your phone? Yeah? Well, wedding speeches are meant to be boring, so everyone has a chance to sneak out for a cigarette.'

Neve decided to sneak out herself and give Max some privacy. She sat on the bathroom floor and had read a chapter of *Lavender Laughs in the Chalet School*, when Max stuck his head round the door.

'It's OK, you can come out now,' he said, and the pout had been replaced with a smile, which was a welcome relief, even if the pout had been prettier. 'Mandy and I are friends again.'

'I'm glad to hear it,' Neve said, and when she tried to sidle past him, he pressed her up against the wall and pinned her wrists above her head for good measure.

'Thank you,' he said, and sealed it with a long, slow kiss that made Neve glad they'd decided to stay in. 'I won't forget this, Neve. Not any of it.'

'You're welcome,' she said, and kissed him back with so much ardour that it took a while for her to realise that Max was trying to disentangle himself.

'It's far too early for *that*,' he said prissily, putting some distance between them. 'There are several items on tonight's schedule that we have to get through before I can let you ravish my innocent body.'

'I thought there'd be mutual ravishing.' Neve folded her arms and tried hard not to pout; there was no possible way she could look as pretty as Max with her lower lip jutting out. 'Did you want to watch another DVD?'

Max was on his knees in front of the wardrobe and rooting through his weekend bag. 'No, you owe me a rematch,' he said, and pulled out a little green box that looked very familiar.

'Um, if you look in my holdall, you might be in for a surprise,' Neve told him, and waited until he pulled out her little green box. 'Snap!'

'I can't believe you brought Travel Scrabble!'

'Well, you did too!'

'Yeah, but I didn't bring the *Oxford English Dictionary* as well. I wondered why your bag was so heavy.'

Neve flung herself down on the sofa. 'We'll use my set,' she decided. 'I wouldn't put it past you to sneak in some extra blank tiles to try and get one over on me and my awesome vocabulary skills.'

'Of course, I am still in a delicate emotional state,' Max said, as he sat cross-legged on the floor on the other side of the coffee table. 'Can I trust you not to take advantage of that?'

'My hangover isn't completely gone,' Neve said, rustling the bag of tiles. 'So I'd say it's a pretty even playing-field.'

Max waited until they'd picked out a letter each to see who'd go first, and when he drew an A and Neve an R, he got a look on his face that was half leer, half glee.

'Oh, Neevy,' he said in a sing-song voice. 'Shall we make this a little more interesting?'

'Define interesting.'

'Best of three. If you win a game, then the loser has to pay a forfeit.' The look was definitely more leer than glee now.

'Define forfeit.'

Max gave a shudder of pure delight at his own cunning. 'The loser has to do one thing that the winner asks them to do. No questions. No arguments. No faffing.'

Neve's eyes narrowed. 'OK, define thing.'

'You know what I mean.' Max stuck his hand in the bag of tiles. 'A sex thing. Something that will get the other one off.'

If Neve had the ability to arch one eyebrow, she'd have been doing it about then. 'Alfred Mosher Butts is turning in his grave,' she bit out and she didn't know why she was so embarrassed because she couldn't wait to get the Scrabble over and done with so they could get on with the sex things, but Max was still in a very unpredictable mood and she didn't think that was going to lead to anything good.

'Who's Alfred Mosher Butts? I swear you just make this stuff up to distract me because you know I'm the better player.' Max arranged his tiles with a beatific smile that made Neve clench her fists.

'He invented Scrabble!' Neve groped for her own tiles. 'Let me remind you that I won last time and I'm probably going to win all three games now and you'll be begging for mercy, so just think about *that*.'

Max *could* arch one eyebrow. 'At your mercy? If that's meant to be a threat then it's not working. In fact, I'm tempted to throw all three games.' He gave Neve a mischievous look. 'We'd better shake on it, Pancake Girl, just to make it official.'

Neve shook Max's hand with every last ounce of strength she possessed, which was a lot, but he just smirked. 'Now, now. It's against the rules to nobble your opponent.'

Max didn't throw the first game. Instead, he left Neve floundering in his wake with a rack full of vowels, while he got the q, z, j and x and used two of them on a triple word score.

His success and her low score, the lowest she'd ever got in a game of Scrabble, was all the motivation Neve needed to get her head in the game. Especially as Max had done a victory lap around the room, even though she'd told him that it was extremely undignified.

She won the second game by a decent margin, and halfway through the third game, when Max realised he was trailing by nearly fifty points, it suddenly became a battle to the death. They were both going to get off at least once so really it was a win/win situation, but that third unclaimed orgasm was a point of principle and they stopped teasing each other, stopped talking and instituted a three-minute time limit on each round.

Even though Max got up to all his usual tricks of using two tiles to make six different words and block off the board, Neve knew she was going to win. Failure was not an option.

She liked to think she was graceful in her victory, unlike certain other people. 'Honestly, Max, it could have gone either way,' she murmured demurely when she beat him by one hundred and twenty-seven points. 'It was just luck.'

'I've never seen anyone get two triple word scores with one word.' Max sounded close to tears. He sighed. 'OK, how do you want me?'

Neve sat back and stretched luxuriously. 'Well, you won the first game. You can go first,' she said magnanimously. He'd spent most of the first two games talking about blow jobs, mainly to distract her, but she wasn't averse to the idea. 'So, what's it to be?'

It was odd how Max could alter the mood between them with just a quirk of his lips. What had been playful suddenly became heavy with tension as his eyes darkened and he caught his lower lip between his teeth.

'Stand up,' he said, no trace of teasing in his voice now. Instead it had a commanding edge that made the breath catch in Neve's throat as she did as she was told.

She stood there, arms swinging nervously as Max walked over to the bed and sat down. 'Now what?' she asked hoarsely.

'I want to see you naked,' and he said it uncertainly, as if he knew he was treading on dangerous ground. 'Please, Neevy.'

Neve shut her eyes. 'I can't,' she said imploringly. 'Pick something else because I won't be comfortable like that and neither of us will have much fun.'

'But I want you to . . .' Max shook his head. 'Come here, come to me.' He spread his hands. 'Just come here.'

Neve stood between Max's legs, even let his hands rest on her hips, but her expression was resolute. 'I don't feel comfortable or relaxed when I'm naked,' she repeated, her voice so low that Max had to lean closer to hear her.

'I want you to be comfortable with me,' he said softly. 'I want you to trust me like I've trusted you with stuff I haven't told a living soul, and anyway I've pretty much seen every bit of you now. Maybe not all at once, but I've seen your body.'

'But it's different when it's dark and we're in bed and, Max, it's not just a bit of cellulite.' She turned her head so she wouldn't have to look at him. 'You can't lose a hundred and seventy-five pounds without it leaving its trace. I have stretchmarks and loose skin, and my stomach looks like corrugated cardboard. Feels like it too.' She felt brave enough to cup his face in her hands because he was still looking at her so sweetly that she thought she might cry. 'I know you don't like me to mention it, but you've been with other women and I can guarantee that out of all of them, I have the worst body, the ugliest and—'

'Shhh, shhh.' Max kissed her hands and he didn't try to shower her with empty compliments that she hadn't been fishing for and wouldn't have believed anyway. 'It's been three months now, Neevy, and you always smell nice and you're funny and you try and take care of me, and do you really think I'm going to get up and go and not come back because you've got bingo wings? Please credit me with some integrity.'

He'd only said 'bingo wings' because he knew it would make her smile, and Neve was. She was even letting him undo the buttons of her blouse, because his speech had touched her and she wanted to believe him. But when his fingers delicately traced the puckered, silvery grooves that were etched into her sagging skin, Neve flinched, and if Max hadn't had one arm around her hips, anchoring her to the spot, she'd have wrenched herself away from him.

'They're *disgusting*,' she choked out.

'They're your battle scars,' Max said, and he wasn't even looking at her disfigured, mottled belly but up at her face, at the eyes she'd widened so she wouldn't start crying. 'You've been through something hard and painful, and it's made you the girl who's standing in front of me right now.'

'Less fat . . .'

'Well, there's that but you're also a fighter and you never forget what it feels like to be on the outside and yeah, you are a bit fucked up, Neevy, but so am I.' He stopped and let his hands drop, so she was standing there of her own accord. 'Why can't you have a little faith in me?'

And when he put it like that, there didn't seem to be any good reason to keep hiding herself. Neve's fingers had never felt so ungainly as she undid the last two buttons on her blouse and then shrugged her arms free and let it fall to the floor. She couldn't tear her gaze away from Max and he was looking her right in the eye, not challenging or daring her, but with a kind of desperation as if he was worried that he'd pushed her too far, too fast.

'It's all right,' she said. 'I'm not going anywhere either,' as she reached behind to unfasten her bra and then took that off too. She didn't think her breasts were so bad now that they'd shrunk and she'd worked enough on her pecs that they didn't droop down towards her belly. But when they weren't encased in underwire and elastane they could hardly be described as perky or buoyant, and they swung merrily, happy to be free as Neve reached down to unbutton and unzip her jeans.

She worked her jeans down her legs, then kicked them off so she was just standing there in her knickers. *Yesterday*, she told herself sternly, *you almost got naked in front of six complete strangers and Max isn't a stranger*. He'd got inside her head and his hands and mouth had touched the place that she was still shielding from him. And really now that he'd seen breasts, belly and thighs, she really wasn't that concerned about him seeing her pussy, especially as she'd suffered great agonies having a bikini wax the day before.

'Look at me,' Max said softly, and Neve realised that her eyes had drifted down to stare blindly at the red polish on her toenails. 'You're almost there, Neve. Come on, get your knickers off, sweetheart.'

She'd been expecting another heartfelt speech, not 'get your knickers off', and she never thought that she'd be laughing as she skinned out of her black lace panties.

And then Neve was naked, in front of a member of the opposite sex. In front of Max. She held her arms out wide so he could see everything and he wasn't looking at her face any more; his eyes were travelling down the body that she'd tried so hard to conceal from him.

'So this is me,' Neve said when she couldn't bear the silence any more. 'I did warn you, and we can pretend that you didn't just say all those things if you want to head for the door or ask me to put my clothes back on.'

Max rolled his eyes so hard that Neve could have sworn his pupils completely disappeared. 'Sometimes I really want to smack you,' he snapped, and before she could point out that there was absolutely nothing funny about domestic violence, Max's hands settled on her hips again. 'Rather kiss you though,' he said, and he was falling backwards on to the bed, and tugging Neve so she landed on top of him with a startled shriek.

He kissed the scream right out of her mouth, as Neve was struggling to lever herself off him, because she was too heavy and she was naked and he wasn't and the whole thing felt utterly ridiculous.

Neve wasn't sure when her struggling turned into squirming and writhing. It might have been at the moment that she started to kiss Max back and he rolled them over. That was better. Much, much better because she could fist her hands into his hair and grind her clit against his thigh, the rough denim of his jeans a source of irritation and delight.

'Take your clothes off,' she demanded, when they came up for air. She hardly recognised her own voice; it was so breathy and bordering on manic. 'How do you want me to get you off?'

Max sat back to pull off his T-shirt and Neve wanted to cry when he moved off her altogether so he could wriggle out of his jeans. But then he was coming down on top of her and they were skin to skin for the first time; all that hot flesh sliding against each other.

'This feels so good,' she gasped, as her breasts shimmied against his chest and she parted her legs so Max could settle between them, gritting his teeth as he realised how ready she was. 'Max? What do you want?'

'I had my turn,' he said, and he hadn't, not really. Because he'd said that the forfeit was to get the other one off and the sight of her naked body certainly hadn't done that. 'What do *you* want? Fingers or tongue or both?'

Neve wasn't in a position to argue any further because he already had two fingers inside her and was rubbing against that spot that made her clench around him and feel as if all good reason was dribbling out of her ears. 'Make me come,' she barked, when he eased off a little and she was capable of rational thought again. 'I don't care how, just do it.'

He made her come with his fingers and his tongue, and she was still coming when his hands were biting into her hips to try and keep her still as she arched against his mouth, until in the end Neve was kicking him away, almost off the bed, because she'd never come as hard as that before.

It was as if the orgasm had made something short-circuit in the over-developed part of her brain that dealt with inhibition, because Neve didn't care that she was naked. She coaxed Max into her arms so she could kiss his jaw, which had felt the full brunt of her flailing legs – his cock wouldn't be hard and wet against her inner thigh if he found her that repulsive.

Neve could taste herself on Max's lips as she kissed him; sleepy slow kisses that felt as if she was moving underwater. But then Max cupped her breast and pinched her nipple between thumb and forefinger, which made his cock twitch and a fresh wave of arousal pierce her languor.

'I think I should put you out of your agony,' she murmured, wrapping her hand around his cock. 'What was it you said? Fingers or mouth, or both?'

'Do you know what it does to me, when you say things like that?' Max groaned and Neve simply smiled because she could see *exactly* what it was doing to him, could feel it beneath her fingertips.

'Well, what's it to be?'

'Do you want to try something new?' Max asked, prising away her hand, one sticky finger at a time. 'But we can only do it for a little bit.'

'Do your worst,' Neve said, because as long as this new thing ended with her eyes rolling back in her head and her heart pounding furiously, she was up for anything that Max had in mind.

What Max had in mind was torment, pure and simple. He fitted himself between Neve's legs again and very carefully, very slowly brushed her clit with the head of his cock again and again.

Then she'd move, because how could she not? And then Max would stop, head thrown back, face set in a grimace and say, 'You have to stay absolutely still, Neevy, because I swear, I will lose it in a minute.'

Neve wanted him to lose it. She wanted it more than anything else in the world, and when he started moving again, always just a few slippery centimetres from where she really needed him, Neve canted her hips and the tip of his cock slipped inside her for a blissful moment that was enough to have her riding out one very tiny, very unsatisfying orgasm.

Max lunged back and she didn't know how he could control himself, when she was one breath away from pinning him to the mattress and riding him to the finish line. She struggled up on her elbows and pushed her tangled hair back from her eyes.

'You owe me for that last bloody game of Scrabble,' she panted. 'No questions, no arguments, no faffing.' Later she'd be impressed at her verbatim recall under extreme conditions, but not then. 'I want you to make love to me.'

'We are making love, there doesn't have to be pene—'

'Don't you dare use semantics on me,' Neve argued. 'Or come up with any more lame excuses. This is not payback for making me get naked and it's not because I feel sorry for you and it's not because of *him*, it's because I will die if you don't. Just once before this is over, I need you inside me.'

'You said, right from the beginning, that you couldn't—'

'Wouldn't!'

'OK, that you wouldn't have sex. That was your one rule because . . . because . . .' Max would have sounded much more convincing if he could even remember why Neve had instigated her no-sex ban and if he wasn't fisting his cock and staring at Neve's pussy.

She spread her thighs a little wider. 'OK, look, if I'm giving up a rule, then you can pick a new rule to make up for it. That's fair, isn't it?'

'Well, no, not really. What if you change your . . .'

'I don't care about that stupid rule any more. Pick. Something. Else.' It wasn't a suggestion; it was an order.

And given the sexual tension that permeated the air like dry ice and the way both of them were breathing heavily, Neve was more than a little surprised when Max gave her a sly, calculated smile. Like he was still capable of not just rational thought, but sneaky, devious thoughts too.

'You have to promise you'll respect my new rule 'cause it's completely non-negotiable,' he drawled, dipping his head down to give her nipple one hard suck, then retreating before Neve had time to cup the back of his head and keep his mouth busy.

'I promise!' He was going to insist that they held hands; she knew and she didn't care.

'I don't want to hear another self-deprecating word come out of your mouth ever again,' he said flatly, as Neve gave a surprised grunt. 'I'm tired of listening to it.'

At any other time, that would have been Neve's cue to let loose a whole stream of self-deprecating words, but Max's hand was between her legs making all those nerve-endings sing again and so she just sighed, 'Fine, whatever. Now, come here,' and she pulled him down on top of her.

There was five frantic minutes of grinding and groping, though it wasn't like either of them needed any more fore-play, and when Max went to the bathroom to get a condom, Neve went with him, plastered against his back, her hand wrapped round his dick again, because she couldn't bear not to touch him.

Even the sound of the foil ripping cranked up the heat and when Max was sheathed, Neve was done waiting. She launched herself at him, ending up in his lap, legs splayed on either side of his, and paused with his cock nestled against her clit and Max's lips pared back in a snarl, because payback was a bitch.

Then she lowered herself carefully so just the tip of Max's cock was inside her and this was where it usually went horribly wrong, but this time it felt so good, and carefully Neve sank down, until he was all the way inside her. Then she stopped.

Max lifted his hips and Neve's eyes snapped open. 'Don't move,' she said breathlessly.

He froze. 'Oh God, am I hurting you?'

She shook her head. 'No. Just . . . I don't want to rush this.'

Neve breathed in and out slowly and it was the oddest, strangest sensation but she could feel herself fluttering around his cock, as if her body wasn't bothered about taking stock of the solemnity of this occasion but was going on ahead without her.

'You're killing me,' Max groaned, his head resting against her shoulder.

'Poor baby.' Neve stroked the back of his neck, then grabbed a handful of his hair as she lifted herself up and then ground back down, because she couldn't help herself. 'You can move. Please. Now.'

'Bloody backseat driver,' Max muttered, his hands cushioning Neve's buttocks as he put her on her back. 'Wrap your legs round me. Tighter than that.'

Neve had always had this vague idea that sex was a spiritual experience that evoked waves crashing on sandy shores and flowers slowly unfurling their petals, but the actual reality was so much more visceral than that.

It was as if each one of her five senses had been designed specifically for sex. She tasted salt in her mouth as she bit Max's shoulder when she told him to go faster and he began to thrust harder and deeper than he had before. And she could hear the headboard of the bed banging against the wall in time with the beat of her heart. Then there was the smell of sex – musky and ripe – and she could see the little beads of sweat on Max's forehead and the sheen across his chest as she looked up at him – Neve knew that she should shut her eyes but she didn't want to miss a thing. But mostly there was touch; their slick bodies moving greedily against each other and his cock rubbing against that spot deep inside her that his fingers knew so well, and then Max told her to touch herself because he was close and Neve wormed her hand between them and she could feel where they were joined, but only for a moment because her fingers wanted to press and rub and then she had to close her eyes because she was coming in white-hot bursts of heat and light and her last conscious thought was that everything that she thought she knew was wrong.

*

402

Then it was later, much later. They'd showered together, even though Neve had had an inhibition relapse but Max had clamped a hand over her mouth when she tried to tell him that. They'd remade the bed because the duvet had been thrown on the floor and someone had pulled the sheet off the bed. And Neve had slipped into her red silk nightie because Rome wasn't built in a day and she couldn't simply sprawl lazily on the bed stark naked now that all her urges had been thoroughly sated.

'So, Neevy? You having fun yet?' Max asked with a grin, which quickly turned into an, 'Ouch! Why the fuck did you do that?'

'I'm offended that you even need to ask,' Neve said, as Max rubbed the spot on his arm where she'd just punched him.

'I suppose it did go pretty well,' Max said, popping a strawberry into Neve's mouth. They were working their way through the platter of chocolate-covered strawberries; Max biting off the chocolate and passing the strawberry to Neve when he was done. 'And I have to say, Neevy, you have some mad skills, and as an added bonus, you haven't asked me if I can introduce you to a publicist I know, or set up a little shoot with *Skirt*.' Max leaned back on his elbows. 'Once, before I'd barely pulled out, this woman said that it had been very nice but she had to get going because she'd left her husband baby-sitting.'

Neve's eyebrows shot up. 'That's not . . . good.' She bit her lip. 'Do you think that you're less scared of commitment now?' She didn't know why she was holding her breath as she waited for Max to reply, and it seemed like a strange conversation to be having after what they'd just shared, but maybe they both needed a reminder that this wasn't a for ever kind of deal. It was an eight weeks and counting sort of deal.

He shrugged. 'I don't know. I mean, yes, we've been dating for a couple of months but it's pancake dating and maybe I'm cool with that because I know it's not going to lead to picking out china patterns and making plans to move in together, is it?'

She knew that, but Neve still felt a pang of regret that Max wouldn't be in her future despite the fact that he was her first lover, the first man to see her naked, the first man to tell her she was beautiful when she was all dressed up or all dressed down or trembling from the ferocity of the first time they'd made love. How peculiar that people could make love, then never see or speak to each other again.

'No, but we'll be friends after this, won't we?' She prodded Max with her finger when he simply grunted. 'You won't get rid of me that easily. I know where you live, Max.'

'Let's see how you feel when you're bedded down with Mr California,' Max said, not looking at Neve as he picked up the last strawberry.

'I'll feel exactly the same way,' Neve protested. 'And don't call him that.'

'Sorry,' Max said, though he didn't sound the least bit repentant. He held the last strawberry just above her mouth so Neve had to lever herself up, one hand on Max's shoulder to reach it. Which meant that she was back in Max's arms before she'd even had time to chew and swallow. 'The post-orgasmic glow looks really good on you.'

'By post-orgasmic glow, I take it you mean red-faced and blotchy . . . Ow! What the hell did you do *that* for?' Neve spat, rubbing the spot on her bottom that Max had just smacked.

'I had to.' Max kissed the corner of her mouth. 'You were being self-deprecating and we have an agreement about that now.'

Neve sighed. 'If you're going to smack me every time I forget, then I'll be black and blue in an hour.'

'You'll just have to try harder,' Max said unsympathetically, his hand sliding up to cup her breast.

'Because I have plans for the next hour that would be spoiled if your arse was too sore for you to lie on it.'

Neve looked down. Then her hand did a quick sortie to make certain that it wasn't just the way that Max's shorts had rumpled. *'Again?'*

Max was already lowering her down on to the bed. 'We've got a lot of lost time to make up.'

Chapter Thirty

It seemed to Neve that the world had split in two. There was the world that had Max in it, where she seemed to spend most of her time naked, but Max was naked too so that worked out rather well.

Then there was the other world that Neve stumbled through, always tired and blinking her eyes in the brilliant sunshine that she couldn't get used to after a cold, grey spring. It was as if she were sleepwalking; only the ache between her legs and her kiss-bitten lips felt real.

When she wasn't with Max and when she wasn't thinking about Max, Neve was glad that she'd waited this long to have sex. Not just because she was old enough to have skipped all the teenage groping and fumbling that other girls went through to get to the good stuff, but because she'd never imagined that she'd be so insatiable.

She should have known really. She was the kind of girl who could never have just one chocolate biscuit, not when there were another twenty-nine left in the packet. When she'd kicked that, she'd got such an endorphin rush from exercising that the staff at her gym had actually staged an intervention because she was in danger of becoming an exerexic.

So it was just as well that she hadn't started having sex at sixteen like most of the girls in her class, because if it had been this good, then Neve suspected that she'd have given up on her GCSEs, never bothered with A-levels, and a degree would have just got in the way of her orgasms.

The only reason she got out of bed to go into work where both Mr Freemont and Rose were finally united in their disapproval of Neve sitting in her back office in a day-dreamy, absent-minded sex-haze, was because Max had to get out of bed. And the only reason that Max got out of bed was because he had an agent, and a book editor and a magazine editor who phoned to shout at him about all the deadlines he was missing.

'I think I've worked out why we're at it like rabbits,' he'd said to Neve one morning, when they'd decided they had time for a quickie, even though Neve was already an hour late for work. 'We wasted two months not having sex and even if we'd only had sex once a day, that's at least sixty orgasms that we've missed out on. We have a lot of catching up to do and we haven't got much time left to do it.'

Neve still managed to make her three weekly sessions with Gustav, because he'd have hunted her down if she didn't, but she yawned her way through them and didn't have the stamina that she used to. 'It's that boy,' Gustav would mutter darkly, when Neve collapsed after five girl press-ups. 'I knew this would happen.'

For the first time in her life Neve wasn't hungry so it didn't really matter that her exercise and training regime had fallen by the wayside. She could just about manage lunch, but having breakfast would have meant getting out of bed half an hour earlier and dinner never seemed to happen because as soon as she got home from work, she was either going round to Max's, or he was on her doorstep and there was just enough time for one of them to say, 'Did you have a good day?' before they were kissing, and kissing just wasn't enough any more.

They'd emerge from under the covers at around eleven to walk Keith to the nearest convenience store to buy a loaf of bread and something to put on it. Neve was existing on a diet of sex, black coffee, spaghetti hoops on toast, cheese on toast, peanut butter on toast, anything as long as it could be spread, heaped or smeared on two pieces of lightly browned bread.

It was four weeks of being joined at the hip (and other more pleasurable places) until they had to do the unthinkable and spend a night apart. Max had a meeting with a publicist, then an awards dinner, and Neve had to catch up on her laundry and spend quality time with Celia. Though spending quality time with Celia meant facing a barrage of questions that made the Spanish Inquisition seem like light relief.

'What has happened to you?' Celia burst out as soon as Neve opened the door. 'I haven't seen you in *weeks* and I heard Charlotte screaming at you about your bed banging against the wall, and since when do you pad around in a vest and knickers, and you have three – no, four – lovebites. How did you get a lovebite just above your knee?'

Neve knew that she should shut Celia down, but when she opened her mouth the only thing that came out was a yawn. So, as she lovingly hand-washed her silk slips in the bathroom sink, Celia perched on the edge of the tub and lectured her about just how stupid she was.

'I know what's going on,' Celia railed as she worked her way through a bag of prawn crackers. 'You and Max are totally doing it. I thought you were doing it before, but now I know that you weren't, because you are totally and utterly doing it now.'

'Celia, don't you ever need to pause for oxygen?' Neve asked, as she hung her midnight-blue nightie over the clothes-horse sitting in the bath.

'Oxygen is over-rated,' Celia said dismissively because they were going off topic. 'This is more than just the two of you bumping uglies. Max doesn't even flirt with the beauty girls when he comes into the office any more and you smile in this sappy way every time I say his name. You're both completely loved up and so, like, is this still a pancake relationship? Or are you serious about each other? Are you going to tell Willy McWordy he's history? What's going on?'

It was actually a really good question: *what's going on?* Neve didn't know because it wasn't something she and Max talked about. They talked a lot about how many days they had left and how much of that time they could feasibly spend horizontal. And they murmured words against each other's skin but they didn't talk about what they were doing and the consequences of what they were doing and whether they should even be doing it in the first place. Which suited Neve fine because she'd spent her entire life pontificating and hypothesising and it had never got her very far.

So she simply turned to Celia and shrugged. 'I don't know what's going on,' she murmured. 'I mean, like, what*ever*.'

As long as she lived, Neve would never forget the look on Celia's face, just before she choked on a prawn cracker. She hadn't even looked that shocked the time she'd discovered that Charlotte had bought the same Chloe bag that she'd spent months saving up for. 'Oh my God, Neevy!' she gasped once the power of speech had returned. 'You've turned into me!'

It was on the tip of Neve's tongue to point out that in order to turn into Celia she'd have to grow seven inches and lose three stone, but she could just imagine Max's reaction, then the sound and fury of the flat of his hand connecting with her arse and she shivered, a good kind of shiver, and smiled. 'Does that mean you're turning into me then, Seels?' she asked mischievously. 'You read any good books lately? And no, the latest issue of *Vogue* doesn't count.'

'Stop smiling like that and don't make jokes about *Vogue* – you're freaking me the fuck out,' Celia moaned, but she seemed to like the new laid-back Neve, even though she was very peeved that new laid-back Neve didn't have a fully stocked fridge and wouldn't dish the dirt on her love-life.

'But is it bigger than a bread-bin?' she demanded after what felt like hours of cross-examination. 'Well, obviously it's not bigger than a bread-bin, but is it bigger than a king-size Snickers bar?'

'I can't actually remember how big a king-size Snickers bar is,' Neve replied, as she heard the front door open, then Max's voice calling out.

'Honey? I'm home. I skipped out after the speeches.'

'He has his own key!' Celia exclaimed, as Neve jumped out of her chair and hurried into the hall.

'You didn't bother to get dressed?' Max asked as he shrugged out of his dinner jacket, which he was wearing with a Clash T-shirt and jeans. 'Well, that's going to save us some time.'

Before Neve could tell him that she had one very inquisitive little sister on the premises, Max grabbed her and kissed her for so long and so hard that Neve completely forgot she even had a little sister.

'Hey, you two, get a room,' the little sister said from behind them. 'Up the stairs, second door on the left. I'm going before I'm scarred for life.'

Neve smiled vaguely at Celia from the security of Max's arms and Max murmured something that might have been, 'Hello,' or, 'Goodbye,' or even, 'Don't let the door hit you in the arse on the way out.'

Neve felt a pang of guilt for driving Celia out of her second home, but she couldn't find it in her heart to feel that bad. She was pretty sure that she'd see Celia every day for the rest of her life, but having quality time with Max, quality naked time, was a very rare commodity.

Then May gave way to June, and it felt as if time was slipping through her fingers. Because all they had left was just over a month. Mere weeks really, if William came back when he said he would, but William had become a vague, blurred figure that Neve couldn't focus on when all she could think about was Max. She'd received two letters from him and countless emails and she'd read them immediately but it was more force of habit than because she wanted to get that giddy high from poring over each of William's words like she usually did. All Neve felt was horribly conflicted as she sent William a quick email claiming: *things are really busy at work. Will write properly when I have a chance.* There were subjects she'd shied away from with William like her weight-loss and her adventures in dating, but she'd never lied to him before, and although it wasn't something she was proud of, it was necessary. William was her golden future and Max was the here and now.

So when Max was sent to LA at twenty-four hours' notice to salvage a cover-shoot for *Skirt*, which was rapidly becoming a clusterfuck between the celebrity stylist, the celebrity photographer and the actual celebrity and her publicist who'd taken to calling Max at three every morning to scream at him, it felt a lot like the end of the world, even if she did get Keith as a flatmate for the rest of the week.

Neve didn't need much persuasion to duck out of work early to accompany Max to Heathrow so they could cling to each other at Passport Control as if he was going off to war.

'I'll be back by the weekend,' Max said, once his gate number had been called, and they were forced to stop smooching.

Neve's face fell. It was Monday afternoon and Saturday seemed light years away. 'You promise?'

'I promise. Even if I have to shoot the cover with my camera phone.' Max cupped her cheek. 'It won't be so bad. You said yourself that you had a ton of stuff to do this week.'

'That would be all the stuff that I was putting off because I didn't want to do it,' Neve said. She straightened the collar of Max's black shirt. 'It feels very strange kissing you with . . .'

'. . . our clothes on?'

'I was going to say with all these people around, but that works too.' Neve knew she should stop pawing at Max, but she couldn't stop herself from trying to smooth down his hair. Getting through the next five days was going to be agony. 'How do you feel about phone sex?'

'I'm very pro-phone sex,' Max said emphatically. 'Also email sex, text sex and wishing that your laptop had a built-in webcam like mine.'

Neve looked up at the departures board. 'Your flight leaves in thirty-five minutes. You need to go.'

Max swooped in for another kiss and just as Neve had decided that another five minutes wouldn't hurt, he pushed her away. 'You go first.'

'No, you go first,' she countered.

'But I can't go anywhere if you're standing there looking so kissable.'

'But if you go first, then I can have at least two minutes longer to look at you before you disappear from view.'

'You just want to perv at my arse,' Max sniffed, then his gaze softened. 'Seriously, you go first.'

'No, you.' Neve didn't know when she'd become one of those sappy, silly girls who used to irritate her beyond all measure when she'd heard them on the bus cooing at their boyfriends on their phones, 'You hang up first.'

At least she wasn't giggling.

'I'm going,' she told Max decisively. 'I have a huge to-do list that I need to get through without you cluttering up the flat and distracting me.'

Max put a hand to his heart and pretended he was mortally wounded, but then they heard his flight being called. 'I really should go,' he said seriously. 'If I miss my flight, I'll be looking for another job.'

Neve thought about having one last kiss, but in the end the only way she could leave was to walk away without looking back.

It was torture to have to slip back into her boring old routine. Eight hours' sleep a night, two hours in the gym consecutive mornings and evenings, three proper meals a day, plus two low-carb, low-calorie snacks, getting to work on time and sitting in the bath with her laptop on her knee and the noise-cancelling headphones firmly in place because Charlotte had got wind that Neve was no longer entertaining a gentleman caller and was putting in extra time with her broom handle.

It also meant that Neve had to deal with her outstanding correspondence. Jacob Morrison had emailed with a summons to his club. He hadn't mentioned the six and a half chapters she'd sent, which could only mean that he was going to let Neve down gently. Or worse, wanted her to hand over everything Lucy-related so he could get a proper writer to do the honours. Or even worse, he hated Lucy's poems and short stories and was washing his hands of her. There was also an email from her father, who was coming into town at the end of the week and wanted to book two tickets for the new Jennifer Aniston film.

Neve decided to get those two obstacles over in one day, so she could block out six hours to ride a tsunami of extreme agitation instead of spreading it out over the whole week. If she saw them both on Thursday, then she could brood until lunch-time on Friday, when she'd stop brooding and start getting excited at the prospect of Max coming home.

There were also the two briefly read letters from William that she'd stuffed into a drawer. But on Thursday morning, which she'd christened D Day (D for difficult and dreadful and dejected), Neve steeled herself to revisit them. Normally she committed to memory every single last syllable, but now as she smoothed out the crumpled airmail paper, she realised that she'd only skimmed them before and could scarcely remember any of the contents.

The belief that one day they'd be together had been such a constant and comforting theme over the three years, that Neve was relieved to find that she wasn't ready to give up on it just yet, as she finally gave William's letters the attention they deserved. What she had with Max was wonderful, but it was never built to last; while what she and William shared was something deeper and more profound than just sexual attraction.

He held her soul in his hands.

Dearest Neve

It's always sunny in California and you can't imagine how boring and monotonous the relentless sunshine can be.

I long for grey, damp days with tea and toast and The Times. *I miss walking in the rain and seeing the world around me all green, glistening and ripe with promise.*

English sun is not the same as the golden light in the Napa Valley or the heat haze hovering over Los Angeles. It's a delicate, ephemeral illusion.

Can you tell that I'm homesick? There are many things I'll miss about LA and I wish I could bring some of them back with me in my carry-on luggage, but I'm so ready to be back in London and whatever the weather, I want to walk with you along the Thames and talk about everything and nothing. Even to share a companionable silence with you would be bliss.

On a more prosaic note, can I humbly request more teabags and a bar of Cadbury's Dairy Milk?

All my love, as always

William

Neve sighed as she tore open the second letter. William's words were no longer the panacea that they used to be, but were like little daggers stabbing into her heart, as if on some level he knew that she'd made room there for Max too.

Dear Neve

Have you forsaken me? You always reply to my letters much quicker than I would have thought possible, given the vagaries of the Royal Mail, but two weeks have gone past and there's been nothing from you in my mailbox.

*I got your email to say how busy you are at work. Once again, I
wonder if being surrounded by those dusty books and files is the
best use of your academic gifts, but this is something we can talk
about when I get back.*

*I'm still yearning for a decent cup of tea and some proper
chocolate (though one of my dearest LA friends has turned me on
to the refreshing delights of frozen yogurt or 'froyo' as I never call
it) so if you could see your way clear to sending me some, I'd be
eternally in your debt.*

Not long now, Neve, before we can share a pot of tea in person.
Much love
William

Neve only had time to read both letters twice, when her
phone beeped. As soon as she saw Max's name on the
screen, her heart sped up, just as it used to when she'd read
William's letters.

Can I shag you senseless courtesy of Orange at 11 p.m. your time?
Max x

Unlike any correspondence from William, all it took was
fifteen words from Max for her breasts to swell and to feel
that spot between her legs start to pulse with longing.

The feelings that Max aroused in her were thrilling, but
they were just about sex. It wasn't romance and it certainly
wasn't love, so there was no need for Neve to feel so guilty
as she texted Max back: *I think that can be arranged! Neve x*,
before she went to get ready for her appointment with
Jacob Morrison.

Chapter Thirty-one

It was very hard to plan an outfit that would take you from afternoon tea and rejection from a super-agent to the cinema with your estranged father.

Neve wanted to look cool and in control and banish all memories of the sweaty, flustered mess she'd been the last time she'd seen Jacob Morrison – or her father, come to that. After one false start with a black wrap dress, she decided her new trouser suit and the cherry-print blouse gave the right impression. Usually she wore trousers with a long top or tunic that covered belly and bum, but after contorting this way and that in the bathroom mirror, she had to admit that neither belly nor bum looked offensive enough to be covered up. It was also the first time she'd dressed for a major event without texting Celia photos of her outfit options, Neve realised, as she clipped the foam wedge to the crown of her head and managed a bouffant ponytail after only two attempts.

Then wearing her Converses, but with her three-inch heels in her bag, Neve stopped off at the Post Office to post William a box of PG Tips, two huge bars of Cadbury's Dairy Milk and a quick apologetic note that she was sorry for the delay and sorry for the airmail silence, and just generally sorry. Neve felt so guilty that she hadn't had time to go to Sainsbury's and get William his preferred Red Label teabags that she sent the package priority airmail for a sum that would have made her eyes water if she hadn't been determined to keep her mascara from smudging. But as soon as she shoved the parcel towards a post office employee, Neve felt as if she was shoving William away to be dealt with at a later date and she could set off to meet Philip with a clear conscience and a fair-to-middling number of butterflies in her stomach.

They holed up in the café across the road from Jacob Morrison's club with a cup of greasy tea each so Neve could listen to the latest instalment of Philip's relationship woes, which were exactly the same as all the previous instalments.

'. . . so he's moved in this little twink who I'm pretty sure has a meth habit,' Philip finished at the end of a rambly monologue listing the many wrongs that Clive had done him. 'Do you really think love conquers all?'

'But do you really love him?' Neve asked bluntly. 'I mean, do you connect on a spiritual level?'

Philip faltered because there was absolutely nothing spiritual about Clive, apart from his vodka intake. 'Well, no, but . . .'

'So is the sex absolutely phenomenal? Like, when you see him, you're not really listening to anything he says because all you can think about is how long it's going to be before you're both naked? You can't eat or sleep because you're thinking about the sex, and all he has to do is send you a text message and you're we— you get an erection.'

'God, no. We haven't had sex for weeks. Clive says that he sees me more as an emotional outlet than . . .' Philip's eyes blinked rapidly from behind his glasses. 'Did you just say erection without even lowering your voice?'

'It's a perfectly acceptable word,' Neve said defensively. 'I think you'd do better to ignore my vocabulary and concentrate more on the actual content.' She took a moment to gather herself. 'You have to dump him.'

'Dump him?' Philip echoed incredulously. 'I can't just dump him.'

'Why can't you? You don't live together, you don't have

any dependants and he makes you utterly miserable. I'd say that dumping him was your only option.'

Philip stared down at his cup of coffee. 'He can be very kind and caring when he wants to.'

Neve refrained from asking Philip to give her three examples of Clive being kind and/or caring. 'I know it's hard with this being your first gay relationship, but—'

'I don't know why you suddenly think you're the expert on gay relationships or any other kind of relationships,' Philip said huffily. Philip saying anything huffily was a huge deal as he hated confrontation. He couldn't even watch *EastEnders* because all the shouting and fighting in and around Albert Square upset him so much. 'You've only been in a relationship for a matter of weeks.'

'Months actually,' Neve said, just as huffily, until she remembered that she was meant to be gathering. 'I know it's not a real relationship but, well, I'm happy, and if I can feel like that in a fake relationship then you should feel like that in a real one. Honestly, Phil, we've been having the same conversation about Clive for three years.'

'Not the same conversation. There are variations on the theme.'

'But the variations are that he's treating you even worse than he was the last time we talked about him. Promise me you'll at least think about telling him to shove off.' Neve pushed away her tea, because it had a rancid, oily aftertaste. 'I mean, if you're not even having sex, then what's the point?'

'Well, there's no need to ask you if *that* aspect of your fake relationship is going well,' Philip said tartly.

Neve waited for her cheeks to heat up, and when they didn't, she decided there was no harm in an enigmatic smile, though it felt more like an ear-to-ear grin. 'I have no complaints,' she said. 'Well, I have plenty of complaints but they're more to do with having to see Jacob Morrison in fifteen minutes.'

'Maybe he wants to congratulate you on your glittering prose style.' Philip finally admitted defeat and pushed his tea away too. 'Then he'll promise that he can get you a six-figure advance and you'll stop coming into work and taking my calls.'

'Hardly,' Neve said, but she allowed herself a few seconds to try to imagine what it would be like if Philip's words came to pass. It seemed so implausible that she gave up. 'And I would always take your calls. Or I'd get my PA to take your calls.'

'You never know, Neevy. People do get agents and they do get book deals. It's not completely unheard of.'

'All I really want is for him to tell me that he's going to submit *Dancing on the Edge of the World* to publishers. Then he'll tell me that while he enjoyed reading my pitiful attempt at writing a biography, I should stick to transcribing. God, I never asked him to read it,' Neve said crossly. 'And I will tell him that. Well, I won't, but I'll be thinking it very loudly.'

'You're being very ornery today, Neve. What on earth has got into you?'

This time the enigmatic smile was more of a smirk. 'A lady never kisses and tells.' She looked at the clock on the wall. 'I suppose I'd better get this over and done with. And will you at least think about what I said? You deserve to be with someone who makes you happy.'

Neve thought that it would take more than one stirring pep talk to convince Philip to break free of decades spent being a doormat. It was hard to change, but it wasn't impossible, and if she kept gently pushing him in the right direction, then maybe he'd break free from Clive's evil clutches and kick his evil ex-wife to the kerb too while he was at it.

She was still grinning at her mental picture of a single, self-assured Philip dancing on the podium in a gay nightclub surrounded by admiring, muscle-bound men as she walked through the dining room of Jacob Morrison's club to what appeared to be his usual table, tucked away in an alcove. He probably preferred that table so there weren't many witnesses when he reduced hapless wannabe writers to tears.

Jacob didn't look up from his BlackBerry as Neve approached, but as he never willingly acknowledged her existence, she was expecting that. She'd also forgotten to change out of her Converses, she noticed as she pulled out the chair, but it wasn't as if he'd asked her there to discuss her choice of footwear.

Neve ordered a pot of tea from a passing waiter, then decided to take the bull by the horns. 'Jacob? Sorry, but I've got another meeting after this.' It sounded better than saying that she was going to see a rom-com with her father.

'Oh, sorry. I think I spend more time on Twitter than I do working,' Jacob said, still transfixed by his BlackBerry and not sounding the least bit annoyed that Neve had decided to speak before she was spoken to. 'How are you? You look well.'

'I'm fine,' Neve said carefully, because she wasn't sure if it was a trick question and that Jacob was just about to hit her with a 'How can you possibly be fine when the chapters you sent me were badly written, poorly constructed and lacking in any discernible content?'

But he didn't. He turned off his BlackBerry then looked up and smiled at her, and Neve couldn't help but state the obvious. 'I didn't know you wore glasses.'

He was wearing a pair of thick black nerdy glasses that made him look a hundred times less intimidating than when there was nothing coming between him and his glare. Jacob touched the frames with a nervous gesture and seemed a little nonplussed. 'Well, I put in my contact lenses when-ever I come to the Archive, even though they irritate my eyes,' he revealed. At least it explained why he frowned so much.

Neve took the bait. 'Why can't you wear your glasses at the Archive?'

Jacob Morrison, literary super-agent, actually squirmed in his chair. If you took away the designer suit and the expensive haircut and the chiselled jawline, he looked like a little boy who'd been caught with his hand in the biscuit tin. 'I used to work at the Archive when I first came down from Cambridge,' he said finally. 'George, Mr Freemont, sat at the next desk and spent a large part of every day mocking me for the thickness of my lenses – when, that is, he wasn't mocking me for my poor cataloguing skills and my general failure as a human being.'

'So he was like that, even then?' Neve asked.

'Worse. I think he's actually mellowed with age,' Jacob said with a smile. 'But Rose used to stick up for me. And there was the time when I did something absolutely unconscionable when I was making him a cup of tea, so it wasn't all bad.'

'What did you do to his tea?'

Jacob shook his head solemnly. 'That's a secret I'll take to the grave or until you get me horribly drunk.'

Neve giggled, and though she'd imagined spending the entire meeting monosyllabic, she spent the next ten minutes firing questions at Jacob so she could get all the dirt on Mr Freemont and report back to Chloe and Philip because Rose had obviously been holding out on them all this time.

Eventually Jacob held up his hands in protest. 'Enough! That wasn't why I asked you to tea. I want to talk about Lucy Keener.'

Every instinct Neve possessed shrieked at her to tense and panic, but she tried to ignore them, because she was here for Lucy first and foremost. Anything else was just gravy, though if Jacob absolutely *hated* what she'd written, she hoped he'd make it quick and relatively painless.

'You said you liked *Dancing on the Edge of the World*,' she prompted nervously.

'I didn't like it,' Jacob said, as Neve frowned because he'd sent her that email, 'I *loved* it. And so did my assistant and my reader and my girlfriend who read it in one sitting and was in tears for the last fifty pages. I think you've discovered one of the great British novels, Neve.'

'I have?' Neve allowed herself to relax a little. 'And the poems and short stories? Did you like them too?'

Jacob nodded. 'I did, very much. Though poems and short stories are a harder sell than novels, but we'll cross that bridge when we come to it.'

Neve decided that the fact that Jacob had said 'we' instead of 'I' didn't mean anything deeply significant. 'So you'll submit *Dancing on the Edge of the World* to publishers then?' She smiled ruefully. 'I know it's out of my hands, but I feel very protective towards Lucy.'

He was frowning at her from behind his glasses and Neve clenched up again. 'Shall we cut to the chase, Neve?'

She nodded despondently.

'The first two chapters you sent were very stilted. They were all tell, no show. I really wanted to get a sense of Lucy's background, where she went to school, who ran the corner shop, what her bedroom looked like – the reader needs to get a sense of who Lucy is so they can start to care about her.'

Neve hung her head. 'Oh, OK. Well . . .'

'But then you got into a rhythm about halfway through chapter three, when her sister Dorothy left home to get married, and I really liked the way you began to build up the relationship Lucy had with her father,' Jacob said, smiling at her. 'I think you're off to a good start.'

'I am?' Neve couldn't keep the surprise out of her voice.

'You are, but don't let it go to your head,' Jacob said sharply, but with another smile to take the sting out of his words. 'Now, I want to submit a package to prospective publishers of *Dancing on the Edge of the World*, along with a completed manuscript of the biography and a collection of her best poems and short stories. I'd like us to work on that together because you have a better understanding of the material.'

'I thought you could maybe divide the poems and stories into decades, so it works almost as an autobiography,' Neve said eagerly. 'Her writing changed so much if you compare her short stories written during the war to the poems she wrote three years after it had ended and Charles Holden had got married. Though I suppose there'd be a chronological gap where—'

'Neve, did you hear what I said?' Jacob asked, with another frown, though she was starting to get used to them. 'I'd like you to finish writing Lucy's biography so I can submit it to publishers.'

'Are you sure? Because I'm not a proper writer. I mean, I had a few things published in *Isis* when I was at Oxford, but that doesn't really count. What if I get stuck? What if I get writer's block?' Neve was just about to run her fingers through her hair in agitation when she remembered that she had a foam wedge resting in there. She settled for wringing her hands instead. 'A whole book – how long is it meant to be, anyway?'

'OK, you need to take some deep breaths,' Jacob advised, summoning a waiter. 'I'll get you a glass of water so you don't start hyperventilating.'

He waited until Neve was clutching on to a glass of mineral water for dear life, before he continued: 'Just think of writing this book as if it were your MA dissertation, but with a lot less literary theory.'

Neve had rolled up at Jacob's club fearing the worst, and now that the worst appeared to be that she had literary representation and the green light to finish Lucy's biography, she wasn't sure how to react. She took shallow breaths and tried to open her mouth to say something. *Anything.*

'Thank you,' she said at last. 'Thank you. I can't tell you what this means to me.'

'Well, what it means is that I've asked you to write a book in your spare time and unpaid. And once it's done, if I can't get you a deal, then you'll never earn any money from it.'

'I don't care about the money,' Neve breathed and it was the absolute truth. Jacob Morrison having faith in her and her writing was more than enough. It was also more than she'd ever expected. 'Oh my goodness, I can casually refer to "my agent" when I talk to people.' She paused as Jacob stared at her as if she was mad. She did feel rather unhinged. 'Not that I would, because people would think I was an utter fool.'

'They really would,' Jacob said. 'I'll get my office to draw up a contract, but shall we shake on it, before we start talking about logistics?'

They spent a happy hour discussing the huge amount of work that Neve had committed to. Not just the actual writing but contacting the Alumni Association at Oxford so she could get in touch with Lucy's contemporaries, and sweet-talking the woman in charge of the Holden family's personal archive into letting her have access to their private papers. Even contacting the Cultural Attaché at the Russian Embassy to shed some light on the two years that Lucy had spent in Russia. It was daunting but it was also very, very exciting.

Even better, Jacob was going to use his influence to wangle her a four-day week at the Archive without a cut in her salary, because any publication of Lucy Keener's work would benefit the LLA and, 'You're practically on minimum wage as it is.'

Just as they were both getting misty-eyed at the wish-for-the-moon possibility of a Lucy Keener biopic with Kate Winslet in the title role, Neve happened to glance down at her watch. She couldn't believe that she'd been there for two hours.

'On dear, I had no idea it was so late,' she said apologetically. 'I have to be in Camden by five.'

Jacob nodded, but he was already pulling out his BlackBerry. 'I'll get my assistant to email you,' he said, as Neve scraped her chair back. 'And I'll take great pleasure in phoning George Freemont tomorrow to tell him that he'll have to manage without you one day a week.'

'Thank you,' Neve said fervently, because she'd been dreading that particular conversation.

'Believe me, it will be a pleasure.' When Jacob grinned and winked at her, Neve decided that it was a good thing that her heart was already taken, because having a crush on your agent would be very unprofessional. 'You'd better run along, you don't want to be late.'

Chapter Thirty-two

Neve had pencilled in the half-hour walk from Bloomsbury to Camden for worrying about the reunion with her father, but she spent all thirty minutes of it on the phone to Philip getting increasingly agitated as she visualised door after door slamming in her face, as the gatekeepers of private family papers and literary archives refused to admit her. In fact, she was so busy wailing at Philip as she turned into Parkway, that it took Neve a second to remember why she was there. Although she was ten minutes early because she was *always* ten minutes early, her father was already standing outside the cinema and giving a flinty-eyed look to the home-less man who was spinning him some sob story in the hope of earning fifty pence. Neve side-stepped the homeless man's shopping trolley, which was full to the brim with bulging carrier bags, and came to a halt beside her father.

'I won't tell you again. Bugger off and get a job,' Barry Slater was saying, when he caught sight of Neve. 'There you are. Let's go in. I don't want to miss the trailers.'

There was a brief hug of bumped noses and banged elbows, before they walked inside. Of course, her dad had already bought the tickets and Neve was dispatched to the toilet ('your mother always goes ten minutes in then spends the rest of the film asking me questions'). When she emerged, her father was standing there with two bottles of water and a small tub of popcorn.

'It's salted,' he said, as they headed for Screen One.

'Can you eat it? Is it all right for my cholesterol levels?'

'I'll have a little bit, but maybe you shouldn't eat things that have a lot of sodium,' Neve said, and she forced herself to look at him properly, without her eyes darting away at the last moment. He was looking good; tanned, without the lines etched into his face that she'd thought were permanent, and his stomach was a lot less paunchy than it had been. 'Mum said you were looking after yourself – it seems to be working.'

Her father patted his gut. 'I miss my beer,' he muttered gruffly, so Neve guessed they were done talking about his cholesterol; she also knew that once they sat down, she'd be under pain of death not to open her mouth.

As she waited for the film to start, Neve wondered what she was doing there. Her father didn't seem even a little racked with guilt over things that had been said and then things that *hadn't* been said. Maybe he was thinking the same thing about her. It was hard to tell with Barry Slater.

Ninety minutes later, Neve was in much better spirits. Jennifer Aniston's hair had been super-glossy, her co-star was handsome in a very rugged way, the obligatory best friend was kooky, the plot wasn't too phallo-centric and it had all ended with a kiss in Central Park in springtime. Neve knew that she should probably spend more time catching up on Eastern European cinema but she really did love a good chick flick.

'Did you enjoy it, Dad?' she asked, as they made their way out of the cinema, her father's hand on her elbow in case she couldn't make it down the stairs on her own.

'It were all right,' he said. 'Though I don't know what that Brad Pitt was thinking of. Imagine leaving a woman like that.'

'I don't suppose we'll ever know the real story,' Neve mumbled because she didn't want to encourage him.

'Got the car parked round the corner. Thought we'd have

dinner at Marco's place,' her father said, and Neve resigned herself to two more tension-filled hours.

They drove to Finsbury Park in a silence punctuated only by Barry Slater's savage character assassinations of every other driver on the road. He also cast grave aspersions on their mothers, while Neve pressed her foot down on an imaginary brake pedal.

She could tell the exact moment that her father relaxed. It was when the restaurant door opened to let out the warm waft of garlic and fresh bread and Marco, the owner, rushed to welcome them inside.

'Signor Slater, it's been too long,' he cried, and then he and her dad were clapping each other manfully on the back and as they made their way to a table by the window, they were greeted by Mr and Mrs Chatterjee who lived next door but one from her parents' house.

Her father's good mood showed no signs of abating, especially when Neve told him that his heart could handle a pizza as long as it wasn't covered in too much cheese, and once her fingers were curled around a glass of red wine, Neve was sure that everything was going to be all right. They'd got off to a shaky start but that was only to be expected after three years of not saying very much to each other.

She smiled warmly at her father as he pulled a crumpled roll of paper from the back pocket of his trousers. 'You brought something to read?' he asked as he opened up *Which? Computing*.

It was then that Neve knew that nothing had changed. Sitting there reading like they'd used to do didn't mean that everything was going to be all right. It meant that her father didn't have a thing to say to her and Neve didn't have a clue what to say to him. She rummaged in her bag and took out *Gay from China at the Chalet School*. If she couldn't have comfort food, then she'd have comfort reading instead.

She hadn't even finished the first paragraph when her

father grunted. 'You're not *still* reading those bloody *Chalet School* books, are you?'

'Well, rereading them, but—'

'Do you remember when your Uncle George found the complete set of fifty hardbacks at a house clearance in Lytham St Annes . . .'

Neve had to stop him right there. 'It was fifty-eight hard-backs, actually.'

'I drove all through the night to pick them up, and when you opened up the box the next morning, you started crying loud enough to wake the dead,' Barry Slater recalled, as if Neve's reaction was still troubling him.

'They were tears of happiness.'

'There's enough reason to cry without doing it when you're happy too,' he said, giving Neve an odd look.

'I suppose,' Neve murmured non-committally as she started reading again.

'I remember *Eustacia Goes to the Chalet School*,' her father announced proudly and Neve was forced to raise her head again.

'How on earth do you remember that? You didn't read them when I was in bed, did you?'

'Give over,' Barry Slater scoffed. 'You told me all about it that time we went to Morecambe, when we had lunch together. Your ma still hasn't forgiven me for that.'

'Just so you know, neither have Seels and Dougie,' Neve said, and she didn't have to force the smile this time; her father was grinning too.

'So, why are you reading those bloody books again when you've got a bloody degree from Oxford?'

So, Neve told him that she'd started rereading them for solace when things had been so stressful at work. Then she told him about the AGM, and when Marco came to clear their dinner-plates, she was telling him about her new writing gig and her newly acquired agent.

'I'm trying not to have a complete panic attack about it,'

she finished, as her father ordered a decaffeinated coffee and a peppermint tea.

'You've always had a knack for telling a story. I remember when you helped Celia with her English homework by re-writing *Romeo and Juliet* and setting it on Coronation Street, not that it did her any good.'

'Oh, I don't know about that. She loves working in fashion.'

Her father sniffed because as far as he was concerned, working in fashion wasn't a proper job and never would be. 'Didn't think we'd have an author in the family. Your nan would be so proud of you, Neevy.'

'Really?' she asked, treading carefully because their truce was so new, so fragile, and her father never talked about his mother.

'She was a very bright woman but her father, that'd be your great-granddad, didn't believe that girls needed an education. He wouldn't let her go to the local grammar when she passed her eleven plus. Then she had to leave school when she was fifteen so she could start paying her way at home. She always regretted that.'

'You must miss her a lot. I mean, she died when you were eighteen and, well, I couldn't imagine what I'd do if anything happened to you or Mum.'

Her father raised his eyebrows. 'You'd cope, pet.'

Neve took a deep breath. 'Look, Dad, I'm sorry about what—'

'I'm proud of you too. Might not always show it, but you're the first Slater to go to university, let alone Oxford, and I can't pretend I know exactly what you do at that library, but don't you ever talk yourself out of opportunities that come your way. You can do anything if you set your mind to it, and I'm not just talking about the book-writing either.'

She was grateful that that was all her father was going to say about her weight because over the last hour, Neve could feel the resentment and the hurt of the last three years slowly ebbing away, fading into the background, even if it wasn't entirely exorcised. 'You know, Dad, it doesn't matter how many letters I've got after my name, I'm still me. I'm not ever going to forget where I came from.'

'You're a Slater through and through,' her father said proudly. 'That's where you get your brains from. I love your ma, but her family, back of the queue when they were handing out common sense, the whole bloody lot of them.'

Once that had been cleared up, all of a sudden it was easy to know the right thing to say, which was, 'Can you come back to my flat? The handle's loose on the cutlery drawer and the shower keeps dribbling even when I've turned it off.'

Barry Slater was never happier than when he could perform some minor household repairs. After Neve had shut Keith in her bedroom because middle-aged men with toolboxes were yet another thing that gave him an attack of the vapours, her dad also rehung a picture, adjusted the time on her oven clock and offered to mount a rack on the hall wall for her bike.

'Get it out of the way, it would,' he remarked as Neve showed him out.

It would get the bike out of the way but it would also make Charlotte think that Neve had done it for her benefit – and that could never happen. 'No, it's OK,' Neve told him. 'It's not really bothering anyone.'

Neve was just about to open the front door when her father put his hand on her arm. 'So, this chap your mother said you were seeing . . . I hope he's treating you all right.'

The chap in question would be phoning in half an hour to talk utter filth down the phone. Neve blushed. 'Of course he is.'

'He better be. Not right, getting you to look after that dog. It could turn on you at any second,' Barry Slater muttered darkly, which was a perfect match for the expression on his face, and just as Neve resigned herself to their reunion finishing on a sour note, he opened his arms out to her. 'You got a hug for your old man, then?'

There never was and never would be anyone who could hold Neve and make her feel so safe and secure. She willingly went into his arms and buried her face in his shoulder so she could smell the fabric conditioner her mother used, and sawdust from where he'd been drilling holes in her wall and this other indefinable, indescribable scent that was her dad.

'Well, we can both get our arms all the way round each other now,' her father said gruffly, and he tried to step back, but Neve just held him tighter, until after several long minutes, he kissed the top of her head and let go. 'I'd better get going. Your ma'll think I've been kidnapped.'

Neve finally opened the street door, and just as her father stepped out, she said, 'Maybe we could go and see a Cameron Diaz film next time?'

'She can't hold a candle to Jennifer Aniston, but I'd like that a lot.'

Chapter Thirty-three

Max flew back to a London that was so sunny even the boarded-up shops on Stroud Green Road looked pretty with the light reflecting off their metal grilles. Neve could almost pretend that she'd been in LA too, as every evening she and Max would eat dinner on his roof terrace, or climb down the rickety fire escape that led from her kitchen to the communal back garden. Neve much preferred his roof terrace because there was no Charlotte pointedly taking her washing off the line and making barbed remarks about Neve and the flimsiness of the patio furniture.

Neve moved through the week befuddled with fatigue because Max was jet lagged and kept waking up in the middle of the night. Of course, once Max was up, he was *up* and Neve would wake on a gasp because he was doing such delicious things to her. It didn't help either that she was going to bed late and waking up early to rewrite chapter seven of her Lucy Keener biography, after Philip had given her some constructive criticism and Jacob Morrison had given her some criticism that was so brutal that it left Neve reeling. When she wasn't immersed in Lucy Keener's world, Neve was either stuck in the Archive's back office or in Max's arms. Either way, it didn't leave much time for sleep.

The rosy glow she'd always taken for granted was now eclipsed by the shadows under her eyes, and the only thing getting Neve through each day was industrial amounts of coffee.

'I can't believe you're still in the sleep-deprived stage of your relationship,' Chloe said one Friday afternoon when she came into the back office to discover that Neve had nodded off in the middle of a tape she was transcribing. 'Hasn't the novelty worn off yet?'

'If you had to listen to Lavinia Marjoribanks jaw on about how she'd have had a more successful literary career if she hadn't spurned the advances of Vita Sackville-West, you'd fall asleep too,' Neve said as she yawned.

'That sounds quite exciting – lesbian shenanigans with the Bloomsbury Set.' Chloe perched on the edge of Neve's desk. 'Does she dish the dirt on old Virginia?'

'Believe me, this woman has such a monotone voice that she could make a threesome with George Clooney and Clive Owen sound like the most boring thing on earth.' Neve rubbed her eyes and sank down on her desk. 'I think I might throw up from over-tiredness.'

'Poor Neevy. Maybe you'd better ask your pretend boyfriend for the night off so you can catch up on your beauty sleep,' Chloe said, as she began to leaf through the pile of *Chalet School* books on Neve's desk. 'My mum would never let me read school stories when I was a kid. She said they were completely reactionary and had no characterisation.'

'That is such a generalisation . . . and Max is *not* a pretend boyfriend. He's a temporary boyfriend, which is an entirely different thing.' Neve stretched her arms above her head. 'I suppose a night on my own wouldn't be such a bad thing, and I can see Max Saturday and Sunday.'

'For a temporary boyfriend, he seems to monopolise all your time,' Chloe murmured distractedly because she was now flicking through *The School at the Chalet*. 'How's the sex?'

'Awesome,' Neve said, because it was and she was too exhausted to hedge.

'Personally, if I had a temporary boyfriend with a

434

glamorous job, who serviced me frequently and orgasmically, I'd be thinking about making him permanent,' Chloe said. 'I mean, this other guy's been away for ages and he's an unknown quantity. Better the devil you know.'

It was the dilemma that Neve kept ruthlessly forcing to the back of her mind, every time it reared up. It seemed like the obvious thing to do, until she remembered that Max didn't do real relationships and even if he did, she didn't want to spend the rest of her life picturing William with the words WHAT IF? above his head in six-foot-high letters.

'I wish men were like items from the deli counter and they came with a "try before you buy" offer,' she grumbled. 'I've spent six years wanting William to be mine. That's nearly a quarter of my life. Besides, I'm only getting Max on his best behaviour because he knows it's temporary.'

'Guess you're damned if you do and damned if you don't. I hate it when that happens,' Chloe said unhelpfully. She tapped Neve on the shoulder with *The School at the Chalet*. 'Hey, can I borrow this?'

'Knock yourself out,' Neve muttered, reaching for the phone. 'I'm going to call Max. At this rate I might actually fall asleep as I cycle home.'

Max wasn't at all offended when Neve cancelled their plans to spend the night together. 'Thank God for that,' were his exact, uncomplimentary words. 'I'm so knackered, I can't think straight. I've spent the last half-hour looking for my iPod until I found it in the fridge.'

'Are you sure that's all right?' Neve asked, because she wanted it not to be all right. If Max couldn't live without her, not even for a mere twelve hours, then maybe it was a sign that her future should have Max in it.

'Of course it's all right,' Max said cheerfully. 'Between you and me, I think Keith could do with some male bonding time.'

Neve thought about their brief conversation all the way home. She searched hard for some double meaning in Max's words to indicate that secretly he was bereft without her. Try as she might, there didn't seem to be any.

As she was chaining up her bike in the hall, she dug out her phone just in case Max had texted her, but there was just a message from Orange telling her that her bill was ready to be viewed online. Neve was still standing in the hall, gazing hopefully at her phone when the front door opened and there was Charlotte.

It was too late to scurry upstairs, so Neve settled for giving the saddle of her bike a proprietary pat and nodding at her sister-in-law. 'Oh, hi.'

'Bike,' Charlotte snapped, her face twisting into its usual grimace. 'Your bloody bike is taking up the entire hall.'

Neve flapped her arms to show there was at least six feet of hall between her bike and the party wall. 'No, it's not.'

It was too close to call who was more surprised at Neve answering back, though Charlotte made a lightning-quick comeback. 'Yes, it is,' she insisted. 'And you left your washing on the line all of yesterday. It's a communal garden, not just yours, and there was no room on the line for anything else because your clothes take up so much space.' She finished with a pointed look at Neve's hips, just in case Neve hadn't got the dig.

'It wasn't clothes; it was my bedlinen,' Neve began. Then she stopped, because trying to reason with Charlotte was like trying to put out a forest fire with a glass of water. 'Look, whatever. I don't have time for this.'

Charlotte was still opening and closing her mouth when Neve turned on her heel and marched up the stairs. As she got to her landing, she could hear Charlotte reach her flat, then close the door behind her with a furious slam that made the whole building shake.

Neve half-expected Charlotte to start pounding away with the broom but then she heard Douglas come in a few minutes later, so she could get undressed and fall into bed on the freshly laundered sheets that Charlotte had been so angry about. After one chapter of *The New Mistress at the Chalet School*, she was asleep.

A couple of hours later, Neve was woken by her ringing phone. She lay there for a second, disorientated because it was still light outside, then reached for her mobile.

'Can't you manage without me for more than two hours?' she asked teasingly, sitting up so she'd sound alluring rather than muffled.

'Neve?' said a vaguely familiar voice, that wasn't the familiar voice she'd expected to hear. 'It's William.'

Her body went from hot to cold in an instant. Even though she was alone in her own bed, Neve felt horribly guilty. If she'd had a naked Max lying next to her, she might actually have died of shame.

'Neve? This *is* Neve Slater?'

'Yes,' she admitted cautiously. 'I wasn't expecting a call from you.'

'For a moment there, I thought I'd dialled the wrong number.' For the first time, William's perfectly enunciated, perfectly proper, BBC English made icy rivulets of fear trickle down Neve's spine. 'How are you?'

'I'm fine. I just . . . erm . . . it's a surprise to hear from you,' she hurriedly improvised, scrambling out of bed so she could pace anxiously. She glanced at herself in the mirror. Her face was sleep-crumpled and her hair was sticking out in all directions.

'I'm sorry, Neve, have I caught you in the middle of something?'

Neve pulled a face at her reflection because William couldn't even begin to appreciate the exquisite irony of what he'd just said. 'No, of course not. I just thought we were going to speak Sunday week. Everything's all right, isn't it?' She frowned. 'You're not back in England already, are you? Because I thought you were aiming for the middle of July and it's not even the end of June.'

'Actually I am. I had to come back sooner than I expected, but I'm flying back to LA tomorrow morning,' William said, as Neve closed her eyes and slumped against the wall. He couldn't be back because she wasn't a size ten and she wasn't ready to finish with Max and she just wasn't . . . ready. 'I know it's short notice, but are you free to meet up for a drink?'

'What – now? Tonight?'

'You know, your voice sounds different,' William remarked and Neve wondered if he could hear the hysteria rising up in her like bile. 'I've been meaning to mention it for ages. Maybe not as breathy as it used to be?'

'Oh, it sounds the same to me. Well, I mean you don't ever really hear your own voice properly, do you? Unless you hear your voice on someone else's answerphone or something,' Neve babbled. She smacked the palm of her hand against her forehead in the vain hope that she might be able to knock some sense into herself. 'Sorry, you were saying? You want to meet up for a drink now.' She squinted at the clock on her nightstand. It was eight thirty. She desperately tried to think of a cast-iron excuse that would get her out of meeting with her destiny when her destiny had turned up weeks ahead of schedule, but her mind refused to cooperate. 'Well, I suppose I could get into town for, say, ten?'

William made a humming noise, like he always did when he was thinking. 'That is rather late, isn't it? It's just I did so want to see you,' he added, and that was just what Neve wanted him to say, had imagined him saying countless times in her head, but it wasn't enough to dispel the panic and the fear and the feeling that she might throw up all over her bedroom rug. 'I don't want to just snatch a hurried hour with you. Would you mind terribly if we left it until I come back for good?'

Neve sagged in relief. Literally. She sank down to the floor because her legs wouldn't hold her up any longer. 'I suppose that makes sense, but it would have been lovely to see you,' she said slowly, and she hated herself in that moment as she'd never hated anyone else. Not even Charlotte. 'Shall we still speak the Sunday after next?'

'Well, that's the thing, you see, I'm doing a little literary roadtrip with, uh, a friend from LA, before I leave the States. A final hurrah, as it were,' William said. 'Actually it's going to be rather fun. We're going to start in California obviously, and visit John Steinbeck's house in Salinas, and of course the Henry Miller Memorial Library in Big Sur.'

Half an hour later, William had eventually arrived at his final destination, New England, where he was 'very excited about going to Concord. Can you believe that Thoreau, Emerson, Hawthorne and Louisa May Alcott all lived there?'

'It sounds amazing,' Neve said, and that at least she could be honest about. She could also allow herself a little fantasy that some time in the future when Max was at best just a friend and, at worst, a painful memory, William would retrace his roadtrip with Neve in the passenger seat next to him, reading maps and insisting that they detour via Amherst so she could lay some flowers on Emily Dickinson's grave. 'I'm so jealous. You'll have to tell me all about it, when you call me from the road.'

'Didn't I mention it? I don't really think I'm going to call until I'm back in London for good,' William said quickly, almost shiftily to Neve's ear, but that was probably because for the first time, she wanted him to have some secrets, some faults and then she wouldn't feel quite so bad. 'I mean, I'll be on the road and staying in ghastly motels and I'll be with my friend, but I'll send you postcards. Lots and lots of postcards.'

'Postcards would be fantastic.' Neve swallowed past the lump in her throat. 'Well, I guess I'll see you soon.'

'You will, and I'll give you at least twenty-four hours' notice next time,' William chuckled and Neve sincerely hoped it was a joke, because she'd need at least two weeks' notice to prepare herself mentally and physically. 'I really did want to see you this visit, Neve, but everything's been such a rush. I had to fly back to the UK at forty-eight hours' notice.'

'That's all right.' Neve tried not to sigh in relief again. 'And I've been busy with work anyway and I'm writing—'

'Yes, I know, beavering away on your dead authors. There was actually something very important I wanted to ask you, but it can wait until we see each other in the fl . . . face to face.'

'What kind of something?' Neve asked. William was being so cryptic that suddenly she was intrigued and all kinds of curious.

'It's a surprise. A really pleasant surprise,' William said. She'd forgotten how warm his voice sounded, so when he spoke to you, you felt as if you were the most important person in the world, or in his world. 'You'll never guess, so don't even try.'

'Not even a little guess?'

'Honestly, it's such a curve ball that I could give you a hundred guesses and you still wouldn't come close,' William said, then he chuckled and Neve smiled too.

'Curve ball? Do you talk American now, William?'

'Fluently, yo.'

They were both laughing now and it was stupid, the curviest curve ball ever, but maybe all her hoping and her hard work had paid off and William felt exactly the same way as she did. And that mysterious question was something along the lines of, 'Neve, will you go out with me?' except that sounded really adolescent and . . .

'So, when I get back from roadtripping, you're first on my to-do list,' the real William was saying and Neve had to tear her attention away from the fantasy William who was turning up for their first official date with a huge yet tasteful bouquet of white roses. 'Around the second week in July.'

That was only three weeks away, and that news completely obliterated all thoughts of first dates and tasteful bouquets from her mind. Even if she could find a surgeon who'd fit her with a gastric band that night, there was no way she could drop two dress sizes and another twenty pounds in three weeks. 'OK,' she said weakly. 'That'll be nice.'

'I can't wait,' William said enthusiastically. 'It's been far too long.'

Neve murmured goodbye, wished William a lovely time on the road, then waited anxiously for the click on the line and the silence that followed. Then she flopped back on the bed and wondered why, when she was so close to getting what she'd wanted, it felt as if she was losing everything.

In order to have William back in her life, she'd have to lose Max.

Not for another three weeks, a voice inside her head whispered, but Neve refused to listen to its insidious whisper. She couldn't string Max along like that; it wasn't fair. She'd been honest with him from the start and she was going to end it with honesty. She was also going to do it quickly, even though she was the sort of girl who could spend five minutes slowly and carefully removing a plaster.

Neve jack-knifed off the bed and without even bothering to change out of the pyjama bottoms and T-shirt that she slept in when Max wasn't around, hunted for a clean pair of socks, shoved her feet into her trainers and headed out the door.

There was a chill to the air as the sun slowly disappeared behind dark, smudgy clouds, but Neve didn't even notice the goose pimples that hatched on her arms as she turned into the Stroud Green Road and began to quicken her pace, until she was running up Crouch Hill at full pelt, even though she'd only ever taken it at a gentle jog before. By the time she reached Max's road, Neve knew she should try and slow down, but her brain didn't want to pass the message on to her legs. She vaulted, actually *vaulted*, over the low garden wall, raced up the path and almost crashed nose-first into Max's front door.

She reached into her pocket for her keys because Max had got a spare cut for her, then realised that her pyjama bottoms didn't have pockets and she'd come out without even locking her front door. As she rang his doorbell, Neve hoped that Max had followed through with his plan to have an early night and hadn't gone out. Then, recalling the way that he could sleep like the dead when he was really tired, she kept her finger on the bell until she heard the sound of feet coming down the stairs.

'That was quick,' Max said, as he opened the door. 'I only texted you five minutes ago.'

'I didn't get your text,' Neve panted, bending over, her hands on her knees.

'Ha! I knew you'd cave first,' Max crowed, then he stepped over the threshold in his bare feet and placed his hand on Neve's back. 'You all right, sweetheart?'

'No,' Neve said, straightening up. Now she was standing in front of him, nothing was coming out of her mouth except her own ragged breaths. He looked so out of her league, even in a ratty T-shirt and a pair of spotty boxer shorts, the sunny smile wiped off his face as he looked at her with concern. That was the thing; Max wasn't out of her league, for the moment he was all hers and Neve knew it was wrong and bad karma would rain down on her by the bucketload but all she could choke out was, 'Will you hold me?'

Max's arms were around her in an instant so he could kiss her sweaty forehead and stroke damp strands of hair away from her face. 'I thought you came over because you couldn't wait to get your hands on me, but something's wrong, isn't it?'

Neve buried her head against his shoulder and hoped that would do for a reply. Max tried again. 'Neevy, did you have another run-in with the sister-in-law from hell?'

And she had, so it wasn't a lie to mumble, 'Yes, yes I did.'

'Anything you need me to kiss better?'

Neve raised her head for another look at Max's pretty brown eyes and the angle of his cheekbones and his crooked nose because there wasn't much time left to commit the details to memory. 'Not really. She didn't leave any bruises, apart from, like, metaphorical ones.'

Even the leer that Max gave her was pretty. 'Well, I could kiss your metaphorical bruises and any other bits of you that you want kissed.' He gestured at the open door behind him. 'After you, sweetheart.'

Chapter Thirty-four

They spent the entire weekend in bed.

Every time Max slipped inside her, Neve would wrap her arms and legs around him as tightly as she could, because they were getting closer to the final time they'd make love. So, each time she became more frenzied, more passionate, though Max didn't seem to mind either the frenzy or the passion. By Sunday evening when he slowly peeled his body away from hers, they were both covered in bites and bruises as they sprawled across his rumpled bed.

'I need to walk Keith,' Max said, making no move to get out of bed. Instead he spooned against Neve, kissing the back of her neck each time she shuddered because their last encounter had been so intense she'd knocked a glass of water off the bedside table with her foot when she came. 'Then we're going to sleep for a full ten hours.'

'You said that last night too.' Neve placed her hand over Max's, which was resting on her belly. 'Then I woke up at two in the morning with you doing very rude things to me.'

'You said it was a lovely way to wake up,' Max reminded her.

'It was, but I'm just saying that you shouldn't issue ultimatums that you have no intention of sticking to,' Neve told him scornfully as she rolled over.

'I mean it, Neve. My dick has gone on strike.' Max put some space between them so he could gaze down at his penis. 'I think I'm broken.'

'It looks fine to me. Would you like me to take a closer look just to make sure?' Neve asked with a grin, as Max gave a girly shriek and shrank back in fake alarm. 'Or maybe not.' She gave Max's flaccid penis a gentle pat, and realised that she'd miss Max's inappropriate humour when they were in bed almost as much as she'd miss having sex with him.

Of course, she'd probably have sex with William but she couldn't imagine much laughter; maybe some quoting of Shakespeare or one of the Romantic poets, but William would never make jokes about his penis . . .

'Why are you looking so gloomy?' Max wanted to know. 'Is it the thought of a ten-hour sex ban? Christ, you're insatiable, woman.'

When Max looked at her like that, still sexy even with his dick all limp, Neve began to consider the unthinkable; going through the door marked b – the door that didn't have a William standing behind it. She'd been so happy these last few weeks in a way that had nothing to do with fitting into a size ten dress or being with William. Max had a knack of making those faraway goals seem unimportant, and if she could be this happy with Max, why break what wasn't broken? And Max seemed happy too . . .

'Just so you know, my girl parts have packed up shop for the night too,' Neve said, rolling on to her front so she could rest her chin on her hands. 'Max, do you like being in a relationship? Do you think you could be someone's second pancake that doesn't get thrown away?'

Max was propped up on one elbow so Neve had a clear view of the indecision that flickered across his face, before he summoned up that smirk, which meant that he was going to fudge the question with some patented Max bluster, because it delved too deeply into places where he didn't want to go. 'Oh, Neevy,' he said playfully. 'There are so many women in the world that it seems unfair on them to tie myself down to just one girl. And not in a fun bondage way either.'

She shouldn't have expected anything else. Even though Max had been absolutely lovely these last few weeks – caring, kind, not even wanting to go out because he preferred to stay in – he'd absolutely refused to discuss his meltdown in Manchester. Or being in therapy. Or if he still felt empty inside. He'd just revert to his usual defence mechanisms, which were the smirk, the sneer and the smartarse remark.

'But say, for example, that William wasn't coming back, what would happen to us?' Neve persisted.

'No point thinking about that,' Max said so cheerfully that Neve went from contemplating a future with him to wanting to smack him. 'He *is* coming back, isn't he?'

'Yes, but say he wasn't, hypothetically. Do you think you and I could have a future?' Neve asked. Max was now staring up at the ceiling so he couldn't see that she'd crossed her fingers.

'Look, Neevy, I promise I'll be a bit mopey when we have to call it quits, but we are going to call it quits when Mr California comes back and whisks you off. Anyway, when you think about it, we have nothing in common. You're scary smart, and reading *heat* from cover to cover is more my speed.' Max angled his head so he could look at her, and he still had that damn smirk on his face as if he wasn't at all heartbroken at the prospect of being Neveless. 'What happened to living in the moment?'

'Nothing happened,' Neve said quickly, because the sooner they changed this awful subject, the better. 'I was just asking.' She hung her head so her hair fell into her face and Max wouldn't be able to see her expression, which she was sure was pretty woebegone. 'Are you going to walk Keith or was that just an idle promise?'

Max swung his legs over the side of the bed and stood up. 'I'm going to make something to eat first. Toast?'

'Yes, please,' Neve said, striving to keep her voice light. 'Two pieces.'

'Four pieces,' Max said firmly. 'We haven't eaten since breakfast.'

'Split the difference and call it three,' Neve insisted. Max's belief that her body could process a lot of carbs after 6 p.m. was one thing that Neve definitely wouldn't miss. 'With just some low fat spread on it.'

'That butter substitute tastes rank,' Max said, as he swatted Neve playfully on the bottom. 'I'll make some sausages and I think there's a can of spaghetti hoops in the cupboard.'

'No spaghetti hoops for me,' Neve said, but Max just waved a dismissive hand as he left the room.

At least she knew now that Max didn't want to be the long-haul guy, Neve thought. That meant that she could put all her focus on William. It also meant that telling Max they were over wasn't going to be that much of an ordeal; he'd take it with good humour and secretly he'd probably be a little relieved that he could go and tell his therapist that yes, he could have a relationship if he wanted one, but actually he didn't. It was a shame, because if he could drop the act and let some lucky girl into his heart, he'd make a wonderful boyfriend.

Neve decided that she had to tell Max before the end of the next week, so she'd have at least a fortnight to properly mourn the end of her pancake relationship. Though she wasn't sure that two weeks was going to be enough to rid herself of the regret and sadness that—

'Neevy! Can you set the alarm for eight?' Max called from the kitchen. 'I'm making you some scrambled eggs too, OK?'

Rolling her eyes, Neve grabbed the alarm clock and set it for half past six. She had a personal training session with Gustav first thing – she'd called him the day before to cancel their Saturday session with a hasty excuse about agonising

447

period pain. Gustav had been really insistent that exercise was the best thing for a cramping uterus, like he'd even know. If she didn't turn up tomorrow morning, or was even five minutes late, Neve knew he'd have her doing jumping jacks and horrible things with kettle bells for two hours straight.

It *had* been tempting to spend the extra ninety minutes in bed, but as if he could read her mind and knew that it was thinking bad thoughts, Neve hadn't even had a chance to wake Max with a kiss when her phone beeped with a text message from Gustav: *Please do not be late – your lady problems must be better by now.*

Gustav was just finishing with another client when Neve emerged from the changing room. She waved at him and got a tight smile in response, which did not bode well for the next two hours of her life.

She'd just started on her warm-up stretches, when Gustav came over. 'Ten minutes on the treadmill as fast as you can,' he ordered. 'I'm going to set up the bench press.'

Neve grimaced at Gustav's back and caught the eye of his previous client, a severe-looking forty-something man whom Gustav always held up as a shining example of dedication.

'Has he got you on the ankle weights yet?' he asked, as Neve started her run off with a very fast walk.

'God, no,' she said, aghast.

'He will,' came the glum reply. 'He's in a vile mood today.'

That was all she needed. Neve immediately whacked up the speed and when Gustav returned she was pounding rubber at twelve kilometres per hour. 'I expected you to be up to fifteen by now,' he sniffed.

The next two hours were everything that Neve had been dreading. Bench presses, dead rows, squats with a forty-pound dumbbell on her shoulders and horrible boy press-ups, interspersed with ten-minute runs at fifteen kilometres to keep her heart rate up.

'Your stamina is not what it used to be,' Gustav told her as Neve lay panting on a gym mat. 'Anyway, it's that time of the month now.'

'I already told you, it was my time of the month on Saturday,' Neve gasped. 'And have I said that I'm sorry that I had to cancel our session? Because I really and truly am.'

'You might have mentioned it once or twice,' Gustav said and he wasn't softening in the least, even though Neve had done everything he told her to without arguing, pouting or rolling her eyes. 'It's actually time for your monthly weigh in.'

The four pieces of toast (because Max had said his toaster couldn't cope with an uneven number of slices), sausages, scrambled eggs, spaghetti hoops and tinned tomatoes that she'd wolfed down the night before felt like a lead balloon in Neve's stomach as she followed Gustav into his little office. But then again, she'd only had a bowl of muesli for breakfast yesterday, hadn't had any dinner on Friday night and all she'd eaten on Saturday was half a pizza and two apples. She wasn't expecting to lose half a stone but she'd settle for two pounds and at least an inch off her hips. Then she had three weeks, or two and a half weeks, to really hunker down on the healthy eating. She'd give up coffee and live on nothing but steamed vegetables if she had to, Neve vowed as she toed off her trainers and nervously approached Gustav's high-tech scales.

The last time she'd been weighed, Neve's magic number was 160 pounds, just under eleven and a half stone. Neve closed her eyes as she watched the little digital counter start to do its thing. It couldn't hurt to cross her fingers behind her back and offer up a little prayer to the Goddess of Dieting.

She heard Gustav give a 'hmmm'. It wasn't a very encouraging 'hmmm'. Neve opened one eye and stared down at the scales in horror.

'It's just a temporary blip on the radar screen,' Gustav said and yes, now he could be nice to her because the number proved that he was right and Neve was wrong. Up to her elbows in wrong.

She wasn't just wrong. She was five pounds heavier. Five pounds! For the first time in three years, the numbers were going up, not going down. She'd broken her dieting mojo and now her metabolism would be even more confused than it already was and the weight would start creeping up and she'd never be in a size ten and she'd have failed and . . .

'Wait!' Neve jumped off the scales. 'I haven't been this morning.'

'Been where?' Gustav asked, and he had no heart because now he was taking the tape measure out of his desk drawer.

'No, I haven't *been*,' Neve hissed, her face flaming. 'I haven't been *open*. So, I'll go and do that and then when I come back . . . I'm soaked in sweat and that has to be making my gym clothes weigh a lot more than they normally would and—'

'Stay right there!'

Neve stayed rooted to the spot because when Gustav barked at her like that, every molecule that she possessed strained to obey him. He wound the tape around the fattest, fleshiest part of her hips but wouldn't let her see the number, then measured around her abdomen, her waist and her breasts.

'Well, your upper waist and chest have stayed the same,' he said and there was no need for him to sound quite so surprised. 'You've put an inch back on your hips and your stomach.'

Then Gustav didn't say anything. He didn't shout or berate her. Or, worse, say that he was disappointed; he just put his tape measure back in its drawer, his features, as ever, cast in granite. But he didn't need to say anything, because Neve was more than happy to fill the silence.

'OK, I ate some things I shouldn't have, I admit it, but there have been days when I've eaten hardly anything.'

'What happens when you skip meals?' Gustav asked in a steady voice.

'My body goes into starvation mode and it clings to my fat and won't let go,' Neve parroted back.

'And what are these things you shouldn't have been eating?'

Neve wished that she'd never blurted that out, but Gustav would have forced the truth out of her eventually. Hips don't lie. 'Bread,' she muttered. 'Lots of bread, sometimes at two in the morning, and spaghetti hoops and . . . and . . . pizza.' Neve collapsed on the spare chair. 'It's not fair! Other girls eat that stuff and skip meals and their weight stays exactly the same. You should see what Celia packs away and she never eats vegetables unless I shove them down her throat.'

'You're not other girls,' Gustav said gravely. 'You can't be the weight you were and expect your metabolism to correct itself after all those years of over-eating.' He patted Neve's knee in a manner that wasn't the least bit consoling. 'It's all right. I don't blame you.'

'Well, I blame me.'

'I see this happen time and time again when my clients let personal attachments come between them and their fitness goals,' Gustav said, as Neve knew he would sooner or later. He leaned forward so he could speak in a whisper, in case anyone heard him break the personal trainer/unfit slob confidentiality oath. 'Take Vaughn . . .'

'Vaughn?' Neve queried.

'He trains before you on Mondays and Wednesdays,' Gustav reminded her impatiently. 'Apart from you, he was my most obedient client, then he falls in love with this girl . . .' Gustav shook his head. 'She's a fat skinny person. Always with the puddings and the pies and the home baking and he puts on weight. Then they have a row and he doesn't just lose weight; he loses muscle tone as well.'

'It's not Max's fault,' Neve said, until her mind drifted back to the night before when she'd asked for two pieces of toast with low fat spread and Max had presented her with a heaped plate of high-fat badness. And he'd made her eat chips and crème brûlée and drink lots and lots of wine, and one time he'd even made pancakes . . . well, he hadn't stood over her and clamped her mouth open, but he'd always been very persuasive with the, 'It won't hurt you just this once,' and, 'It's almost Treat Sunday,' and even, 'By the time I'm done with you, you'll have easily burned a day's calories.' Max wasn't a feeder, but he was an enabler and that was almost as bad.

'Are you still committed to losing weight?' Gustav asked.

Neve stared at him in amazement. 'Of course I am!'

'Because we could work on a maintenance programme rather than a weight-loss regime,' Gustav continued.

Neve flailed on the chair in sheer, ineffectual disbelief. 'I'm nearly twelve stone. I'm still medically overweight. I want it off! I want *this* gone!' She pinched one of her thighs so Gustav could see the rolls of fat that she was never going to shift at this rate.

'This five pounds, it's nothing. You go back to your diet and exercise plan and pfft! It's gone in a fortnight.'

Neve put her head in her hands. 'William will be back in London in two and a half weeks.'

'William? I cannot keep track of all your men,' Gustav tutted.

'There's only two men and I absolutely cannot see Max any more,' Neve said because the 165 pounds on Gustav's scale had made the decision for her. 'Before Max, there was William and the goal that I'd be in a size ten dress by the time he got back from California and, quite frankly, the only way I'm going to get into a size ten is if I have intense, hard-core liposuction.'

'Neve!' Gustav moaned in protest. 'I've been clear about

this from the start. You do this for you, not for a man. Any decent man should love you for who you are, not how much you weigh.'

'I'm not doing it for a man,' Neve said, though to her ears it sounded hollow because Neve knew decent men, and instead of loving her in all her rotund glory, they'd always gone for the skinny boho girls at Oxford who wrote really, really bad poetry. And then there was Max who had his pick of model-thin, beautiful girls to go home with every night, but he hadn't loved Neve for who she was, rather than how little she weighed, because he didn't love her at all. But when she took William and Max out of the equation, then the truth was that she could never expect any man to love her despite her weight, when she didn't love herself. 'I didn't start *this* because of William, you know that, but yes, his return coincides with a desperate need to hit at least one hundred and forty pounds on the scales. Do you think I could weigh ten stone and still get into a size ten?'

Gustav didn't look convinced. 'If this William is the one, he'll wait and you can concentrate on your diet and exer—'

'It's been six bloody years already!' Neve realised she was almost shouting and tried to lower her voice. 'What about that extreme diet for really obese people before they have major surgery so they don't die from complications with the anaesthetic? Can I do that for a few weeks?'

'You're not listening to a single word I'm saying,' Gustav rapped back. He was perilously close to shouting too. 'If you dare even think about some fad diet or laxatives or surgical intervention, because I will know, Neevy, then you'll be looking for a new personal trainer.'

'You wouldn't!'

'Oh, I would. I will strike you off and I will warn all the other personal trainers in north London not to work with you. I have contacts,' Gustav added grimly and normally Neve would have laughed and told him that he was sounding a little too *'Allo 'Allo* to be taken seriously, but she was so busy glaring, and hating Gustav and Max and her metabolism and yes, herself, that she got up, snatched her stinky trainers from the floor and stalked out of the room.

Chapter Thirty-five

'Max, it's over. William will be back in two and a half weeks and we both knew that this was going to end sooner or later. Besides which, you've set my health and fitness regime back by months, and even if William wasn't coming back, I'd have to finish with you,' Neve said sternly.

She looked at Celia. 'How do you think that sounds?'

'Bloody terrible!' Celia exclaimed, scrunching up her face in disapproval. 'Christ, Neevy, let the bloke down gently.'

'Breaking up with someone is really hard,' Neve muttered, sinking down on her ancient swivel chair, which creaked in protest, because she was five pounds heavier and it couldn't take the strain. 'Could I write a letter instead?'

'No! What is wrong with you?'

'You know what's wrong with me.'

Celia knew because five minutes after leaving the gym, Neve had phoned her close to tears and spitting with fury until Celia had promised that she'd come round to the Archive in her lunch-hour even though she always said that she didn't like being surrounded by dead people's things.

Now she was perched uncomfortably on a hard-backed chair trying not to breathe in too deeply because she also insisted that the basement reeked of mildew, which wasn't true, and if Mr Freemont had overheard her, he'd have washed her mouth out with liquid hand soap. Mildew was every archivist's worst nightmare.

'Look, I know you're upset about the weight thing,' Celia mouthed the last two words, 'but you can't dump Max when you're like this. You have to calm down. And stop being so mean! We're talking about *Max*.'

'I know exactly who we're talking about and don't say his name like that, all reproachfully as if I'm being completely unreasonable.' But now that the shock of the unexpected weight gain was levelling off, the petulant tone of her voice was starting to sound a little unreasonable to Neve's ears.

'It hasn't been all bad. You've seemed really happy and he's been sexing you up 24/7 and also, not to make this all about me, but he's one of my superiors at *Skirt*. You go all psycho on him, then one word in Grace's ear and she'll have me colour-coding hair slides for the next six months. Do you have any idea just how many hair slides there are in the fashion cupboard? I don't deserve that.'

'Well, I suppose not,' Neve agreed slowly. 'He did make me happy, but I think he made me *too* happy so I let my guard down and now look at me.' She opened her arms wide so Celia could get a good look at the spread of her hips. 'Getting a pretend boyfriend was hard enough and now I don't have a clue how to get shot of one.'

Celia had been surveying the stacks of yellowing paper on Neve's desk with a moue of distaste, but now she turned her full attention back to her sister. 'He knew Willy McWordy was coming back, so lead with that, then bang on for a bit about how great it was but you both knew it couldn't last and you hope you can still be friends, blah, blah, blah. Lather, rinse, repeat. How does that sound?'

'I don't actually do the "blah blah blah" bit, I take it?' Neve asked, as she scribbled down what Celia had just said. Celia didn't reply, but gave Neve a long-suffering look. 'OK, so I'll let Max down gently – but what am I going to do about this?' She pointed at her thighs, encased in denim and straining the seams way more than they had yesterday.

'How do you feel about colonic irrigation?'

'Er, I don't really have an opinion one way or the other,' Neve replied, though she was already considering it. Having a rubber hose up her bottom was a small price to pay if she could lose five pounds in one sitting. Not that she would be sitting if she had a rubber hose up her bum.

'And you love all those raw juice drinks, don't you?' Celia continued. 'Like, with wheatgrass and wheatgerm and little Japanese berries.'

'Well, I suppose . . .'

'Then I can help you with the weight loss,' Celia said proudly. 'You can go on the Hardcore Cleanse for our Health Editor.'

Neve could feel the tiny flame of hope begin to flicker; it was either that or her tummy rumbling because she'd done a full workout on an empty stomach. 'What's a Hardcore Cleanse?'

The Hardcore Cleanse was the latest New York diet craze being trialled in London. Cleansees signed up to have fresh juice delivered by courier every three days so they could drink juice for breakfast, lunch and dinner, along with herbal tea, raw vegetables and a medicine chest full of vitamin supplements. 'The publicist says it's great for weight loss, detox and also you'll feel more energised and mentally alert,' Celia explained. 'Everyone in the office wanted to try it, even though you have to have a colonic the day before you start and sign a medical waiver.'

Signing a medical waiver wasn't the deterrent it should have been. These were desperate times. 'Why doesn't anyone in your office want to do it?'

'No one could actually get the juice down without heaving,' Celia admitted ruefully. 'All three drinks taste pretty rancid. Even smelling the orange lunch juice made me retch.'

'I'll do it!' Neve said eagerly, because she'd always had a cast-iron constitution. Their mother had once made a casserole with some diced chicken two days past its use-by date and Neve had been the only Slater who hadn't spent the next twenty-four hours either puking or pooing. 'Sign me up, sister!'

'It would only be to reboot your metabolism,' Celia warned. 'Even the publicist said you should only do it for two weeks maximum, then you have to start reintroducing solids.'

'Fine! Call your Health Editor right now and book me in for the colonic. This afternoon, if possible.'

Celia already had her phone held aloft. 'And you promise you'll be nice to Max when you tell him he's history?'

Neve flushed guiltily. 'That stuff I said before? I didn't really mean it. I was just lashing out. He's been so sweet to me and I . . . I still want him to be part of my life. I mean, we weren't so emotionally attached that his heart's going to be broken. We'll still be able to be friends, won't we?'

'Yeah, sure, course you will,' Celia said soothingly. 'Being pals with your ex, what's the harm in that?'

It was easy to remember Max's favourite things. Neve wore a green dress that Max said made her eyes change colour. She roasted a chicken, even though she wouldn't be eating it because the Hardcore Cleanse publicist had told her she could only eat raw vegetables until she started her Cleanse. There were four bottles of fancy imported lager chilling in the fridge, and as Max and Keith walked through the door, Neve was just sliding the Clash's *Greatest Hits* into her CD player.

'There you are,' she said shrilly as she walked into the hall.

'There I am,' Max agreed with a smile and he leaned forward to give her a kiss. Neve ducked awkwardly so his lips just grazed her cheek, because it felt wrong to get all smoochy when she knew what was coming. 'You OK? You seem a bit twitchy.'

The twitchiness wasn't just nerves. Neve hadn't eaten

anything all day except two carrots, and the smell of the chicken was making all the moisture in her body migrate to her mouth. She knew exactly how Keith felt as he sat there, his tongue lolling as two slobbery lines of drool hung from his slavering mouth.

'I'm fine,' Neve assured him with a tight smile. She stared at the toes of his Converses because dumping Max wasn't something she could rehearse any more. Not when he was taking up her narrow hall with his long, lean limbs and the clean, sweet smell of hair gloop and his grapefruit-scented bodywash and looking adoringly rumpled in his saggiest jeans and a faded red T-shirt. 'I made roast chicken and there's lager in the fridge.'

'God, I could get used to this kind of treatment,' Max said, as she turned to walk into the kitchen. Then his arms were around her waist so he could nuzzle her ear. 'So, we're going to have a proper evening meal at a proper time for once?'

Max was. Neve was going to chew on some rocket leaves and try not to look resentful. As it was, she could feel herself stiffening in his embrace. 'Please, Max . . . I need to check on the chicken.'

'You're so tense. I'll give you a back rub later,' Max promised, still with his arms around her so they had to shuffle to the kitchen. 'Oh, I spoke to Mandy, she says hi.'

Stop being so nice to me, Neve thought despairingly, as Max finally let her go so she could open the oven door. The ordeal that lay ahead would have been so much easier if he'd been in a filthy mood when he'd come in and had been short and snappy with her. Or if she was still in a filthy mood about the five pounds that he'd helped her to gain, but . . . no, she wasn't going to go there.

Maybe it had been a stupid idea to feed Max before she gave him the 'let's be friends' speech. It smacked a little too much of the condemned man eating a hearty breakfast, but it wasn't as if he was going to be absolutely devastated. Though Neve hoped that he'd be a little bit devastated because what had started out as awkward and artificial had become something real, something precious – to her, at least.

'Why are you only eating leaves?' Max suddenly asked, and Neve looked up from her bowl of rocket and radicchio leaves to see that Max had devoured half a chicken and was now giving her his full attention.

'I'm really not that hungry,' she muttered, and it was true. Her stomach had spent most of the day loudly protesting the new regime but now it felt as if there was a huge knot clogging up her intestines. 'And I've decided to go on a detox.'

Max sighed. 'Please don't start that crap all over again. Do you think that deciding to detox counts as self-deprecation, because if it is, I know just the cure.' He stared at the palm of his hand meaningfully and Neve began to wonder if, as well as a good meal, she should treat the condemned man to one last romp. 'A chicken leg or a spanking. Your choice.'

Food or sex; that was what it really came down to. She could stuff her fat little face with Max and never, ever get to have sex with William – though she never really thought about William in a purely physical sense . . .

'Neevy, what's it to be?' Max asked playfully, nudging her foot with his toe. 'You digging in or bending over?'

'No! Max, I don't want any chicken and well, if you want to do *that* . . . we need to talk first.'

'That sounds ominous.' Max put down his lager and folded his arms. 'Is this about me leaving the loo seat up again?'

Neve shook her head. 'Max,' she said. 'Max . . .'

'I've done something really bad, haven't I? Did I pee on the seat, then not put it down? Is that why you keep saying my name in a really forlorn way, like I haven't just let myself down, I've let you down too?'

'No. Max . . .' Neve looked up at the ceiling in supplication because she just couldn't seem to get past repeating his name. She was really starting to reconsider the whole letter scenario. 'I want you to know that I really care for you and I consider you to be one of my closest friends.'

That was better. It was a whole sentence, even if the words were all sticking together, and Max wasn't grinning quite so widely now; he was listening intently, which was good. Sort of.

'And I hope that you'll always be one of my closest friends.' Neve came to a grinding halt now that she'd got the friend part of her speech out of the way. Another swift look at the ceiling and a deep breath. 'William called me the other day and he'll be back in London, um, in just over two weeks' time, so, you know, I think we should just be friends now.'

Max didn't say anything at first. He was too busy peeling the label off his lager bottle. 'So when exactly did he call you?' he asked in a mild voice. 'What day?'

'Um, Friday, I think.'

'The Friday before the weekend we just spent together?'

Neve looked at the top of Max's head, which was still bent over his lager. 'Yes. I was going to tell you then but I wasn't—'

'So you and Mr California are all ready to rock and roll?'

It was hard to get a handle on how Max felt about this new development. He wouldn't look at Neve and his voice was devoid of any real expression. Neve looked at her half-eaten bowl of leaves, then at Max and wondered if the two of them were really mutually exclusive. How would she react if Max flung himself at her feet and begged her to stay with him?

'Well, he says he has something really important to ask me but I'm not sure what it is,' Neve said carefully. 'So where does this leave us? What do you want to do?'

'The rabbit food is for his benefit, then? Have to be perfect

461

for Mr California?' Max enquired with an edge to his voice.

'I've put on a lot of weight over the last month,' Neve explained, trying hard not to sound accusing. 'So, even if William wasn't coming back, I need to concentrate on my health and fitness programme again.'

'Well, that's that then,' Max said, standing up and putting his lager bottle down on the table with more force than was strictly necessary.

'That's what?' Neve stood up too. 'How do you feel about this?'

'I don't feel anything either way.' Max was already marching out of the kitchen and up the half flight of stairs to the bedroom, so he could start scooping up the little pile of socks and shorts that had become a permanent fixture. 'Can you go and get my toothbrush and my razor?'

For the first time in a long time, Neve was scared to touch him. 'What are you doing?'

'What does it look like I'm doing?' Max demanded as he shoved his clothes into his bag. 'You can keep those Salinger books, by the way. I'm never going to read them.'

'But they were a present,' protested Neve. In all the possible outcomes she'd imagined, this hadn't been one of them. At the very worst, she'd thought Max would storm out in a huff to walk Keith. Then he'd come back half an hour later and they'd talk it out and agree to be friends. In fact, all the possible outcomes that Neve had envisaged had ended up with them remaining buddies. But Max stuffing his goods and chattels into his Vivienne Westwood duffel bag was horribly, irrevocably final. 'Please, Max. Can we sit down and talk about this?'

'There's nothing to talk about.' Max shouldered past Neve on his way to the bathroom. 'It was a pancake relationship. Like you keep constantly reminding me, the first pancake gets thrown away. I'll be out of your hair in less than ten minutes.'

'It doesn't have to be like this,' Neve said, standing in the bathroom doorway and watching as Max snatched up his shaving kit and his toothbrush and his shower gel, because hers was rose-scented and too girly for them to share. 'You're obviously upset. I am too.'

'There's nothing for either of us to be upset about,' Max said tightly. 'You got what you wanted from our little fling and now you're ready to move up to the big league. Congratulations.'

'But you were happy to go along with it,' Neve reminded Max, blocking his exit when he stepped forward, because she wasn't going to let him leave like this. 'You said you weren't cut out for a real relationship. Do you still feel the same way?'

Max stared her down, nothing teasing or soft in his eyes. 'Our little experiment has proved, once and for all, that I don't want or need a relationship. They're completely over-rated.' He put the fingers of one hand on her shoulder and applied enough pressure to get Neve to move out of the way. 'I mean, what's so fucking great about a relationship? You have to think about someone else all the time and all you get in return is regular sex. Really not worth it.'

'You're just saying that,' Neve choked as Max hurried down the stairs and scooped up Keith who'd come out of the living room to see what all the fuss was about. 'If William wasn't back, you'd be perfectly happy to carry on as we are.'

'Oh, would I?' Max sneered, struggling to tuck Keith under his arm as he tried to heft the duffel bag over his shoulder and open the front door at the same time. 'Yeah, keep telling yourself that, sweetheart, if it makes you feel any better.'

'Why are you being like this?' The end of her sentence was drowned out by the slam of the front door behind him.

Neve sank to the floor, knees pulled tight against her body. She didn't know how long she sat there but when her legs began to cramp, she slowly stood up and wandered through the flat. In ten minutes, Max had managed to eradicate all signs that he'd ever been here: sat on her sofa with his feet resting on the coffee table and refused to relinquish the remote control; perched on one of her kitchen chairs drinking tiny cup after tiny cup of espresso; slept in her bed, his arms tight around her, both of them a little sweaty, a little breathless from making love.

Max was gone.

PART FOUR

I Just Don't Know What To Do With Myself

Chapter Thirty-six

Having a plastic tube inserted into her fundament so that approximately fifteen gallons of water could be flushed in and out of her colon really took Neve's mind off Max marching out of her life the night before.

The only emotion that Neve could summon up was excruciating embarrassment. Or maybe it was shame? Even though the offending area was shrouded in a fluffy white towel and the colonic hydrotherapist spoke in a soothing low tone as she massaged Neve's abdomen, they both knew that the reason she was there was the water gushing out of her bottom.

'You might feel a slight cramping sensation over the next two hours but that's just your colon reshaping itself,' Neve was told, once the therapist had decided that her colon was squeaky clean, and she was back in her own clothes. 'Did you read the information sheet?'

Neve nodded. She'd given it a cursory glance during the sleepless hours she'd spent pacing and moping and crying.

'Well, remember not to drink alcohol or operate heavy machinery,' the therapist said as she showed Neve to the door of the smart Primrose Hill townhouse, which didn't look like the sort of place where such nefarious practices were carried out.

As Neve stepped out into the muggy heat of a hot June day, she wasn't prepared for the head rush that made her stagger and clutch on to the wrought-iron railings for support. She stood there, blinking her eyes because the leaves on the trees looked greener and shinier, and over the roar of traffic and the sound of a piano playing from an open window, Neve was sure that she could hear the engines of the plane she could see circling in the sky above, which surely hadn't been that blue before.

When she'd left her flat that morning, she'd felt hollow and bruised, but now she felt clean and purged, and, well, maybe still a little bruised but that was more the after-effects of the colonic rather than heartache. Neve pushed off from the railings, surprised that she had a swing in her step and a renewed sense of purpose.

Max was gone and that had always been part of the plan. And instead of obsessing about the manner in which he'd gone, she needed to remember that he'd had to go so there were no obstacles between her and William, apart from the twenty pounds she still had to lose. Neve patted her stomach, which felt flat for the first time in living memory. She'd probably already lost the five pounds she'd gained and still had another two colonics booked as part of the Cleanse; also, the therapist had said that some people lost as much as ten pounds each time.

Neve felt a surge of sheer delight as she imagined losing thirty pounds in a fortnight just from having her colon deep-cleaned. She beamed at an elderly woman who gave her a wide and tottery berth, then ran all the way round the corner to where she'd chained up her bike so she could hurry home and wait for the delivery of her Hardcore Cleanse juices.

Water was a recurring theme over the next week.

Neve had to plan her days carefully to make sure that she was never more than ten minutes away from a toilet. The Hardcore Cleanse did exactly what it said on its fancy black and white packaging. She drank. She peed. She drank. She peed. She was getting through two rolls of Andrex Quilted Velvet every day.

But it wasn't just the peeing. The euphoria was now feeling less euphoric and more manic. Happily, the Cleanse coincided with Mr Freemont's annual fortnight in Broadstairs. This was Rose's cue to embark on a marathon reorganisation and swab-down of the Archive. She swore it had nothing to do with dispelling the lingering stench of Mr Freemont's BO and more to do with having the opportunity to throw out the yellowing, desiccated piles of paper that he claimed were vitally important.

Normally Neve put up a spirited defence against dumping all those files in the recyling bin, but now she was happy to work off some of her Cleanse-sponsored energy by lugging boxes outside and scrubbing down floors and surfaces with hot, soapy water. But as soon as she plunged her rubber gloves into the bucket, she'd have to stop and run to the loo. She couldn't even pass a pond or an ornamental water feature without the power of autosuggestion working its magic on her bladder.

The other benefit of Mr Freemont's annual holiday was that they took it in turns to have three-hour lunch-breaks and one afternoon off a week, so Neve had plenty of time to run laps around the law courts and do press-ups in the office. She didn't dare set foot in the gym as she was pretty sure Gustav had had her membership revoked after she'd sent him a furious email formally severing their trainer/client relationship during one of her more manic episodes.

Mostly Neve tried to keep busy so she wouldn't miss Max. She was sure Max was managing just fine without her, and when she was running laps, scrubbing floors, making contact with Lucy Keener's old classmates from Oxford and happily imagining the moment when William clapped eyes on her for the first time in three years and murmured throatily, 'God, Neve, when did you get so beautiful?' she was doing just fine too.

The only time that she wasn't fine was when it was dark

and hours before her next juice and she couldn't sleep because she was a ball of nervous energy. Then, Neve had nothing else to do but miss Max so badly that the lack of him was a tangible, physical pain.

One morning when Neve wasn't frantically googling *Hardcore Cleanse + side effects* she even found herself on Amazon buying Max and Mandy's WAG novels and paying the extra for next-day delivery.

She devoured *Gucci and Goals*, in one long gulp. Brandy Ballantyne wasn't even a thinly disguised Mandy McIntyre. She *was* Mandy from the top of her *blonde head, the exact same shade as the creamiest, palest vanilla ice cream that Brandy couldn't eat because she was lactose intolerant, to the tips of her French-manicured toenails, which Brandy knew was much more classy than the tarty red her friends preferred.* But it was Max's voice she could hear in every line, his vodka-dry sense of humour shining through as Brandy got herself into all manner of amusing scrapes, from being falsely accused of shoplifting a pair of Gucci boots to running across the pitch at Old Trafford during extra time in hot pursuit of her pet Pekinese, Tiffany, in her hunt for a footballer boyfriend.

Neve read *Penalties and Prada* the next day even though she had promised Rose she'd sort through a teetering pile of Archive material. When Brandy married her star striker fiancé Damon, Neve found herself tearing up, and *Armani and AC Milan* had Neve so overwrought that she wasn't sure she could finish it. Brandy was starting married life in Italy after Damon's multi-million-pound transfer deal, and for all his bullshit about not believing in relationships, Max wrote about love as if it was something he'd personally experienced: *Brandy forgot about the cruel jibes of the other WAGs when she'd rocked up to the VIP box in her thigh-high, seven-inch-heeled Stella McCartney boots because there was Damon larger than life and twice as handsome on the big TV screens dotted around the stadium. The sun was glinting off the highlights in his hair and he'd stripped off his shirt so he could douse the muscled planes of his chest in water and he was smiling and looking up in the direction of the VIP box as if he could see her distress and wanted to let her know that he was on her side and always would be. He was her man and nothing else mattered.*

Unfortunately the next book in the series, *Burberry and Bootees*, wasn't out for another few months so Neve was forced to borrow all of Celia's back issues of *Skirt* so she could read everything that Max had ever written. She knew that she was on the fast track to indulging in all sorts of clichéd break-up behaviour like ringing Max's phone and his BlackBerry and his landline just to hear him say cheerfully, 'I can't come to the phone, you know what to do after the beep,' or pacing a well-trodden path outside his flat. She'd planned to use this down-time before William returned to mope and reflect on their break-up, but Neve had never expected to wallow this hard.

Her head had known that Max was just a trainer relationship, but it seemed as if her heart had never got that memo. Or maybe it was because Max had been her first boyfriend that she felt torn in two and Sellotaped back together. If she'd gone through these rites of passage in her teens, then she'd probably be blasé about them by now.

Like Yuri, who'd gone out with the graphic designer for two months and was only mildly annoyed that he'd turned out to be a wrong 'un.

'Why aren't you more upset?' Neve demanded as they sat in the back garden on a sultry Sunday evening, ten days into her Cleanse. 'I mean, you've cried at least once, haven't you?'

Yuri shook her asymmetric fringe out of her eyes. 'Nuh-huh! Not wasting any tears on a douchebag who couldn't keep it in his pants for three days while I was at a skateboarding festival in Manchester.'

'I don't understand how you can be with someone and share beautiful, intimate moments with them and then not give a damn that it's ended.' Neve turned gimlet eyes on her. 'God, Yuri, do you even have a heart?'

'Dude, you're getting really, really snippy again,' Yuri told Neve.

'I can't help it!'

'It's all right,' said Celia from the patio doors that led from her kitchen straight on to the decking in the back garden. 'She's due another juice. She'll be all right once she's choked it down, won't you, Neevy?'

Neve nodded and tried to muster a weak, wavery smile as Celia walked towards her with her evening Cleanse and a saucer with four lemon quarters on it. 'I will but this is not just a Cleanse withdrawal. I have genuine reasons to be in a very bad mood.'

'Of course you do,' Celia clucked, as she shoved the Cleanse bottle at Neve. 'Now, for the love of God, get that down you.'

The green morning juice wasn't so bad. It had a clean, fresh taste that only slightly resembled the washing-up liquid that her mother had once squirted in her mouth after Neve had questioned the existence of God. And she was actually acquiring a taste for her lunch Cleanse, which was neon orange and tasted of carrots and lentils. It was only her last juice of the day that was a problem because it was a brown sludge that . . .

'God, that shit smells like bongwater,' Yuri announced, squinching up her face and sliding down the wooden bench so she was as far away from it as possible.

Neve lifted the bottle to her lips and tried to ignore the fetid smell – there was really only one way to do this. She closed her eyes, tipped back her head, pinched her nostrils and tried to pour the juice straight down her throat so she could bypass her taste buds altogether. As soon as she wrenched the bottle away, Celia thrust a lemon quarter into her hand so Neve could jam it in her mouth and suck hard.

'Just like a tequila shooter,' Celia said proudly.

'Brrr!' Neve shook her head and waggled her arms, and once she was sure that the juice wasn't going anywhere but down her alimentary canal, she stilled. She didn't feel quite so angry any more. 'That's better.'

'Speaking as someone who eats raw tuna for fun, that stuff is ungodly,' Yuri said. 'You cannot live on three gross drinks a day. No wonder you're snapping all the time; your blood sugar must be in minus numbers.'

'The juices are giving me a daily intake of a thousand calories and I'm allowed to eat two small portions of raw veggies.'

'Big whoop.' Yuri eyed Neve up and down. 'You look thinner. How much have you lost?'

'I don't know,' Neve replied, because she was too scared to get on the scales and discover that the Cleansing and the colonics and the constant peeing had all been in vain. 'But I can take my jeans off by stepping on the hem and waiting for them to slide down.'

'Maybe it's time to invest in a new pair?' Celia suggested excitedly. 'I've got a discount card for this great denim boutique in Hoxton and you can try on the True Religion jeans I've been coveting for years but can't buy because my arse is too flat.'

'I'm not buying any clothes until I'm in a size ten,' Neve said firmly. She stretched her arms above her head. 'Do you want me to wash your kitchen floor again? Or I could clean your bathroom, if you'd rather.'

'You in a good mood now?' Yuri asked slyly.

She was definitely getting there. 'Why? What do you want?'

'A birthday party on Saturday in this very garden,' Yuri said. 'And I can't make any promises that I'll clear everyone out and turn the music down at eleven o'clock sharp.'

'I don't mind, but Charlotte might have something to say about it,' Neve said, angling a glance up at the first-floor windows even though she'd heard Charlotte and Dougie go out earlier.

'Dougie's putting her on a plane for Ibiza as we speak,'

Celia informed her smugly. 'As if Charlotte and her chavvy friends need to spend a week making themselves even more orange.'

'A whole week?' Neve clasped her hands together in prayer. 'Thank you, God.' Charlotte and her broom had been delighted that Max was no longer around so they could make up for lost time by banging on the ceiling every five minutes.

'You can invite some friends if you like,' Yuri offered magnanimously. 'But no one over the age of thirty-five and definitely not that Gustav.'

'Who phoned me earlier today and wanted to discuss staging an intervention on you,' Celia revealed. 'And no, I didn't say you were on a brutal regime of stinky drinks and colonics. Oh, that reminds me, will it be triggery for you if we ask you to make some cheese straws?'

'Not triggery at all.' For the first time in her life, even when she'd had swine flu, Neve had absolutely no appetite. 'Are you inviting anyone from the office, Seels?'

'Only the assistants and the interns that I really like, and Gracie said she might pop along, but everyone else is far too up themselves for a party in a north London garden.'

'Have you invited *him*?' Even with her blood sugar temporarily restored, Neve couldn't trust herself to say Max's name, because even thinking it in her head was usually enough to bring the gloom crashing down on her.

'After what he did to you? Of course I didn't! And no, I don't know how he is, because he's in LA just like he was the last ten times that you asked me,' Celia said. 'I promise you the party will be a Max-free zone.'

Which was a good thing, although Neve's heart refused to accept that and it had perked up just a little at the thought of seeing Max again. Maybe even walking over to him and touching his arm, so they could drift to the quiet corner of the garden which the dog roses were trying to colonise, and talk things out, becoming friends again. 'You can invite him if you like,' Neve said, and she knew that she didn't sound even a little bit casual, more like utterly desperate. 'I don't mind.'

'He's dead to me,' Celia snapped. 'Apart from when I'm at work and I have to do what he says because he has "Editor" in his job title.' She squeezed Neve's knee. 'You could invite Willy McWordy, if you like.'

'He's still roadtripping and I really don't want our reunion to happen when there's a chance that one of your friends will be throwing up in the flowerbeds,' Neve said. 'And I'm not a size ten so I can't see him just yet.'

'You're going to be finished with your suicidal detox programme before the party, right?' Yuri wanted to know. 'Because I love you tons, but I can't have you glaring into the vodka punch. It will kill the vibe.'

Celia looked pointedly at Yuri, who shrugged. 'I'm just saying.'

'You've only got another three days, haven't you?'

'Well, the publicist is giving me another two weeks of juices at a fifty per cent discount to say sorry for the mood swings,' Neve admitted and braced herself for the outrage that she could see Celia working up to.

'You're only meant to do it for two weeks,' she reminded Neve sharply. 'Two weeks! That was the only reason that I told you about it.'

'The publicist says that they have clients in the States who've done it for much longer than that,' Neve muttered.

'She's a publicist. She's paid to tell great, fat lies. We agreed that this was just about kick-starting your metabolism again, not as a permanent replacement for solid food.' Celia gave her sister a reproachful look. It was such a good look that it could have softened the stoniest heart, but Neve just folded her arms and stuck out her lower lip in a mutinous pout.

'I don't care,' she gritted. 'It's my body and so what if I can't sleep, and I'm a bit moody and yes, the brown juice smells like bongwater though I've never actually smelled bongwater so I'll have to take your word for it. If this gets me into a size ten then it will be worth it.'

'But . . .'

'Dude . . .'

'Shut up! I don't want to hear it because neither of you can even imagine what it's like to be trapped in a prison of *fat* and until you do, you've got nothing to say to me on the subject, so zip it!'

Celia zipped it for a few long moments, her lips pressed so tightly together that she looked like she might explode. Then she couldn't contain herself any longer and opened her mouth so she could let rip. 'You might have been a size fourteen when you were shagging Max but you were a damn sight more happy then than you are now. And I'll tell you something else: you were a hell of a lot less spotty too!'

Chapter Thirty-seven

Neve had always thought of Celia as soft and pliable like Plasticine but she proved absolutely rigid and unbendy over the next week. She resisted all of Neve's entreaties about her body, her choice, remained unmoved even when Neve spent an evening dragging the lawnmower round the garden, nearly amputating a couple of toes in the process, and received 247 freshly baked cheese straws on the Saturday afternoon with a blank face and an icy, 'Thanks.'

'I've had my run,' Neve said chirpily to show she didn't bear any grudges. 'And before I shower, I thought I'd help you make the flat party-friendly.'

'You don't have to do that,' Celia said without much conviction. The only time she or Yuri ever had clean glasses was when Neve refused to listen to their claims that the alcohol sterilised the germs and washed them up herself.

They worked in silence, or rather Neve ferried breakables and designer clothes and accessories to Yuri's room, which had a lockable door, took out five black bags of rubbish, vacuumed, arranged crudités and dips on silver-foil platters and popped to the pound shop to buy more nightlights.

Meanwhile, Celia and Yuri had wardrobe crisis after wardrobe crisis, until it was seven and they were both wearing the same outfits that they'd started in: Celia in a fitted polo shirt and a pair of high-waisted denim shorts and red braces, and Yuri modelling a blue-and-white striped playsuit that looked like a Victorian swimming costume.

Neve was careful to look at them with a neutral expression on her face. Maybe when she was a size ten, she might start dressing more outlandishly, but somehow she doubted it.

'Everything's done,' she said in the same bright voice she'd been using all afternoon. It was exhausting to have to keep the pep so peppy. 'You just need to make the punch.'

'Thanks, Neevy. You're a total star,' Yuri said, gazing around their lounge with wonder. 'I never knew we had a rug under all those magazines.'

'It was nothing,' Neve said, looking at Celia. 'Always happy to help out.'

Celia sighed and Neve could tell from the defeated way that her shoulders slumped that her sister couldn't keep up the effort of being mad at her. 'Thank you,' she said. 'Really, thanks a lot. Everyone would be crunching under old pizza boxes if it hadn't been for you.'

Neve nodded and Celia nodded back, and neither of them had to say anything else to know that Celia was still furious about the Cleanse but she wasn't furious at Neve any more, and Neve understood the difference. 'OK, I'm going upstairs to get changed now.' Neve paused. 'Cherry-print blouse, dark wash straight-leg jeans and heels?'

'Flip-flops,' Celia said firmly. 'This is a house party, not a nightclub.'

By eleven o'clock, the Scoins from next door had complained about the noise three times and all four members of a minor indie band had turned up, so the party could be considered a rousing success.

Celia and Yuri's friends were an intimidating bunch of fashion and design types who had distressed haircuts, distressed clothes and liked music that hurt when you listened to it. They were all perfectly pleasant to Neve, because being Celia's sister gave her an automatic pass, but she could see their eyes sliding away from her after a couple of minutes of polite conversation. Her cherry-print blouse, straight-leg jeans (which were now baggier and saggier than her 'just around the house' jeans) and Primark flip-flops just didn't cut it.

Neve sat on the stairs with Philip and Rose. Chloe and her boyfriend had long since been sucked into the noisy throng of people in the ground-floor flat and this way Neve could prevent anyone from gaining access to the top two floors. She wasn't particularly bothered about Dougie's flat, especially as his contribution to the party was four cans of Budweiser, but she wasn't having anyone fornicating on her landing. Besides, from her vantage point on the stairs she could race up to her flat to use the loo, whenever nature called. Which it did, with alarming frequency.

'And ever since I told Clive that I couldn't have his toxic presence in my life any more, he's been absolutely devoted,' Philip was saying with a fond smile. 'It really worked, Neve.'

'You have to treat them mean to keep them keen,' Rose sniffed, pulling her shoulders back and adjusting the neckline of her sparkly gold dress so her cleavage was better displayed. One of Yuri's skateboarder pals kept wandering into the hall to exchange lingering smiles with Rose, even though he was at least half her age, and Neve had a feeling that her friend wouldn't be getting the night bus back to Bayswater on her own.

'I didn't tell you to dump him so he'd have a nasty shock and start being nice to you. I said it because he's a vile, evil toad of a man,' she reminded Philip crossly. She was long overdue her third, bracken-scented juice, but she'd promised Yuri she'd drink it as late as possible so she'd be even-tempered just as the pubs emptied out and the party really started kicking off.

'You're a regular ray of sunshine these days, Neevy,' Rose said. 'It's not your juices, it's giving up meat. I've never met a happy vegetarian.'

'I've been vegetarian for fifteen years,' Philip said

peevishly and they started bickering about the pros and cons of a vegetarian diet as they did once a week on average. Neve had heard it all before: Hitler was a vegetarian and Philip couldn't be that dedicated because he'd eaten two pigs in blankets at the Archive Christmas party three years before.

She looked at her watch. It was just after eleven and she really should have her juice before she knocked her colleagues' heads together. Neve had one hand on Philip's shoulder as a prelude to standing up when Max walked through the open front door.

Neve felt her body give a quick jerk of joyful recognition because it had been almost two weeks since she'd last seen him. Max was tanned a deep golden brown, which accentuated his cheekbones and made his tousled hair look lighter. He was wearing his nicest jeans, the ones he called his Sunday best, which hugged his long legs, and a rumpled blue and red plaid shirt. And he was grinning, eyes twinkling, until he looked up and saw Neve at the top of the stairs, neither sitting nor standing, but crouching awkwardly somewhere in between.

She didn't know how Max could do it, but by the time she'd blinked the grin had thinned and he was sneering at her. That was when Neve noticed that he was holding hands with a tiny blonde girl with delicate everything; the gentle sweep of her eyebrows, her perfect, tip-tilted nose and lips that looked like a sodding rosebud. Lips that were whispering something in Max's ear as she stood on tiptoe so Neve had a clear view of her perfect, bare legs in short-shorts and perky little breasts straining against her white wife-beater. Neve was forced to acknowledge the painful truth that she could glug down Hardcore Cleanse juices from here until kingdom come and she'd never be tiny and sylph-like and a slip of a girl that men would want to protect and cherish, in the way that Max was doing; he had his arm curled around the girl's minuscule waist in case a stiff breeze knocked her over.

Rose and Philip were still negotiating the finer points of vegetarianism, not even realising that Neve's world had stopped. Max raised his eyebrows in greeting but didn't say anything. He didn't have to – his smug smile said it all for him.

Then, thank God, Max and his delicate nymph were slipping into Celia and Yuri's flat and Neve was freed from her paralysis to stumble up the stairs to the sanctuary of her own rooms.

She didn't cry, which was a minor miracle. But she felt like crying and never stopping. 'Don't you dare,' she said out loud. 'Max is free to see whoever he wants and you have no right to be jealous or upset because he's not The One and that's why you let him go. William is The One.'

Giving herself a stern talking-to didn't do much good. Neve could feel her bottom lip quivering and the first tear start to trickle down her face. She wiped it away impatiently. No wonder she was so emotional. The juice would make everything better.

It didn't – mainly because Neve had forgotten to have a lemon quarter to hand. Eyes watering, she reached for the fruit bowl, but had to stop and retch for what felt like for ever. There was no time to even cut a lemon in half; Neve jammed the whole fruit into her mouth and bit down hard.

It suddenly struck Neve just how ridiculous her life had become when she was standing in her kitchen sucking on a lemon so she wouldn't throw up her evening meal, which had come from the empty bottle standing on her kitchen counter, while downstairs her former lover was entwined around a girl who probably weighed ninety pounds dripping wet.

And just what was her former lover doing here anyway?

Rather than going back downstairs the way she'd come and risk bumping into Max and *that* girl again, Neve opened her kitchen door and raced down the rickety metal stairs to the garden, nearly breaking her neck as she fell over entwined couples.

It was easy to spot Celia; she was a head taller than all the other girls and her legs gleamed ghostly white in the darkness, which was illuminated by the flickering tealights that Neve had lugged back from the pound shop.

'Seels!' Neve shouted while there was still half a garden between them. Celia's head turned in her direction. 'Why is he here?' Neve panted. 'Why did you invite him?'

'Why did I invite who?' Celia asked.

'Max! He's here with some skinny girl who's wearing a pair of shorts that are so tiny, she might just as well have turned up in her knickers!'

Celia looked down at her own short-shorts, but decided she wasn't going to go there. 'I didn't invite him, Neevy, I swear,' she said earnestly. 'How dare he gatecrash our party? Do you want me to throw him out?'

Neve contemplated having to spend the rest of the party skulking in her flat rather than risk running into Max. Or worse, having to brazen it out and pretend that she wasn't bothered. But then she thought about Celia turning up for work on Monday and probably getting an official warning for throwing the Editor-at-Large out of her house. 'Well, I suppose it's OK, but feel free to accidentally spill something over him.'

'I will,' Celia muttered, running a hand through her already dishevelled hair. She seemed preoccupied and Neve was just about to ask her if everything was all right, when she spotted Dougie standing right behind Celia – and from his tense face and Celia's distraction, she realised she'd barged into the middle of something.

'What's going on?'

'Nothing,' Dougie said too quickly. He was already moving past Celia, who shot out a hand and grabbed his arm.

482

'Not so fast, dickweed!' she told him. 'Guess what he was doing, Neve?'

It could have been any one of a number of things. 'What?'

'Look, Seels, this is none of your business . . .'

'He was sucking face with one of Yuri's friends,' Celia burst out, eyes wide with an outrage that Neve completely shared.

'You weren't?' Neve gasped. 'But you're married!'

Dougie threw his head back and made a sound that was half growl, half groan. 'So? Both of you hate Charlie, so don't start acting like you care about her feelings.'

'Still doesn't give you the right to perv on my mates.'

'Did I mention that you're married?' Neve pointed out again. And she didn't care about Charlotte; in fact, she hoped that she'd get swept away by a freak tidal wave while she was in Ibiza, but Neve was still angry on her behalf. It had to be another weird side-effect of the Cleanse. 'You made vows, solemn vows, to be faithful and she's been gone for no time at all and already you're hitting on other women like she doesn't mean anything to you at all. You're sullying all the special moments you've shared together. You should be ashamed of yourself!'

'Well, I'm not!' Dougie suddenly roared, and Neve saw a crowd of people gathering to witness the Slaters going at it, which was a family tradition they usually kept behind closed doors. 'You two hate her – well, try being married to her and see how long you last!'

He pushed past them, knocking Neve into Celia as he went, and when Celia's arms tried to close around her, Neve frantically wriggled free. She couldn't bear to be touched right then.

'He's despicable,' Neve ranted. 'Behaving like that when he's married, even if I do hate Charlotte.'

'I know you do. I do too,' Celia said carefully. 'Are you sure this isn't more about Max and those lame diet drinks, which I haven't even got the energy to get on your case about.'

'I wish I'd just concentrated on losing weight and hadn't got side-tracked with all that rubbish about pancake relationships, because Max was just a waste of time and effort.' Neve tossed back her hair angrily. 'He can go out with whomever he likes. I am so over him!'

'Neevy – I hear what you're saying.' Celia was looking over Neve's head and frowning. 'Can we talk about this later? Go upstairs and drink a shake or something, and don't let Yuri see that you've gone all dark side again.'

Neve's journey back up the fire escape was even more perilous when it was hard to see where she was going with a red mist swirling in front of her eyes.

Why were men so predictable in such an unpredictable way? Just when you thought you had them figured out, they'd pull some sneaky, low-down move, which made you see them in a new, highly unflattering light.

It wasn't enough that Dougie had married Charlotte. Now he had to go and cheat on her too, so she'd have even more reasons to make Neve's life an utter, living hell.

Even William was driving her to distraction as she tormented herself wondering about his big, important question that he hadn't asked her because it was impossible for them to be on the same continental shelf at a mutually convenient time.

And then there was Max, Neve thought, as she wrenched open her kitchen door. Turning up with Miss Hot Pants just so he could rub Neve's nose in the fact that he was used to a far higher calibre of girl in his bed.

'God, I hate them all!' she shouted, snatching up her empty juice bottle and hurling it across the kitchen where it collided with her corkboard and dislodged half a dozen flyers. 'Bloody, bloody hell!'

'Still not using the f-word, then?' said an amused voice – and there was Max standing in the doorway.

Neve's first thought was that it was a pity that she'd already flung the only suitable missile she'd had to hand because throwing it at Max would have been much more satisfying.

And her second thought was: 'How did you get in here?' she demanded, hands on hips.

Max held up her spare key because he'd left so abruptly that they'd never had time to hand back door keys or change locks or any of that stuff which would have ensured that Max wasn't currently standing in her kitchen uninvited.

'You should have knocked.'

'I did knock – there was no reply,' Max said calmly, as if her furious voice and squinty-eyed scowl weren't affecting him in the slightest.

'So you thought you'd just come barging in, did you?' Neve advanced, hand outstretched. 'Give me the key and then you can go back to the party that you weren't invited to and find the little blonde you came with.'

She had to be looking pretty terrifying at that moment, red-faced and vibrating with rage, but Max stood his ground and didn't even flinch when Neve was near enough to jab her finger at his chest.

'Don't do that, Neevy,' he said equably. 'It's kind of rude. Anyway, my therapist said I should try to re-establish an open, honest dialogue with you and that the way a relationship ends is just as—'

'Oh, she did, did she? So you just turn up here uninvited, with some *waifish* girl who's everything I'm not?'

'Jane's a friend. A happily married friend whose husband works with Yuri and followed us in once he'd had a chance to go to the offy.'

Neve snorted in derision; a much snottier snort than she would have liked. 'Do you always hold hands with your friends' wives?' As soon as the words came hurtling out of her mouth, Neve wanted to take them back. As it was, she couldn't really blame Max for staring at her so disdainfully.

'So now you're an expert in holding hands, are you? Anyway, I thought you'd be wrapped round Mr California.' Max turned his head so he could look out into the hall. 'Where is he?'

'He's not— it's none of your business where he is.'

'He's not here?'

'No,' Neve admitted reluctantly, and she took a deep breath to try and centre herself, but when Max's fingers looped round her wrists, she gave a nervous start and tried to jerk free. 'What are you doing? Get off me!'

'You were jealous when you saw me with Jane, weren't you?'

'No! I wasn't! I just thought it was impolite that—'

'Bullshit,' Max murmured in her ear, and his breath tickled and made Neve shiver as if it was the depths of winter and not a sticky summer night. 'You were jealous, just like I'm jealous at the thought of you and Mr California together.'

Neve felt the anger begin to fade. 'I wanted to explain but you were just *gone*. You went so quickly it was as if you were never here at all.'

Max's hands were still round her wrists but now they felt comforting. 'I wanted you to give me a sign . . .' He closed his eyes and when he opened them again, Neve could see her own sadness reflected back at her. 'If you'd given me any reason to hope, I'd have staged a sit-down protest.'

'But you didn't give me even the slightest indication that you wanted us to make a proper go of it.' Neve tried to look cross but her heart wasn't in it. 'I dropped enough hints.'

'No, you didn't. You asked me if I was ready to be some other girl's second pancake,' Max told her. 'Then a few days later, you tell me *he*'s coming back and it's time for me to go.'

'I never said it like that,' Neve protested, struggling to get her hands free again because just standing so close to Max and having this conversation was too intense when she had all these emotions that she hadn't dared let herself feel bubbling up again. 'Every time I thought about William coming back, I'd think about you and how I didn't want us to end. It's complicated . . .'

Max still held her, his thumbs stroking the spot on her wrists where her pulse was thundering away. 'Uncomplicate it then. Did you miss me?'

'Of course I did! I've missed you so much, I *hurt* from it.'

Then, and only then, did Max release her but it was only so Neve could wind her arms around his neck because they were kissing. She couldn't say who leaned in first, but all of a sudden there was the familiar but shocking touch of lips on lips.

It started off glacially slow as if they needed time to re-acquaint themselves, but with the first glide of Max's tongue into Neve's mouth, it became fast and greedy and they were clutching at each other, hands delving and unbuttoning, teeth biting, then soothing the pain away, and Neve could feel her legs buckling as Max pulled her down on to the black and white linoleum and, then he was hard on top of her, his lips driving her crazy as he kissed a path down her neck.

'When I saw you on the stairs before, I'd forgotten how beautiful you are,' he whispered against her skin.

'Spotty, not beautiful,' she corrected gently, running her finger along his crooked nose. 'Now you, you're beautiful.'

'I even missed your inferiority complex.' Max smiled and shifted against her, so she could feel his cock pressing along the seam of her jeans where her clit was throbbing frantically.

'Not being inferior. It's a point of fact. I'm covered in zits,' Neve said and she didn't know why she felt the need to share that with Max but then she was glad that she had because he was kissing each one of the angry red bumps along her forehead and chin and cheeks, even though a few of them were starting to suppurate. 'Don't do that, it's completely unhygienic. Kiss my mouth instead.'

Neve didn't even care that they were going to have sex on her kitchen floor. She only cared that Max was all fingers and thumbs as he tried to prise his wallet out of the back pocket of his jeans, which were halfway down his legs. She sat up to help but then had to clumsily scramble to her feet and kick off her own jeans, which were pooled around her ankles.

'Do you want to move this to the bedroom, then?' Max asked, leaning back on his elbows so he could look at her standing there in her unbuttoned blouse and knickers.

And maybe they were destined to be together because Neve didn't think she could ever be this relaxed and unclothed with anyone else. But she'd think about that when she wasn't hopping from one leg to the other. 'I need to pee!' she yelped, because it had been ages since her last juice and it always went right through her and now that she was upright, she realised that she'd been holding it in for ages. 'Now! Don't go anywhere!'

She also could never share information about her bodily functions with anyone who wasn't Max, Neve thought, as she washed her hands and stared at her face in the mirror. She was so flushed that her spots weren't even that noticeable and she liked the way she looked when she was with Max; all kiss-sore and saucer-eyed. She could hear him crashing about in the kitchen and a loud, 'What the fuck!' as she opened the bathroom door and was just about to order him to her bedroom in a come-hither voice, when she saw that he was rooting through her fridge, in his hand the empty Cleanse bottle that she'd thrown across the kitchen.

'Max?' she said uncertainly and he paused, head still in her refrigerator.

'What the fuck?' he said again, his voice muffled, then he straightened up and in his other hand was the wire bottle cage containing tomorrow's three juices. 'What are you doing with this shit?'

'Well, I'm detoxing, it's why I'm so spotty,' Neve said carefully. 'Lots of toxins build up over time and your body can't shift them and your energy levels get all out of whack and—'

'You're doing this to lose weight, aren't you?'

And that was a surprise, why? 'You know my goal is to be a size ten. It's not like I made a secret of it.'

Max tried to shrug but his shoulders were so stiff with anger that it was more of a jerk. 'And what was wrong with what you were doing before?'

'It was taking too long.'

'Oh, so you're on a clock. Funny that going on a juice fast just so happens to coincide with Mr California's triumphant homecoming,' Max scoffed and Neve didn't know how he could stand there still naked, still half-hard and totally at ease as he laid into her, while she was suddenly wishing that they were doing this fully clothed. If they had to talk about her body, then she didn't want her body so prominently displayed.

'Look, I put on five pounds when I was with you.' No matter how hard she tried, her words sounded like an accusation. 'I'm not like other girls. I can't just lose five pounds by cutting back on sweets and crisps. It takes more effort than that.'

She couldn't bear it any longer but entered the kitchen hunched over to hide her belly and thighs as she groped one-handed for her jeans.

'That is not a good enough reason to choke down this crap!' Max waved the bottles of precious liquid about, to make his point, and Neve held her breath as they bumped around in their wire cage. Even with her 50 per cent discount, they were still fifteen pounds a bottle.

'Can you put them down? Gently, please,' she begged, easing one foot into her jeans. 'And can you turn round while I get myself dressed?'

Max thumped the bottles down on the table so hard they bounced, and when Neve whimpered in protest, he exploded. His face got so red and angry that she wouldn't have been at all surprised to see cartoon steam coming out of his ears. 'You are not drinking this crap!' he howled. 'Two people died in New York doing this bloody Cleanse.'

'They probably had underlying medical problems,' Neve muttered.

'What the fuck is wrong with you?' Max shouted. 'Really, what do you think is going to change when you're in a size-ten frock? What's going to be different?'

Neve didn't answer at first because she was fastening her jeans and she needed time to think, although really this should have been a no-brainer. 'I'll be different,' she said eventually. 'I'll be happier. I'll be normal.'

'I don't know how you can be the smartest person I've ever met and also the most stupid,' Max snapped, as he pulled on his jeans. 'What's going to magically happen between now and you being a size ten that's going to make you different and happy and normal?'

'I *will* be different,' she said fiercely, as if saying it with enough vehemence was enough to make it so. 'The only reason you want to keep me fat is because you can't handle being in a relationship with someone who's slim enough and pretty enough to make demands on you.'

'That's crap,' Max spluttered.

'What's crap is you making judgements about me when you're far from perfect yourself,' Neve shrieked, her voice so shrill that it scraped her throat. 'You go to your therapist and jaw on about your intimacy issues when the only issue was your uncontrollable urge to sleep with girls solely because of what they looked like. You're the shallow one, not me!'

'I'll tell you something about those girls. Not one of them, not the models or the actresses, went on about the way they looked as much as you do,' Max said. He wasn't shouting any more, but spitting the words out like bullets. 'You're not self-deprecating, sweetheart. You're the most self-involved, narcissistic person I have ever met.'

'I bet you don't even know what narcissism means!' Max might not have been shouting any more, but Neve certainly was. 'At least William's on my intellectual level.'

'It's never going to work between you two, you know that, don't you?'

It was like having a glass of icy-cold water suddenly thrown in her face. Max was completely still, no longer stabbing at the air with his fingers to make his point, but standing there with his hands in his pockets.

'Yes, it will,' Neve said as she quietened down too.

Max started walking towards her, his face so intent and serious that Neve took a step back. Then he changed direction so he was standing in front of her corkboard and could give one of the photos that was pinned to it a derisive flick.

'No, it won't,' he said, his hand covering the picture of Neve and William taken at a garden party in Oxford. It was the only photo from back then that Neve could look at without cringing. She and William were sitting on a bench and she was smiling awkwardly for the camera, while William was in half-profile and gazing at her with such tenderness that having Max's hand obscuring their faces made it seem like he was also obliterating the happy memories she had of William. 'This isn't any more real than we were.'

'You don't know what you're talking about,' Neve said witheringly, her eyes shooting daggers into Max's back as he stooped to give the photograph a closer inspection. 'What William and I have . . . well, I wouldn't expect someone like you to understand.'

It wasn't often that Neve chose her words solely for the damage they could inflict, but she still felt a twinge of satisfaction as she saw Max's spine stiffen; however, when he turned back to her, his expression was thoughtful.

'There's nothing *to* understand.' Max cocked his head. 'All you've got there is a lot of long words and hot air. The most you'll ever do is hold hands. Pity it takes more than that to get you off though.'

Neve went hot, then cold, and back to hot. Hotter than a thousand, flaming, fiery suns. 'Get out!'

It wasn't crockery or anything sharp and pointy that might take out an eye, but Neve scooped up Max's shirt from the floor and threw it at him. He caught it one-handed, which was even more infuriating. 'Well, there's nothing here worth staying for.'

She never wanted to see him again, and Neve was sure Max felt exactly the same way but it wasn't that simple when he had to put his socks and sneakers back on while she stood there with her hands on her hips, eyes narrowed and this terrible rage bubbling and brewing so she had to tense every muscle she possessed so she wouldn't suddenly find her hands wrapped around his windpipe.

It was a short march to the front door, which she wrenched open. Two of Celia's friends were sitting on the stairs smoking a joint and not bothering to hide the fact that they'd been eavesdropping because they nudged each other and giggled until they saw the look on Neve's face. 'Go away,' she hissed through clenched teeth, then pressed herself against the wall, as Max brushed past her.

She was all ready to slam the door behind him, in a way that would have Charlotte claiming copyright infringement, but Max came to a halt in the hinterland between her flat and the stairwell. 'One last thing,' he said evenly.

Now what? Then light dawned. 'Your key? I'll give it to—'

'Even if you starved yourself down to a size zero, you're always going to be a fat girl, Neevy,' Max whispered in her ear, as she shrank away from him. 'You don't know how to be anything else.'

His words felt like a knife plunging into her belly again

and again, twisting this way and that way, tearing skin and flesh, so all Neve could do was press the flat of her hand hard into her stomach to try and ease the pain.

Max was set to step smartly past her and be gone, be done with her, but at the last moment, he turned his head so he could look her straight in her tearing eyes. Neve could see the realisation hit him like a speeding train. That of all the terrible things they'd just said to each other, of accusation and counter-accusation angrily flung around, Max had crossed a line he didn't even know had existed.

'I shouldn't have . . .' he began clumsily. 'I take that back.'

Neve bent her head so she wouldn't have to look at him and waved her hand in the direction of the hall, cowering back when he raised a hand to touch her cheek.

'Look, I'm sorry,' he said, and he still wouldn't go. Not unless she made him. 'Will you say something?'

Neve reared forward, hands hitting Max square on the chest so she could push him out of the door backwards. 'Fuck off!' she said, and slammed the door in his shocked face.

Chapter Thirty-eight

After the rage, came the deluge.

Neve had known that the violent mood swings couldn't last for ever, but she hadn't imagined that they'd be replaced by an attack of melancholy that had her taking to her bed because she couldn't see the point of getting up.

Although she called it melancholy because it conjured up images of Victorian ladies swooning back on chaises longues, while their concerned mamas dabbed at their foreheads with handkerchiefs soaked in eau de cologne, it felt a lot more like depression.

A big swirly depression that was a blend of the mean reds, the black dogs and a very blue period so that everything looked bruised, especially the dark circles around Neve's eyes because she couldn't stop crying. It was all she could do to get out of bed to take delivery of her juice, drink her juice, go to the loo after the juice had taken effect, then crawl back to bed and cry herself to sleep.

Despite what Max had said, Neve wasn't stupid. She knew that her melancholia was in large part due to the Cleanse, but all of it, the peeing, the acne, the mood swings, the dry heaving, would be worth it if the pounds had melted away.

She still hadn't weighed herself because she was scared of the absolute, incontrovertible truth that she'd find on the scales. None of this would have been worth it, if all that she'd lost were a couple of pounds and the goodwill of friends and family. The only thing that Neve knew right now was that she didn't feel as if she was taking up any less space in the world.

But feeling like that wasn't anything new or anything that Neve didn't deal with on a daily basis. What was tearing her into tiny little pieces, so she didn't think she'd ever be whole again, was the fight with Max.

There was the shame of all the hurtful, hateful things she'd said because she was angry; she hadn't really meant them but it was too late to take them back now. Of course, he'd said hurtful, hateful things right back, but she'd deserved them. Apart from the one hurtful, hateful thing that she couldn't dismiss, couldn't put down to the heat of the moment.

You'll always be a fat girl. You don't know how to be anything else.

It was the sordid, secret truth that Neve had always shied away from before it could become fully formed. Max had made it real, because after a few short months, he knew her better than anyone.

That was the worst thing about having a relationship with someone, even a pretend relationship. You opened up, let someone in, and when it was over, they had all the ammunition they needed to completely destroy you. When Max had spoken about her fat before, on the night she'd got naked for him, he'd said that it had fucked her up, but what they both knew was that she was still fucked up and likely to stay that way for ever.

Being a size ten had assumed such mythical proportions for Neve, but what if it didn't change anything? What if she was still an outsider, still not normal, still a freak?

It all kept ricocheting around Neve's brain, making her head ache and making her cry, until the fifth morning of her confinement, when she woke up with tears rolling down her cheeks yet again.

'Enough!' she said out loud, forcing herself to sit up. 'This has to stop.'

She got out of bed on shaky legs, stripping the sheets and bunging them in the washing machine, before heading to the bathroom to shower off five days of bed sweat and tearstains.

Then, wrapped in her old size thirty towelling robe, which doubled as a security blanket, and swigging from her bottle of breakfast Cleanse, Neve switched on her phone. Celia had contacted the Archive to tell them that Neve had summer flu, because 'I've tried the old "I've got a broken heart" excuse and it never works', so there were several peevish enquiries from Mr Freemont as to when she was coming back. There were also less peevish enquiries from Rose, Chloe and Philip, which should have filled Neve with warm fuzzies that there were still some people who weren't blood relatives who liked her, but she was all out of warm fuzzies. But when she saw that she had a missed call and a voice message from William, it was like a beacon of hope in a post-apocalyptic landscape.

Neve fingered a particularly painful spot on her chin as she listened to William's breezy message. 'Neve? William here. I'm back in London. Let's meet as soon as humanly possible. I have news that won't keep and I can't wait to see you. Call me.'

With a hand that shook slightly, Neve returned William's call, without giving herself time to reflect on the ramifications of such an audacious move. She needed to change, and right now having William back in her life was the only way she knew how to make that happen.

'Ah, it's the elusive Ms Slater,' he said, before Neve could even spit out a hello. 'Where have you been? I called you Sunday and it's Thursday now. Even in LA, three days is industry standard for returning calls.'

'I've had flu. Summer flu,' Neve explained in a rusty voice.

'Oh, poor thing. Must be why you sound so croaky. Are you better now?'

Physically she was getting there. Emotionally, she was sure that a strong gust of wind might knock her over. 'I think I'm ready to start getting up and about now.'

'Well, that's why I've been trying to get hold of you. I'm going out of town this weekend,' William said.

Neve looked up at the ceiling in despair. *Not again*. 'Oh. So when will you be back this time?'

'No, I absolutely have to see you before I go,' William said firmly. 'How about tomorrow evening?'

Neve looked down at her unshaven legs, and prodded her towelling-swathed belly. Then she traced the bumpy surface of her face, until she remembered that the last time William had seen her, she was twice the woman she was now. Anything had to be an improvement on that. 'Tomorrow, as in Friday tomorrow?' she clarified.

'The very same,' William said with a slight chuckle that warmed his clipped vowels. 'Do you mind awfully coming south of the river? I know what you north Londoners are like.'

'Well, the South Bank is usually as far south as I go,' Neve admitted, already seeing her and William strolling along the Embankment hand in hand, because with William she'd hold his hand on the very first date. 'Would that be all right for you?'

'God, you're so parochial, Neve,' William sighed, then he chuckled again, as if her unwillingness to cross the Thames was absolutely adorable. 'OK, shall we say seven at the Royal Festival Hall Members' Bar? It's on the sixth floor; the view is absolutely breathtaking.'

'That sounds lovely,' Neve agreed. 'Well, I'll see you then, I suppose.'

'I can't wait,' William said. 'And I have two surprises for you, so prepare to be astounded.'

He rang off and Neve sat on her lumpy red bucket chair in a daze for a few long moments as she contemplated the new direction her life was about to take. Change was good.

It was just what she needed – William was just what she needed – so why did it feel as if William was less her destiny and more a way to get over Max?

Neve stood up, intending to change into her running gear and pound the paths of Finsbury Park until she cleared her head. Then she caught sight of herself in the mirror. It was all she could do not to scream out loud as she peered at her face and the pustules that seemed to have multiplied while she was talking to William. Actually, the spots were the very least of it.

She needed an extreme makeover. She needed some really intensive spot cream. She really needed a haircut and she needed Celia like she'd never needed her before.

Neve had never truly appreciated Celia's talents. She never understood what Celia was going on about when she declared that shoulders were the new legs or justified spending four hundred pounds on a pair of over-the-knee boots because they were 'very on-trend'.

But she'd never had a fashion and beauty emergency on the scale of the one she was having now, and Celia, God bless her, was ready and able to rise to the occasion.

She came home from work with a bulging bag of potions, unguents and creams, courtesy of the *Skirt* Beauty Department, and slathered Neve's face in a paste that smelled like horse manure but was *guaranteed to eradicate 98 per cent of most facial blemishes overnight*.

Celia had even made appointments for Neve to have a mani-pedi, cut and blow dry, and her armpits, legs and bikini line de-Hobbited, before she met Celia in the *Skirt* fashion cupboard at three the next afternoon.

'I'm going to call in some clothes for you,' Celia said, because on Planet Fashion, the clothes came to you, rather than the other way round. 'What were you thinking in terms of outfits?'

'A dress,' Neve mumbled because it was hard to move her

mouth when her face was covered in blemish-eradicating cement. 'A nice dress. What are those very long dresses called?'

'Maxi-dresses,' Celia replied. 'Um, don't really think you've got the length of leg for one of them. You'd be swamped.'

'Hardly,' Neve snorted.

'Don't! You'll crack your zit mask. That stuff costs a hundred and fifty quid a pot,' Celia snapped. 'And don't start with all that "find me a burka" stuff either. What size are you now?'

Neve decided that shrugging wouldn't move any facial muscles. 'I was mostly a size fourteen before I started the Cleanse.'

'It's hard to tell what's going on under there,' Celia complained, pulling a face as she indicated Neve's voluminous dressing-gown. Then she pulled a different, more conflicted face. 'Look, Neve, you know I love you, right? Like, I love you to *pieces* and I want you to be happy, and if you think that Willy McWordy is your route to happiness, fine, then I'm on board . . .'

'But?' Neve prompted, because she could tell that the whole point of the speech was to get to the 'but'.

'But you have to promise me that you'll stop the Cleanse, because apparently people have died from it, and you're not you any more and I miss you,' Celia finished with a sniff, because she was close to tears.

'I know,' Neve said softly, because she'd come to the same conclusion during the last stages of her Bed-In. Anyway, once she saw William tomorrow, the truth would be out. Hopefully not being a size thirty-two would make up for not being a size ten. 'I've got juices for tomorrow and then I'm done.'

'You promise?'

'I promise!'

'Do you promise on Mum and Dad's life?' Celia

demanded. 'No, hang on, do you swear on Jane Austen's grave?'

'Seels! I do. I promise. I'll use up tomorrow's juices and then I'll start reintroducing solids,' Neve said.

'OK.' Celia seemed satisfied with Neve's sincerity but was frowning at her sister's swathed body. 'I still need to know your size. Why don't you go and weigh yourself, then I'll take your measurements.'

'Can't we just go on guesswork?' Neve begged.

'Aren't you even a little bit curious about how much you've lost?' Celia asked. 'I mean, your face looks really thin and what I can see of your chest looks bony.'

Neve was almost dying from curiosity but there were also huge amounts of dread mixed in with it. The longer she put it off, the more she might have lost. Especially if she waited until first thing in the morning – well, first thing *after* she'd had a really long run. 'I don't know,' she said hesitantly.

'It should go without saying that I won't tell a soul. Not even Ma,' Celia declared, getting up from the sofa.

'Especially not Ma!' Neve gasped, and she was getting up too and following Celia out of the lounge even as she tightened the belt on her dressing-gown.

Neve was beginning to think that Celia might have been replaced by the pod people on her way home from work, because she sat on the edge of the bathtub and displayed huge amounts of patience as Neve fussed with the scales; moving them back and forth, until she'd centred them to the left of the weird little dip in her bathroom floor.

'OK, I'm getting on them now,' Neve said unnecessarily. She took a deep breath and shucked off her robe, then stood there in bra and knickers.

Celia kept her eyes fixed on a spot to the right of Neve's elbow. 'Um, the sooner you get on them, the sooner you can get off again.'

Neve shut her eyes and stepped on the scales. They were fancy, expensive scales that gave her weight in pounds and kilograms and had nearly given her a hernia when she'd lugged them back from John Lewis. She shuffled around on them, until her weight was evenly balanced.

'Don't say a word,' she ordered Celia, her eyes still tightly shut. 'Look at the display and don't tell me what I weigh, just tell me if it's lower than one hundred and sixty-five pounds.'

She could hear Celia grumbling good-naturedly under her breath. 'Yes, yes, it is.'

'Is it lower than one hundred and sixty pounds?'

'Wouldn't it be easier if I just told you how much you weighed?'

'Just answer the question, Seels.'

'Yes, it's lower.'

'Is it lower than one hundred and fifty-five pounds?'

'Yes, and Christ Almighty, we're going to be here all night at this rate,' Celia said in an exasperated voice. 'You weigh one hundred and fifty-one pounds. What's that in English?'

'Ten stone and eleven pounds,' Neve said, her eyes snapping open as she stared down at the number. She jumped off the scales, then got on them again, pressing down with the soles of her feet as hard as she could. The number wavered and for one delicious moment it went down to one hundred and forty-nine pounds, before settling back to where it had been. 'I've only lost a stone in three weeks.' She sighed. 'If I hadn't spent five days in bed with my muscles atrophying, I'd probably have lost even more.'

'I love you and I'm not judging you but I am so close to stabbing you through the heart with your tweezers right now,' Celia growled. 'You've lost fourteen pounds, which is fantastic though I'm not in any way condoning that stupid Cleanse – and don't think this means you can back out of your promise, because you can't.'

'I'm not going to, but I should have lost more than that. I had three colonics!' Neve stared down at her thighs, which looked as solid as ever. 'I don't know where this so-called

501

stone has gone but it definitely wasn't from my bottom half.'

Celia was already scooping up the tape measure that Neve kept on her bathroom shelf. She slipped it around Neve's chest, and before they could go through the same rigmarole all over again, she called out numbers. 'Thirty-six!' She moved down to Neve's waist. 'Thirty!' And then she was wrapping it around the widest part of Neve's body where belly bulge became hips became bottom. 'Forty!'

If she'd lost three inches off her hips, then why did they still look like she could birth quadruplets? Neve quickly slipped back into her dressing-gown and once it was securely fastened, she felt better. 'Well, this is all good news,' she said, and tried to sound as if she meant it. She should mean it, but from where she was standing, directly opposite the huge mirror that took up most of one wall, she didn't look any different.

Chapter Thirty-nine

Neve had never been in the *Skirt* office before, preferring to wait downstairs in Reception whenever she met Celia from work. But that afternoon she was escorted to the seventh floor of the Magnum Media building by Celia's latest intern, a doe-eyed, elfin-cropped boy called Seth, and led through a large open-plan office, which she'd expected to be populated by willowy, model-y fashion-magazine types. Reassuringly, there were lots of normal-sized bodies wearing normal clothes and even the remains of a birthday cake on a table as Neve walked to the back of the office where the Fashion Department held court.

Here, there were very thin women wearing the kind of clothes that Neve could never fathom but which Celia always described as 'directional'.

Neve had had vague introductions to all the members of the Fashion Department on numerous occasions but she was never entirely convinced that they remembered her. She was also deeply ashamed of her baggy boot-cut jeans and tunic top, which were completely undirectional, so she was relieved to see Celia standing in the doorway of the fashion cupboard, all ready to usher her within its hallowed portals.

That wasn't the only reason. 'He's not here, is he? Max, I mean,' Neve said in a furtive whisper, as soon as Celia closed the door.

'He never comes in on Friday afternoons,' Celia said. 'In

fact, another half-hour and this place will be a ghost town.'

'But it's only three o'clock!'

'And your point is?' Celia folded her arms. 'Let's have a look at you.'

Neve stood there awkwardly, hands hanging limply by her sides. She felt entirely frazzled after a day of back-to-back beauty appointments, which weren't so much fun without a gaggle of WAGs there to hold your hand or keep your champagne glass topped up. The bikini wax had been particularly harrowing, and as for the hairdresser . . .

'He was very bossy,' Neve told Celia, who was scrutinising her tousled but shiny waves of hair. Neve hadn't even known her hair had the ability to wave. 'He absolutely refused to give me that bouffant ponytail I like. He said it was so last year.'

'Well, it kinda is,' Celia said, without much sympathy. 'Your hair looks great. *You* look great!' She seized Neve's hand and waggled it about as if she could inject some perkiness into her through the power of touch.

'I just keep hoping that William will ring and cancel on me. Then I wonder if I should ring and cancel on him,' Neve confessed, sinking down on to a stool and gazing around her. The cupboard was actually a huge room lined with clothing rails, which were crammed with garments in every colour and every fabric imaginable, from leopardprint chiffon gowns to red wool coats. There were shoes paired in neat rows under the rails and a series of cubbyhole cupboards and shelves loaded with bags and crates of accessories. It was like being in Celia's box room, which she grandly referred to as her 'walk-in wardrobe' but to the power of a thousand. 'I don't know whether to throw up or burst into tears, quite frankly.'

'It's been a rough few weeks,' Celia murmured tactfully. 'And well, this is huge, isn't it? Three years of prep work to get you to this moment. You are a little bit excited, aren't you?'

'Yeah, well, I'm trying to be. I suppose there's a thin line between nervous hysteria and excitement.'

'That's the spirit,' Celia told her dryly, as she started to rifle through a rack of dresses. 'I called some stuff in for you, but more importantly, grab that plastic crate. Second shelf to the left, third crate along. Didn't like to say anything last night, but your bra is too big. I reckon you should be about a thirty-two DD now.'

Celia reckoned right and then after double-checking that the door to the cupboard was locked, Neve gingerly approached the rail of clothes.

She rejected 90 per cent of them without even trying them on. She wasn't wearing anything sleeveless, anything with a hem that finished above the knee and certainly not anything with a garish floral print. That left three dresses hanging there.

Neve tried on a multi-coloured patchwork dress with a square neck, but its drop waist bunched at her hips. Then there was a vertically striped frock, which she thought would be slimming, but it made her look like the inmate of a prison camp. As she approached the last dress, both she and Celia were holding their breath.

It was a wrap dress, made of a chocolate-brown silk jersey. Compared to some of Celia's more outrageous outfit options, it felt like an old friend. Neve slipped it on and fussed with the bell sleeves until her upper arms were adequately covered, then tied the waist sash in a bow. Only then did she deign to look at herself in the mirror that was propped against the only available piece of wall.

She looked . . . all right. More than all right. In fact, more all right than she'd ever looked, apart from the evening in Manchester when she was adorned in sequins and had big hair and a glow that had nothing to do with the huge amounts of make-up she had on. The dress skimmed over belly and bottom and made Neve's waist look positively minuscule, and if it weren't for her bare feet and her bare face and the way she was gnawing on her bottom lip, she'd look elegant and sophisticated.

'I think this works, don't you?' she said at last.

'Just so you know, that's a size eight, Diane von Fursternberg dress that you're looking absolutely gorgeous in,' Celia squeaked, then she actually tried to pick Neve up and swing her round, but thankfully she came to her senses as Neve fended her off. 'You did it, Neevy! You bloody well did it!'

'Well, that's an American size eight, which is really a twelve and it's a wrap dress so it doesn't count.'

'A size eight designer dress,' Celia said again, with heavy emphasis. 'How does it feel?'

Neve did a slow 360 degrees. 'I didn't think that size twelve would feel this flabby,' she said at last, pinching her tummy rolls. 'And I'm not a proper size twelve, I cheated my way into a size twelve.'

'For fuck's sake, Neve! Can't you be happy and just take a moment to bask in that happiness?'

Neve tried with all her might – and just as she felt the first flicker of euphoria, she heard the echo of his voice.

You'll always be a fat girl. You don't know how to be anything else.

'I'm trying, Celia,' she said imploringly. 'I was fat my entire life, I've been a size twelve for all of five minutes. It takes some adjustment.'

'You know, there was about a month when you were all loved up with Max and you never talked about your weight, or complained about what you looked like, or went on and on about how much better your life would be if you were a size ten,' Celia informed her sister savagely. 'God, I think that was the happiest month of my life.'

'Seels, that's not fair!'

'What's not fair is that I've gone to all this trouble blagging beauty appointments and calling in clothes for you, even though I'm meant to be sorting out three fashion shoots, and you haven't even said thank you.'

Neve hung her head. 'You're right. I'm so sorry.' As well as the fat girl jibe, hadn't Max also said that she was the most self-involved person he'd ever met? 'I swear I'll make this up to you.'

Celia looked unconvinced. 'You don't need to do that, but would it kill you to crack a smile?'

Neve obediently lifted up the corners of her mouth. 'How's that?'

'Like you've just had your wisdom teeth taken out,' Celia said, but she sounded less sulky, and when Neve stuck her tongue out, she grinned. 'It's just as well you're my sister, otherwise I'd have killed you by now.'

'I do appreciate this, Seels, and now that William's back and we can be together, I'll be happy,' Neve said, even as she wondered why her happiness had to be dependent on someone else. Shouldn't she be able to find happiness from within?

Celia certainly seemed to think so. 'I can get happy just from logging on to net-a-porter.com and adding expensive clothes to my wish-list,' she said. 'Or listening to Gloria Gaynor really loud. Or eyeing up gross men on the tube so they get all hot and bothered because they think they're in with a chance. Happiness really isn't that hard to find.'

'You're obviously more evolved than I am.' Neve fluffed out the skirt of her dress. 'This is actually very pretty. What shall I wear on my feet?'

'Oh, I picked you out these great Alaia sandals,' Celia enthused, her attention immediately diverted away from Neve's total happiness fail as she dropped to her knees so she could rummage through the rows of shoes on the floor. She pulled out a pair of perilously high sandals with delicate taupe leather straps. 'I had to put gaffer tape on the soles, so try to avoid any wet floors.'

Neve didn't dare argue about the wisdom of putting her

in a five-inch heel. She even sat quietly and docilely on the stool while two girls from the Beauty Department smeared products all over her comparatively pimple-free face. Neve was told that the smoky-eyed look was even more last season than bouffant ponytails and that they were going for a dewy, natural look.

The dewy, natural look took over an hour to achieve, but when the beauty girls finally returned Neve's face to its rightful owner, she was forced to concede that it had been time well spent.

Her skin looked as flawless, if not more, than it had done before she started detoxing. She had a radiant glow, her eyes were enormous, and her glossy pink lips seemed more pouty than usual.

She looked like a girl who'd get second glances as she strolled through the metropolis in her chic outfit, swinging her tan leather bag (Celia had confiscated Neve's battered satchel) and giving the impression she was someone with places to be and people to see. And actually she *was* that girl . . . with a panicked shriek, Neve looked up at the clock and realised she had half an hour to get from the *Skirt* offices in Marble Arch to the South Bank in the middle of the Friday rush hour.

'Seels, everybody, thank you so much,' she said hurriedly. 'There will be payback but I have to go. The Bakerloo line will be rammed!'

But Neve never discovered how rammed the Bakerloo line was because using public transport was strictly forbidden when you were wearing borrowed designer pieces.

Celia came down to the street with Neve to help her flag down a black cab and maybe Neve was channelling the kind of girl who'd normally wear a dress like this, because as soon as she stuck out her arm, a taxi did an illegal U-turn and pulled up alongside her.

'Thank you, thank you, thank you,' she gasped, already half in and half out of the taxi.

'I think you're all paid up on the thank-you front now,' Celia sniffed, giving Neve a quick hug. 'Now, remember, don't talk about diets and detoxes. Stick to boring books by dead dudes; should have him eating out of your palm.'

They were holding up the traffic so Neve had no choice but to shut the door and sink back on the seat as Celia stood at the kerb, waving and grinning like a loon.

Now that Neve was all gussied up and on her way to meet with destiny, there was no time to do anything but fret. From being her *raison d'être*, in the last few months William had begun to recede from the forefront of her mind and become something that she'd deal with at some unspecified moment in the future.

But the future was now, and even as she tried to think about William and possible topics for conversation, all Neve could think about was Max.

As she'd been herded out of the *Skirt* offices by Celia, she'd glimpsed a large picture of a Staffordshire Bull Terrier tacked to the wall: Keith posing for a picture and looking pretty cheesed off about it too. Just as Neve was hit with a wave of longing for Keith, she'd seen the desk with magazines neatly stacked on it, the sparkly pink spines of the WAG novels, a tub of Brylcreem perched on top of them and a framed black-and-white signed picture of Madonna – Max's desk. She'd wanted to stop and run her fingers over the things he'd touched, the things he looked at every time he sat there, but Celia's hand had been at the small of her back as she hustled Neve towards the lift and there hadn't been time.

There wasn't time now, when the only man she should be thinking about was William. Max had only been a starter boyfriend so she could make some rudimentary relationship mistakes and learn from them. In which case, romance with William should be a breeze, because she'd made so many mistakes with Max and she *had* to have learned some lessons from them, otherwise she'd have nothing to show for all those months, except a heart that was bruised and battered.

Thanks to her cabbie's love of illegal U-turns and the fact that he'd faithfully promised 'the missus I'll be back in Poplar by seven thirty sharp', Neve was deposited at the back entrance of the Royal Festival Hall at exactly ten minutes to seven. She had time to go to the bathroom and check that her make-up was still fulfilling its remit to be both dewy and natural-looking, which it was, though the waves in her hair were beginning to wilt, then slowly climb up six flights of stairs so she wouldn't arrive at the top all sweaty and out of breath.

As Neve waited at the reception desk, her hands weren't even shaking, though her toes in her borrowed sandals were clenching compulsively and she was having trouble breathing out. And breathing in for that matter.

When a waiter arrived, Neve found that she could hardly choke out William's name and the time of his reservation, so she was staggered that she still knew how to put one foot in front of the other to follow the man across the long, light room.

Her gaze was fixed rigidly on the waiter's back so when he came to a halt by one of the window tables, it was all Neve could do to peer shyly over his shoulder – and there he was; there was William calmly folding his copy of *The Times* and looking directly at her.

Chapter Forty

'Good God,' he said. Then he said it again, 'Good God.'

The waiter melted away and Neve was left without anyone to hide behind and she'd never felt this exposed and vulnerable before; not even on the waxer's couch or standing naked in a hotel room in front of Max.

She raised her hand in a feeble, half-hearted wave and decided that she might as well enjoy the stunned look on William's face because his shock at her transformation was vindication. Proof that getting up at six in the morning to go to the gym and forsaking cakes and chocolate and other sweet things and even pouring those wretched juices down her throat had all been worth it.

William's eyes ran over her again and again, then finished at her feet, where her toes were still all scrunched up because she couldn't remember how to unscrunch them.

'It's me,' she said at last, because William wasn't saying anything.

William jerked in his seat as if he was trying to force himself out of his inertia. It must have worked because he was rising gracefully to his feet.

'So it is,' he said smoothly, his hand resting on Neve's waist for one thrilling moment as he brushed his lips against her cheek. 'I'm sorry. I didn't recognise you. Have you changed your hair?'

Neve patted her hair, which was getting less tousled with every minute that passed. 'Well, yes, I suppose,' she said, as

William pulled out the chair opposite his so she could sit down. She hadn't expected him to demand to know exactly how much weight she'd lost, but the comment about her hair seemed rather disingenuous, she thought, until William sat down and smiled at her. It was a warm, genuine smile as if everything in his world was all right, just because she was sitting there.

He hadn't mentioned it because bringing up someone else's weight, or even their lack of it, was uncouth. He hadn't wanted to embarrass her.

She smiled back at him, and then his hand rested on hers for one fleeting second. 'It's been too long, Neve.'

In her head his beauty had dimmed, grown duller with time but Neve could see that her golden boy was still as golden as ever: his floppy blond hair lightened by the Californian sun, eyes bluer now his skin was so tanned. He was wearing a crisp white shirt and jeans and looked less Brideshead and more preppy, as if he'd strolled across a rolling New England lawn to get there, instead of taking the District line from Fulham Broadway.

'I've missed you so much,' Neve said, and William smiled again – and in that moment everything that had happened in the last few months was swept away, didn't matter, had never existed. There was only William. 'Three years, Will. Don't ever go away for that long again.'

'I won't, I promise,' he said, and this time his hand rested on hers and stayed there as he beckoned a waiter over. 'Shall we have champagne?'

Neve still felt almost sick with nerves, and a glass of champagne would have taken the edge off. Even better, they could have toasted their future, eyes meeting, glasses clinking, but she hadn't eaten solid food in weeks and Neve didn't want to run the risk that after two good swallows she'd be so drunk that she'd strip off her clothes and do a victory streak. 'Just water for me,' she said. 'With four lemon halves on the side.'

William had been in LA so long that he didn't blink an eye at her odd request or flinch when she squeezed all four lemon halves into her glass so the water went cloudy. 'You always were an odd little thing,' he murmured.

He made her quirks sound endearing, rather than neurotic, Neve thought gratefully as she took a sip. 'So, how have you been?' she asked. 'Tell me everything.'

He began to talk and after a minute, Neve settled back in her chair, finally able to relax. She giggled a little as William described one of the students in his tutor group and nodded sympathetically as he began to recall his battles with the Dean.

She'd been staring at the London Eye for ages, trying to track its almost imperceptibly slow rotation when Neve realised that William was now talking about lyrical poetry and she was squirming restlessly on her chair. It was the bloody Cleanse. She'd been due her evening juice hours ago so it was no surprise that she was so distracted. She straightened up and widened her eyes so she could pay attention to what William was saying.

'. . . and can one separate Pound's fascist ideology from his creative output, or are the two intrinsically linked?'

She was damned if she knew. Neve smiled vaguely. William smiled back and kept on talking, which was fine with Neve because she could rest her chin on her hand and watch the way his firm, sculpted lips moved as he made words come out of them.

He was so handsome. The kind of handsome that made her feel as if she still wasn't worthy, but when William smiled at her, as he was now that he'd reached the end of his monologue about Ezra Pound, it was like being bathed in sunlight.

Though that might have been more to do with the huge windows that took up an entire wall so Neve could gaze down at the people ambling along the banks of the river, see pleasure-cruisers chugging along the water . . .

'Neve? Am I boring you?'

She was forced to turn her attention back to William and whatever he was talking about now – she didn't have a clue. 'No, of course you're not,' she assured him. William was frowning at her as if he suspected that she hadn't been listening to a single word he was saying. 'Please go on.'

'I was just talking about the differences between academia in Britain and America, although by America, I mean the West Coast. As you know, I did my lecture on the Romantic poets at Amherst and it was received with a lot more intellectual rigour,' William said, and Neve noticed that he'd popped the collar of his shirt and kept swiping his bottom lip with his tongue as he talked.

God, I would never want to be naked with him. The thought popped into her head unprompted. It wasn't a new thought. It was a very old thought, though usually it was more of a blanket *God, I would never want to be naked with anyone, even a qualified doctor.*

I wouldn't want to see him naked either. This was new territory, because now that she thought about it, Neve had never pictured their naked bodies colliding, writhing or gently undulating against each other, the way naked bodies did when you and the love of your life were all ready to consummate that love and make it official.

Neve studied William intently, who beamed at her now he could see that she was giving him her rapt, undivided attention. He was beautiful, he was smartly dressed, he was fiercely intelligent – and she absolutely did not fancy him.

She wasn't fidgeting in her chair because she had that sweet ache low in her belly; it was because she was bored and restless. She tried to remember back to those long Oxford afternoons in William's sitting room, where they'd sit and talk for hours. Neve had been certain that she'd loved him then, but now she wasn't so sure. She'd loved to look at him, that much hadn't changed, and she'd been flattered by his attention, the time he gave all to her, but not once had she ever wanted him to pull her down in front of the roaring log fire (which had smoked more than it had roared), tear off her clothes and make frenzied, passionate love to her.

It couldn't have just been a crush. It was the real thing. It had to be.

William had finally finished picking holes in the American schools system, and to test out her new, alarming theory, Neve squeezed her elbows together to give herself a cleavage and looked at him from under her lashes, a half smile on her lips.

The only time she'd ever tried that out on Max, and then it had been completely unintentional, he told her never to do it again, especially not in Caffè Nero, because he was five seconds away from dragging her to the loos and doing something that would get them banned from every Caffè Nero in the country.

William gave her breasts a reflexive glance, his eyes lingering for a brief moment that should have had Neve tingling and suddenly getting short of breath, but she felt nothing. Not even when his leg brushed against hers as he shifted position.

Neve sighed and folded her arms. 'So,' she said. 'You told me you had two surprises in store for me, so maybe you should start with this big, life-changing question you have to ask me?'

When William asked her out, or God forbid, declared his love, she'd feel it. She had to.

'Are you sure you're ready for it?' William asked playfully.

'Please, William, I'm in an agony of suspense here,' Neve said, and she was dry-mouthed and slightly trembly but she couldn't tell if it was anticipation, dread or Cleanse withdrawal.

'How would you feel about coming to live with me in Warwickshire?'

'I beg your pardon?' Neve spluttered, because it fell

somewhere between being asked out and a marriage proposal.

'Well, not *with* me, but it would mean relocating,' William said, and Neve wanted to scream at him to get to the bloody point. 'I'm taking up the post of Senior Lecturer in the English Department at the University of Warwickshire and you're going to be my research assistant.'

'I am?' All Neve felt was relief that William wasn't asking her something that would lead to both of them getting naked. Relief and inestimable amounts of confusion. 'Aren't most research assistants PhD students?'

'I talked to the Dean of Post-graduate Studies and he's more than happy to accept you on to their PhD programme,' William revealed proudly. 'I'm sure you'll have no trouble getting funding and, of course, I can help you out with a small stipend, though you won't be able to supplement that with teaching until your second year. I thought you could expand on your MA dissertation for your thesis. What was it on again?'

'Between the Wars: Reclaiming the Feminist Novel,' Neve answered in a small, tight voice because William should have *remembered* the title of her MA dissertation, considering she'd written him enough letters about it. 'Sorry, William, forgive me if I'm being dense, but what made you think that I wanted to start working on a doctorate thesis?'

William looked at Neve as if she wasn't just being dense, but wilfully and deliberately dense. 'Well, you can't be my research assistant unless you're a PhD student,' he explained impatiently. 'I know you wanted a couple of years off, but every day you spend in that library is a day that your intellectual muscles are atrophying.'

'It's not a library, it's a *literary archive*,' Neve snapped. 'I like working there and I flex my intellectual muscles every day, thank you very much.'

'Of course you do,' William said appeasingly. 'Or you

think you do, but that's only because you've gone so long without the vigour of daily academic debate.'

They had vigorous daily debates at the Archive, but they were mostly about which cardigan Our Lady of the Blessed Hankie would be wearing when she turned up five minutes after they opened or guessing the origins of the new stains on Mr Freemont's tie.

'I like working there,' Neve repeated firmly. 'I like the people who work there and I get to do different things every day. I'm even going on an advanced book repair course in the autumn and I'm wri—'

'But I'm planning to write a book,' William interrupted, taking the words right out of her mouth.

'Oh . . .'

'Ah, I thought that might persuade you where all else failed,' William said. 'I think I might like to write a couple of volumes on the correlation between Romanticism and the Modern Age.'

'But Romanticism isn't my speciality.'

'Yes, but you wouldn't be writing it, I would,' William reminded her. 'Though of course, I couldn't do it without your help.'

'William . . .'

'I thought we'd work on a synopsis and the first three chapters, then start shopping it to agents and—'

'William!' Neve had to say his name very sharply so they could talk about her. 'I'm already writing a book. Well, I've started anyway.'

'*You're* writing a book?' There was no need for him to sound quite so incredulous, or look faintly amused. 'A novel?'

'No, it's a biography of Lucy Keener and I'm editing her poems and short stories, though my agent thinks that we might publish them separately, after he's got a deal for her novel,' Neve said, and she'd wanted to impart her news with pride but William had a furrowed brow and he didn't look particularly ecstatic, so she kept it down to an apologetic mumble.

'You have an agent?' William asked, with a faint edge to his voice.

'Yeah . . . well, Jacob Morrison. He worked at the Archive when he came down from Cambridge and now he's on the Board of Trustees.' Neve shrugged. 'It might not come to anything, but—'

'No, it's wonderful. I'm very happy for you; it just took me rather by surprise,' William said. He swallowed hard as if he was gulping down on his own disappointment and pique, but then he gave her one of those smiles that she'd lived for when she was at Oxford. 'Well done, you.'

'I'm sorry,' Neve said, and now it was her turn to cover his hand and squeeze his fingers. 'I didn't mean to suddenly hit you with it. I was going to write and tell you but I've not been such a good correspondent over the last few months, have I?'

'Well, it sounds as if you've had a lot going on,' William said. He entwined his fingers with hers and the only thing that Neve felt was sadness that she'd wasted so much time loving a William who existed only in her head. 'You're not really going to make me forage for myself in the wilds of Warwickshire?'

They went back and forth for nearly an hour, William extolling the virtues of the University of Warwickshire's English Department, the beautiful countryside, the thriving arts scene and how he absolutely couldn't manage without her, none of which were the selling points they should have been.

Neve was still trying to process the shocking information that she wasn't madly and passionately in love with William, but even if she still was, 'I'm a London girl, born and bred,' she insisted. 'Warwickshire's the country and the country's full of big lumbering animals that smell awful and I don't do wellies.'

William smiled again, though by now it was lacking its usual wattage. 'I wouldn't mind if you wanted to tinker with your book in your own time.'

Hadn't he heard a single word she'd said? Neve narrowed her eyes and was all ready to snap out another, much more explicit refusal, when she saw William's eyes flit appreciatively over her again. Was this his way of saying that he wanted to be with her in a mutually supportive literary relationship like Elizabeth Barrett and Robert Browning, or Scott and Zelda Fitzgerald? Though that hadn't worked out well for poor old Lizzie or Zelda. 'I'm afraid I must regretfully decline your kind offer,' Neve joked feebly, as William frowned.

'This doesn't have anything to do with your, er, *transformation*?' He waved a vague hand in the direction of her size twelve body. 'I'm trying to understand, so forgive me if I don't put this very elegantly, but now that you look the way you do, do you feel as if you don't need to try so hard on the intellectual front?'

As soon as the words were out of his mouth, Neve could tell that he regretted them. Though that might have had something to do with the way she was glaring at him. '*Excuse me?*' she spat, and as Dougie and Celia always pointed out, it didn't matter that Neve never swore because she could make 'Excuse me?' sound like 'Go fuck yourself.' 'You think I did all *this* so I could give my over-taxed brain a rest? Is that what you really think?'

William's hands fluttered ineffectually. 'Neve . . . I'm sorry. That came out all wrong, I was rather scared that it might.' He brushed his hair back from his forehead. 'So, coming to Warwick with me is a categorical no?'

She nodded, still so angry with him that she didn't trust herself to speak.

'You're full of surprises this evening,' William said, reaching up to fiddle with his collar because her fury and her glaring had left him discomfited. 'It's not just the way you look – you've changed since I've been away.'

'It's been three years,' Neve said, and she made a conscious decision to let her anger go. It wasn't worth it and William wasn't to blame for failing to live up to her expectations of him. There wasn't a man alive, not even the Dalai Lama, who could be *that* perfect. She didn't measure too highly on the perfect scale either. 'I don't think all the changes I've made have necessarily been for the better.'

'I think that's called getting older.'

'Well, whatever it is, it sucks.'

They sat there for a while, neither of them saying anything. Neve began to wonder how long she had to sit there, before an appropriate length of time had passed and she could make her excuses and leave. Meeting up with William had been nothing but one agony after another and she needed to be on her own to lick her metaphorical wounds, pack away all those silly adolescent dreams and come to terms with the knowledge that if William wasn't her golden ticket, then all she had to look forward to was a life that didn't have Max in it. A miserable, lonely little life.

Neve lifted her head to tell William that, or at least mutter something about a subsequent appointment, but William wasn't even looking at her. He was gazing across the room. Then he suddenly smiled.

Neve thought she'd memorised all his smiles, but she'd never seen this one before. William looked incandescent as he lifted his hand and waved frantically at someone.

Neve peered over her shoulder to see a girl coming towards their table, her own smile just as luminous as William's.

William stood up, in time for the girl to throw her arms around him. 'Baby,' she said in an American accent. 'I missed you.'

'I missed you too,' William said, and even his voice sounded different: softer, lighter, happier. 'The afternoon seemed to last an eternity.'

The girl giggled, then giggled some more as William

tickled her waist as he let her go. The only person who wasn't smiling or giggling or doing anything but sitting there with a frozen look on her face was Neve.

William went off to find another chair and Neve tried to smile but it felt more like a grimace as the girl gave her a friendly but slightly blank look, as if she hadn't expected to find Neve sitting there.

She was beautiful. Maybe the most beautiful girl that Neve had ever seen in real life. She was tall and slim, not just slim, but lithe and toned with long, naturally wavy caramel-coloured hair that she pushed back with a nervous hand so Neve could get a better look at her face, which was perfectly symmetrical, free from make-up and gorgeous. Neve marvelled that they could both have eyes, nose and mouth, but while hers were wholly unremarkable, this girl's features looked as if they'd been sculpted by some divine hand.

And, of course, she was wearing faded blue jeans, a white T-shirt and flip-flops with an easy elegance that made them look like haute couture, while Neve was sitting there in a borrowed dress and bra, a pair of Spanx, sandals that were cutting into her feet, hair that was getting lanker and limper by the second and a natural look that had taken two people an hour to achieve.

'There you are, baby,' William announced proudly, placing a leather chair in front of the girl, as if he'd personally gone all the way to the Conran Shop and carried it back on his shoulders. 'What would you like to drink?'

The vision wanted a glass of Chardonnay, William was ordering another bottle of lager and Neve knew that she couldn't get up and go, not for at least another half-hour, but she couldn't sit there sober.

'I'll have a glass of Sauvignon Blanc,' she told the waiter. 'A large glass.'

'So, Amy, this is Neve, who made my last three years at Oxford bearable,' William said, as Amy proffered a hand for

Neve to shake. 'Neve, this is the other surprise I wanted to tell you about. I'd like you to meet Amy, my very dear friend from LA who's, well . . . somehow I've managed to convince her to . . .' William took a deep breath. 'I'll try that one again. Neve, I'd like you to meet Amy, my fiancée.'

Neve's hands were sweaty but Amy didn't flinch as they shook hands, only smiled uncertainly. 'Oh! Neve! But you're *so* pretty,' she said, then giggled nervously. 'I mean, William's told me so much about you.'

That's funny, Neve thought. He's told me absolutely nothing about you.

'You never said . . .' she began accusingly, because there had been all those letters and not once had William thought to mention that he was head over heels in love with another woman and planning to plight his troth, but then she stopped. There had been some oblique references to a close friend and something about frozen yogurt. Amy looked like the kind of girl who'd be evangelical about . . . what was it? *The refreshing delights of frozen yogurt.* Neve willed her hectoring, spiteful inner voice to shut the hell up. At least, William had implied, whereas there were many, many things she hadn't felt the need to enlighten him about with even a vague hint.

The waiter arrived with their drinks and Neve practically snatched her glass off his tray and took a swift gulp. She could feel the alcohol sizzling all the way down to her empty stomach.

They were both looking at her nervously as if their future happiness depended on her reaction to their nuptials. There was no point in sitting there feeling bitter and jealous when she'd already relinquished any claim on William.

Neve raised her glass so her wine was transformed into liquid gold as it was backlit by the spectacular sunset outside. 'Congratulations,' she said. 'I hope you have a very long, very happy marriage.'

Amy giggled again and William let out a breath. He had

every right to be nervous – in all the time that he was giving her the hard sell on upping sticks and leaving her job to follow him to the Midlands, he hadn't thought to tell her that she was going to play third wheel.

'I wanted it to be a surprise,' William explained weakly.

'Well, mission accomplished,' Neve said, because just one good gulp of wine was enough to make her light-headed and loose-tongued. She turned to Amy. 'Anyway, it's a *lovely* surprise. So, how did you two meet?'

They'd met in a coffee shop where Amy was waiting tables. Not even because she was taking acting lessons and had grand ambitions to get spotted by a talent scout or an agent but because, 'I figured I could either wait tables in Des Moines, Iowa, or I could wait tables in Hollywood.' Amy had mucked up William's order of a chai latte and a bran muffin, and it had been love at first sight. Then during their roadtrip, because, of course, he'd taken Amy on his literary odyssey, William had realised that he couldn't bear to leave Amy on the wrong side of the Atlantic and had gone down on one knee in the hallway of Rowan Oak, William Faulkner's former home in Oxford, Mississippi.

Neve wanted Amy to be a bitch so she could hate her, just a little, but she wasn't. She was sweet and disarming, as if she didn't know she was so beautiful she could get away with being neither. The only downside to Amy was her giggle, which was starting to grate on Neve's tattered nerves, and her serious lack of book smarts or street smarts or any other kind of smarts.

'I thought it always rained in England,' she told Neve. 'But it's *so* sunny. Do you think it will be sunny in War-wick?'

'Baby, I told you, the second w is silent,' William said. Amy still had her head turned in Neve's direction so she couldn't see him rolling his eyes or looking at Neve with a rueful smile that she was supposed to return.

But she didn't. So Amy wasn't the sharpest tool – William

still wanted to marry her. Despite all his intellect and know-ledge of fourth-wave feminism, he'd still chosen beauty over brains; wanted to settle down with a girl who was gorgeous and giggly but who would never be able to even pronounce Heidegger, let alone debate the finer points of *Being and Time*. And he'd had the nerve to tell Neve that her drastic makeover had decreased her IQ points.

Neve smiled vaguely at Amy as the other girl chattered away excitedly about how she couldn't wait to see War-wick and felt another pang of regret that William had fallen a few more inches off his pedestal. She'd spent all those years obsessing and pining over William's mind and beauty, but she'd never even noticed what he lacked.

He wasn't funny, he wasn't perceptive, he didn't get her, not at all, and God, he wasn't Max.

'. . . dating, Neve?'

She blinked as Amy said her name and realised that her glass was almost empty, the room was spinning around her and they were both looking at her expectantly.

'I'm sorry,' she said. 'I didn't quite catch that.'

'Amy was just asking you if you were dating anyone?' William explained, giving his fiancée a stern look. 'You're not in California any more, baby. Generally, it's impolite to ask strangers personal questions the first time you meet them.'

'Oh, sorry, Neve. I didn't mean to be rude.'

'You weren't,' she said, giving William a reproachful look. 'I've known William for years so if you two are engaged, then we're not strangers, are we? We're friends who don't know each other that well . . . yet.'

Amy nodded. 'I'd like that.'

'Me too,' Neve said, and she was surprised to find that she meant it. She felt a little sorry for Amy, swapping the sunny West Coast for a smaller, greyer life in a town where she wouldn't know anyone except William. 'Warwick's not that far from London on the train.'

'That's very kind of you,' William said, though he didn't sound like he was about to turn cartwheels at the thought of them becoming BFF.

'You must be dating,' Amy persisted, as William sighed. 'William's always saying how smart you are but he never told me that you were *so* gorgeous. I mean, like, I saw pictures, but y'know . . . you don't look *anything* like that now.'

'Amy . . .' William sighed again and she turned to him with a helpless shrug and a hurt look.

'I've lost a lot of weight since William last saw me,' Neve said, her voice lacking any pride in the achievement. 'I wanted that to be *my* surprise.'

'Yes, well, it suits you,' William said uncomfortably, because he didn't want to acknowledge this new, *gorgeous* Neve as the girl he used to know. Neve understood that now. If he had loved her at all, even in the smallest way, it had been for her brains and her slavish devotion to him. Having to confront the fact that Neve was more than just brains, that she might actually be a sexual being, had to be as much of a headspin for him as it was for Neve to discover that she didn't love him and that even if she did, he wanted to spend the rest of his life with someone who wasn't her.

It was all so painfully, horribly awkward that Neve wanted to slide off her chair and hide under the table. Instead she smiled inanely, Amy giggled and William summoned up a slightly manic grin, as he squeezed both their hands. 'So, goodness, isn't that fantastic? My two best girls finally get to meet each other.'

Amy and Neve both murmured in agreement and Neve wasn't sure how much more of this she could take because it was just so . . .

'Anyway, Neve, you never said if you were dating or not?' Amy asked again, and Neve suspected that the other girl was more desperate to plug the gaping hole in the conversation rather than get the lowdown on her love-life.

Besides, this was the part that Neve had rehearsed over and over again, though when she had, it was William asking the question. And she'd reply in a casual, insouciant way so he'd know that she wasn't the silly, fat girl he'd left behind. She was a woman of the world.

'I was seeing someone.' She manoeuvred the words past the huge lump in her throat. 'But it didn't work out.'

'Oh, that's too bad,' Amy cooed. 'Did he have commitment issues?'

Neve swiftly shook her head because she wasn't sure that she was even capable of speech any more. It was all too much. The expectation, the disappointment and, worst of all, now that William was no longer a distraction, all she could feel was the pain of not having Max.

'It was all my fault,' she said, her voice trembling. 'I ruined everything and he said terrible things and I deserved every single one of them.'

She stayed for another hour, another glass of wine, and she could see William surreptitiously glancing at his watch and Amy biting her lip and shooting him anguished looks as Neve talked about Max. She managed to steer clear of any mention of pancakes, but telling William and Amy about the myriad ways she'd screwed up and how much she missed Max still gave Neve plenty to talk about.

Halfway through, she noticed the way William was looking at her – that soft, tender look she remembered so well. But the scales had fallen from her eyes and she recognised it for what it really was: pity. Not even sympathy, which would have been kinder, but pity – and that was when she started to cry.

In the end, William lied and said that he and Amy had made dinner reservations in Fulham. Neve knew he was lying because his face flushed and he tugged at his shirt collar and Amy blurted out, 'I thought we were just going back to your place,' but she wouldn't have wanted to be around herself either.

They led her out of the bar and down all six flights of stairs, hiccuping softly because she was all cried out now.

'Shall we walk across the bridge to Embankment?' William wondered aloud, as Amy tucked her arm into Neve's. 'Or is Waterloo all right?'

'I have to get a cab,' Neve sniffed. 'I have gaffer tape on the soles of my sandals.'

She wasn't sure, out of the three of them, who was more relieved when she was finally deposited in the back of a black cab and crossing the river back to north London.

As luck would have it, she got a chatty driver who wanted to talk about the appalling season Arsenal had just had. Neve suspected that she started crying again because it was the only way to get him to shut up.

'Bad break-up, love? He's not worth it.'

He is. Max is worth every single tear, she thought as they turned into Stroud Green Road. Through blurred eyes, she looked at the wig shop and the funeral directors, before she saw the friendly glow of Tesco's.

'You can let me out here!' Neve yelped.

She lasted for thirty seconds of gaffer-taped soles slapping against hard pavement, thin leather straps cutting and chafing her skin, before she unbuckled her sandals and walked into Tesco's with bare feet.

The security guard gave her a dirty look as she took a basket but Neve didn't care. She didn't care about anything any more. There was this hollow ache inside her and she knew of only one way to fill it, because being a size twelve sucked like nothing had ever sucked before.

At least when she was fat her flesh had shielded her from the world. People hadn't seen her, they'd just seen her fat, and as far as they were concerned, her fat meant that she was lazy and stupid and it had been easy to exceed their expectations. It was impossible not to when the bar was raised so low that it had almost touched the floor.

Her fat had been a Get Out of Jail Free card. Her fat was

to blame for the jobs she didn't get and the love affairs she'd never had and all the slights and rejections and the failures. If she wasn't fat, then there was nothing left to hide behind. *She* was the problem. Neve understood now that when she'd been a size thirty-two, she'd been insulated and protected and safe. She'd give anything to feel like that again.

Chapter Forty-one

A box of Tunnock's Tea Cakes was the first thing she tossed in her basket. Neve looked down at them and hesitated. Then her stomach growled, her heart ached and her throat felt raw from crying. She was *so* doing this.

Her mind made up, the rest was easy. Brightly coloured bags of crisps, salt and vinegar, cheese and onion, and bacon. How had she managed to live without bacon-flavoured crisps for so long? Chocolate Hobnobs, chocolate digestives, chocolate cake liberally smeared with thick chocolate butter-cream frosting – anything as long as it was chocolate. There was cheese too, which she'd grill and pile on to thick sliced white bread and coat in tomato ketchup. A tub of Ben & Jerry's Chunky Monkey ice cream and one of Phish Food too while she was at it – and she hadn't even been down the confectionery aisle yet. Neve hurled fistfuls of chocolate into her heavy basket and tucked a huge bottle of full-fat Coke under her arm on the way to the till.

Then she walked home, the pavement cutting into the soles of her feet, but she didn't care. What was a little more pain when you were already one gigantic ball of hurt? When you'd wasted years of your life loving someone who only existed in your head, and in your desperate pursuit of that love, you failed to see that you already had some-thing that was real and special and utterly precious?

Neve stumbled up her garden path, tutting furiously when she had to put down her precious cargo and fish for

529

her keys. The house was in darkness and as Neve fumbled for the light switch, three heavy carrier bags awkwardly clutched in one hand, she stumbled, stubbed her toe against the wheel of her bike and screamed as it toppled off its kickstand and crashed against her legs.

'Oh, for God's sake!' Neve was trapped between the wall and her bike, her foot pinned under the handlebars. She didn't even have room to put down her shopping, but had to huff and puff like a little piggy as she lifted the bike off her foot and sent it clattering back against the opposite wall.

Neve hopped on one leg, as she tried to simultaneously put down her bags and clutch her injured foot. Her toes felt as if they were crushed beyond all repair, and as she doubled over from the weight of her shopping, the shooting pains in her foot made her want to throw up because she had a very low pain threshold and . . .

'What the fuck are you doing?' From darkness came light and Charlotte's voice screaming down the stairs. 'Can't you fucking do anything quietly?'

Neve glanced up to see Charlotte's malevolent face peering over the banisters. She ignored her because now the lights were on she was able to look down at her foot in all its mangled glory. She slowly unpeeled her fingers from around her foot to find that her big toenail had lifted up and blood was oozing out.

'Oh God,' she mumbled, and she wanted to steel herself to investigate further, to see just how firmly attached her nail was, but even the abstract thought of an unattached toenail made her shudder – and anyway, Charlotte was storming down the stairs.

'What is your problem?' Charlotte demanded, before she'd even reached the bottom. 'I can't live with your constant noise and you left your washing on the line all day like you're the only one who wants to use it. You're selfish! You're, like, the most selfish person I've ever met.'

'I'm sorry, Charlotte,' Neve snapped. 'I'm a little busy here.'

'If you didn't leave it there, you wouldn't have fallen over your bike in the first place,' Charlotte snapped back, stabbing an angry finger into Neve's chest for emphasis. 'And you wouldn't have fallen over it, if you weren't such a fat cow.'

'What did you just say?' Neve said, her voice eerily calm, which was odd because on the inside she was screaming.

Charlotte *was* screaming. 'Are you deaf as well as stupid?' She jabbed her rigid finger into Neve even harder. 'You're as fat and disgusting as you were at school. I can't believe I ended up living underneath Neve the Heave.'

Neve swallowed hard, took a deep breath and stood there motionless, so still that she could feel the hot, humid air of the night stir around her. 'Get your hand off me,' she said in a constricted voice that didn't even sound like her.

'Oh, what are you going to do about it?' Charlotte sneered.

Neve didn't even feel her hand come up, not until her palm cracked against Charlotte's cheek, the blow jarring all the way up Neve's arm and rocking the other girl into the wall.

'I am not fat! I am not stupid! How fucking dare you? What gives you the fucking right to treat me like crap?' Each word was punctuated by a blow, as she pounded her fists against any part of Charlotte that she could reach as her sister-in-law twisted and flailed in her efforts to get away from her. 'I hate you! I hate every bone in your fucking miserable body.'

Charlotte was screaming right back at her and when she realised that Neve wasn't going to stop, she fought back, punching her way out of the corner that Neve had boxed her into.

They crunched over Neve's shopping but Neve didn't care about anything other than gouging Charlotte's eyes out and getting her hands round her throat so she could stop her hateful, vile words once and for all.

'I'm going to fucking kill you!' she shouted, until she realised that Charlotte wasn't shouting back and that the banging she could hear was coming from next door where it sounded like the Scoins had a battering ram aimed at the party wall.

It was enough to catch Neve off-guard and Charlotte lunged at her, not to scratch or hit but to wrap her arms tightly around Neve. 'Stop it,' she said sharply. 'Just stop it, Neevy.'

Her legs didn't want to hold her up any more so Neve sank to the floor, Charlotte still holding her as she sat there, shaking and panting heavily. Slowly she came back to the present, where her face was buried in Charlotte's neck and her foot still hurt and she had a hundred other aches and pains both inside and out.

'Let me go,' she said, struggling to free herself.

Charlotte didn't budge. 'Promise you won't try and strangle me again.'

'I promise,' Neve said. Her words must have passed muster because Charlotte's arms fell away, leaving Neve feeling curiously bereft as she raised her head and looked right into the eyes of her enemy. Or the left eye because the right eye was red and almost swollen shut. 'Oh God, did I do that?'

'Yeah, and it hurts like hell,' Charlotte said – she sounded surprisingly unconcerned. 'It's OK. I split your lip.'

Neve put her hand to her mouth and gingerly prodded her bottom lip; her hand came away bloody. Her wrap dress had unwrapped and she was about to peer down her legs to see how her big toenail had fared in the mêlée, when Charlotte picked up a tub of rapidly melting Chunky Monkey.

'What is all this crap?' she asked, gesturing at the debris that littered the hall floor: broken biscuits and crisps burst free of their packets, tomato ketchup arcing across the wall so the entrance looked like a scene from a splatter movie.

'It's my food,' Neve said defiantly. 'I bought it and I'm going to take it upstairs and eat it. All of it.'

'No, you're not,' Charlotte said. 'You can't eat stuff like this any more 'cause it will make you fat again.'

'Well, according to you, I'm still fat so what difference does it make?' Neve braced her legs and tried to stand up, but it proved too much effort. 'Stop being nice to me. It's not convincing and it's not going to make me see the error of my ways and guilt me into saying sorry to you.'

Charlotte didn't say anything at first. She stretched her legs out in front of her and gave Neve a thoughtful look. 'You *are* noisy . . .' she began.

'And most of the time I'm as quiet as a bloody mouse,' Neve hissed. She hated feeling angry all of the time, so she was turned inside out and back to front but never right way round again. It was exhausting. 'I've sat upstairs before, not moving, hardly even daring to breathe, and you've still banged on the ceiling with your bloody broom.'

'Yes, but—'

'But nothing! It's my home! I'm meant to be able to shut the door and escape from the world, but I'm scared to even make a cup of tea because it sets you off. And FYI, I'm perfectly entitled to use the washing line a couple of days a week and walk up the stairs to my flat and—'

'You don't know what it's like living underneath you,' Charlotte insisted, but she wouldn't look at Neve; she stared at a squashed loaf of bread instead. 'Every sound carries.'

'Sure it does, and if I'm so noisy, then how come you never start on Celia and Yuri who slam doors and play loud music and you never made a fuss when you knew Max was there?' Just saying his name and remembering how it felt to have him with her was an ache that would still be there long after her lip stopped throbbing and her toe no longer felt as if it was damaged beyond salvation. 'You're just a bully. You always have been and you always will be.'

'I'm not a bully.' Charlotte sounded indignant. 'We just don't get on, that's all.'

Neve stared at her in disbelief. 'We don't get on because

you waged a hate campaign against me at school; you called me that awful name and you took my clothes after PE and you got your friends to spit at me. And OK, when you married Dougie I didn't exactly roll out the welcome mat but it's not as if you ever apologised. Why won't you admit it?'

Charlotte wrinkled her nose. 'When we were at school . . .' She looked up to the ceiling for inspiration. 'I was really unhappy and picking on you made me feel better.'

'Is that the best you can do?'

'I'm trying to explain,' Charlotte said, pulling a face. 'I'm not good with, like, words and stuff. My dad had left and I went out with Dougie for two weeks and then he dumped me *and* I got put in Remedial English. I was such a loser so I just made out that you were a bigger loser and it made me feel better.'

'But why *me*?'

'Well, you were Dougie's sister and it was easier to take it out on you than him – you talked posh and you always had your head in a book.' Charlotte, at last, was beginning to look sheepish. Neve would rather she looked ashamed, but she'd settle for sheepish. 'And I knew you wouldn't fight back.'

'And I was fat,' Neve reminded her.

'Well, see, you weren't,' Charlotte said. 'I mean, you were a bit porky, but you weren't fat *fat*. Not to start with.'

'I've always been fat *fat*,' Neve said tartly, but, for once, that wasn't important. 'So, why did you decide to reinstate your reign of terror?'

'What?'

'Why have you been bullying me again?' Neve asked quietly.

Charlotte looked away again, then winced as she levered herself up and got to her feet. 'Look, we need to clear up this mess.' She swivelled around to look at her Juicy

Coutured rear end. 'I've been sitting in ice cream and—'

'I asked you a question, Charlotte.'

'I know you did.' Charlotte walked towards the stairs. 'You can come up to mine, if you like.'

Neve really didn't have a choice, so she followed Charlotte into the first-floor flat that she'd never been in since it had been converted.

It was bland and impersonal; a symphony of magnolia and oatmeal, taupe and cream. Almost as if Charlotte and Dougie had decorated it solely for the purpose of having a neutral interior that would appeal to prospective buyers because neither of them planned on sticking around that long. The only personal touch was a wedding photo on the mantelpiece. Charlotte and Dougie were standing on either side of the Elvis impersonator who'd married them in Vegas. Neve had never seen Charlotte look so happy as she beamed a gummy smile while Dougie stood there looking red-faced and uncomfortable.

Charlotte walked into the lounge with a roll of black bin bags and a bucket of hot soapy water. 'Shall we sort out the hall?'

They worked quickly and silently as they dumped the ruined food in the garbage bags and stacked them by the front door. Then Neve washed the ketchup off the walls as Charlotte tackled the pools of melted ice cream.

Then they were back in Charlotte's flat, sitting at her kitchen table, drinking tea. Charlotte had changed into a clean tracksuit and had a bag of frozen peas pressed against her eye, and Neve had her foot propped up on her chair, her big toe padded with gauze and a towel draped over it because they'd both agreed that even looking at it made them both want to dry heave.

It was progress of a sort.

Just as Neve decided that she'd lost her advantage and Charlotte would never confess the rest of the awful truth, she put down her mug and looked steadily at Neve.

'Dougie doesn't love me,' she said. 'I don't think he ever did, not really. Just married me to prove to your dad that he was a proper grown-up.'

Suddenly Neve didn't think she wanted to hear the rest of Charlotte's confession. Not if it was going where she thought it was going.

'I'm sure that's not the case,' she said weakly.

'Nah, it is.' Charlotte rested her elbows on the table. 'I've loved him ever since Year Nine and I thought if I loved him enough, then eventually I could make him love me back.'

'It doesn't work like that, does it?' Neve was thinking of William; all that energy she'd expounded on loving him. The thing about love was that it caught you unawares, turned up in the most unexpected places, even when you weren't looking for it.

'You can say that again,' said Charlotte, getting up and walking to the freezer to swap the frozen peas for frozen carrots. With her back to Neve, she said, 'He's shagging someone else. Lots of someone elses.'

Neve shut her eyes. She didn't want to feel sorry for Charlotte and she was sure that Charlotte didn't want her sympathy, but she could empathise. When Amy had turned up earlier that evening, she'd been annoyed, had even felt a little betrayed, but it was nothing compared to the agony she felt at the thought of Max with someone else. He'd probably shagged lots of someone elses too by now.

'I'm sorry,' she said, and she meant it.

'You don't have to be,' Charlotte said matter-of-factly, pulling out the chair and sitting down again. 'He drinks too much and he stays out all night and I don't say anything. Then I scream at him for all kinds of stupid shit that doesn't matter because I'm too scared to talk about the stuff that does matter.'

'Because then he might say he doesn't love you and walk out for good,' Neve guessed.

Charlotte looked at her in surprise. 'Yeah. How did you

know that?' She gave Neve the ghost of a smile. 'You're really, really smart.'

'Oh, in some ways I'm really, really stupid,' Neve said. She put down her mug and folded her arms. 'This has got to stop. Neither of us can live like this. You have to stop making *me* feel like shit because *you* feel like shit. Does that even work?'

'Not really,' Charlotte said, and then she started to cry.

It was horrible. Neve could tell that Charlotte was humiliated at the thought of crying in front of her, because she curled in on herself so Neve couldn't see her face through the curtain of hair. She kept trying to swallow down the sobs, which just made them sound even more desperate and pitiful as they were wrenched from her.

There was nothing Neve could do, so she did nothing. She simply sat there quietly, and when it seemed like Charlotte was done, she got up, soaked a piece of kitchen roll under the tap and gave it to her, her hand on Charlotte's shoulder for one brief moment.

Charlotte carefully dabbed at her cheeks. 'It really hurts to cry when you've got a black eye.'

'Hurts to drink hot tea with a split lip,' Neve offered and they shared a weak smile.

'You know what, Neevy? He won't even hold my fucking hand when we're walking down the street. How fucked up is that?'

'It's very fucked up.' Neve glanced up at the clock. It was past midnight, which was early considering that she felt as if she'd lived several lifetimes over the last few hours. 'It's late. I should be going.'

'Are we friends now, then?' Charlotte asked doubtfully.

'I think friends is pushing it.' Charlotte looked a little put out by that. 'Shall we just say that we've called a truce with a ceasefire effective immediately?'

'You what?'

'We don't actively hate each other any more.' Though

Neve wasn't sure that she exactly liked Charlotte, she no longer thought of her as evil incarnate either. 'Sound good?'

Charlotte nodded. 'Yeah, I mean, I can't see us hanging out at Nando's or nothing but we're cool.'

'Great.' Neve stood up. 'I'm going upstairs and I'm not going to tiptoe around any more, just so you know.'

'Like you even could with your toenail hanging off,' Charlotte scoffed.

'You never said it was hanging off! You said it had just come away at the sides!' Neve peered down at the gauze, which was streaked with pink, and felt every single one of her internal organs judder in revulsion. 'God, I think I'm going to be sick.'

She started hobbling towards the door. Charlotte had disappeared into her bedroom, but just as Neve stepped on to the landing, she reappeared. 'I want you to have this,' she said, handing Neve a neatly folded pile of velour. 'Just to say I'm sorry and all that.'

Neve looked down at the sherbet-pink fabric. 'Is this . . . ?' She couldn't finish the question, because, really, there were no adequate words.

Charlotte nodded. 'It's one of my Juicy Couture tracksuits.' She looked a bit misty-eyed at the thought of parting with it.

'I can't accept this,' Neve said firmly, because tracksuits were solely for the gym and anyway, it was pink.

'I'll be dead offended if you don't.' As threats went, it was a winner as Neve knew only too well what an offended Charlotte was capable of.

'It won't even fit me,' Neve protested. 'You're much smaller than I am.'

'Don't start all that again,' Charlotte snapped. 'I only said you were fat 'cause I knew it wound you up. You're not, OK? You know that, right?'

'Well, of course I know that, but I've been on this detox Cleanse which is the only reason that I'm this, well not slim, but *unfat* at the moment.'

Charlotte's face was contorting into familiar, scornful lines. 'What are you talking about, you silly cow?' she demanded. 'I've been a size fourteen since I was fourteen and you've been the same size as me for months. Maybe even smaller.'

Neve looked Charlotte up and down. Charlotte was curvy but it was slim and compact curvy. Not jiggly, wiggly curvy. 'But you *look* much smaller than I do.' She shook her head. 'Honestly, I don't know any more. I can't tell if I'm fat, if I'm slim or I'm somewhere in the middle.'

'You know what your problem is? You think too much about stuff,' Charlotte summed up. 'I try not to think about stuff at all. Now just take the bloody tracksuit.'

Neve took it because their ceasefire appeared to hang in the balance. Besides, she couldn't wait to see Celia's face when she modelled it for her.

Back in her own flat, Neve walked into the bathroom and started the shower as she stripped off the DVF dress, took off her borrowed bra and unrolled her Spanx.

Showering was a tricky business standing on one leg with her injured foot poking out of the shower curtain so she didn't get the dressing wet. The hot water rained down on her, washing all the product out of her hair and the natural look off her face.

Neve stepped out of the shower and after she'd wrapped her hair in a towel, she tucked another around her and began to slap on body lotion in a half-hearted fashion. Combed out her hair. Brushed her teeth. Scrutinised what was left of her zits in the mirror. Dabbed some cream around her eyes because Celia was absolutely adamant that it was never too soon to stave off the appearance of fine lines.

She turned away from her reflection and was just about to scurry from the bathroom, when she stopped, turned and faced the mirror again. She stood there for a long time, her apprehensive face staring back at her, then unfastened the towel and let it fall to the floor.

Oh my God, you look awful!

It was her first thought – an automatic reaction to looking at herself naked. Though when she thought about it, Neve couldn't remember ever looking at herself naked. She tended to get out of the shower with her back to the mirror and would only turn around when she was enveloped in a bath sheet. If by some accident she did look in the mirror while she was naked, she quickly averted her eyes so all she had was a vague impression of acres of wobbly, dimpled flesh.

Tonight she was going to stand naked in front of the mirror for as long as it took for all the self-doubt, self-loathing and self-delusion to dissipate so she could see what other people saw when they looked at her.

It took a while for her shadow self, the Neve of three years ago, to fade away. It took even longer to stop focusing on one specific area of her body and take it all in.

Actually, you don't look that *awful.*

She looked like a woman who was something less than who she used to be and she could see the war it had waged on her body. She was never going to have taut, toned, smooth flesh. Never going to happen. The loose skin on her thighs, stomach and arms was mottled like salami. Her breasts looked like balloons that were beginning to deflate and there were silvery pink stretchmarks cobwebbed all over her body.

The longer she looked, the more Neve could see. When she turned round and peered over her shoulder, there were her shoulderblades, the line of her spine, two buttocks instead of the four she used to have, and when she tensed her legs, there were muscles in her thighs, in her calves. She had a tiny waist, wrists and ankles, and when she raised her arms above her head, the flesh pulled and tightened.

It wasn't a perfect body but it was the body she deserved.

Not just from every bar of chocolate or bag of crisps or laden plate of food that she'd eaten. This body was also testament to all the hours in the gym, and cycling up hills on her bike and glugging down two litres of water a day and learning to love vegetables and fruit that didn't come as an optional extra with a pastry crust. She'd earned this body.

This body could do a faultless Downward Dog and run for the bus and fit into a cinema seat. She could cross her legs and squeeze between tables in a crowded café. She could go into any woman's clothes shop on the high street and buy something to wear, without being banished to the plus-size section at the back of the store.

This was her body and she had to stop giving it such a hard time.

But even as she took stock, Neve knew she wasn't always going to look like this. Being a size twelve was an illusion. As soon as she started eating and drinking regularly again, she'd gain back most of the weight she'd lost on the Hardcore Cleanse. She waited for the wave of panic to drag her under, but it didn't. She just stood there on her white bath mat staring at herself, and the longer she stared, the more ordinary her body became. Familiarity was robbing her flesh of its power to paralyse her.

So she'd start eating again and put some weight back on until she was a size fourteen, or even a size sixteen – she'd let her body make that decision for her. Then she'd stalk Gustav until he agreed to take her back and they'd get her down to a size twelve again safely and responsibly before they began to work on a new maintenance programme. Neve had no doubt in her mind that Gustav would take her back, though she'd probably have to sign a sworn affidavit that she would never knowingly drink another cleansing juice as long as she lived.

Neve said one last silent sorry to her body, then wrapped the towel around her and padded into the bedroom. She was finally beginning to understand that her fixation on being a size ten had been another excuse to spend her life in preparation, instead of living it and taking risks and maybe getting hurt in the process.

The outside stuff was easy really. Neve knew what she had to do: three meals a day, two light snacks and at least an hour of rigorous exercise five or six days a week. What she needed to start working on now was the inside stuff because, obviously, she wasn't right in the head.

She wasn't going to let the urgent need to have her brains descrambled become another excuse for living a half-life. In the morning, or *later* in the morning at any rate, she was going to walk up the hill to Crouch End to see Max.

Neve knew he'd be a much harder sell than Gustav. She'd start by apologising profusely, upgrading to grovelling and genuflection if Max remained unconvinced. And if that didn't work, then she'd put her arms around him and kiss him over and over until she'd persuaded him that he belonged to her and she belonged to him and pancake relationships were so very last season and they were both ready for the real thing.

That was why she got into bed naked, because it was the kind of thing that a girl who was relationship-ready did. Neve lay there in the darkness trying to sleep but mostly tossing and turning and thumping her pillow.

Now that she'd made all these big, important decisions about what her life was going to be like, Neve wanted to start right away. Even the thought of facing Gustav's Teutonic wrath was as exciting as it was nervy, and the prospect of tracking Max down in a few short hours was terrifying – but just to see his face again would be like all the birthday and Christmas presents she'd ever had combined and tied with a big red bow.

But mostly Neve couldn't sleep because she was hungry. She was so hungry that it felt as if her stomach was about to start eating itself, which it probably was because it had been twelve hours since her lunch-time juice and there was nothing to eat in her kitchen apart from two lemons and a jar of horseradish.

There was no reason why she couldn't go back to sensible eating right now, Neve reasoned, as she flung back her summerweight duvet. There was a shop on Seven Sisters Road which stayed open all night and she could buy a loaf of granary bread and a box of eggs. They might even have some tomatoes and she could make an omelette.

Neve pulled on underwear, then grabbed her new pink Juicy Couture tracksuit. It was nearly three in the morning so she wasn't going to bump into anyone she knew. As she pulled up the zipper on the hoodie she had to take a moment to appreciate how soft and plush it was. Comfy too. No wonder Charlotte liked them so much she had one in every colour.

She carefully threaded her injured toe into a flip-flop, grabbed purse and keys and tiptoed down the stairs. Stomping down them in the wee small hours would definitely violate the truce.

As she crept along the hall, there was nothing on her mind but the tomato omelette and two pieces of toast she was going to eat in thirty minutes' time. Twenty minutes if she really hurried.

But when she opened the street door and saw a hunched figure sitting on the steps, Neve knew the omelette could wait.

PART FIVE

I Close My Eyes And Count To Ten

Chapter Forty-two

Max turned around as Neve stepped through the door.

'Hey,' he said, his arm tight round a frantically squirming, yelping bundle of dog.

What are you doing here? How long have you been sitting outside? It's the oddest thing but I was going to hunt you down in a few hours. There were a thousand things Neve wanted to say but she just sat down on the step next to him and replied, 'Hey.'

Keith's joy was too great to be contained. He struggled free of Max's grip so he could bound up and down the garden a few times, before launching himself at Neve, front paws on her shoulders so he could give her face a thorough tongue bath.

'Who's my special boy?' Neve cooed, once he'd settled with his head on her knee so he could gaze up at her adoringly. 'You are, aren't you?'

She didn't know why Max was there and why he wasn't saying a word, but then again, she was sitting there feeling tongue-tied and absurdly shy. All she did know was that even though neither of them had changed position in the last five minutes, their thighs were pressed against each other.

Summoning up every last ounce of courage she possessed, Neve glanced at Max; even the sight of his wonky nose in profile made her want to catch her breath. Instead of lying in bed listening to her stomach roar, she should have been composing a 'For the love of God, will you have me back?' speech in her head so that . . .

'What happened to your toe?' Max asked eventually.

'My bike fell on to my foot. I'm hoping if I keep it tightly dressed then my nail might reattach itself. It had lifted right up off the nailbed when—'

'Jesus! Stop! Don't say another word,' Max begged, his body one huge spasm of horror. 'That's just gross.'

'I know,' Neve agreed happily – happy because they were talking, even if it was about her necrotic toenail.

'And what happened to your lip?' Max asked, because he was looking at her face now, which was illuminated by the lamp-post across the road. 'Where did you get that scratch on your cheek? Did your bike fall on you from a great height?'

'You think I look bad, then you should see Charlotte,' Neve told him as Max's eyes widened. 'We had a fight. A proper, full-on deathmatch. She's got a black eye and a sprained wrist, but I'm not sure that was my fault. I think she skidded on some of the melted ice cream.'

'Are you all right?' They both watched his hand lift towards her face and then stop in mid-air, before he dropped it again.

'I'm fine,' Neve said. And she'd thought that she was and that everything was going to be OK, but he wouldn't even allow himself to touch her and now she wasn't so sure.

She was just wondering if she should move up her schedule to the part where she threw her arms around him and kissed him into compliance when Max cleared his throat. 'So, anyway, I broke up with my therapist.'

'You did?'

'I did,' Max said grimly.

'Oh? So, does that mean that she might have space for a new client, because I think I need some help from a trained mental-health professional,' Neve said. She had to keep talking and sooner or later, she'd get round to saying what she wanted to say. 'I broke up with Gustav too but I'm going to make him take me back because I—'

'Look, Neevy, I don't care if you're a size ten,' Max cut right through her babble and gently pushed Keith's head on to her other leg so he could curl his hand over her knee. 'If Mr California only appreciates you if you're skinny, then he doesn't really appreciate you at all.'

'I saw him today,' Neve said, and when Max stiffened and tried to move away from her, she grabbed his wrists and held on for dear life. 'He wants me to move to Warwickshire with him.'

It was interesting watching Max's face collapse in on itself. Interesting, encouraging, but also hard to look at because within seconds, Max had got his features under control, set his face into a hard, harsh mask.

'Congratulations,' he said stiffly. 'Can you let go of me?'

Neve shook her head. 'No, I can't.' She tightened her fingers hard enough to leave bruises and Max didn't make a word of protest, just sat there with a face full of barely restrained fury. 'See, he had it all worked out. I was going to chuck in my job, enrol into the doctorate programme at the University of Warwick so I could also be his research assistant for some dreary book he wants to write. This was before I even found out that his fiancée was coming too. I—'

'He's engaged?' Max interrupted. Neve hadn't thought it possible, but his face became even tighter, more closed off. 'That really must have fucked up your masterplan.'

'You're not listening! You keep interrupting before I get to the important bits,' Neve complained. 'Will you just shut up and let me say this?'

'Say what? You wasted weeks on a starvation diet because you didn't know that Mr California was otherwise engaged?'

'*Shut up!*' It was verging on a scream. 'I mean it, Max. Promise to keep your mouth buttoned tight.'

'OK, I promise,' he sighed, but with a lot of eye-rolling,

and Neve would have preferred to have him in a more conciliatory mood when she handed him her heart to do whatever he wanted with it.

'Now, where was I?' She hoped that Max couldn't feel her fingers trembling around his wrists as she tried to retrace the threads of her conversation. 'Before his fiancée arrived, before he implied that I'd given up on being smart for being slimmer instead, as if the two things were mutually exclusive, I sat there listening to him talk and talk and I realised something really important.'

'What?' Max asked sulkily, before he remembered he was under strict instructions not to make a sound. His mouth snapped shut.

Neve decided to let it go. 'I realised I didn't want to be naked with him – and not because of my legion of body hang-ups, it was because I didn't fancy him. Then I wondered why I didn't fancy him because William . . . well, he's handsome and super-intelligent and I thought I was in love with him for all those years but it turned out I was in love with the idea of William. The actual reality was a bit of an anti-climax.'

She finally released Max's wrists so she could run her hands through her damp hair. Max must have sensed that she wasn't done, because he sat quietly, his eyes trained on her face.

'I thought, well, William would never shove the word WAG into pop songs to make me laugh and he wouldn't bite the chocolate off chocolate-covered strawberries for me and he'd never, ever watch a film with Sandra Bullock in it, unless it was a Shakespeare adaptation and then he'd spend the entire film listing all the historical inaccuracies and he'd never go down on me for half an hour because he'd lost a game of Scrabble. Point of fact, I can't imagine William doing anything that would mess up his hair, and he's started popping the collars of his shirts and have I mentioned that he's not you? He's not you, Max, and that's why I'm actually really pleased that he's engaged and he's moving to Warwickshire so I don't have a constant reminder of what an idiot I've been.'

Neve had run out of steam and breath by now, so she leaned back on her elbows and glanced anxiously over at Max, who didn't seem to realise that she was done and he had permission to speak again.

He was staring down at the ground, lost in thought, and she wanted to touch him, even more than she'd wanted him to touch her and tell her that everything was going to be OK. That they were going to be OK.

'I went to a bar tonight where I know I can always pull a girl,' Max said diffidently and her heart plummeted. Had he come round simply to tell her they could be friends after all? 'I met a nineteen-year-old model from Texas called Karis; blonde, blue-eyed, legs up to here,' Max gestured to his chest. 'Pulled down her jeans to show me the butterfly tattoo on her arse. It was the easiest thing in the world to go to her place in Notting Hill to have sex with her and get you out of my system.'

'Oh.' She traced patterns on the stone step with her fingertip as she felt her world crumble into tiny pieces that could never be put back together again. 'So did your scheme work, then?'

'I don't know,' Max said. 'I didn't even make it as far as the Westway before I realised that I didn't *want* you out of my system. I like having you in my system.'

Neve hardly dared hope until Max's hand cupped her chin and turned her face towards him. 'Why did you sack your therapist?' she asked.

Max grinned a little shakily because neither of them were in a place where they could start throwing around carefree smiles. Not yet. 'Because she was crap,' he said. 'I'm used to her telling me I'm not capable of being in love because of my intimacy issues that stem from my relationship with my mother, but I wasn't going to let her talk shit about you.'

'What did she say about me?'

'That you have an unresolved Electra complex,' Max revealed, as Neve hissed in sheer outrage. 'To be honest, I'm not even sure what that is, but she also said you were emotionally retarded and you're not. You're the kindest, most empathetic person I know, and she's a woman whose most meaningful interaction is with her cat. I should never have taken advice from a cat person. I mean, what do they know?'

'I'm going to have her struck off!' Neve vowed, clenching her fists angrily. 'She's got no right to say stuff . . .' She stopped because Max was giving her an exasperated look. 'So . . . are you and me OK now, then?'

'I think we're getting there.' They were leaning into each other now, heads bent and almost touching. 'Look, full disclosure, I wouldn't be happy if you were a size thirty-two again, but I'd rather have you that size than not have you at all. Don't you get it, Neevy? What you look like is just one part of who you are – but it's not *all* you are.'

'I know.' She covered Max's hand with her own and hoped that she'd never have to let go. 'You have to believe me, I know that now.'

'And you should know I have zero tolerance for that fucking stupid Cleanse or any other fad diet you were considering, but I'll go running with you, unless it's raining, and I won't force you to eat carbs after six.' Max brushed his cheek against hers. 'How does that sound?'

Then Max pulled away so he could look at her and Neve was sure that she didn't have to say anything because her answer was written all over her face.

'It sounds good,' she whispered. 'So, do you?'

'Well, do you?'

Neve pouted. 'I asked first.'

'Of course I do,' Max said firmly, and his hand wasn't on her chin any more. His thumb was brushing along the scratch on her cheek from Charlotte's engagement ring. 'Not as your friend. And not like we were before because I realised something else tonight. Something about pancakes.'

'What about them?' This was one of the most meaningful moments of her entire life; it felt as if her entire future hung in the balance, but at the mention of pancakes, all Neve could think about was how hungry she was. It wasn't very romantic.

'We both got so obsessed about that first pancake being thrown away that we forgot something really important,' Max explained, and he looked incredibly pleased with himself. 'That first pancake tastes just as good as all the other ones. It's not its fault that it was first in line and the pan wasn't hot enough so it got a bit lumpy and misshapen.'

'And when you're really famished that first pancake tastes better than all the ones that come after it,' Neve said, and then she couldn't wait any longer. Her arms were around Max before she'd even finished forming the thought, but his arms were around her too in that exact same moment.

Just having him there to hold, warm and solid and real, was enough for five seconds, and then she was peppering his face with kisses – his forehead, his eyebrows, the tip of his crooked nose, along his cheekbones until she reached the glittering prize of his mouth.

Sometimes Neve thought that her appetite was the most robust thing about her, and she didn't kiss Max so much as she devoured him. Graceless, messy kisses without any thought or reason, but simply because she hungered for him. Kissed him with everything she had and everything she was, and she didn't know why she could kiss Max and have him kiss her back with the same fierceness but still be greedy for the next kiss and the one after that and the one after that and the one . . .

'Stop,' Max said, laughing as he pulled back, because Keith had invaded the gap between them and was trying to get in on the kissing by licking whoever's face was closest.

'We don't need to do this on your doorstep. I'm not going anywhere.'

'Promise you won't. Not ever again. I hate it when you're not here,' Neve said as she tried to shoulder Keith out of the way. 'Come inside.'

'Where were you going at nearly three in the morning, anyway?' Max asked, standing up and holding out his hand, so he could tug Neve up too.

She flushed a little. 'Well, I was going to the all-night shop on Seven Sisters Road to get some food because I haven't eaten in weeks,' she admitted, and she didn't want to ruin this before it had even started again, the same way she'd ruined it last time. 'This is just a one-off. I'm done with detox cleansing, I swear, but I'm also done with eating crap at weird hours because we can't get out of bed. Except for right now, because I am seriously contemplating cutting off my own hand and lightly sautée-ing my fingers in extra-virgin olive oil.'

Max stood poised on the step above her, brow furrowed as if he was trying to reach a decision about something. Probably that he didn't want to be with her enough to deal with her dietary restrictions any more. 'OK, then. If that's the way you want it,' he said, as if he was done deciding. He jumped down the steps, picked up Keith's lead and headed for the gate, while Neve stood there watching in disbelief.

It didn't hurt any less having your heart broken for the second time. In fact, it hurt more, and . . .

'You coming, or what?' Max called, already walking down the street. 'We'd better get a move on or they might have sold out of that disgusting bread that's all seeds and nothing else.'

With a hand clutched to her heart, which had had more than enough shocks in the last twenty-four hours, Neve hurried after Max and Keith.

'You're such a drama queen,' Max complained when she caught up with him. 'No one could be *that* hungry unless

they'd survived a plane crash and been stranded on a
desolate mountain-top for days and the only thing standing
between them and death was gnawing on one of their dead
travelling companions.'

Neve punched him on the arm. 'Are you joking? If the
shop turns out to be closed after all, I expect you to sacrifice
a couple of fingers for the cause,' she said, as she slipped her
hand into his.

New York Valentine

Carmen Reid

LOVE IS IN the air!

Personal shopper Annie Valentine has a dream job in the heart of fabulous Manhattan.

Daughter Lana is lost in the heat of first love, but has she fallen for a heart-breaker?

In London husband Ed faces a scandal at work and knows, in his heart, he needs Annie back.

What's a girl to do when her true love is in London but her new love is New York?

Does it have to be fashion or family, or can Annie Valentine have it all?

'Cleverer than the average slice of chick-lit and much
more entertaining too'
HEAT

A fabulous read. A sexy read. A Carmen Reid.

9780552163170

Sleeping Arrangements

Sophie Kinsella
Writing as Madeleine Wickham

Chloe needs a holiday. She's sick of making wedding dresses and her partner is having trouble at work. Her wealthy friend Gerard has offered the loan of his luxury villa in Spain – perfect.

Hugh is not a happy man. His immaculate wife seems more interested in the granite for the new kitchen than in him, and he works so hard to pay for it all, he barely has time to see their children. But his old schoolfriend Gerard has lent them a luxury villa in Spain – perfect.

Both families arrive at the villa and get a shock: Gerard has double-booked. An uneasy week of sharing begins, and tensions soon mount in the soaring heat. But there's also a secret history between the families – and as tempers fray, an old passion begins to resurface . . .

'Lightness of touch and witty observation
make this a perfect holiday read'
SUNDAY MIRROR

9780552776752

Forbidden Pleasures

Jo Rees

They were tempting fate – but will the winner take all?

From **Las Vegas** and **Dubai**, to **Shanghai** and **London** – in the glamorous world of international gambling, fortunes rise and fall on the roll of the dice or the turn of a card.

Addicted to sex and coke, pleasure-loving It Girl **Savannah** seems to have it all – except the one thing she wants, the approval of her cold and powerful father, Michael.

Lois, a tough, ruthlessly ambitious ex-cop, runs the gambling business of Michael's greatest rival. No one has been able to get between her and her rise through the glamour and wealth of the casinos . . . not even her young daughter.

Will they realize what is really important, before the greedy and corrupt world of gambling consumes them forever?

9780552156240

Prep

Curtis Sittenfeld

'Curtis Sittenfeld shares with Salinger a knack of capturing, in effortless prose, a teenager mindset . . . It feels important . . . Most vitally of all, it feels like adolescence'
THE TIMES

LEE FIORA IS a shy fourteen-year-old when she leaves small-town Indiana for a scholarship at Ault, an exclusive boarding school in Massachusetts. Her head is filled with images from the school brochure of handsome boys in sweaters leaning against old brick buildings, girls running with lacrosse sticks across pristine athletics fields, everyone singing hymns in chapel. But as she soon learns, Ault is a minefield of unstated rules and incomprehensible social rituals, and Lee must work hard to find – and maintain – her place in the pecking order.

'*Sweet Valley High* as written by George Eliot . . .
A highly accomplished novel'
INDEPENDENT ON SUNDAY

'A class act . . . *Prep* deserves pride of place on
any summer recommended reading list'
NEW YORK TIMES

'Critics have compared author Curtis Sittenfeld to Salinger and Plath. But her novel *Prep*, about boarding school, pegs her as a name to watch in her own right'
TIME

9780552776844

Wild Things

Jo Carnegie

Lights, camera, *SCANDAL!*

Meet the glamorous cast of WILD THINGS

Sophia – the leading lady who gets what she wants. And she wants

Jed – the village's gorgeous gardener, living with devoted girlfriend

Camilla – sweet-natured and desperate for a baby, unlike her sister

Calypso – fiercely ambitious, and unimpressed by the penetrating gaze of

Rafe – dashing leading man, who quickly wins over Calypso's grandmother

Clementine – whose only desire is for them all to go away, so Churchminster can win **'Britain's Best Village'**!

9780552160865